them, and make them feel what her characters are going through. From start to finish, her novels are beautifully written, teaching her readers more about faith and love whilst also presenting them a story they'll cherish for a long time to come."

— Anna Hutchinson, Aspiring Author on the *Faith to Love Series*

"This story is filled with God's abounding grace, love, and redemption. Cleopatra does an amazing job at pulling you not only into the story but the characters. You not only want to know everything but be part of the community this story takes place in. It takes a special talent to do that as a writer, and she accomplishes this flawlessly. Be prepared to laugh, be surprised, and even tear up with this book. Definitely recommend it!"

— Kelly-Ann, Book Blogger on *Healing Their Hearts*

"In this warming story of faith, family, and crisis, Margot masterfully brings us into real-life scenarios. Witty dialogue, tender moments, and the importance of leaning on God are strongpoints of the Mckays—a family who stayed strong together, even when everything else was falling apart."

— Willowy Whisper, Author of *Angel Gate* on *The Floods Came*

With You I Am

To Jay,
I hope you enjoy
Wynn + Noelle's story!
— Cleopatra Marzot ♥

With You I Am

CLEOPATRA MARGOT

Faith to Love Publishing

To my mom, for never hesitating to give me constructive criticism and pushing me from good to best by guiding me to what ultimately led to this book. For never failing to support my writing, even when I struggle to find my way. For always being there for me, no matter what. For your (sometimes not-so-subtle) pushes to go in God's direction and not mine.
I love you.

Bryant family Tree

John Bryant: 64, Son of Henry and Emma (deceased) Bryant; former Balsam Falls Chief of Police turned homeschool dad turned inn owner; married to Jackie Watters Bryant; father of Sarah, Wynn, Marshall, and Ember; grandfather to Sadie and Will

Jacqueline Watters Bryant: 60, Daughter of Benjamin (deceased) and Margaret Watters; former attorney of family law turned homeschool mom turned inn owner; married to John Bryant; mother of Sarah, Wynn, Marshall, and Ember; grandmother to Sadie and Will

Sarah Joy Bryant Taylor: 34; Happily married to a former South Carolinian and marketing expert Chris(topher) Taylor; stay at home homeschool mother to four-year-old Sadie and eleven-month-old Will(iam)

Wynn David Bryant: 31; Unmarried (but not for long…?); CEO and co-owner of Bryant Brothers Construction

Marshall John Bryant: 27; Unmarried (but being pressured into marrying his best friend since childhood Jessica Johnson, sister of town chief of police, Seth); co-owner of Bryant Brothers Construction

Ember Lauren Bryant: 19, Unmarried (but fantasizing about her future husband, using Christian romance novels to craft her Future Husband Standards); works part-time at the Serendipity Inn, part-time at Cozy & Grounds Coffee House, and volunteers at the library

CHAPTER

One

"If I were to build a house, I wouldn't put a balcony going off the bathroom." Ember perched on the corner of Wynn's desk, munching on a cinnamon roll as she looked at a blueprint. "I mean, who in their right mind would walk out in a towel onto a balcony? No one. The answer is no one."

Wynn Bryant glanced up at his younger sister. "That balcony is off a bedroom, Em. Not a bathroom. And besides, Marshall drew up these plans, so if it was, you'd have to talk to him."

"Ohh." Ember nodded slowly. "Okay. Now I see it. Well, in that case, when can I move in? If I pitch in on building it—physical labor, I mean—can that count as payment?"

"Um, no. It's already got an owner." He rolled over to his printer, grabbed the printout, and wheeled back to his desk. "But if you let me have the other half of your cinnamon roll, I'll take you to lunch at Farm to Table."

Ember hesitated. "You're serious?"

"As the fact that that balcony is off a bedroom and not a bathroom, yep."

"And will this lunch include dessert?"

"Sure."

Ember set the to-go container from Cozy & Grounds on his desk. "I'm in. Do you have any water around here? Where is Marsh, anyway? He tried to take my cinnamon roll before I'd even had so much as one bite. And he didn't offer me lunch."

Wynn leaned back in his office chair, pinching off a bite of soft, gooey dough. "He had to help Dad with something, I think. Water's in the mini fridge in the break room. I believe it just got stocked."

"I'll be back." She hopped off and disappeared through the doorway.

Wynn glanced around his office. The plaster walls were painted a light gray, the hardwood floors the original from this building and sanded then stained dark brown. *Dark Walnut* had been the stain color Mom recommended, and the one they'd gone with. Photos of previous projects they'd done were framed and hung on the wall by his bookcase. His L-shaped desk took up a decent portion of the space, and two chairs sat opposite of it. A whiteboard with haphazard notes about the house for single mother Jenna Williams stared at him from across the room.

It wasn't a huge space, but the building on Main Street had been affordable and its somewhat rundown state had given Wynn and his brother the chance to organize everything how they'd wanted to. Aside from Wynn's office, there was Marshall's office, a break room, and the lobby that doubled as a meeting space. Bryant Brothers Construction was a business that survived by helping others, and their intent was for clients to feel welcomed upon walking through the doors. So far they'd accomplished that in the decade they'd been in business.

Ember strolled back into the room, bottle of water in hand, this time plopping down in the leather wingback chair across from him. "So, when is this house going to be done? Once the snow stops falling? Because that might be never, and I won't complain because I love snow and soup and all things cold weather."

"All we've got left is to finish the interior and a few things outside, but we're still waiting on a total thaw to do any landscaping." Wynn finished off the cinnamon roll and tossed the empty container in the trash can under his desk. "Move in date will hopefully be the end of March, possibly early April. We'll just have to see how the weather cooperates."

"It still amazes me how your contractor brain works." She took a swig of water. "I mean, I do good to construct a blanket fort on a rainy or snowy day with Sadie. A real house—I'd be lost. Not gonna lie."

Wynn lifted a shoulder, let it drop. "You learn as you go. Technically, a blanket fort is probably more complicated than a blueprint for a house or the building of a house itself. You don't have solid materials for the fort."

"True enough. Are you planning to come to the city council meeting tonight? Rumor has it the mayor's got it in his head to restore the community gardens in time to have Spring Fling there."

"When did this come about?" Wynn straightened in his chair, interest piqued. The Gardens and building that accompanied them had been abandoned long ago, and nobody had decided to take the project on. But if Wynn could get on as a contractor... "Do they already have plans made, or is it just an idea?"

"Well, well, well. I didn't know my big brother was so into gardening. You sure never help out this much with the inn's gardens in the summer."

"The Gardens aren't the part I'm interested in. Well, not really. I'm interested in the building that accompanies them."

"All I know is that the council plans to discuss the idea tonight. Probably hoping to boost tourism even more, which I don't quite understand considering it was up as of last month, but whatever. Pretty sure Dad's planning to go."

Wynn grabbed a pen and sticky note and jotted down a reminder to swing by The Gardens this afternoon sometime. "You going?"

"Probably not. Helping Mom bake some stuff for the nursing home. I think Sarah and Sadie are helping us too." A grin crinkled the corners of her brown eyes. "The Bryant men could take on the city council meeting. Unfortunately, the women there would probably be swooning over, and I quote, 'Balsam Falls's most eligible bachelors.' Excluding Dad."

He scoffed. "Yeah, right. Besides, Marsh is seeing someone. Okay, no, he's not, but he should be."

Ember twirled a lock of dark hair around her finger. "Hey, you don't have to tell me. I'm well aware of the connection between those two lovebirds."

"If you're referring to me and Jess," Marshall said, poking his head in the door, "we are not lovebirds. We're good friends."

"Um, we have eyes, Marsh," Ember retorted. "I see those longing looks across the dinner table. How you buy her groceries and drive her out of town when she needs to go somewhere."

Marshall dropped into the chair beside Ember. "I told you, we're friends. What's wrong with that?"

"You sure you want to open that can of worms?" Ember asked. "Because I have plenty of reasons. If you have any work at all to do today, then—"

"No, I don't want to," Marshall interrupted. He directed his gaze towards Wynn. "Did you hear about The Gardens? Revitalizing them, apparently. Gonna be discussed at tonight's city council meeting."

Wynn peeled the sticky note free and grinned. "Already one step ahead of you. I want to drive by, maybe get out and look at them. I know we've got this house—"

"The one with the balcony off the bathroom."

Ignoring Ember's comment and Marshall's creased brow, he continued. "But it could be a good project. At least look into it, if nothing else."

Marshall nodded. "Exactly what I was thinking."

CHAPTER

Two

Considering they were already into March, spring was coming a lot faster than it took to plan an event. Noelle Carter had handled event coordination at her late grandfather's company for four years now, but never had this kind of prospective job come across her desk.

Dear Ms. Carter, the handwritten letter read. *My name is Leonard Mason (my friends call me Leo), the Mayor of Balsam Falls, Nebraska. You may be wondering how exactly I discovered your work, but in our present day, we have incredibly helpful technology and somehow my assistant managed to track you down. Your grandmother, Estelle Carter, lived here in town for many years. Her greatest joy, so I'm told, was tending to our community gardens. They have been neglected now for going on two decades, but the city council and I have started to consider having our town's annual spring event there. The place would have to be restored, of course, but I'm sure it would be doable. Would you be interested in coordinating the event? Your portfolio is simply splendid. Please*

*advise. Thank you for taking the time to read my letter. – Mayor
Leo Mason*

Noelle folded the letter again and rose, crossing her office to stare out the floor-to-ceiling windows overlooking downtown Jackson. Late afternoon sunshine glinted off neighboring buildings, and traffic moved on the street several stories below. Pretty soon, on a Friday like it was, people would be getting off work. Flocking downtown to dine out, see a movie, or, not Noelle's favored activity, hang out at the bars.

It was instances like this when she wished Grandpa or Grandma were still alive. If not for any other reason than simply to guide her in the right direction. Tell her that yes, taking the opportunity to get out of Mississippi and do a totally different project would be a good idea. Only a handful of months ago, Grandpa had sat right here in her office in his signature charcoal suit and white dress shirt and told her he thought she was growing stagnant in her current position. That the glitzy city parties and sometimes too-picky clients were tarnishing her passion for this job.

He'd died of a heart attack three days later.

And she'd had no choice but to inherit the role of CEO at Carter, Inc., not to ponder what could be if she tried something different.

But now…

Heels clicking on the cool, light gray wood floors of her office, Noelle returned to her desk and reread the letter again. For probably the twentieth time since her assistant had brought it in this morning. What was it about this mayor's letter that affected her like it did? Was it the mention of her grandmother? She vaguely remembered hearing stories about Balsam Falls when she was younger, but not major details. Grandma had loved her gardens, that much the mayor did know. Up until her passing four years ago, she'd kept the gardens beautiful at home, even though she and Grandpa could've easily hired out the work.

A restoration project, though? Noelle could orchestrate an event for five-hundred guests, no problem. But restoring something?

That was outside of her wheelhouse. Grandpa had done the occasional woodworking project and she'd watched him, but she'd never done anything like what the letter foreshadowed. A place neglected for twenty years had to be in pretty bad condition.

And yet, Noelle was curious.

It couldn't hurt to try calling and hope the mayor would be available, right? She wasn't locked into a contract, nor had she even agreed to thinking about it. Well, the latter may technically be false, but whatever.

Noelle tapped in the number Mayor Mason had scribbled on the bottom of the page and lifted her phone to her ear, nerves bunching inside her.

On the second ring, a man answered. "Leo Mason speaking."

"Yes, uh, hello, Mr. Mason." *Get it together, Noelle.* "My name is Noelle Carter. I received your letter this morning."

"Oh, Ms. Carter, yes. I'll be honest, I didn't expect to hear from you so soon. Well, I mailed the letter at the beginning of the week, but anyway."

Noelle fingered the paper, already creased from unfolding and refolding it so many times. "You were correct about my grandmother being from Balsam Falls, but I didn't realize her involvement with your gardens."

"It was well before my time as mayor but yes, I've been told she was very involved with them. Apparently she planted, pruned, watered—you name it, she probably did it. Somebody took decent care of them for a while after her, but like I mentioned, they haven't been kept up for twenty years."

"That's quite a long time. When you say restore, is it only the gardens?"

"No, no. There's a building there, an event space if you may. That would have to be renovated, of course, as would the gardens. I'm sure the fountains and pots and all that are probably outdated." He paused, and muffled voices came across the line before he spoke again. "I was just informed that at least one, if not more, of the fountains are broken."

Noelle tapped her chin, gaze fixed on the picture of her grandparents sitting on the corner of her desk. "I see. You do realize I'm an event coordinator, correct? I know next to nothing about landscaping or renovating or whatever."

"Of course. But if you could be here while it's being restored, I'm sure that would help your creative juices and such."

"That may be true," she conceded. "And when is the event?"

"Traditionally we hold it downtown every year at the end of May, but it would be really nice if it could be hosted at The Gardens this year. If we go any later than May, it would be more of a summer event, and we've already got one of those."

"Yes, that makes sense." Squinting, she tried to mentally calculate how long she'd be absent from headquarters by looking at the calendar hanging on the wall behind her. "And is this a done deal, or just a topic of discussion?"

"We plan on discussing it at tonight's city council meeting," Leo said. "By the end of the meeting, we should know if it's a go or not. We'll have to get a budget drawn up and see if there's any permits to obtain, but the city does own the property."

Noelle squeezed her eyes shut, hoping she wasn't acting too impulsively. "Okay. If the council decides to move forward with it, I'll do it. Getting out of the city might be nice. And if the idea is nixed, well, thank you for thinking of me."

"Wonderful!" Merriment laced his hearty voice. "Can I call you in the morning? I know tomorrow's Saturday, but that way we could get the ball rolling. Of course, we can pay for your travel expenses if that's something you'd prefer. And we have a great Bed & Breakfast in town. I'm sure a special rate could be worked out."

"If it's a go, I'd prefer to know tonight. That way I can start getting arrangements made on my end. And that's very kind of you, but you don't have to do that. I can take care of it."

"Of course. Well then, I guess I'll be speaking with you again soon, Ms. Carter."

"Please, call me Noelle. And yes, I look forward to it."

The call disconnected a moment later and she lowered her phone to her desk, processing what she'd just agreed to. If she left tomorrow—provided the council voted in favor of the project—she'd be in Nebraska for close to three months. A full quarter of a year. Granted, there wasn't anything here that she couldn't hand off to someone else or take care of remotely. So unless something came up between now and whenever Leo Mason called back, there was no reason she couldn't swing it. Truthfully, it wasn't so much about the income the prospective job would bring in so much as the chance to visit her grandmother's hometown. Where she and Grandpa had—

Wait.

They'd gotten married in Balsam Falls, Grandpa and Grandma. Noelle had been raised by her grandparents, grown up here in Mississippi. But she was fairly sure they'd been married in Balsam Falls. If there was one thing about her past that Grandma always loved to talk about, it was her fairytale wedding. William Carter had been the sole son to Alistair and Regina Carter, owners of the Carter Hotel in downtown Jackson. But as the story had been told, Grandpa had sacrificed his role as heir to marry Estelle Richmond. They'd ended up back in Jackson not long after getting married, but Noelle was certain the ceremony had taken place in Nebraska.

Surely she could find the photo albums she and Grandma had flipped through when Noelle was little. She glanced at the clock on her computer monitor. Quarter to five. Close enough. Technically, she was the boss now and that came with the benefit of arranging her own schedule. Came with a lot of responsibility and sometimes a few headaches, but she'd grown up at Carter, Inc. Had no intentions of letting it crash and burn simply because leadership had been passed down to her last November. Didn't matter if there was someone wanting to buy the company ever since she'd stepped into her new position.

She powered off her computer and tidied up her desk, eager to get home, have supper, and dig through the boxes in her hall closet. Hopefully the albums hadn't been looked over when she'd cleared the estate and sold it last year. As a single woman, she hadn't needed the space of her childhood home, plus it held too many memories. With both her grandparents gone, she had been ready for a fresh start. So, she'd sold it, found a cute house near downtown, and rented that for the time being.

Gathering her purse, the letter, and her phone, she left her office and crossed the hall to her assistant's office. "I'm heading out a little early today, Lucy. Got a couple personal things to take care of."

Lucy Scott glanced up, her eyes widening behind her glasses. "Oh. Okay. Hey, before you go, about the Perry event—"

"Hand it off to Grant." Noelle looped her bag over her shoulder. "He can take care of it. Not too difficult of a project, and he can call me if he has any questions."

"Wait, what's going on?" Lucy tilted her head, her dark bob brushing her shoulder. "You're up to something, aren't you?"

"What? No. Well, okay, so I have a potential project." She couldn't help but grin. "In Nebraska."

Lucy opened her mouth. Closed it. "Wow. I can't say I expected that. What kind of project?"

"One that includes restoring gardens and an event space, and I don't know what else other than that it's my grandma's hometown and they supposedly have a great B&B. If the city votes in favor of proceeding, I'd probably be leaving tomorrow. Sunday at the latest. And I'd be gone through the end of May."

"*May?*" Lucy squeaked. "Noelle, it's practically spring and people are probably going to be—"

"Again, hand them off to Grant. Besides, I don't know if it's actually happening or not. But if it does, I'll still be reachable. Phone, email—just not in my office. I'm going to Nebraska, not the moon."

Lucy nodded slowly. "Right. Okay, then. Do you want me to look into flights?"

"Actually, I was thinking I would drive. But thank you."

"I, uh…. I just don't have any words."

Noelle laughed. "It's sudden, yes, but maybe it's what I need. After Grandpa died…" She straightened her shoulders, blinked away the tears. "I think I just need to do it and not look back. If it flops, well, I guess it flops. But I won't know unless I try."

CHAPTER
Three

How taking a walk around The Gardens to see what Wynn and his brother had agreed to last night had morphed into a family field trip, Wynn wasn't sure. But it had, and there was no changing it now. When the Bryant family made their minds up about something, there was no way to un-make them.

"I think this one is definitely broken." Ember nudged an empty flower pot along the cracked sidewalk with the toe of her Adidas tennis shoe. The pot crumbled partway down one side. "Oops. But hey, I wasn't wrong."

Wynn shifted his sleeping eleven-month-old nephew to his other shoulder. "Most of them are probably that way, judging by how they look. Which fountain did Mayor Leo say was broken for sure?"

"The big one everybody's standing around, more than likely." Ember tucked her hands into her jacket pockets, the semi-mild early March sun glinting off her dark hair. "I mean, it's just a guess, but since Mom, Dad, Sarah, Chris, Sadie, and Marsh are all—"

"Yeah, I get the point," Wynn interrupted. "Are you planning to help with demo? Or why else is everyone here?"

"Why wouldn't we all be here? This is a big deal. Mostly because we actually get to be in on everything that's happening, and that's way more fun than speculating about it. What are your plans, anyway?"

"We literally just put in a bid at the meeting last night and it got accepted. Mainly because the mayor was too excited to wait for any other company to bid on it. There hasn't been any time to make plans yet."

She made a face. "Wynn, if I had a project like this, I probably wouldn't have been able to sleep last night because I would have so many ideas. For inside and outside. Just *think* of everything you can do with this place."

"Unlike you, I enjoy my sleep." He squinted at the fountain where the rest of his family congregated. Was it cracked all the way down that one side? "Remind me again why you won't come on as interior designer for Marshall and I? It would be more fun than hiring Sally Darren for every project individually. You could literally have your own office if you wanted. It might be tight, but we could swing it."

"I'm nineteen, Wynn, and have no degree or anything. You're better off hiring Sally. She's the most elite designer around here."

He frowned. "Neither Marshall nor myself have degrees. We're licensed contractors, that's it. Seems to me we've done pretty well."

"Yeah, but you're thirty-one and Marsh is twenty-seven. People trust you and have seen your work. I'm the family baby—literally."

"And how old were we when we started Bryant Bros.?"

"That's really not—"

"I was twenty-one and he was seventeen." Wynn halted and stepped in front of his sister, forcing her to stop as well. "People love you, Em. You somehow charm everyone you meet. If you worked for us, or with us, I should say, it wouldn't matter what education you do or don't have. I've seen your sketches. And I've implemented some of your ideas into various projects."

"Hey, Wynn, I have an idea about this fountain," Marshall called, giving Ember an opportunity to slip around him.

Wynn sighed and pivoted, forcing his thoughts to the back of his mind. If his sister wasn't interested, so be it. He couldn't change her mind. She was young. There was plenty of time for her to find something she wanted to pursue.

He picked up his pace, glancing around the outdoor part of The Gardens. Flower pots were scattered throughout the overgrown area, some of them upright and some overturned, others in broken heaps of ceramic. Fountains both big and small and probably all not functioning had been positioned with a bench beside each one and, under weeds, a circular tile pattern underneath.

The best part, though, was that Falls Lake was easily visible from wherever a person was standing on the sloped lawn that ended at the edge of the lake. One could witness a gorgeous sunset this way. Even if the event was at the end of May when days were lengthening, he doubted it'd be wrapped by nine or ten at night. Not if it panned out like the mayor had expressed he'd like it to.

Sparklers, fireworks, and s'mores had been only a few of the ideas. None of which, especially the first two, could be done before dusk fell.

Not that the firework one would pan out no matter what time of day. Wynn hadn't missed the grunt of protest from town chief of police Seth Johnson when Mayor Leo had mentioned the idea. For once Wynn kind of sided with Seth. He couldn't imagine the paperwork that would accompany trying to obtain a permit for one night of fireworks at the end of May. Nor the cost associated. And, come to think of it, where would they even be able to purchase them? Stands for the Fourth never went up until the end of June. Granted, there was Barry Darren, Sally's husband, and he'd handled other events' fireworks in the past, so that was always a possibility.

"What if we broke up the existing fountains and used that to repave the sidewalk?" Marshall asked once Wynn reached them. "I mean, trying to refurbish these may or may not work very well, and that way they'd still be incorporated into the new and improved gardens."

Wynn tilted his head back and forth, considering. "That, or we could use the pieces to make tabletops. If the city is planning for this to be an operating event space, they'll probably want tables."

"Ooh, would you use that clear stuff with them?" Mom's brown eyes sparkled as she glanced up at her husband. "Oh, John, what is that called?"

Lines creased Dad's forehead. "Epoxy resin?"

She clapped her hands together. "Yes, that. Like how they make those river tables with those pieces of wood, you know? The fountains all have these colored tiles inside that would be *gorgeous*."

Huh. Wynn hadn't noticed those, but now that his mother had pointed them out, yeah, they'd be perfect for a tabletop.

"Good idea," he said. "But it wouldn't be like the wood and epoxy one you were talking about. Two totally different materials."

Mom nodded. "Yes, of course. I know. If you need any more great ideas, you know where to find me."

"It's a pretty fountain." Sadie, Wynn's four-year-old niece, ran her little hand over the uneven and probably splintery rim of the fountain. A pale pink tutu style dress peeked out from under her mauve Columbia coat, her black leggings and green frog rainboots clashing with both. "Maybe it'll work again, right?"

Chris, Sadie's father, squatted down next to her and gently pulled her hand away. The resemblance between father and daughter was undeniably obvious. Sadie's dark hair and dark eyes matched Chris's, as opposed to Sarah's dark blonde hair and blue eyes. "Probably not, Sadie bug. But I bet your uncles are going to put in a newer and even better one."

Eleven-month-old Will moved in Wynn's arms, his sleep-heavy eyes slowly blinking open. Wynn started swaying the baby back and forth, either to soften the blow of waking up or to lull him back to sleep. Unlike Sadie, Will was fond of his naps. Something that came in handy when Wynn was deemed babysitter for the evening when Chris and Sarah went out on a date. At least his house was on the same street as the inn, so he was close by. Usually Ember or Mom liked to drop by and help out, especially when Wynn was on a deadline for work.

"Uncle Wynn, is this gonna be an enchanted garden?" Sadie moseyed over to him, her head tilted back as she clasped her hands, eyes big, brown, and so very hopeful. "'Cause then we can have a carriage ride. Wouldn't that be so pretty?"

For only being four, she was able to pronounce her words incredibly well. Sarah would attest that to homeschooling and that it allowed Sadie to learn at her own pace.

"I'm not sure, but we can definitely consider the idea," Wynn replied, winking at his niece. "Do you think you could draw me a picture of it? That way Uncle Marshall and I could know exactly what we'd need to do."

Sadie nodded enthusiastically, her rain boots thunking as she bounced on up the path, singing a song from one of the movies they'd probably watched more than once. Popcorn and princess movies went remarkably well together, Wynn had learned over his uncle-ing years.

He glanced up to find his mother grinning at him. "Oh, no. I know what that look means."

"All I'm saying is that you're over thirty now, and there are plenty of nice girls out there," she said, using that certain voice she used when giving this certain speech. "You'd make a wonderful husband and father."

"Thank the Lord I'm not thirty yet," Marshall quipped, tapping the toe of his cowboy boot against an overturned pot. "Maybe I'll get married on the eve of my thirtieth birthday, just to get on Mom's nerves a little. Did you know that, in the Bible, it wasn't uncommon for men to be around forty before they married? I mean, Isaac and—"

Mom shook her head, waving a finger at her youngest son. "Just because you're not thirty doesn't mean you're exempt from my little chat. And I appreciate your biblical knowledge, however that still doesn't mean much. Certainly not in your case. In fact, I know exactly who—"

"Don't say it," Marshall interrupted. "Again, for the millionth time, Jess and I are friends and we'd both like to keep it that way."

Sarah snorted, her arm wrapped around her husband. "You're so wrong about that. She likes you and you like her, but you're too worried you'll 'mess up' your friendship." She grinned up at her husband, to which he responded with a kiss to her forehead. Like they were newlyweds instead of just having their sixth wedding anniversary in January. They were like the super couple of super couples both in appearances—Chris was tall and lean, Sarah was average height and fit—and in parenting, work, and all other areas of life. Chris's remote job at a marketing firm from his home state of South Carolina allowed them flexibility and a generous but not over-the-top yearly income. "Let me tell you, marrying your best friend is the best idea ever. I'm living proof."

"What if we shift our focus back to the project our sons are taking on and let God handle the rest?" Dad placed his hands on Mom's shoulders, chuckling as he steered her back onto the sidewalk. "Do you have any ideas in that brilliant mind of yours, my beautiful wife?"

Wynn fell in step beside Ember, Marshall on his other side, and laughed as Mom continued to list off matchmaking ideas. Maybe they could have a singles event at The Gardens, she suggested, or Wynn and Marshall could have an open house to celebrate their ten year business anniversary.

Come to think of it, they probably should have some kind of open house for that, but he wasn't keen on the idea of it being matchmaking based. Potential clients who needed house projects or a house itself? Yes. Women who were interested in coming solely to flirt with him? No, thank you.

CHAPTER

four

How was a girl supposed to pack for a three-month-long work project in a small Nebraska town? Correction: a work project that included *renovations*. No, she hadn't been hired to do that part of it, but maybe she could help out some, right? After having HGTV on in the background all day today, she knew some new things about renovating. She could definitely hop on the design train—it wasn't required to have any special education or degree for that, according to the Google search she'd ran somewhere between doing a load of laundry and figuring out what to take along.

This was still considered a business trip, so she'd selected a variety of clothing that she'd wear to the office, like ankle pants, a couple blazers, some blouses, business-casual dresses and, of course, heels. Then, because spring was approaching, she'd added casual clothes like shorts, skirts, T-shirts, dresses, jeans, and whatever stuck out to her. If she needed something, she could probably order it online or get it in Balsam Falls. A quick browse of the town's website had made her even more excited to hit the road tomorrow. Balsam Falls had a plethora of fun boutiques, plenty of town activities, and lots of restaurants from what she'd seen. She had little doubt it'd live up to the small-but-not-too-small vacation lake town it was made out to be.

Noelle pulled her mug from the microwave and lowered her chamomile tea bag into the hot water, bobbing it up and down like a puppet. She'd loaded her suitcases and miscellaneous things into her rental after supper, which meant she now had some time to unwind, enjoy her tea, and ponder exactly how this was going to work. The logistics were in place: Carter, Inc.'s current projects were passed to Grant in her absence, Noelle would still be reachable if someone needed to, and she'd be back by June first.

She was more stumped on this event Balsam Falls had hired her to coordinate.

Fuzzy socks on, hair washed and up, and tea in hand, Noelle slid open the screen door and stepped out onto her small backyard patio. She could enjoy the sunset while she thought about...well, everything.

What would Nebraska sunsets be like?

Sky awash with bright oranges and pinks and a fiery sun in the middle? Or would they be more pastel colors, the sun a little more subdued?

Something she'd enjoyed doing with Grandpa and Grandma was watching sunsets from their second story balcony. Grandpa had spun tales of how when the sun went down and the moon came up, the sun was simply taking a nap. God had designed it that way to represent when humans were supposed to rest and when they were supposed work or play. Grandpa, however, hadn't completely followed his own guidance, because Noelle had heard him padding around in his office after she'd gone to bed, working. To provide a living like he had for her and Grandma. To build the company he had.

Noelle rested her head against the back of the Adirondack chair, legs tucked under herself. Her grandparents had been entrepreneurs, and they'd raised her to want to be one. Yes, she'd "worked" for Carter, Inc., but it had been her grandparents' company. Something she'd been passionate about. Something she *was* passionate about.

And now she was CEO of the company, a title she still wasn't entirely sure she deserved. Grandpa had made it look effortless, even the late nights and early mornings. He'd been so...smooth and respectful in his business practices, from hiring to firing to everything in between.

Noelle felt like she was jumping the gun when hiring someone and hurting someone when she fired them.

Sure, she had a backbone. She wasn't technically intimidated by anyone in the corporate world she worked and lived in, but more scared of letting her late grandparents down.

"Oh, Noelle, just the person I wanted to see."

Noelle straightened as her neighbor, an eighty-something woman by the name of Lily Collins, ambled over from her own patio. The woman wasn't Grandma, but she'd helped fill the void after losing Grandpa last year. Invited Noelle for tea and scones, given her a Christmas present, and even went for walks with Noelle on the more mild evenings. Lily's husband had passed away several years ago, and her kids were scattered all over the US. One of her grandsons played in the NFL, Noelle did know that much, and another was in the Coast Guard.

"I heard you're leaving me tomorrow," Lily continued, pulling her bright coral cardigan snug around her slender frame, her matching toenails peeking out from her bedazzled sandals. "Or was that just a rumor?"

"No, I'm afraid it's not a rumor." Noelle motioned to the open chair beside her—it'd been in the tiny shed when she was first exploring the house, so she kept it out just for Lily—and wrapped her hands around her mug as Lily sat. "I've been hired to coordinate an event in Balsam Falls, Nebraska. At the place where my grandma tended gardens. The town is planning to restore the whole property, I guess."

Noelle had told Lily about her grandparents, what they'd loved to do and how they'd sacrificed and how important their love had been to her. The only person she'd confided in, really. Not that she didn't have friends. She did. Just not...ones she felt comfortable sharing everything with. Maybe it was because she hadn't grown up like other children who were raised by their parents and went to school instead of being homeschooled.

She still wouldn't change her upbringing.

Sometimes, yes, she wished her parents had been or still were or could be a part of her life. But that didn't mean she resented the amazing childhood she'd been blessed with.

"Tell me about these gardens." Lily broke into Noelle's thoughts, orange sunset bathing her shoulder-length white hair in light. "You've mentioned them before, of course, but now you actually get to see them."

Noelle took a sip of tea before responding. "Grandma tended to them when she was young and all the way until they moved to Jackson, I think. She and Grandpa got married in front of one of the fountains there. Because of the town having The Falls and Falls Lake—both tourist attractions—the water fountains were a big part of them. But they haven't been kept up on the inside or the outside for twenty years. I tried to find some pictures online. No luck. I did find my grandparents' wedding photo, though."

"So you weren't kidding when you said they were restoring them."

"No, I think they need some pretty big renovations." Noelle felt the corners of her mouth lift. "I may have had HGTV on all day while I got stuff ready to go."

Laughter lines fanned out around the older woman's blue eyes. "There's the Noelle I know. Maybe you'll get to swing a hammer or something like that while you're up there."

Noelle chuckled. "I admit, tearing down walls looks kind of fun to me. Not that anyone should trust me to do that. They really shouldn't, now that I think about it."

Lily leaned forward and patted Noelle's sweat pant-clad knee. "Don't be so certain about that. Perhaps the walls you'll be tearing down won't be solely physical ones. I've found that, more often than not, our best inspiration or soul searching comes when we step into unchartered territory. This, I believe, qualifies as just that."

CHAPTER
five

Snow in November or, more importantly, December? Fifty-
one forty-nine-percent chance, odds not in favor of a white
Christmas. Snow in March when Wynn had a house to
finish? Hundred percent chance. They'd gotten four inches
overnight and flakes were still floating down from the dreary gray
sky outside. Wynn was supposed to be at the jobsite this morning,
but at this rate, none of the landscaping plans they'd wanted to
work on would be doable.

"Wynn? You there?"

Jerking his focus from the snow falling outside the coffee shop
window, Wynn glanced at his friend. "What?"

"Do you have a girlfriend I don't know about?" Seth Johnson
narrowed his eyes accusingly. "You were pretty far gone just now.
Come on, what's her name?"

"I don't have a girlfriend, Seth."

"Then what's with the faraway look?"

"The fact that this snow hinders our work on Jenna's house.
That the city council voted to go forward with restoring The

Gardens." He took a sip of his coffee. "That Mom and Dad's thirty-fifth wedding anniversary is next month."

Seth frowned. "I'm still not so sure about that whole restoration thing. I mean, the place hasn't been touched in twenty years. You'd be better off using it as a haunted park or something during the month of October. Or just bulldozing it. Then I wouldn't have an onslaught of teens seeking a thrill to deal with."

"You have to admit that you're a *little* bit intrigued by the idea, though."

"Far as I know there isn't a law stating that."

Wynn leaned back in his chair. "I get what you're saying. It has been a while since the place has been touched. But it's a business opportunity for me, so you might understand my enthusiasm here."

"Fair enough," Seth conceded. "You gonna plan the Spring Fling too?"

"Ha. No. Apparently someone from Mississippi is handling that. I wouldn't know the first thing about planning a party."

"Sounds like you're gonna have to learn, if your parents' anniversary is coming up." Seth rose a dark brow. "Thirty-five years, huh? That's a long time."

"Are you implying that I'm old?"

Seth rolled his eyes. "No. Well, maybe. But the point is that you'll have to plan some sort of party for them. Or your sisters will, but I doubt you'll be let off the hook from helping some."

"Yeah, but at least that would be a little more low key. They'd probably task me with making appetizers or something. I'm the most concerned about Jenna's house, I'll admit. If the snow doesn't let up soon..."

"She doesn't have to have landscaping to move in. I mean, it's a brand-new house in a much better neighborhood than where she currently is. I highly doubt she'll be picky."

Wynn grinned. "Now who's all funky? You like her."

"Wha—No. I've helped her. Interfered when necessary because of my *job*."

"You know, you sound like Marshall when it comes to your sister. Denial, denial, denial. You of all people should recognize that."

Seth's expression shifted to a full scowl. "We aren't here to discuss my love life, Bryant."

Wynn let out a low whistle. "That statement implies you actually have a love life. Wait, is it you that has the secret girlfriend?"

"No. Definitely not." Seth finished off his coffee and pushed away from the table. "While it was fun discussing your terrible party planning skills, I have work to do. From the sounds of it, so do you."

"Nah. It's just all fun. All the time."

"You tell yourself that." Cynicism laced Seth's words.

Wynn stood and slipped his phone into the pocket of his jacket. "They say that if you affirm something enough it comes true."

"Yeah, well, 'they' say a lot of things."

"True point. You know, Seth, sometimes you're just such an inspirational speaker. Remind me again why you don't take those speeches on the road?"

Seth shook his head as they moved towards the door. "Funny. Remind me why you didn't go into stand-up?"

Wynn reached for the door handle and opened it for none other than Jenna Williams and her kids. He did his best to hide his grin as Seth stepped aside to allow them in. His buddy could deny it all he wanted, but it was pretty clear his feelings weren't solely out of duty to the young mother. Jenna's ex-husband, Pete, had been less than deserving of the titles husband and father. Which was the polar opposite of Seth—if he'd forget about his own scars and open up.

And, if he took stock of the potential "couple" together like his mother or grandmother would, they did look good. Seth, with his tall, lean frame and serious personality. Jenna, with her petite frame and undoubtedly strong mindset.

"My mommy said I can get a cimanon roll," Jenna's four-year-old daughter, Ella, told Seth. "Do you like cimanon rolls, Office Seth?"

Pink colored Jenna's cheeks as she rested a hand on her daughter's head of dark curls. "Her version of Officer," she explained, mostly to Wynn. Obviously Seth had heard it before. "I'm sure Officer Seth has plenty of work to do today, El, so we better let him go."

"As a matter of fact, I do like cinn—" Seth was cut off by a wail from Jenna's youngest child, two-year-old Eli.

"Hey, you're okay," Jenna soothed, pressing her lips to the boy's forehead. "Mommy's got you, baby boy."

"If your mother doesn't mind, I'll cover the cinnamon rolls today." Seth held his hands out. "I can take him, Jen."

Tears welled up in Jenna's eyes as she passed her son to Seth's open arms. Wynn smirked at Seth as they walked by, to which Seth replied with a shake of his head. So much for the aforementioned "work" he'd mentioned only minutes ago.

Wynn stepped out onto the sidewalk, a gentle quietness surrounding him as snowflakes drifted down. He tucked his hands into the pockets of his leather jacket, walking the short distance down the block to his truck. He'd swing by the jobsite and check in with Marshall, then come back to the office and get some paperwork squared away. A sometimes unfortunate part that came with being the older brother, but he couldn't complain. Not really.

At the last second, Wynn took a right onto Falls Drive. Marshall could hold down the fort for a few more minutes. It couldn't hurt to swing by The Gardens. Some of his best inspiration came from being on the property, whether that was an empty lot, an already-in-progress site, or a renovation project.

This could be considered the latter, and based on what he'd seen Saturday after the council had voted to proceed Friday, he was going to need all the inspiration he could get.

CHAPTER

Six

Some things aged well—like cheese or wine—but this place clearly had not.

Noelle stepped around a pile of glass and dust and dirt that'd apparently been swept into a heap and then abandoned like the rest of the place. She was beginning to second-guess her decision to accept the key from the mayor—a man who had to be in his sixties and was even more exuberant in person than over the phone—to come and see The Gardens before going to the Serendipity Inn. She'd wanted to leave Saturday so she could have some quiet time to settle in, but Sunday had been the official departure day, so here she was. Standing in a place that could easily qualify as a haunted house.

She'd never been interested in that sort of thing and didn't plan to start now. She had agreed to planning this event, though, so she just needed to forget about the cobwebs woven into every available corner or doorway. Or that portrait painting whose eyes seemed to follow her everywhere. If it was up to her, pretty much everything would have to go.

There was one neat thing: the fountain that looked like a mirror. Even though it was dry—frankly, Noelle would be a little freaked out if the fountain was operative after twenty years of neglect—it was pretty. A little filthy and maybe broken, but still pretty. Simple, to the point. Unlike the clutter of boxes and items scattered around the rest of the place.

Noelle crossed the semi-large room to a closed door and tried the handle. Locked. Kind of expected that. She pulled the key Mayor Mason had given her from the pocket of her jacket. Wasn't the right key.

"How can I get you open?" she murmured to the emptiness of the place.

Of course, nobody answered. She paced back across to try and come up with some brilliant—*that.* The mirror fountain reflected her image and reminded her of the bun she'd put her hair in this morning before hitting the road. Pulling a bobby pin free, Noelle crossed back to the locked door and inserted it. After a little wiggling, the lock released and the door swung open to reveal another room of boxes, more cobwebs, and a large window that was grimier than she'd want to mess with.

Noelle stepped inside, drawn to the box labeled *Fine China.* For the most part she preferred modern day living, but there were a few things about the past she wouldn't mind making normal again. Such as how both men and women dressed, the standard—

A loud thump caused her to whirl around.

"No, no, no," she mumbled, rushing across the room to the door that'd closed on its own.

Noelle wiggled the door handle, tried to figure out how to unlock the door. No such luck. Apparently, it was only unlockable from the outside, and any person with a functioning brain would have tipped the kickstand down. Too late for that now. Maybe driving twelve hours yesterday and then three more today hadn't been the wisest.

She couldn't exactly call anyone to help her out of this situation she'd trapped herself in. Other than the mayor, she hadn't met anyone else, and even if she had, it wasn't like she'd know them well enough to call. What would she say? *Um, hello, I just locked myself into this room at The Gardens and it's really cold and I can't get out.* Not the best way to make new friends.

Her gaze moved around the room. Maybe there was something to pry that filthy window open and get out that way. Since the door was so nice and large and solid, she didn't think busting it down would be a particularly good option, if that was even possible. Her five-foot-five stature wasn't exactly built for that.

Back to the window scenario. Noelle found a box marked *Kitchen* and opened it, coughing as a plume of dust billowed up. Why the heck there was kitchen stuff for a kitchen-less building was beyond her. She moved a bag of cookie cutters out to reveal a cast iron frying pan.

"Aha!" Noelle pulled the pan from the box. "Your handle will make a fine crowbar." That was a term she learned Saturday during her HGTV marathon while she packed. Felt kind of good to have a slightly more expanded knowledge of the construction world.

Step one was to figure out the best way to use the handle. Up or down? If she flipped the pan upside down, the handle might curve in a better direction. That decided, Noelle wedged the handle under the seal of the window and leaned into the pan.

Didn't budge.

"Okay, let's try—"

A thump came from the main room and she froze as footsteps moved around. Somebody else was inside. Had she left the door unlocked? What if it was some kind of burglar that'd been watching her this whole time? Or, better yet, what if this was all a setup? Sure, the mayor seemed like a very nice man, but didn't they all? Unlikely, maybe, but very possible.

She bounced on the pan again.

No budge.

Again.

The footsteps got a little fainter. Either they were going to leave or, and if her earlier assumptions were correct this option was more likely, they wanted her to think they were leaving.

She really needed that window to open.

At least she'd donned tennis shoes, leggings, and a jacket today. That'd make running for the safety of her car much easier. Not that she was a runner. Yoga was much more up her ally. The occasional jog. Definitely walking. She wasn't opposed to doing a few bicep curls here and—

Noelle let out a scream as a mouse scampered across the windowsill. The pan clattered to the ground as she jumped and clamped her hands over her mouth. Footsteps neared the door.

No, no, no.

This was bad. Very bad.

Heart racing, Noelle retrieved the pan and flattened herself against the wall, hoping against hope the mouse had made itself scarce because of all the racket. Her breath quickened as the doorknob rattled. It was locked, though. She should be safe.

Then it turned. *Oh, no.*

Forcing her fear-induced limbs to cooperate, Noelle lifted the skillet, ready to thump the intruder if push came to shove. Which, considering the door was opening right this very moment, she needed to unfreeze her legs too. She was pretty certain her plan to utilize the skillet would be null and void if she was frozen in place.

"Hello?" *A man's voice.*

"Step foot in here and I will use this." Why, why, *why* did her voice wobble like that? She took a step forward. "I—I have a frying pan. A skillet. A cast iron skillet."

"Ma'am, I don't—"

Noelle forgot about trying to escape this room. She shoved her weight against the door to close it, hoping he would take the hint to not underestimate her.

It, very much like that traitorous window, didn't budge.

God, if You're there, some kind of divine intervention would be helpful right about now.

Cast iron skillet still wielded and ready like a baseball bat, Noelle backed away. Maybe if she pretended like she'd given up he'd do the same. Maybe it'd help.

It didn't.

The door opened all the way and there was a tall man that took up the whole doorway and Noelle decided to forget her original plan. She made a run for it, skillet in hand, and darted around the man to go out the door. Perks of being a small person, this was.

Then she ran straight into a wall.

Noelle groaned, then shrieked when the wall moved. She backed away, her eyes widening as they slowly focused on the navy blue-clad figure before her. The badge on his chest.

Oh, just let me sink into nothingness now.

"This is your idea of a break in?" the cop asked.

Noelle felt so very lost. Also, why had he left the door open? Snow swirled in and caused her to shiver. It was March. By now at home temps were crawling into the sixties. She had not been prepared to drive into a winter wonderland. She wasn't a winter wonderland expert by any stretch of the imagination, and that was a fact.

"Well, pardon me, but the vehicle outside has California plates, Seth." That came from the other man. The one who'd apparently come up behind her. Who was apparently on a first name basis with the officer, because the tag on his chest read *S. Johnson.* "By the way, I don't recommend sharing what your weapon is. Kind of ruins the purpose of it."

Noelle couldn't seem to form words as she risked a glance over her shoulder. *Oh.* The man she'd termed as a burglar was definitely not of a typical burglar appearance. This man was tall, his brown hair closely cut on the sides, longer on top, and dusted with snowflakes. Broad shoulders. Amused blue eyes. Quirked lips. Wearing jeans, cowboy boots, and a t-shirt with flannel layered overtop, a brown leather jacket to complete the look.

"Also, that weapon of choice is very *Tangled*-esque of you," he continued.

"I, uh..." Noelle slowly lowered the pan, unwilling to fully surrender it right away. "You know *Tangled?*"

Oh, for the love of movies. That was the first question she asked him?

The officer shifted his weight, crossing his arms over his chest. Clearly he had better things to do. Noelle couldn't say she didn't. By now, if she hadn't locked herself in that room, she could've been on her way to the inn. Better yet, at the inn already.

"It was Sadie's favorite movie at one point." He glanced at the cop. "What are you irritated about? That I interrupted your cinnamon roll da—"

"Don't say it, Bryant," the cop warned. The intruder-not-intruder's name was Bryant? Beneath the gruff tone, Noelle sensed a little bit of humor in the cop's voice, though. His height worked nicely on the whole intimidation front, and Noelle had a feeling that humor could shift to threatening quite quickly. "Ma'am, since you decided against using your skillet on us, do you mind explaining why you're here? This is private property."

Okay, so the dry humor she'd detected wasn't as amusing when directed at her. "I—I have a key. My name is Noelle Carter, and I'm here to plan the event that's supposed to take place here at the end of May. Mayor Mason gave me a key, so I figured I would come by here before going to the inn."

"And the California plates? Word is you were coming from Mississippi."

Oh, of course. "It's a rental," she hurried to explain, gaze bouncing between the two men. Both very tall, but one wore a more granite-like expression and the other appeared as though he wanted to burst out laughing. "What? It's true?"

The Bryant man held his hands up. No wedding band. So who was the aforementioned Sadie? And why had she noticed his bare ring finger? "Hey, I never said it wasn't."

Heat worked its way into Noelle's cheeks now that her initial fear or shock or whatever it was had worn off. "Um, so, if you don't need anything else from me, I think I'll just be going. Oh, I have the key though, so you'll both have to leave also. Too, I mean. You'll have to leave too. Before me." The cold was getting to her. Making her tongue freeze up.

"Name is Seth Johnson, by the way," the cop said, offering his hand. "Local chief of police."

Noelle accepted his hand, trying not to let her embarrassment show. "Noelle Carter. Which I already said."

Seth smiled lightly, though it didn't fully reach his mossy blue eyes nor fully crease his shadowed jaw. "Nice to meet you. See you later, Wynn."

Wait, was his name Wynn or Bryant?

"Sorry for breaking up your date with Jenna," the man—Wynn, apparently?—called after the cop. He received a grunt in response, then glanced at her. "You can loosen your death grip on the handle now."

Instinctively, she tightened it. "But h-how do I know this isn't a setup? I mean, you could've called that cop in to cover up your criminal behavior and make it look like you're a good guy so then I trust you and I don't know, let you take me away."

He chuckled. He actually had the audacity to *chuckle.* "Watch a lot of crime shows, do you?"

A gust of wind reached in and curled its fingers around her, but she refused to shiver. She did not need him knowing that she was cold and therefore her mind was probably not operating at full capacity. "Are you trying to gauge how much I know about a criminal mind?"

"No. It was just a question based on your assessment of me. An inaccurate assessment, by the way."

"Actually, Hallmark is more my style." She inched towards the open door. "Not that you needed to know that. You didn't. I'm just gonna go now, okay? Forget this all happened, yeah?"

He nodded at the pan, his hands tucked in the pockets of his jeans. "Planning to take that with you? I believe they consider that theft. Then who'd be the criminal?"

"No. I was planning to drop it just before I ran out the door." That was a lie, but really it was probably a good idea.

"I don't recommend running out the door. Or anywhere."

"Okay, if you're insinua—"

"I'm not insinuating anything. It's icy underfoot and you have tennis shoes on. Also, your car probably won't get you very far."

Noelle straightened, her height seriously lacking in comparison to his. What was he, six-two? Six-three? "I made it all the way here, thank you very much. Have a good day, Mr. Bryant."

With that, she turned and marched out the door, gasping as biting snow peppered her cheeks. *Don't turn around. Whatever you do, do not turn around. You can march out of here and just go to the inn and forget this ever happened. The inn is—*

She turned around halfway to her car when she realized she had no idea where the inn was located.

"That was quick," Wynn quipped when she walked back in. He hadn't moved an inch, and was it her imagination or did he look even more amused? And even better looking, now that her pulse had slowly started to return to normal.

"I don't know how to get to the inn," she admitted, chin tipped up. "So, if you could just tell me how to get there, I'd appreciate it."

He seemed to weigh the idea for a moment, then, "No."

"No?" she sputtered. "What do you mean, *no?* This isn't funny."

"You're going to the Serendipity Inn, right?"

She nodded. With reluctance. Nothing like saying exactly where she was going. Good looking or not, she didn't fully trust him.

"I'll take you. Got a four-wheel-drive truck. I know the family who owns it pretty well."

"What the—No. Uh-uh. If you think I'm going to ride in your vehicle and trust you, you're wrong. Not happening. My car and I will be fine."

He rose a brow. "Really? What, do you want me to call my mother or something for a reference? The police chief didn't do enough?"

This would be so much easier if he wasn't as smooth as water down a parched throat. "Officer Johnson didn't exactly sing your praises."

44

"Seth and I have been friends since we were little. He doesn't sing anyone's praises."

"If that was supposed to convince me, it didn't."

Wynn sighed. "Look, I don't know you, you don't know me. I get it. But trust me, I've lived in Nebraska my whole life and if you don't have a vehicle suitable for winter weather conditions, you shouldn't drive in them. Take it or leave it."

She really, really, did not want to give in. Sure, it was a small town and he seemed like a nice guy, but didn't they all? Wasn't there a saying somewhere about the good-looking ones being the bad guys or something?

"I'll call my mother," he repeated, that amusement back in his expression. "She might be doing something right now, but I'm sure she'd stop to tell you some, oh, let's see here, reassuring facts about her favorite son."

Noelle rolled her eyes. "No, thanks. I'll be fine. Really, I will be."

"All righty then." He moved to exit the door, then peeked back inside. "Usually the lady goes first, but since you kind of ordered Seth and I to go so you can lock the door, here I am going. Good luck with the drive, Ms. Carter."

The nerve! And yet, Noelle had zero reason to be mad about his leaving because, yes, she had told him and Seth to leave first so she could lock it. But still. She hadn't *ordered* them to go. They— or, in this case, solely Wynn—could've easily waited for her. There was a fairly slim chance of her being able to push him out if she really wanted to go there.

It still irked her that the door had apparently been unlocked for him. How did that work?

With a final glance around, Noelle stepped back into the icy mix, pulled the door closed and locked it. She tucked her chin into her jacket and crossed the lawn to her waiting car, breathing a sigh of relief once inside.

Key in the ignition, Noelle turned it and cranked the heater, then pulled her phone from her pocket. She could find the Serendipity Inn just fine. No, she *would* find it just fine.

Case in point, her destination was the inn, and she planned to get there.

———— ✍ ————

CHAPTER

Seven

By the time a sign for the Serendipity Inn came into view, Noelle's knuckles were probably permanently white and her GPS was probably no longer on speaking terms with her.

Noelle breathed a sigh of relief as she pulled into the parking lot beside a white SUV, even though her stomach growled. A glance at the dash clock said it was quarter after twelve, meaning it'd taken her a half hour to travel all of maybe a half mile. But she was here, Wynn Bryant hadn't followed her that she knew of, and she'd made it without asking for assistance. Really, it wasn't even snowing much now. Just blowing hard. Not that she was a winter weather expert or anything. It may have been a good idea to check the forecast before leaving Mississippi, but since it was March she'd expected spring-like temps.

If this was Nebraska's version of spring, this event she'd been hired to coordinate wasn't going to be like the tentative ideas she'd been imagining.

That wasn't her present predicament to focus on, though. For a moment she simply took in the view of the two-story house, amazed at the architecture of it. A long porch wrapped around the side of the first level like a welcoming embrace, and even through somersaults of blowing snow she could see an indigo door. Maybe a porch swing or two?

Pale gray siding was contrasted by white trim, wooden window shutters, and that blue door. Smoke curled out of a large white brick chimney extending from the shingled roof, and a sign reading *Serendipity Inn* dangled from the eve over the porch. Based on the brick paved sidewalk leading up to the porch steps, their landscaping once spring came—they did have spring in Nebraska, right?—would be just as cute as the exterior of the house itself. Her little house in Mississippi, though fun-sized and cute, totally paled in comparison to this. Even her childhood home—a regal, colonial-style home constructed of red bricks, complete with white pillars—had a different air to it. This was just…beautiful. Serendipitous, given the name.

In short, no, she wouldn't have a hard time living here for three months. Leaving may be another story.

Noelle turned the car off and gathered her purse that doubled as her backpack. She decided against trying to lug her other luggage in while the wind whipped like it was. Both her laptop and her phone were in her bag, and she wouldn't need a change of clothes for now. A heavier coat might be nice, but that would have to wait. She didn't own as heavy of one as she'd like. Even Christmastime in Jackson was usually mild.

Tucking her chin yet again, she crossed to the porch and reached the door. Which was much heavier and bluer up close than she'd thought. She gave it a good pull but it didn't move. What was it with her and doors or windows today?

It wasn't until the third attempt that she realized it was a push door.

A nap may be first on the list, right after food. Food was definitely her highest priority after checking in.

Immediately upon stepping inside, she was greeted. By warmth, the delicious scent of apple, and one very furry golden retriever.

"Well, hello there," she laughed, letting the door close. "You are adorable. Yes, you are."

The outside of the house was nothing compared to the inside. Dark, walnut floors and pale walls. Wooden beams crawled across the ceiling overhead of this entryway hall, stairs to the right. A doorway by the staircase peeked into a sitting room, and the closed door to the left was probably a closet. Noelle caught a glimpse of the kitchen down the hall behind the check in desk, and a living room beyond that.

"Nova, come over here." A petite, middle-aged woman with dark hair walked into the entryway, reaching for the dog's collar. "I'm sorry. She's harmless, but she will attack you with kisses and tail wags. Can I help you?"

Noelle scratched the dog's silky head. "She's adorable. I love dogs. I just don't have the time or space to have my own. And yes, I'm here to check in. The reservation should be under Noelle Carter."

"Ah, yes. We've been excited for you to arrive." The woman released the dog, who sat down with her tail wagging, and led Noelle to the desk with a sign reading *Check In Here* overhead. "My husband John and I own the place. My name is Jackie, by the way. How were the roads in this weather?"

"Oh, they were okay. Not that I'm used to this kind of weather. I admit, I expected warmer weather."

Jackie accepted Noelle's debit card. "Came as a surprise, actually. Nebraska weather can be unpredictable. Could be eighty degrees tomorrow and it would be considered normal. Weird, but still normal to us. Here's your card back, as well as your key. You'll be in room three for your stay."

"Your house is beautiful. I love the airy feel." Noelle had seen some impressive event spaces, been to some five-star hotels, but this place just seemed special in its own way. "I have to say, it beats a hotel."

"Well, thank you. John and I—and our children, of course—want this place to feel like home away from home for our guests."

"Considering I've only been here for a few minutes, you've accomplished just that. Oh, do you know of any place to get lunch? I should've picked something up in town, I guess."

Jackie fluttered a hand. "Nonsense. We've got a fully stocked kitchen. Get settled in your room—my youngest son, Marshall, will bring your luggage up—and then I'll have some food ready for you in about twenty minutes or so. Is there anything to stay away from?"

"Nope." Noelle scooted her bag up on her shoulder, fighting back a yawn. "I'm not a picky eater. Although, I'm not really a fan of broccoli."

Jackie laughed, crinkling the corners of her dark brown eyes. "Honestly, neither am I. I'll steer clear of any baby trees. Your room is up the stairs and the second door on the left."

"Wonderful. Thank you so much."

CHAPTER

Eight

Wynn took his boots off on the mat inside the back door before walking into the kitchen and dropping a kiss on his mother's cheek. "Hey, Mom. Woah, what smells so good? Wait, is that your spaghetti? I didn't miss a special meal or anything right?"

She patted his stubbled cheek. "You're a little charmer today, I see. And no, I'm just getting a little something made for our new guest. Noelle Carter got here today. Pretty little thing."

Oh, he remembered vividly how pretty she was from only an hour and a half ago. Wide blue eyes that'd been full of spit and vinegar. Blonde hair that was probably pretty long if not for the bun she'd arranged on the top of her head. Wearing clothing that was most definitely not fit for a wintery day in Nebraska.

In hindsight, she kind of looked like Rapunzel from *Tangled*. Sort of ironic, considering the whole cast iron skillet scenario.

"Wynn? Did you hear me?"

He snatched a golden brown piece of garlic toast from the cookie sheet on the counter. "I did."

Mom rose a dark eyebrow. "And you didn't deny what I said?"

"Hard to deny when it's the truth."

"All right. What's going on? Usually you—"

A crash came from the entryway vicinity. Wynn glanced at his mother, who looked equally as baffled as he felt. Maybe Nova had gotten into something. It was odd she hadn't come to greet him when he came in. Toast in hand, Wynn wove around the marble topped island and through the open concept archway, then down the hall.

In a heap but still moving—and groaning with the movement—at the bottom of the wooden landing was none other than Noelle Carter herself.

He shouldn't laugh. He really shouldn't. It would be rude to laugh.

He cleared his throat instead.

Noelle's head jerked up and surprise followed up by confusion flickered through those big eyes of hers. Huh, she must've taken her hair down. It tumbled in loose waves around her shoulders now. A few strands fell in front of her face as she pushed to a sitting position.

"You?" Accusation punctuated her words. "What are you doing here?"

"Noelle?" Mom came up beside him, dish towel in hand. "Oh, dear, are you all right? What happened? Wynn, you could help the girl to her feet."

Lips twitching, he held out his hand. She hesitated, then, and whether because his mother was standing there or because she genuinely wanted his help he didn't know, she grabbed ahold. He hoisted her to a standing position and held her hand until she took a wobbly step back.

"I, uh, probably shouldn't wear these socks on those steps next time," she said slowly, pink seeping into her cheeks as she straightened her gray Nike pullover and brushed that hair from her cheeks. It was definitely long. And pretty. *She* was pretty, his mother had been right about that. "My foot slipped when I was nearly to the bottom and, well, you know the rest, I guess."

"I have to ask," Wynn said. "Do you always make grand entrances? I mean, first it was the whole frying pan thing, and now this."

And there was that feisty expression from earlier. Yeah, minus the excessively long hair—hers did nearly reach her waist in the front, though—she resembled Rapunzel quite efficiently. "No, I don't, thank you very much. Did *you* follow me here?"

"Follow you here?" Mom looked back and forth between them, her brow creased. "What do you mean?"

Wynn grinned. "Yes, Ms. Carter, whatever do you mean?"

"I told you I could get here just fine on my own and I did." Now she adjusted her hair again, which actually only made it fall in front of her face. Again. "You didn't need to come see if I got here because you have a fancy truck and my car wouldn't do. But it did and I'm here just fine."

"I'm confused," Mom said. "Did you two—"

The door opened and all three of them turned as Ember walked in, brushing snow from her long, dark hair.

"Hey, big brother," she said, seemingly oblivious to Noelle standing there as she took off her woolen gray mittens. "Mom, I'm supposed to tell you that Marshall can't come to help with cleaning today because he supposedly has other work to do. Where is Nova at?"

Wynn was fairly sure he could see the moment when it clicked in Noelle's mind that the inn was owned by his parents. A fact that, yes, he had purposely kept from her earlier. She'd already been very untrusting of him, so why not have some fun with it? Only partially the reason, of course. He didn't want to blow the mayor's plans of hiring this event coordinator by running her out of town before she'd even had the chance to really see it. That was the reason he'd also withheld the fact that he and Marshall's company was handling the renovations. Hopefully she wouldn't renege when she did find out.

"You're..." Noelle's gaze moved between the three of them, then narrowed in on him. "That's a dirty trick."

"What are you talking about?" Mom asked. "You two have met?"

Wynn smirked. "Indeed we have. She tried to whack me with a cast iron skillet. Didn't succeed, in case you were wondering."

"Sometimes I myself would like to whack you with something like that," Ember mumbled as she poked her head into the front sitting room off the entryway. "Nova! Get your booty on out here."

"So you're his mom," Noelle said observingly. "Which means your parents own the inn and *you* didn't tell me that."

He nodded. "Astute observation."

"You guys met?" Mom repeated. "When?"

"I decided to swing by The Gardens before going to Jenna's house, and suddenly a loud scream came from the one room," Wynn explained. "The door to that room was unlocked, so I decided to check it out. Called Seth first, to be safe. Ms. Carter here was waiting for me on the other side with a skillet. Then she darted out and Seth happened to walk in, so they collided. Seth left shortly after, I offered to give her a ride here, and she turned me down. Here we are. End of story."

Ember's eyes widened. "Wow. I'm kind of impressed. Mom, do you know where Nova is? I'm going to take her to the library with me, and that's kind of hard to do if I don't have her."

"She was just around here somewhere." Mom gestured for Ember to follow her. "We'll find her. Noelle, there's food ready—spaghetti and garlic toast. Wynn here can get a plate for you and I'll come in once I'm done with Ember."

If she wanted to protest, she didn't. Wynn nodded down the hall and allowed her to go first, both their socked feet thudding dully on the hardwood floors. Mom must've made an apple pie or apple crisp because he caught a whiff of cinnamon-y apples contrasting the tangy tomato sauce. He had his mother to thank for the cooking skills he did know, which were amazingly more expansive than both his sisters'. One of which was married with two children.

Noelle let out a gasp when they walked into the kitchen, then pivoted to face him. "This house just keeps getting more amazing. I cannot believe this kitchen."

He watched as she ran her fingertips over the marble countertop, her gaze taking in the space. It was impressive—he'd give her that much. Lightly stained white oak cabinets lined a backsplash-tiled wall and wrapped around the side wall like an L, with a matching wood-disguised hood over the stove. Appliances that'd been updated a few years ago, all of them stainless steel. His personal favorite was the six burner stove with a double oven underneath; a pricey appliance but so, so very worth the investment.

Situated in the middle with a second sink was a massive island—cabinets around half and barstools the remainder. A breakfast nook that'd doubled as a study corner when he was younger had been nestled into a semicircle of windows overlooking the expansive Falls Lake. And then there were the French doors that opened to the back deck and the same view. The long wooden table between the kitchen and main living room could seat up to twenty people, perfect for the breakfasts the inn provided.

So yeah, he could see why she'd be amazed.

"Seriously," she continued. "I don't think I've ever seen a more beautiful kitchen. Can I just move it into my house?"

Wynn opened his mouth to respond but she spoke before he could.

"Don't answer that." Color bloomed in her cheeks and she slid a pointed toe across the recently swept hardwood. "That's a terrible question. Besides, it wouldn't even fit in my house, to be honest."

"I'm sure Mom would let you use it while you're here."

Her brows raised. "About that. You lied."

Wynn snorted as he grabbed two white plates from the exposed shelf above the double wide stainless steel sink. "I never once lied."

"You said that you"—she made air quotes—"'knew the family who owned the inn very well.'"

"Exactly. Not a lie." Spaghetti on each plate, he drizzled sauce on top then retrieved the fresh parmesan from the fridge and a grater from the island drawer. "Parmesan?"

Her eyes widened even more. "Yes, please. And you kept the information from me, so you can practically consider that a lie. Also, can I have two pieces of toast?"

"Certainly. And to be exact, it wasn't a lie because I do know them very well." He slid a plate across the island to her. "They just happen to be my family instead of good friends. By the way, Mom makes her sauce spicier than I do, so just be warned. It's good, just kind of spicy. Says it keeps her young."

She twirled her fork in the spaghetti, a sort of concentration on her face as she lifted it to her mouth and took the bite. Part of him would be amused if it was really, extra spice this time. But at the same time, he hoped she enjoyed it. The rest of her day, maybe partially because of him, had been a little iffy.

"Wow." She took a long drink of water from the glass he'd filled for her. "That's spicier than I thought it would be. But it's good. Really good."

Wynn readied his own bite. "Mom'll be happy to hear that. If you think this is good, though, you should try her lasagna. Not as spicy, but it's meatier, cheesier, and she puts her personally homemade noodles in it."

"That sounds like absolute heaven," she mumbled, her eyes closed as if picturing the meal he'd described. "My grandma loved to cook. I wish I'd picked up more skills from her, but I was more interested in going to the office with Grandpa. Don't get me wrong, I loved being with her too, but there was something about being in downtown Jackson..." She shook her head and twirled another bite, but didn't lift her fork. "Anyway, enough about me. What do you do? Other than scare the daylights out of people and call the cops on them."

He made a face. "To be fair, I'm not the one who made you scream. I was on my way to check out the back outside and then turned around *because* of your scream."

"No," she conceded, "that was a mouse that scared me. I'm not scared of them, though. Not really. Unless, like today, one decides to run out in front of me when I was already freaking out because I'd locked myself in a room and there was a stranger moving around outside the door. But usually I'm okay with the little creatures."

"So, hypothetically speaking, if a mouse scampered across your bed, you'd be fine with it?"

"Well, no, but wouldn't anybody be a little freaked out if there was a mouse in their bed?"

"Touché."

She took the bite she'd readied, then angled her gaze up at him after she'd swallowed. "Were you trying to avoid answering my question? Because it won't work. I'll ask you again."

"My younger brother—"

"Marshall?"

"Uh, yes. How did you know that?"

"Your mom mentioned that he'd carry my luggage in for me. Which may not happen since your sister—Ember, was it?—said he wouldn't be back to clean today or whatever. But I'll get it. After I put shoes on, of course. I only brought tennis shoes and some more business-y shoes, so I decided to wear only socks down here to eat. Didn't expect you to show up. Anyway, back to what you were saying."

Well, she was an observant one. A little odd, but observant. "Marshall and I own a construction company. Mostly to build homes for those in need, but we take on other projects too. Built a new gazebo for the town square a couple years ago after a wind storm claimed the old one. Designed and built the rooftop dining area for Farm to Table, as well as renovated the interior and the side outdoor dining space, oh, six or so years ago."

"Outdoor dining?" Intentional or not, her gaze darted to the nook windows. "People sit outside in this?"

"No. Well, yes. The rooftop is closed for the winter, but both the indoor and the other section are open year-round. The outside part is covered for the most part, and they use heaters. It's not cold and snowy like this all the time, though, you know."

Apprehension huddled in her expression; narrowed eyes and pursed lips. "It's March and it's snowing and blowing. Spring starts in a couple weeks."

"True. Some of our biggest snowstorms hit in March. But it also melts pretty fast most of the time." He paused for a bite of garlic toast. "Wait till summer. You'd realize that, for how cold it can be, it can get *hot*. A hundred degrees isn't uncommon for July or August. Seriously."

"I won't be here then, but who knows? Maybe I'll visit again. My grandma was from here, plus I was looking up Balsam Falls on Saturday and you guys have some neat attractions."

He nodded. "We do. A lot of sporadic activities pop up, but we have Spring Fling, Summer at the Falls, Fall Harvest, and then our downtown Christmas celebration, each of those annually. Plus lots of shops and walking trails and all that. Falls Lake is a big attraction. People love that in the summer, plus there's a lot of folks who only own summer homes and come for those months. We can get pretty touristy when warm weather hits."

"Okay, make that several trips back," she said with a slight laugh. "It sounds like The Gardens are the only unkempt part of town."

Wynn shook his head. "No, we've got an iffy side of the tracks, per se, just like pretty much every town does. Trailer houses, lower income areas, that sort of thing. The Gardens is one of the only more 'downtown' areas that's rundown, that's true. Not for much longer, though."

"I didn't see much of it while I was there, but I can see why my grandma loved the place so much. She took care of the literal gardens, I guess. And she and my grandpa got married there."

"You talk about your grandparents a lot..." Wynn trailed off there and directed his focus to his place. When had he eaten so much of his spaghetti?

"They raised me." She answered his mostly unasked question matter of factly, as if she was used to answering that way. "My mom—their daughter—is an actress. She and my dad weren't

58

married, I guess. Grandpa and Grandma didn't want me raised in Hollywood, so they raised me. Other than my mom's name, I don't really know anything about my parents."

Words eluded him for several seconds. He hadn't assumed she was rich and spoiled or anything like that, but he'd expected her to have parents who'd provided a cushier upbringing. Or at the very least, ones that were around. His family hadn't always been as fortunate as they were now monetarily, but her words just came as a shock to him. To grow up without parents... He couldn't imagine. Even if everything materialistic was stripped away, parents were parents. The people who were supposed to have your back, who were there to raise you until you grew up, got married, and started your own family. Even then they were meant to be grandparents.

Instead, Noelle had been raised by her grandparents solely.

"That's..." He pursed his lips. "I don't know what to say."

She lifted a slender shoulder. "It's okay. I mean, I have to say I'm grateful they didn't force me to grow up in LA. And my grandparents were fairly youthful people in the sense that they kept active and loved to do stuff. Seriously, it wasn't bad at all, and I don't want to make it seem like it was. My childhood really was a good one." She smiled then, as if saying *Conversation closed, please let it go.* "So, what're you working on now? A gazebo for the restaurant you were talking about?"

Wynn chuckled, still partially distracted by the previous topic. "No. We're currently building a house for a single mom. Her ex-husband isn't the most considerate guy around, I'll tell you that much. Hoping to have Jenna and the kids moved in by the end of this month. April at the latest. We've mostly got landscaping and a few interior touches left. Believe it or not, we had a mild enough winter that we could do a lot of work through it. Not like spring, summer, or fall, but we're almost finished and we started last fall, so there is that."

Her brows furrowed. "But how do you...fund it?"

"Some of it is donation based—the town loves to pitch in on projects like this, and our church will organize fundraisers. We also apply for grants and all that fun stuff. Plus, our local lumberyard and even a few bigger stores that aren't local will work with us on pricing a lot of the time when we're doing a project like this. As the book of Matthew puts it, 'Ask and you shall receive, give and it will be given to you.'"

"Wow. That's really amazing." She took another sip of water. "And after this house?"

He grinned, unable to stop himself. "Actually, funny thing is, Marsh and I pitched a bid to the city council. Our crew, mainly him and I until Jen's house is done, are handling the renovations for The Gardens."

And just like that, he wasn't the only one speechless.

CHAPTER
Nine

Had she ever actually seen someone frown? Like, in books when the author used *he* or *she frowned*, was it applicable in real life? Because if so, she was frowning right now.

Noelle groaned as she rolled over in the king-sized bed, satiny white sheets cocooning her like a swaddle blanket. She squinted one eye open to see the clock on the bedside table. 6:31 a.m. Maybe she could just roll back over and—

That awful, obnoxious noise blared again, the one that had caused her to frown in the first place.

What even was it? Not a siren, unless Nebraska had drastically different sirens than Mississippi. It kind of sounded like a cow being tortured. Or a goat. A chicken? How was she supposed to know? She'd grown up in the city and the only animals she'd been around were the dogs they'd had. Cassie, an Australian shepherd until Noelle was nine and then Olive, a golden retriever till she was twenty-one. She wasn't familiar with farm animals.

Left without much choice, she pushed the heavy ivory comforter aside and crawled out, goosebumps rippling her bare arms and legs. Maybe she should've opted for warmer pajamas than shorts and a T-shirt since she'd driven into a snowstorm yesterday. But then, she hadn't really brought anything else because again, it was nearly spring.

Noelle crossed the room and pushed open the floor-to-ceiling curtains, allowing morning sunshine to filter in. Normally she was a morning person. That bed had just been abnormally comfortable and warm and...

And that was the most beautiful view she'd seen in twenty-six years of life.

Okay, that might be an exaggeration, but *wow.*

Only a couple hundred feet from the back of the inn was a glittering blue lake that stretched on and on, trees and houses peeking out from the banks she could see. Snow blanketed the land and seemed to make the water that much more stunning and blue. Though she didn't see the sun—this room must be western-facing—she could tell it was fully out today. She was tempted to step out onto her own private balcony just to fully soak in the view, but a glance at her clothing and the snow outside the French doors had her changing her mind.

She stared at the view—the one she'd get to wake up to every morning for three months—for a few more minutes before she forced herself to turn and get ready for the day. How had she missed it last night? Maybe because the curtains had been closed and she'd decided against opening them because she was working? Which was unfortunate, because it had probably been a beautiful sunset.

Today's itinerary consisted of a meeting with the mayor and Wynn and Marshall Bryant to discuss how they were going to go about this project. The mayor, fine. Marshall Bryant, well, she hadn't met him, but he was probably fine. Wynn Bryant, though? It was unnerving how smooth the man was, and she'd only interacted with him three times. First at The Gardens. Second when he showed up at the inn. And third when he'd brought up her luggage and supper last night. She'd intended to go down and see what Balsam Falls had to offer food-wise, but then she'd started drawing up sketches and putting ideas on paper and before she knew it there'd been a knock at the door, her watch reading quarter after six.

Jackie's pot roast had been just as incredible as her spaghetti.

Dressed in skinny, dark-wash jeans and a loose purple T-shirt with a cardigan, she slipped out of her room. The aroma of breakfast wafted up from downstairs and Noelle felt her stomach growl in response. Or was it another farm animal she heard? Did Nebraska have wolves or bears? Why hadn't she looked up climate or wildlife before coming?

After making it down the stairs successfully and safely, unlike yesterday's awful stumble that she could still feel in her tailbone, she rounded the distressed wood banister and headed toward the kitchen. Wynn had told her they served breakfast from six-thirty to nine, and to come to the kitchen for it. He hadn't appeared to be teasing at that point.

Maybe if his eyes weren't so ridiculously blue and he didn't have such an effortlessly amused smile it would be easier to ignore him...

Noelle rounded the corner. And promptly halted.

On that massive marble island that was the size of her whole kitchen back home sat a feast. One of breakfast foods ranging from scrambled eggs to bacon to toast to muffins. Three pitchers were lined up, one filled with water, then apple juice and lastly orange juice. Something was steaming in a bowl between the bacon and the eggs. Hash browns?

At the extra long dining table constructed of rustic-looking wood and stained a light color, with light coming through the block of windows behind it—there was that exquisite view again—people sat, some eating and others carrying on conversations. She could pick out Ember, Wynn's little sister, from yesterday but the other eight or ten people must be other guests. Jackie was chatting with an older couple, a pot of coffee in hand.

"You made it down for breakfast."

Noelle startled at the sound of Wynn's voice behind her, causing her to slam her hand into the door jam. He really needed to stop scaring her, even if nobody else had noticed. She tried to muster up the sternest expression she could as she turned, but words wouldn't come. Not when he was standing barely two feet from her in jeans, bare feet, and a long-sleeved white T-shirt, the tips of his brown hair still damp from a shower. And that amusement... She cleared her throat.

"I did." Squeaky but not terrible. She straightened. "You told me I shouldn't miss it, so here I am. And it looks delicious."

He tucked his hands into the pockets of his jeans, tilting his head toward the kitchen. "Go ahead, since the lady wasn't able to go first yesterday. Oh, and you should try the bacon. I made that. Brought it just this morning."

Oh, yes, she'd forgotten that he'd mentioned he could cook. A quality she'd need in her future husband. The food she prepared wasn't exactly like this, and even though she liked the idea of cooking, she hadn't really been successful in her attempts up till now.

Wynn Bryant, however, wasn't a man on her radar. He was probably unavailable, anyway. His lack of wedding band didn't necessarily mean anything. Some men didn't wear a ring after so many months or years following the wedding, or he could just be dating someone. Engaged, even. Probably was. *Hopefully* was. That'd make it easier to ignore his fresh and very masculine cologne or soap or whatever that was and his obvious physical strength.

And for the record, Noelle would prefer her future husband to keep his band on.

"Oh, Noelle." Jackie hurried over, sporting a black and red plaid apron. Were those Christmas tree dish towels in the kitchen? "I'm so happy to see you joining us. Wynn must've relayed my message last night."

Noelle nodded. "He did, and I'm glad. This looks amazing. I'm not sure where to start."

"With the bacon, obviously." Wynn's warm breath tickled her ear, sending a shiver of awareness down her spine, and he stepped around her and dropped a kiss on his mother's cheek. "Morning, pretty lady. Missed you when I brought the bacon."

Jackie shook her head, but Noelle didn't miss the maternal delight in her eyes. "Not sure how, but I raised this boy right. As far as breakfast goes, grab a plate and help yourself. We've got plenty of food and plenty of room at the table for you, so eat up. You probably have an exciting day ahead."

Wynn passed her a plate with three slices of perfectly crispy looking bacon and winked. "A very exciting day, considering she gets to work with Marsh and I. And Mom, it's March. Time to transition the decorations."

Ah, so they were Christmas trees and not only because of the snow outside.

"Yes, yes, yes." Jackie set the coffee pot back on its rest and stirred the eggs. "I'll get there, Wynn. We *did* switch out everything outside of the kitchen. Pardon me if I like Christmas."

"She's a Christmas year-round kind of person," Wynn explained, leaning his hip against the cabinet, arms folded over his chest. *Yes, he was certainly muscular.* "But soon, like the temperatures, this place will be full of springy stuff. Just you wait."

CHAPTER
Ten

"A nd that's the plans that I have." Noelle folded her hands in her lap, her foot bouncing up and down.

Why was she wearing heels? They'd been sitting in the meeting room at Bryant Bros. for an hour now and Wynn had yet to figure it out. The snow had already started melting, yes, but heels? It made no sense.

"So you're thinking of having a full meal?" Mayor Leo leaned back in his chair, ankle crossed over his opposite knee as he regarded Noelle. "Instead of appetizers?"

"Well, no... I mean, kind of, but no. I just think that having something beyond appetizers may leave a more lasting impression on the guests." She darted a glance in Wynn's direction. "I mean, I know this is just a town event and not a fundraiser or anything, so appetizers might be more affordable. Which makes sense."

"Hold on just a moment..." Mayor Leo rose, his checkered yellow and blue button up pulled taut over his portly midsection. "You said fundraiser. Why don't we turn it into one? Yes! We could turn it into a gala, even. Choose a charity or—" he gestured towards Wynn and Marshall, seemingly picking up speed "—we could even donate the proceeds to you guys' company to use on your next project."

Marshall glanced sideways, then straightened in his chair. "Uh, we're not a charity, Mayor Leo. Got the W-9 and a memory bank overload from tax season to prove it."

"Yes, but you always do fundraisers for projects and you're the ones handling the restoration." The mayor returned to his chair, steepling his fingers on the wooden tabletop. "Or we find a different charity, but this could be a brilliant idea. Bring in music, have food, and encourage people to dress up. Summer at the Falls is a casual event and so is Fall Harvest. The Christmas gala is in the winter, so it's a fancy indoor event. But why not an indoor/outdoor one? People would love to have something after a cold winter."

"I, uh, well, we could do that," Noelle said, biting her lip. Man, she was cute when she was nervous. Not that it mattered. Considering she didn't seem to be his biggest fan, it definitely shouldn't matter. "I mean, I can easily switch things around. I've obviously planned parties for barbeque-simple or gala-fancy."

"But this changes the whole concept of the event," Wynn cut in, not sold on the idea. "People in town look forward to that barbeque-simple event, to use Noelle's words, every year. Just because we're changing the location doesn't mean the event should change. Like you said, we've got our Christmas gala. That's enough for one year in a town like Balsam Falls."

Noelle scrunched her brows together, determinedness in the tilt of her jaw. Oh boy. "And why can't there be two fancy events? Are you against dressing up or something, Wynn?"

"I mean, considering I'm a guy, I just really don't get into tutus or ball gowns." He flashed her a smirk. "I much prefer swing dresses, to be honest."

"Oh, my—" She rubbed her forehead. "Please *never, ever* say that again. You're way too... Never mind. I think the gala is a wonderful idea, and The Gardens will be the perfect place for such a thing once they're all fixed up."

Marshall shrugged. "Sounds good to me."

Ouch. His own brother and business partner had just gone along with the abrupt change of plans. That one was a betrayal, but then again, Marshall had been moody all morning and he'd been "working" instead of coming to supper last night. Probably something with Jess, unless something had happened at Jenna's house site that Wynn wasn't aware of. And the chances of that were slim to none.

Mayor Leo looked at Wynn. "So? Are you in?"

Did he have any choice but to be in? "Sure, I guess. We're just handling the renovations anyway, so that's fine. Nobody hired me to be the event planner."

Noelle let out a little laugh, then covered her mouth and coughed. She found that funny, did she?

"Are you all right, Ms. Carter?" Mayor Leo asked. "Do you guys have some water around here or something?"

Wynn started to stand, then sat back down when Noelle waved her hand dismissively. She let out a final cough into her elbow before smiling a smile that did very little to disguise her amusement.

"Well, then, I suppose we'll have another meeting after you alter the plans to fit these new ideas." Mayor Leo stood and reached for his coat, shrugging it on over his charcoal sports coat. "Here are keys to the building for all three of you, and let me know if you need anything else. Otherwise, you're free to proceed with the project."

"Oh, before you go, I did have one question." Even when standing, Noelle wasn't all that tall. Nor was she very big. "Is everything supposed to stay there, or can things be replaced? Like fixtures and the fountains and benches and whatever else there is."

Mayor Leo seemed to consider that for a moment. "As long as you all have the best interests in mind—which I believe you do—then no. You're free to make any necessary changes or updates you see fit."

That meant the table idea Mom had voiced Saturday would be viable. It also opened up a whole plethora of doors to what they could do. Wynn was already trying to think of what walls needed to stay up in the building and if any could be torn down. If so, it would go a long way in making the small-ish space feel a lot bigger and more open than it currently was. As far as the outside, a good clean-up would go a long way in improving the curb appeal it was currently lacking. Cosmetically speaking, most everything would need to be updated.

"Are there any other questions before I go?" Mayor Leo glanced around the room. "I have a meeting with Joanna Crawford about the Chamber meeting there next week, so I have to get going. Oh, I could speak with her about catering. Unless you'd like to, Ms. Carter."

"Please, call me Noelle. And I wouldn't mind talking to her, if you don't mind."

"Of course, of course." Mayor Leo waited for a moment and, when nobody asked any more questions, he nodded his goodbye and left.

"That went well," Noelle said as she folded her laptop and slid that and a thick notebook into her bag. "I hope this doesn't affect your reno plans, though."

The word *reno* coming from her lips sounded nearly as foreign as her slight Southern accent. "Nope, it doesn't change anything about our reno plans," Wynn replied, adding extra emphasis to the word *reno*. " Besides, we're not the one coordinating the event. That's all you."

"Yeah, about that..." Noelle's lips quirked to one side. "I was wondering if I could be there some while you guys are working? I figure that might give me some inspiration. And I could do some work too, if you want me to."

He rose his eyebrows. "You, help with renovations?"

"That's what I just said, yes."

"Do you even have any shoes or clothes fit for it?"

"Um, yes. I do."

"And that's why you didn't wear shoes downstairs yesterday?"

She made a face. "Who would wear their work shoes downstairs just to eat? But if you don't want me to, that's fine. I'll understand."

Why, oh why was he a sucker for that hint of vulnerability in her eyes, that uncertainty lurking in her voice? Maybe because she was an out-of-towner who knew very few people in town? Probably not, because he was fairly sure she could hold her own.

"You can be at the job site," he said at length, pushing to his feet. "So long as you don't wear those shoes during renovations. Ever."

Noelle stood, bag looped over her shoulder, and mock saluted. "Sir, yes, sir."

Marshall snorted as he grabbed a bottle of water from the mini fridge but said nothing, then disappeared down the hall to his office. What was up with him?

"Hey, Wynn?"

"Yes?"

"That sound at the inn this morning...was it a cow?"

Wynn's brows lowered. "A cow?"

"Yes. It woke me up."

"Oh, you mean Libby?" He grinned as he folded his arms over his chest. "That's my sister's rooster."

Her eyes widened. "Your sister has a pet rooster?"

"Ember isn't exactly a normal person, and yes, she does have a pet rooster."

"Oh. Wow. I guess I...um, yeah." She zipped her jacket up— still not warm enough for today's fifty degree temps. "I'm, um, just gonna go now and I'll see you...later."

Wynn rose a brow as she hurried over to the door and left. Well, that had been interesting. If this was any indication of what the next months were going to be like, they certainly were not going to be dull.

CHAPTER
Eleven

Noelle leaned back in the chair at the desk in her room, feeling a little rush of excitement. After the change in event style she'd been both filled with ideas and yet not sure where to start. So she'd simply sat down after eating her to-go supper from the restaurant Wynn had mentioned and tried to keep her expectations low.

And now, three hours later, she had a brand new plan drawn up.

Hopefully Mayor Leo and Marshall and Wynn would like it. Noelle wasn't concerned about the first two so much as Wynn. He hadn't exactly been thrilled about making it into a formal event, and even though he had agreed, it wasn't an enthusiastic *yes*. Which meant he needed to be convinced, and Noelle planned to do just that.

Right now, though, she was hungry. She should've gone to the market she'd spotted downtown Balsam Falls while she was there. Why hadn't she done that? Her stint at the coffee shop—a modern but still lake-y feeling place—had been unproductive. Not because of the environment, but she'd just been stuck.

Still didn't reason for her not going to the market.

She stood and stretched her neck, then pulled a hoodie on before leaving the room. It was a little after nine, but hadn't she spotted a little snack pantry somewhere downstairs? Something to tide her over till breakfast would be better than nothing.

As quietly as possible, she descended the stairs, mindful of the other guests that may or may not be sleeping. It was a Tuesday night, so there probably wasn't much by way of entertainment. Or maybe there was and she was being unnecessarily quiet. Oh well. She'd get her snack and go back to her room, guests sleeping or no guests in house.

Socks dull on the hardwood, she padded down the hall, glancing around. Where had she seen the sign for the pantry? Was she mixing the pantry from the hotel she'd stayed at on the way here to a nonexistent one at the inn? That was entirely possible, which was also sad because then she would have to go to bed without a snack. Surely there was something around here. Perhaps in the kitchen area…

Noelle tucked her hands into the big front pocket of her sweatshirt and stepped into the kitchen. Sconces on either side of the breakfast nook provided dim lighting, but nobody else was in here. She took another step in and spotted a sign she hadn't noticed earlier that hung by the first row of cupboards to her left. Probably because Wynn had snuck up on her this morning, and his presence didn't allow her to focus on much else.

The kitchen is open for use to all our guests free of charge, but we ask that you please write down on a sticky note what you use so we can get some more. Happy cooking! – Jackie

They just trusted their guests with this beautiful kitchen? Noelle wasn't a worrier, but wow. That was a level of trust she wasn't sure she'd be able to attain very easily. However, since the Bryant family clearly had, she could figure out something to whip up. Or maybe she'd get lucky and find a granola bar or some crackers somewhere. Surely they had at least saltines, right?

Cooking really just wasn't her strong suit, and it was moments like this that she was reminded of that.

Just as she opened the first cupboard, movement near the doorway caught her eye. She leaned back in time to see Wynn walk through the door and oh, Lord have mercy, but he was wearing glasses. Glasses and a gray T-shirt and sweatpants and had she mentioned glasses? She went back to poking through the cupboard of cleaning solutions to process that information.

Glasses. He wears glasses.

"If you think that cupboard makes you invisible, it doesn't." The sound of leather shifting meant he'd claimed one of the upholstered barstools. *Great.* "Noelle, I know it's you. Are you purposely looking for cleaning supplies?"

Shoot. With what she hoped was a totally neutral expression, she closed the cabinet door and turned. "I wasn't hiding. And the sign says the kitchen is open to guests, so I was just looking for a bedtime snack, then I'll head up to my room. Do you, uh, have saltine crackers or something?"

"Do you make it a habit of consuming Clorox for a snack? And yes, but I can do better than that." Setting his notebook down, he stood and rounded the island, nodding at the barstool he'd deserted. "Have a seat. Are you opposed to ice cream, chocolate syrup, peanuts, or maraschino cherries?"

"No, but really. You don't have to—"

He was already pulling out the ingredients he'd mentioned, so she decided to simply stay quiet. Who was she to complain about a man who was preparing an ice cream sundae for her after nine at night? A man wearing glasses who looked really good in glasses and she had yet to fully wrap her mind around that fact. He must wear contacts during the day? Also, was it her or did they make his eyes even more blue? Were color-enhancing glasses a thing?

For her own good, she let her gaze wander and somehow it ended up on the notebook sitting in front of her. Wait, was that a sketchbook? She glanced up at him. "Did you draw this?"

He licked chocolate syrup from the pad of his thumb, not looking at her. "Huh? Oh, those. Yeah. It's nothing fancy though."

Noelle flipped the page and raised her brows. "Nothing fancy? These are great. I mean, I draw up rough sketches for my events, but they're nothing like this. Seriously, what are these for?"

"It's nothing," he repeated, sliding a white ceramic bowl across to her. "You should probably eat that before it melts. My grandma made the ice cream, so it doesn't have all those preservatives to keep it firm for long."

Noelle took a bite and let the creamy blend of ice cream and chocolate meld together on her tongue for several blissful seconds before revisiting The Notebook again. "I'm not gonna let you off the hook so easily. What are these for? They look like little cottages."

Wynn sighed, dragging his spoon through his ice cream. Then he came around and took the chair beside her, causing his cologne to waft straight to her nose. Yes, those glasses, color-enhancing or not, made his eyes even more blue. Perhaps it was the just right thickness of the black rims around them. Whatever it was, it was kind of unfair that they made him more attractive. Why couldn't he wear those thin, wire-framed ones that had to be too narrow to see through?

Somehow she didn't think even those would be unattractive enough to detract from his lean, handsome face.

"I've had this little idea to build a few cottages on an empty lot on the lake and sell them, but it just isn't viable right now." He shrugged and scooped up a bite. A bite he didn't lift to his mouth. "The land is the first hurdle, because it belongs to George Fleming, and he's notorious for not being flexible in business. Secondly, I lied. I don't want to sell them to just anyone. Or at all. I'd like to provide them as a summer vacation spot—or fall or winter or spring, I guess—for people who can't afford it. Families, single parents, whatever. And, because a lot of times all six rooms here are booked, we could use them as additional rental spaces. But, like I said, it's not viable right now, so the only place they'll exist is that sketch pad."

She allowed a few minutes to pass, both of them eating their sundaes, before saying anything. "Then why not take Mayor Leo's idea? The proceeds can go to your company and then that'll be a good start for this project. We could even figure out another fundraiser or two, if you want."

"Our business isn't a charity." He took his last bite of ice cream, then rinsed his bowl and spoon and put them in the dishwasher. Offered a tight smile as he grabbed his sketchbook, closing it. "Have a good night, Noelle."

"Wynn, wait." She hopped off her stool and moved to the doorway, prohibiting him from exiting. Though, really, he could probably move her out of his way with his pinky alone. He was much taller when she didn't have heels on. "I didn't mean to upset you. I'm sorry if I did. I just—"

"Seriously, Noelle, it's fine." Another forced smile. "I'll see you tomorrow at The Gardens. No heels."

The humor did little to make her smile as he stepped around her, his arm brushing hers, and his footfalls echoed down the hall.

Noelle sagged against the doorjamb. Wynn Bryant had dreams, and who even knew about them?

Judging by how he'd shut her down just now, nobody but her.

CHAPTER
Twelve

The wall Wynn and Marshall were currently slugging sledgehammers through was nothing compared to the one that'd been constructed ever since Noelle's inquisition of his sketchbook a couple days ago. Like, it'd been built within a matter of seconds, and she'd felt it throughout the past forty-eight hours. They'd spent Wednesday and Thursday completely emptying the space out to make way for demolition. And even when Marshall cracked a joke, Ember dropped by to help, Sarah brought Wynn's adorable niece—Sadie was *not* his daughter, and according to his sisters, he was very single—or when his parents came by, it did nothing to thaw the chill between them.

Which wasn't really her fault. He'd set the sketchbook there, open for her to see. He'd caved and told her of his dream. He'd then constructed the wall between them.

That said, it was a little disconcerting knowing he wasn't seeing anyone, even though it shouldn't be. There was no reason for it to be. It wasn't like she was interested in him.

"Knockety, knock." Jess Johnson—the police chief's younger sister, whom Noelle had been introduced to last night—walked through the door, carrying a white box. Apparently she was five years younger than her brother, and she currently worked as the head baker for the coffee shop, which meant she had most afternoons off. "I brought muffins for anybody interested. Hey, Noelle."

Noelle's interest perked at the mention of a carb-loaded food. Her muscles had never been as sore as they were from hauling boxes of papers and old, broken things to the Dumpster the past couple days. But that wasn't enough to make her regret volunteering to help. Otherwise she'd just be sitting around and probably checking in at Headquarters too often for Lucy's liking. Tomorrow was Saturday, though, and she planned to use the weekend to do a little exploring.

"Well, if they decide not to come out, so be it." Jess set the box on a sawhorse and opened the lid. "There's banana nut and blueberry. Take your pick. You guys have been working hard. This place looks awesome."

Noelle selected a banana nut muffin and peeled back the semi-transparent brown wrapper. "There was a lot more stuff in here than I remembered. Then again, I wasn't quite able to just look around on Monday."

"My brother told me about what happened." Jess tucked her hands in the rear pockets of her jeans, her lips quirked. "Trust me, he's not nearly as intimidating as he seems. He just likes to think so."

"Who, Marshall?" Wynn emerged from the room Noelle had locked herself into, his ballcap backwards and his sweaty gray T-shirt hugging his broad shoulders. Muscles rippled in his forearm as he leaned his sledgehammer against his jean-clad leg and reached for a blueberry muffin. "Jess, when my brother finally comes to his senses and marries you, promise me you'll make these muffins every day for your favorite brother-in-law."

Jess rolled her eyes. "Very funny. Where's Marsh at, anyway? I need to talk to him."

"Checking something about the window in there." Wynn shrugged and shoved another bite in his mouth. "Guess that leaves more muffins for us."

If Noelle wasn't a part of the *us*, he didn't indicate so as Jess nodded and left in search of Marshall. Maybe the aforementioned invisible wall had been a figment of her imagination. Maybe Noelle had mistaken Wynn's drive to get work done for a cold shoulder. He was clearly focused when it came to his projects.

Except the one that nobody probably knew about.

Noelle cleared her throat. "Listen, Wynn, I'm sorry about the other night. It's none of my business, and I didn't mean to pry."

He glanced at her, studying her through those steady blue eyes of his. "I know you didn't."

That was it? "So…you're not upset with me?"

"Nope." He finished the last quarter of his muffin in one bite. "Why?"

"You just seemed like, I don't know, you were mad or something at me." She peeled more of the wrapper back, but not to eat any of it. Her stomach was a little unsteady right now. "Never mind, though. It doesn't matter."

Tossing his wrapper in the trash can, he blew out a breath and adjusted his cap. "Okay, it made me uncomfortable. Nobody, excluding you now, even knows about the idea whatsoever. I've warred between wanting to tell my family, but for some reason, I just can't. Not if it's not doable, and it's not."

"So, since you said that, do I have permission to say something?"

He eyed her ruefully. "Am I going to even have a choice?"

"Well, no, probably not." She averted her gaze to the smudge of dirt on her Brooks. "It's just—You and Marshall build houses for people who need them and not because they pay for them but because the community backs you. They support you. Why would this project be any different?"

"Those projects are funded that way, yes, but people are going to be living in the house full time. The donors and investors know

78

who the people are. The project I told you about is one, a vacation spot for no one person, and two, possibly a way for my family to have additional income. Neither of those things match our current jobs."

"That's not true. Unless your plans have already changed, you said that you wanted to offer them as vacation spots for people who can't afford it. That's right in line with what you're doing now. I mean, take Jenna's house. A single mom with two little kids who can't afford a better place to live and you guys build her a house? One I haven't seen yet, but I'm sure it's beautiful. You can't tell me the community wouldn't support you on this too."

Wynn perched on the sawhorse beside the muffin box. "It's not that they—"

"There's a but in there and I'm gonna interrupt you before you can get to it." Noelle set her uneaten muffin back in the box and pulled her phone from her pocket, opening her notes app. "I know I probably overstepped by doing this, but in my spare time I put some ideas into my phone. Just simple ones that... Sorry, I definitely overstepped, judging by your expression."

"My expression?"

"Yes, your expression. Maybe men don't get it, but how you look says a lot about how you feel. Kind of like how you can say the same words but your tone can convey the message in a totally different way." Heat filled her cheeks as she turned her phone off and found herself wishing she'd kept the muffin so she could shove as much as possible into her mouth.

"Noelle, relax. Whatever you thought you saw, it wasn't accurate. I'm open to hearing your thoughts, but not right now and probably not the rest of today. We've got a lot to do here, and then at Jenna's house." He stood to his full height and rose his brows. "Not going to interrupt me again. Okay. Anyway, do you have any plans tomorrow?"

Noelle's spirits picked up and she hoped her tone was normal, considering she'd just given him a mini lecture on precisely that. "I planned to do a little sightseeing, but otherwise, no. Not that I even know what to look at. Or for. The Falls look really neat. I mean, I have the lake view from my room, so that's not a big checkpoint on my list or anything."

"Do you always ramble if you're nervous?" Lines crinkled his eyes as he smiled and motioned to her face. "And don't tell me you weren't nervous, because I've heard your talk on facial expressions, and you're blushing."

So much for nonchalance. "I don't have an appropriate response for that."

"Well then, let me be your tour guide tomorrow. You tell me your ideas; I'll show you around town. Sound good?"

"I, uh..." A giddy, probably too-eager happiness bubbled inside of her at the idea of Wynn Bryant, kind of annoying but equally as intriguing, being her personal tour guide. For a whole day. Or at least she assumed as much. "Sure. Yeah, that sounds great."

"Awesome." He pulled his work gloves from his rear jeans pocket. "Go ahead and eat your muffin, then get back to work. Under direct supervision, I'll even let you swing the sledgehammer."

Her eyes widened. Was he flirting with her? "What, are you gonna duct tape my hands to it so it doesn't go flying?"

Wynn laughed and oh, but the sound of it was enough to make her smile. "That's a good idea, actually. Maybe. I'll let you take one swing before I make that judgement. I mean, we're not keeping the wall, which means the worst that happens is you make a bigger hole than intended on one shot. No big deal. But first, eat your muffin. Trust me, you do not want to miss out on Jess's baking."

— ⌒⟋⟍⌒ —

CHAPTER
Thirteen

After a hot shower and changing into clean clothes, Wynn padded barefoot down the hall to his kitchen. The hamburger and chips Mom had dropped off for him, Marshall, and their crew had tasted great but digested quickly. Now that the snow was gone except for a few bigger piles, they could get things rolling. Landscaping was supposed to start in a couple weeks, and interior-wise they were nearly finished. His initial move-in goal could very well be moved up, especially if they put in a few extra hours every workday.

Having the additional project of The Gardens probably didn't help, but they weren't about to turn back now.

Wynn opened his fridge and found himself smiling despite the near-empty state of the appliance. Since when had he been running so low on refrigerated foods? He usually kept his kitchen fully stocked for moments like now when he wanted to whip something up for himself or for those instances when his family decided it was Impromptu-Supper-At-Wynn's Night. Something that seemed to happen at least every two weeks, if not more, despite their standing tradition of having a family supper every Saturday at the inn when they could.

Settling on simply reheating a slice of lasagna from the other night, he grabbed the Tupperware container and closed the fridge.

What would happen if he invited Noelle to join them for supper tomorrow after their sightseeing?

He nearly dropped the lasagna when he saw his younger sister standing in front of him.

"Hey, big bro." Ember raised her brows. "You're gonna heat up some lasagna for me? You know, suddenly the reason you're my favorite brother makes perfect sense. I'll get out the plates and forks. Is that dopey smile of yours for me?"

Wynn pivoted slowly as his sister opened the cupboard door above his sink. "Ember, when did you get here?"

She selected two round hand spun clay plates. "Uh, like, a minute ago. Are these clean? They look dirty."

Wynn set the lasagna down and took the plates, still recovering from the near heart attack he'd had less than sixty seconds ago. "Yes, they're clean. Rinsed and put through the dishwasher and back into the cupboard. *Why* are you here, I probably should've asked. It's almost nine at night."

"It's a Friday. I'm your sister. Live a little. And why can't I just drop by here and there?" She squinted at the two forks in her hand. "Seriously, you need to get your dishwasher checked. These are so not clean."

"Seriously, they're fine. And yes, dropping by is fine, but I know you. Unless you want something or have something to tell me, you don't just 'drop by.' Last time you did that you wanted me to persuade Mom to change the inn's decorations and look how well that went. I'm really not as big of an influence as you think."

Ember set the forks down and claimed one of his four island barstools. "Technically, that's not true. We switched the décor in the kitchen today. It looks *so much better* for this time of year."

"What do you have to say? Come on. Just say it."

"Okay, fine." She flipped her long, dark hair over her shoulder. "I got the inside scoop."

Wynn frowned as he dished up two plates of lasagna. "On what? I wasn't aware of any scoop to get inside."

"Of Marshall and Jess," she said matter-of-factly, as if he was supposed to know that. "Why Marsh is so moody. Tell me you noticed that much, at least."

"Marshall's moodiness? Yes, I noticed. I work with him every day, remember?"

Ember nodded. "Yes, yes. Anyway, the deal is that Jess is leaving. Not forever, I don't think, but for two years or something. She's going to some fancy culinary school in Paris or something, and she leaves at the end of this summer. Whatever you do, don't ask me to pronounce the name of the school, because I can't. I tried."

Wynn absently pulled the first plate from the microwave and slid it across the marble island to his sister, processing that information. Jess was leaving? For *culinary* school? Sure, the girl was an incredible baker and people needed to try her pastries, but she was going all the way to Paris to study something she already knew? Wynn wasn't nearly as close to her as his brother, but that did not sound like the Jess he knew.

"Oh, and I don't think it's technically her choice," Ember added, forking a bite into her mouth. At least she swallowed before continuing. "Not that she said so, but I'm pretty sure it's Meredith's idea, and you know how much she and Elias couldn't *stand* that Seth became a cop. Probably wanted him to be a doctor or lawyer or an astronaut. To be fair, police officers are technically on the common list for little boys and what they want to be when they grow up. I still don't know what I wanna be, and I'm technically an adult." She mock shivered. "That's a scary word, adult. But considering you and Sarah and Marsh have done okay in adulthood, I have a pretty good chance of being fine."

"And you found that out about Jess how?"

"Oh, I talked to her. She came over to make some cookies—I promise that was not a ploy to get this information—tonight, and it kind of just came up naturally. To be honest, she doesn't sound particularly thrilled about it, which is why I'm pretty sure it's her aunt's idea." As if needing to take a breath, she set her fork down and reached for his Yeti. "This is water, right?"

"No. Whiskey."

Ember gave him a look.

"Yes, of course it's water, Em. Probably."

She rolled her eyes and took a long drink, then blew out an equally as lengthy breath. "You know what, Noelle's right. You don't talk very much."

Wynn lowered his eyebrows. "Huh? You talked to Noelle?"

"Oh, yeah. Did I forget to say she helped us make the cookies?" Not pausing long enough for him to respond, she tapped her fingers against his tumbler and continued. "Well, she did, and we were talking about The Gardens—that's actually when Marsh and Jess got brought up—and she said that you guys had a date tomorrow."

He choked on his lasagna and lunged for his Yeti to take the sting from his throat. "She said what?" he croaked out.

Ember snorted out a laugh, shaking her head. "I'm kidding, I'm kidding. Relax, bro. She said that you were gonna show her around tomorrow. But to be honest, since she didn't stay on the subject for very long, she probably wishes it were a date."

"Ember."

His sister held her hands up. "Hey, don't shoot the messenger. I'm just saying. So, where are you gonna take her? I recommend a drive to The Falls, maybe a picnic lunch there, followed by a short hike now that it's nice enough out. And if you really wanna be a romantic, take her to Farm to Table and sit outside. I'm single and that patio alone makes me feel romantic."

"It's not a date, Em, and I don't know what we're going to do."

Actually, he did. He was planning to take her up Falls Drive to the empty lots he'd told her about. Something that he couldn't exactly tell his sister, since she wasn't aware of his sketchbook of ideas for cottages. Three of them, to be exact, and they'd each be two bedrooms and two bathrooms. Nothing fancy, just like he'd told Noelle.

"And there it is again," Ember's all-too-knowing voice broke into his thoughts. "That smile I partially wished was because you were excited to see your favorite sister but also not because that would be really awkward, considering the kind of smile it is."

Wynn scowled at her. "It's not like that, Em. I'm showing her around town, not taking her to the courthouse to marry her."

"Hey, Mom would be really happy if you did the second option."

"Wrong. She wouldn't be really happy because she wouldn't get to plan my wedding."

Ember waved her hand dismissively and hopped off the barstool, ruffling Nova's golden head. "Nah. She planned Sarah's, and let's be honest, she's already planning Marsh and Jess's despite this little hiccup called Paris. You'd be fine to elope. Can I take Nova home with me?"

Wynn followed his sister to the door and leaned against the wall. "No, you can't take her home. You asked that last time and got the same answer. And not to be redundant, but no, fine or not I won't be marrying Noelle tomorrow. Or ever, I mean. She's not from here, and I'm not leaving here. That's only one of many reasons."

"Oh. My. Word." Ember pulled his door open and shot him a look. "That's the absolute worst excuse in the book. I cannot believe we're even related sometimes."

"What, because you're so experienced in love?"

Ember's hair blew in front of her face, but it didn't hide her exasperation. "I consider myself not personally an expert but externally one. I mean, take Chris and Sarah—"

"You didn't set them up, Em."

"I was her maid of honor."

He couldn't help but smile. "I love you, Ember, but no. It's not a date and I most certainly will not be coming home wearing a wedding band."

"Does that mean Nova can come home with me to help soften the blow?"

"No."

Ember let out a huff and dropped her chin, turning to go out the door. "Fine. I'll be fine. Totally okay. Might eat a pan of creamed corn and watch Hallmark all night long, but I'll be good. Great, actually."

The fact that creamed corn to Ember was ice cream to most other people would never get old. "Good night, Em. Love you."

She tossed a *love you too* over her shoulder before turning onto the sidewalk from his walkway. Wynn stood on his porch and watched until he could see that she'd gone in the inn's side door. She may be a lot of crazy things, but firstly she was his sister, and her safety was his responsibility as her older brother. Who was he kidding? He was protective of Sarah and she was four years older than him *and* married with two kids of her own.

Wynn stepped back inside and closed his door. Nova had made her way back into the living room and curled up on the end of the sofa, her favorite spot. He'd raised her from puppyhood for the last eight years, and she was as much a part of his life as his family and his business.

"Jess is leaving later this year," he told the golden retriever as he too sat on the couch. He reached for the remote, but his hand landed on his sketchbook instead. *Then there was that.* "You know, Nova, I have a feeling there's a lot of change coming."

Nova looked at him, then stood and turned so her head could be in his lap, her big brown eyes looking up at him. White had slowly started replacing the rich golden shade on her head, but he knew she was patiently waiting for summer so she could go on endless walks, spend lazy days outside, and swim to her heart's content in the lake. Her age wouldn't stop her from participating in her favorite activities if she had anything to say about it.

"I know, girl." He rested his hand on her head, tipping his head against the back of the sofa. "It'll be good in the long run. Maybe humans ought to take a lesson from you guys and learn to relax more."

Of course, Nova didn't respond unless you counted soft snores a response, but Wynn smiled.

Things would be okay. They would be.

Even if change had to run its course for however long it was necessary.

CHAPTER
fourteen

A gentle breeze twirled through the rolled down truck window, causing loose pieces of Noelle's hair to tickle her face, but she couldn't bring herself to care. Not when there was some country song playing lightly in the background, Wynn was humming along, and the day was predicted to be sunny and sixty-five. She had no idea what he planned to do today—she did hope he'd take her to The Falls—but she also couldn't make herself care too much about the details.

Today was an opportunity for her to tell him her ideas and for him to show her around his hometown. Her grandmother's hometown. And she wouldn't jeopardize that by breaking the comfortable silence.

Especially not when her tour guide had such a nice voice, a low, sort of country sounding one, even when he was solely humming.

No, today was going to be a good day. She just had a feeling. She also had a soreness in her legs, abs, and arms that reminded her of the physical labor she'd done this week. That alone was reason enough to enjoy her weekend—whatever that was going to entail.

For the moment, it was letting the cool morning breeze blow in her face, similarly to how Wynn's golden retriever had her head stuck out the back window.

"I hope you don't mind a little walking." Wynn broke the silence after the song ended, glancing over at her. He was wearing a pair of Oakleys, though, so she didn't get to see his actual eyes, which was kind of a bummer. "Most people don't mind the tourist view of The Falls, but as a local, I prefer something different. And, from knowing you all of five days now, I have a feeling you're not most people."

Since the previous moment had been broken, she tucked those wayward hairs behind her ear. "You guessed correctly, and no, I don't mind a bit of a walk. Maybe it'll help stretch my sore muscles a little bit."

Wynn chuckled as he reached for his Yeti tumbler—a plain stainless steel one. "Found a few muscles you didn't know you had, huh?"

"Try a lot of muscles I didn't know I had." Just talking about it made that sort of satisfying ache, well, ache. "But it's a good thing, I guess. Probably even better than any gym or at home workout."

"Depends." He paused at a stop sign, then took a right onto Beechwood Avenue. "If you're like me, some of the construction world means handling paperwork, which means you're at a desk and if you *don't* go to the gym or workout at home, you wouldn't have much muscle at all."

Either he did minimal paperwork or he worked out close to every day, because Wynn Bryant was certainly not muscle-less. Not by a long shot. A lot of guys in the corporate world could take a lesson from whatever Wynn's workout regimen was. Most—not all, but most of them were either very small and very thin or very not small and very not thin. One extreme or the other.

Wynn was in the ideal category: Tall, muscular, and not afraid of physical work.

"I grabbed some snacks and a couple water bottles, plus a few hiking necessities from my place before I picked you up, so if you're hungry or thirsty, let me know." Easing off the gas, he pulled into what looked like it was a sheltered parking lot. One most people probably wouldn't notice if they weren't paying attention. "Oh, and I also brought you a shirt to wear over your jacket. It'll warm up, but not for a while. I hope you don't mind it being a men's size."

Noelle's eyes widened behind her own sunglasses as she got out of the truck. He'd packed snacks and water and extra layers of clothing? He seemed like the always-prepared-for-anything kind of man, sure, but still. She hadn't quite expected *this*.

Although, her first clue probably should've been when he told her he was taking her to the non-touristy viewing spot.

"Here you go. Like I said, it'll be big, but at least you'll stay warm." He pulled a gray and blue flannel shirt from the back seat of the Chevy and handed it to her. "I'll take the backpack. The trail isn't paved or anything, but it's been used enough that it's not like braving the wilderness. Also, cell reception is nada. Any questions, or should we get started?"

Maybe it was the March sunshine on her cheeks or the scent of coffee, sawdust, and fresh air that screamed *Wynn* coming from the shirt currently embracing her like a warm hug, but she simply shook her head no. That was true, though. She had no questions, only a sudden sense of exhilaration. A sudden want to go on this adventure, regardless of her sore muscles or the fact that she'd never been hiking like this before. Not through both coniferous and deciduous trees and probably plenty of animals.

"All right, then." He guided his golden retriever out of the truck and wrapped her leash around his hand, then shut the truck door and nodded towards a trail that peeked out at them. "Off we go. You'll be able to hear the waterfall a while before you see it, so don't get too excited. It's about a mile walk."

Good thing she'd outfitted herself in tennis shoes, leggings, and a T-shirt under her jacket. "Note taken. Nova looks ready to go."

"Nova's ready for anything involving the outdoors," he said with a laugh as they started walking, him on the left and Noelle to his right. "She's eight, but her personality says otherwise."

"We had a golden retriever for a while when I was younger," Noelle said, her vocal cords having decided to start functioning again. "He was the best dog a person could ask for. I remember falling asleep using him as my pillow, not even under my covers or anything. Of course, I was always miraculously tucked in by morning."

Wynn said nothing, as if sensing she had more to say.

"My grandpa tucked me in," she continued, averting her gaze to the budding trees along the trail. "Grandma would read to me and tell me stories, and then Grandpa would come in a little afterward and tuck me in. Or, on the dog-pillow occasions, I guess he'd completely move me around."

"They sound like wonderful people," he said softly.

Noelle allowed a few moments to pass, inhaling the fresh scent of nature. "They were. My grandma passed away when I was twenty-two, and, um, Grandpa died last November."

There was another pause of silence and then, much to Noelle's shock, Wynn reached out and squeezed her hand gently. "I'm sorry, Noelle. That's never easy."

Before she could comprehend it, he'd slipped his hand from hers. But not before she could note the warmth of his, despite its roughness. She pulled in a long breath, folding his shirt's cuffs in her hands, and exhaled slowly. "Thank you. They're...better off now."

He glanced down at her, and again she wished he wasn't wearing those sunglasses. "That doesn't necessarily make it easier."

"No," she conceded, "it doesn't. Enough about me, though. You mentioned your grandma made the ice cream—which was delicious, by the way—that we ate the other night?"

Amusement quirked the corners of his lips. "Yes. My grandma Margie—Mom's mom—made that. About the only thing she's trusted to make, honestly. She and my grandpa on Dad's side are still living. He's got an equally, uh, feisty personality but in different ways. Grandma is more of a matchmaker, a say-anything-on-her-mind, kind of person. Grandpa is better in the kitchen, and he can and will whoop you in pretty much any card, board, or physical yard game. I usually avoid playing against him, and if I can't be on his team, I just avoid playing in general."

Noelle laughed. "Sounds like an interesting time—Wait, is that the waterfall? I know you said I'll hear it a while before I see it, but is that what I hear?"

"That's what you hear, yes." He adjusted Nova's leash, and the dog strained on the end of it. "We've got about fifteen minutes and you'll be able to see them."

Renewed excitement replaced the somberness of the topic of her grandparents' and she picked up her pace a little. Even the way her muscles complained wasn't enough to make her want to slow down. It was too beautiful out here to wish she was anywhere else.

As if sensing her eagerness, Wynn withheld from initiating any further conversation, but the way he matched his strides to hers and warned her if there was some kind of hurdle to step over spoke volumes with hardly any verbal words. At a certain point, he even took the whining Nova off her leash—probably because they were far enough from any kind of civilization—and told her to stay close. The golden seized the window of freedom by darting ahead to sniff at brush lining the trail or to run rather than walk, but she always circled back to check on them.

"Watch your step over this log." Wynn crossed it first, then offered his hand to Noelle. "We'd love to move it out of the way, but then we'd have to get equipment up here and it would likely create a scene, so we just step over it."

Noelle raised her voice over the increasing volume of the waterfall. "Is it only your family that—"

Her sentence crashed to a halt as she, too, stopped. Stunned by the view in front of her. Foamy, beautiful water fell over the tall wall of uneven slate, creating a swirly blue-green pool at the base before it continued down the slim river. Mist dampened the air, clinging to her face and sunglasses and creating a rainforest-like feel. From this vantage point—literally as close as a person could get without being in the water—The Falls looked massive and gorgeous and... *majestic.*

"Wynn..." The word was more like a whisper, probably too soft to hear over the incredible display before them.

He removed his sunglasses, tucking them on the pocket of his shirt, and slid the backpack down to the ground. "Here we are. Hungry? If you want, there's a big rock we can sit on. Have a snack, drink some water. Admire the view."

Noelle still felt near-speechless as she followed him to a large, mostly flat boulder. He pulled a blanket from the backpack and laid it out, followed by a bag of Cheetos, apple slices, and two bottles of water. If she wasn't so awestruck by The Falls, she probably would've laughed at the combination of snacks he'd packed. Not that she could laugh, because they both caused her to stomach to grumble.

"Have at it." He sat on the rock beside her, stretching his long legs out on the surface, and grabbed a slice of apple. "One healthy and one not healthy has to balance it out, right?"

"I can't say it doesn't."

They munched on the snacks in silence, giving her an opportunity to fully admire the view. The brush and greenery had dwindled and pebbly sand led up to the riverbank like a beach. Trees still crowded around as if whispering their secrets, their gnarled, barely budded branches knitting together in a canopy overhead that allowed only select rays of sunshine to filter through. She had no doubt that, once leaves and flowers bloomed, this place would be downright magical.

"During the summer, my family always comes here once or twice to swim," Wynn said, eyes on the waterfall. "We have the lake, of course, but this is a different kind of adventure. Marshall and I—sometimes even Dad and Ember—usually go behind the waterfall, but Sarah and Mom have always preferred to stay out in the open. The only time Sarah went back there was when she wanted to show off when she and Chris, her husband, were dating. She ended up freaking out and nearly sliding down the rocks, but

I guess she still did it. Right now, though, the water is freezing. In the summer, it's the perfect temperature for swimming in."

Noelle glanced at him. "Sounds like fun. I can't say I'd go behind, though. I like to err on the side of caution."

"You?" He smirked. "No. You're kidding."

She rolled her eyes and reached for another Cheeto. "Ha-ha, very funny. But yes, I do. Not always. A lot of people would say my grandparents were overprotective, but that's not how I see it. Not really, anyway." She hugged her knees to her chest, little memories sliding through her thoughts like Clark Griswold and the projection kit in the attic. "My grandma homeschooled me, which meant I was able to go to the office with Grandpa. There was this lady that worked there when I was about nine—her name was Phyllis—and I went through a phase where I was slightly obsessed with lipstick. I always watched Grandpa stamp stuff, you know, but I didn't have any stamps in my backpack. I did, however, have this lipstick in there that Grandma either unintentionally put in or just trusted me with. While Grandpa was in a meeting one day, I wandered around and found this stack of envelopes on the corner of Phyllis's desk. She was out at the time, and they weren't marked or anything, so I decided to 'stamp' them. Turns out they weren't marked yet, but employee bonuses were already sealed in them. Case in point, I never had lipstick in my bag again. I'm pretty sure that's also the most adventurous thing I've done since then. Guess I just decided to play it safe."

Wynn chuckled, scratching Nova's head as she leaned against the side of the rock. "Homeschool kids are just that creative, huh? I'll bet none of those employees had ever received such a pretty envelope."

"Sure, something like that. What about you? Wait, let me guess. High school star quarterback. Graduated top of your class, but mostly because of your good looks and your grades had nothing to do with it."

He arched a brow, eyes sparkling. "You think I'm good looking?"

94

"That wasn't the point." Even if her cheeks flushed and she looked away.

"You're right. I did graduate top of my class." He took a swig of water. "But only because I was the only one in it. All of us were homeschooled, hence my comment about homeschool kids being creative."

"Seriously?"

"Yep. Well, Ember wasn't in the beginning, but that's because she didn't have the option."

"Your parents just decided the first three got the advantage and she didn't?"

He shook his head. "Ember was adopted. I was already twenty-two when they did, and she was nine. That's why there's such a big age difference between even her and Marshall—eight years."

Noelle was temporarily speechless. She hadn't been around all of them together at once, but their whole family was just that: a family. Ember really did look like she could be a sibling, resembling Jackie with her dark hair and dark brown eyes. But she wasn't one. Not biologically.

"Dad was a cop in town for twenty years, chief of police for fifteen of them," Wynn continued, "and Mom practiced family law. They were later twenties when they got married, and they had Sarah the year after, then me three years later, and Marshall four years after that. When I was nine, my dad was in an accident. Crushed his legs because of the impact. He was hospitalized for six months, and told he may never walk again. Not without surgeries and doctor visits and meds and all that, and that wasn't even a promise that he'd gain his mobility again. Mom had obviously already stopped working after she had us, so our sole income was that of Dad's salary, meaning they had no means of income. But they had three kids, medical bills to pay, and all other living expenses. There were people that stepped in and cooked for us or cleaned or did laundry or bought us groceries, but the bottom line was that there was no money coming in. We were barely staying afloat, and Mom was pretty much a single parent during Dad's hospitalization.

"At a certain point, Mom was forced to get a job. Sarah and I tried to help—she was twelve and Marshall was five—by doing what we could, but we eventually had to move in with our grandparents. And then Dad made a decision to screw everything the doctors had told him and leave the hospital." Wynn turned to look at her, and the emotions in his eyes nearly made her wish he . still wore his sunglasses from earlier. "He made a full recovery with no more surgeries, no more doctor visits, and no more over the counter meds. He and Mom prayed together, they researched herbs and natural remedies, they made a workout schedule to strengthen his legs, and they pushed out every last bit of negativity. To earn another side income other than what she was making from her receptionist job at an attorney friend's practice, Mom started making meals and people donated money to eat them. Obviously she didn't have any culinary training or any of that, but it became more well known. It was a year after Dad's accident that the inn came on the market. Dad had already decided he wouldn't go back to his job—even though I know he missed it—and they made an offer. It's been open ever since. My parents became business owners and wanted to raise their children to do the same."

"Wynn, I . . ." She swallowed, both amazed and suddenly more respectful of the Bryant family as a whole. "That's incredible."

"Don't get me wrong, there's doctors that do want to help people. But in my experience—or Dad's, I guess—sometimes you've got to do the work yourself. You cannot sit around and pray for God to fix it all by Himself. Not impossible for a miracle, but most miracles come by way of choices to make different decisions than the common population." He lifted a shoulder and let it drop. "Dad's living proof of exactly that."

96

CHAPTER
fifteen

Spilling his family's history hadn't been a part of Wynn's plans for the day, but after Noelle had shared a little more about her own past, he hadn't been able to stop himself. There was something freeing about it, even if they'd both been mostly silent ever since. It wasn't a tense silence but a thoughtful one. Even Nova, who'd rebelled against his instruction to avoid the river, was sleeping quietly in the back seat.

He turned back onto Falls Drive after coming back down from his family's private viewing place of The Falls and drove until he reached the empty lots. There were plenty of shops—boutiques, home décor, etc.—downtown, but he had a feeling this would mean more to Noelle. Besides, he'd promised to listen to her ideas and so far that hadn't happened.

Parking alongside the curb, he shut off the ignition. "Okay, here's the lots that I was talking about. Owned by Balsam Falls's most, let's see here, cutthroat businessman. Fleming owns Falls National Bank which, by the way, is not national at all. So not only does he have a *lot* of pull in this town with some people, but he also isn't exactly a fan of my family. He's not the only one, of course. Just one of the most influential."

"Why wouldn't he like you?"

Wynn left her question hanging and got out to open her door, unsure of how much he was willing to disclose. "Some of the more…wealthy people, per se, around here don't love what my parents have built for the past twenty years or so. What Marshall and I have built in the past decade. Dad didn't come from money and Mom did—that was the first reason, way back when. Then the accident and what followed—second reason." He tucked his hands in the pockets of his jeans as they came to a stop in the middle of the bare lots, a breeze off the lake ruffling his hair. "But their continued and still growing and flourishing success? That's one sustaining reason. On the flip side, a lot of people do love our family and what my parents built. We have some families that have been coming since that first year the inn opened. And some of them drive from a distance to get here. I'll have to show you the guest book sometime."

"So the good people outweigh the bad, except for the fact that these lots in particular are owned by the mean businessman, right?"

He laughed. "That's one way of putting it, I guess. I mean, I get it. This is prime real estate, what with it being right on the lake and all. But if Fleming knew that I, the son of John and Jackie Bryant, was interested, I'm pretty sure he'd be less interested than a fish would be to live on land. That, or he'd jack the price up even higher, and it's already priced too high."

"Then let me make an offer," she said, her jaw tilted slightly. A posture he'd found meant she wasn't going to be easily talked out of something. "Other than my grandmother having been from here, I'm not known around here."

"No."

Her expression shifted to something like annoyance. "Wynn, my grandpa built a highly successful—"

"Party planning company. Not an investment company."

98

"Actually, Carter Inc. isn't solely *event planning*. Grandpa made some wise investments in his lifetime, and that resulted in success in many areas. Now that I'm CEO, yes, it's mostly event coordination, but we've helped fund and kickstart a few companies, so it's like three-fourths event coordination and a quarter venture capitalism. Those kickstarted businesses, for the record, are doing very well. For the most part."

Wynn really didn't want to discourage her, but there was no way he was going to let her invest on this property. "Let's hear those ideas you were talking about."

"You're changing the subject."

"You're stalling."

She rolled her eyes, but she pulled her phone out—its bright pink case matched her form-fitting jacket—and passed it to him. "There's not a lot there, but that's my list so far. Mind if I walk around? Wait, we're not trespassing, are we?"

"Trespassing? No. Why?"

"Well, I'm guessing you certainly didn't call up George Fleming and ask to come look at his property. So we'd be trespassing."

He tried his best to hide his smile, something easier said than done. "Noelle, it's an empty set of lots that are for sale. No, we're not trespassing. You're free to roam about the cabin."

"Can George see us? Where's his house?"

"Noelle, relax."

Finally, she turned, but he didn't miss the hesitancy in her steps as she walked towards the bank of the lake. He'd never really not noticed, but it struck him just how pretty she really was. With that long, golden hair and his shirt tied around her waist, she looked adorable.

He forced his gaze to her phone in his hand, to her neat little bullet point list.

- *Make the cottages wheelchair accessible, in case any kids with disabilities would get to come*
- *TELL YOUR FAMILY ABOUT THE IDEA*

- *Make the cottage exteriors look like the inn so people would maybe make the connection between them?*
- *Did I mention to tell your family about the idea???*

Wynn shook his head as he turned her phone off and released a sigh. Telling his family about it sounded great in theory, but what if he couldn't swing the project? What if they had enough funding to get only partway finished? Then what?

"So?" Noelle reappeared in front of him. "Like I said, it's not much, but it's a start. Of course, if your family knew about it, I bet they'd love to share their ideas with you. Ember seems to have a knack for design. Your mom said she designed your backyard outdoor space, and even though I've only seen it out the window, it looks really cool. And Marshall is probably really good with architecture stuff like you are."

"It's not that simp—"

"You told me about your dad and the accident and what followed," she interrupted, her tone firm. "What if he would've said, 'It probably won't work' or 'I can't do this anymore'?"

"They had a family to support. And the inn didn't cost them crazy amounts of money in the beginning."

"So? There were all the medical bills, kids to feed, other bills. Maybe the inn didn't cost a lot monetarily when they bought it, but your dad could've easily decided to believe he wouldn't walk again. But he didn't. They took a risk, Wynn. Both of them, your mom and your dad. To me, you don't seem like the kind of guy to play it safe and ignore the possibilities. Wasn't opening your own business a risk?"

Wynn rubbed a hand over his jaw. "Come to supper tonight. Every Saturday we have a family meal at the inn—most guests are out to eat or something."

"And you'll bring it up then?"

"No. But I'll think about it."

Her face fell.

"Listen, I hear what you're saying, but there's a lot of factors that play into the possibility of these cottages. You're right—I'm not usually afraid of risks. But I do need a little time to process this one."

"I can accept that."

"Supper?"

"Probably not. I don't want to impose on your family time."

"Jess comes nearly every week, and even Seth comes every so often when he's not working." He passed her phone back to her, hoping she'd say yes. Why he wanted that, well, he wasn't about to go there. "Please?"

But before she could respond, his own phone vibrated in his pocket. He pulled it out, heartrate increasing as he glanced at the screen. A text from Ember.

Emergency at the inn. Where are you at?

CHAPTER

Sixteen

Wynn wasn't sure what was more alarming: Seth's cruiser parked in front of the inn or Ember's rooster standing guard on a pile of filthy towels near the front door. His sister's text had caused several scenarios to race through his mind, most including at least one cop car but none including Libby and towels. Especially not Libby on a pile of them.

He'd flashed back to that day on the porch swing with Mom and Sarah and a squirmy Marshall. Mom had been reading them a book after lunch and before naps when one of Dad's officer buddies had come by, his expression solemn. He'd asked to speak to Mom alone, and Wynn had been able to hear their hushed voices through the open window, even though Sarah had carried on the reading of the book.

Still caused Wynn to feel helpless all these years later.

"Wynn?" Noelle's voice broke into his thoughts. "Are you okay?"

Clearing his throat, he shot her a smile and removed the key from the ignition. "I'm good. Hang on a sec and I'll get your door.

Ember is usually vague in texts, so who knows what happened. Probably something that doesn't qualify as an emergency."

Even though she probably didn't believe him, he wasn't lying. Ember really was vague while texting. Something that didn't come in handy when discussing Christmas or birthday presents or surprises of any kind. Speaking of, his parents' thirty-fifth anniversary was coming up and they'd yet to plan anything. He should probably bring that up sooner than later, since none of his siblings had done so.

They'd just reached the first step when the door swung open and Ember flew out, towels piled in her arms. Sopping wet ones, streaked with grimy dirt. *What in the world?*

"Finally." Ember shooed Libby away with her foot and dropped the towels on the pile. "You took forever to get here. Did you think a flood was just gonna dry up by itself?"

"Wait, what? A flood?"

"Yes, a flood. I texted you."

Wynn went in the door behind Noelle, confused. "You texted that there was an emergency at the inn, not what the emergency was."

"Well, it's a flood. Room three."

Noelle's room. He glanced at her, but her expression did little to tell him much of anything. Either she was skilled at hiding her feelings, or it really didn't faze her at all. Which was kind of hard to believe, considering Ember had just said Room 3 had flooded. To what extent, he was about to find out.

Ember pulled her hair back into a sloppy ponytail as they started up the steps. "We got all your stuff on higher ground, Noelle. It's not flooded anymore, technically, but everything on the floor is soaked. Marshall and Jess ran to get a couple extra fans and dehumidifiers. We're hoping the floor won't need to be replaced, but no guarantees. Dad shut the water off, and Mom called Tim Warren. I think he's on his way over to check it out."

"Uh, okay... And you didn't think of maybe mentioning that in your text?"

"I typed that out while I was taking a pile of *soaked* towels downstairs."

Wynn decided against stating that *flood* was much easier to type out than *emergency*. Growing up with one, and then two, sisters, he'd learned when it was best to keep his mouth shut. Most of the time. There were still instances when, yeah, something slipped out unintentionally, but for the most part he'd learned to hold his tongue.

"What happened?" His gaze took in the room, noting the small amount of stuff on the bed that must be Noelle's. She traveled a lot lighter than the females in his family.

Dad emerged from the en suite bathroom, drying his hands on yet another towel, and Seth came out behind him. Per usual, his expression was unreadable, his hands resting on his tactical belt. Why was he even here? It wasn't like he was a plumber, and judging by his lack of enthusiasm—something that rarely peeked out, unless it included Jenna Williams and her kids—he hadn't come to simply follow Dad around and sop up water.

"Pipe burst in the bathroom," Dad said. "Didn't realize it till everything was flooded. But the water's off, and Tim's on his way, so hopefully it's an easy fix. We were able to get everything dried up pretty quickly."

"Is there another hotel in town or something?" Noelle asked. "I can find somewhere else to stay for a couple nights, or however long I need to."

Dad opened his mouth, but Ember spoke before he could. "That's probably not necessary. You could always stay in my room. I can bunk at Wynn's. Right, big bro?"

"Uh—"

"Oh, no, I couldn't intrude on you like that." Noelle tucked a strand of hair behind her ear. "Really, it's fine. I can totally find another place to stay. I don't have much stuff, so it's no big deal."

"What's this talk of you finding some place else to stay?" Mom appeared in the doorway beside Noelle, a stack of fresh white towels in her hands. "It's not that bad in here, is it? How long will it take to fully dry out?"

Dad shrugged. "Depends. It probably will only take tonight, maybe tomorrow. Hopefully it's an easy fix, because we have to have the water off right now, meaning nobody upstairs has any water."

"Oh dear. Well, Wynn, you have a couple spare bedrooms." Mom glanced at him, then Noelle. "Then you'd just be next door, so you don't have to move very far. Marshall and Wynn could move your things for you. Ember could stay there too, if that would make you more comfortable."

"Hey, that's a great idea." Ember turned to look at him, her eyes sparkling. "We can have a party at Wynn's. I've never quite understood why he needs all that space to himself. Who knows? I might just move on in with him, considering he makes such good meals. So do you, Mom, but I'm sure Wynn here gets lonely all by his lonesome self."

"Considering I work five to six days a week, and we—"

Ember waved her hand dismissively. "Details, details. Does that sound okay to you, Noelle? If not, I'll totally understand."

Noelle darted a glance up at him. "Seriously, I wouldn't want to impose on you like that. I'm fine with finding a hotel."

"I'm fine with it." Because really, could he be not okay with it? "Seth, what are you doing here? Let me guess, you came to write me up for something I didn't do because it's nearing the end of the month? Get your quota in?"

"Ha, well, actually I am here to talk to you," Seth replied. "Originally, that is. Then I got roped into helping your dad play plumber and here we are."

Dad laughed. "Something like that, kid. I'm gonna head downstairs for when Tim gets here. Marshall and Jess coming back today?"

"Anything involving my sister is kind of like a wild goose chase." A hint of a smile quirked Seth's lips—another one of his soft spots: his little sister. "In other words, she probably got a brilliant idea and it'll just snowball from there. But she always eventually finds her way."

Was it just Wynn or did Seth mean something deeper by that last sentence? Maybe he was wrong, but Wynn couldn't imagine Seth was too keen on the whole Paris deal. He'd gone against the grain by becoming a police officer, just like Ember had said, and he probably wished his sister would stand up to their aunt and uncle. Which, knowing Jess, was very unlikely.

"How about you two have your little chitchat while I help Noelle get moved over to your house?" Ember nudged Wynn towards the door. "Is supper still on for tonight, Mom?"

Mom pursed her lips. "Anyone up for pizza night? If so, text me what flavor you like so I can order it from Giorgi's. If not, tough luck. You're on your own."

"I'll take supreme, since you're ordering," Seth said. Was he actually grinning? He must've seen Jenna at some point earlier. "Where do you want to talk, Wynn? Preferably somewhere private."

Wynn rose a brow. "If that's the case, you're in the wrong house."

CHAPTER

Seventeen

"A nd here's his—" Ember made air quotes "—'tea cabinet.'"
Noelle's eyes widened. "Tea cabinet?"

"Hard to believe such a manly man such as my oldest brother drinks tea? Yeah, I know, but the proof is in the pudding." Ember grinned. "Or, in this case, in the cupboard."

"Wow. Impressive."

"Yeah. So, that's the house. You're sure you're all right with this? I probably could've been less pushy about it, but my mouth and brain don't always coordinate what to say before I say it. Probably not my best attribute."

"I think it's kind of brave," Noelle admitted. "Maybe you could take over some of my more difficult clients. Because let's face it, some people just really need to hear the blunt truth. And unfortunately, I'm not the type of person to do that."

Ember laughed. "Hey, I'm up for it. Hang on a sec, and I'll be back. I think the washer just went off with those sheets." She disappeared down a hall that housed two bedrooms—one temporarily Ember's and the other Wynn's—a bathroom, a home office for Wynn, and a laundry room.

Noelle glanced around at the open concept layout of the kitchen/living room area. To the left of the white stucco fireplace was a window seat, a cubicle of books underneath. French doors that opened to a back deck and lakefront view were on the other side. A woven rug with various shades of blue, ranging from baby blue to navy blue, softened the hardwood floors, with simple leather furniture and a wooden coffee table on top. Two chairs and one sofa, all three a light mocha color. A flatscreen hung above framed photos on the wooden mantle.

As for the kitchen, well, it was just as nice. Light brown cabinets, a marble island, concrete countertops on top of the cabinets lining the wall, and stainless steel appliances. Nowhere near the size of the inn's, of course, but it was beautiful. Simple, modern yet cozy, and reasonably spacious. Not at all difficult to picture cooking something in.

If, of course, a person knew how to prepare more than grilled cheese.

She spun around when the front door opened. Wynn walked in with Nova, but there was a certain set to his shoulders that wasn't normal. As if whatever the police chief had wanted to discuss had weighted them down somehow.

"Hey," he said with a smile. One that didn't reach his eyes.

Noelle folded her jacket's cuffs in her palms. "Hey."

"Did my sister give you a tour?" He opened the fridge and grabbed a jar of jam, then held up his hand. "You don't even have to answer that. I already know the answer. Where is Em, anyway?"

Unsure of whether to sit on one of the barstools or not, she simply stood near the end of the island. "She was washing some sheets."

"Ah. Gotch—Wait, why?" A crease formed between his brows, giving him an adorably befuddled look. "The beds were made."

"You'd think that, after Mom and Dad being in the hospitality business for over twenty years now, you would've picked up on some of it," Ember said with a shake of her head as she walked out and claimed a barstool. "Nobody has slept in those sheets for who knows how long, so yes, I'm washing them. I may be nineteen, but I am responsible, thank you very much."

"I see." Wynn got out a box of crackers, butter, two plates, and two butter knives. "Anybody want some? Mom said she's going to be ordering the pizza for six, because they're talking to Tim and seeing what they can do to try and prevent from having to get new floors."

Ember patted the stool next to her. "You can sit down, Noelle. I'll take a couple crackers, since you asked. What'd Seth want to talk to you about?"

The question caused Wynn to pause briefly mid-butter-slather, Noelle noticed as she sat, but he snapped back and continued buttering the cracker.

"Well, apparently he got a call about some trespassers on those empty lots of George Fleming's," Wynn said evenly, glancing up. "Apparently Fleming thought it was me and Noelle."

Noelle choked on nothing. " *What?*"

Wynn wordlessly grabbed a glass, filled it, and passed it to her. With a perfectly articulated smirk that highlighted that angular, clean-shaven jaw of his. "Just kidding."

"I am so confused," Ember said slowly, looking between them. "You were there? Why? And what're you kidding about?"

"That." Wynn moved onto the jam. "No, he had something...else to talk to me about. It's not important."

That, or he wasn't comfortable talking about it with Noelle around. It wasn't like she was family or anything. They were simply being over-kind and letting her stay here, which was really quite unnecessary. Maybe she could just excuse herself and...escape to the outdoors. Where to from there, she didn't know, but at least then she wouldn't be intruding.

"He asked me if I'd be willing to mentor a kid," Wynn said quietly, setting the knife down and bracing his hands on the edge of the counter. "A thirteen-year-old African-American. Lives over on Lake Street with his little sister and his father in the trailer park.

Apparently Seth and his team have been monitoring the situation but I guess the dad isn't an extremely upstanding citizen. You didn't hear that from me."

Noelle wasn't sure what to say, and even Ember was silent, though her mouth did open and close several times. What was a person to say about a situation like that, anyway? Sure, Noelle hadn't had her parents in the picture, but her childhood had certainly never been hard. Did it sting that her mother had chosen a career over her own daughter? Yes. Had she ever wondered why her father hadn't stuck around? Of course. But she'd never, *ever* doubted that she was loved or if she'd be taken care of. Not once, and she was twenty-six years old.

"I'm not sure why he asked me, though." Wynn resumed his jam-spreading, gaze downward. "I'm nobody special, not to mentor a kid who's probably had to grow up to way too fast. Honestly, Seth would be a better person for that."

"I disagree." Ember snatched a cracker and took a bite, chewing thoughtfully. "You could teach him plenty. Think about when Dad had his accident. I mean, I wasn't even alive at the time and definitely didn't know you guys yet, but you were, figuratively speaking, the man of the house when he was hospitalized. And everyone can see how awesome you are with kids. As much as it pains me to say this, I'm pretty sure you're Sadie's favorite. So trust me, you're qualified for it."

"I was nine years old when Dad's collision happened, Em." He slid a plate over to each of them, three butter-and-jam crackers on each. "Sarah was older than me."

"No, really? Wait, that's how that works? A sibling born before another sibling is older than the one born after them? No way. That's crazy."

Noelle nearly choked on her cracker.

"Hilarious," Wynn drawled, his expression hinting that he found it anything but that. "That's all good and well, but seriously. I'm not the right person to mentor him. Besides, I've got too much on my plate to have another project added to it."

Too much on my plate to have another project added to it. The cracker she'd just choked on turned to sawdust in her mouth. He hadn't said it directly, but Noelle could read between the lines. The cottages were a no-go. Maybe he'd been joking about the trespassing scenario—at least, she hoped he was—but between that and his statement about work, the message was clear.

She shouldn't have started dreaming up ideas and plans for a project that one, wasn't hers, and two, wasn't a done deal. She couldn't blame Wynn—he'd never told her that he'd even tell his own family about the idea, let alone pursue the project.

"...don't mind supreme pizza, right?"

Noelle caught the end of Wynn's sentence and blinked. "Say what?"

He gestured to his phone. "Mom asked if you were all right with supreme. It got majority vote."

"Oh, I, um, that's fi—"

"If you want a different kind, just speak up," he interrupted. "Or you can pull up the menu online too. They've got several different combinations."

She found some semblance of a smile and shook her head. "Supreme sounds good to me."

"You sure?"

"Completely."

"*Most* people would be inclined to use the ladder to get down," Dad said, using that tone he always used when telling stories. "But not Marshall. No, he wanted to do it more 'heroically' by jumping down from the treehouse. Fortunately, it was only five or so feet off the ground, but he had a fairly sore tailbone afterwards, if I remember correctly."

"Hey, in my defense, I did land on my feet," Marshall said, glancing at Jess—who was, shocker, sitting beside him at the outdoor patio table—as if she'd back him up. "I just didn't stick the landing. And I was only six. How was I supposed to know better?"

Sarah smirked, bouncing Will on her lap. "You really want someone to answer that, Marsh? Because, technically, a six-year-old is capable of knowing he should, like Dad said, use the ladder. It was literally *right* there."

"Okay, then, how about the time Wynn flushed Goldie down the toilet?" Marshall countered, grinning. "I still don't know how someone doesn't notice a goldfish swimming around in the toilet. And actually, were you just flushing the toilet for fun, or what?"

Wynn shook his head, aware of Noelle's curious gaze from across the table. "No, no, no. *Sarah* had her goldfish 'swimming' there while she cleaned his bowl, and Mom asked me to clean that toilet because we had company coming over that night. I can't be the only one who flushes the toilet before cleaning it out."

"Oh, honey, you might be surprised." Mom's twinkling eyes and wide smile matched that of pretty well everyone else around the table, thirteen people in all. "But Goldie had been around for quite some time, so he probably wouldn't have lasted much longer anyway."

"Actually," Grandma said, waving her hot pink fingernails around emphatically, "if you take proper care of them, goldfish can live up to twenty-five whole years. How old was Goldie at that time? Maybe he would've lived longer after all."

Sarah nodded. "See? Somebody cares about my fish's wellbeing. Thank God dogs aren't flushable, or Wynn couldn't be trusted with them either."

"Okay, explain to me why you would put it in the *toilet* to swim," Wynn said dryly. "Why not, say, the sink? The tub? An *ice cream* bucket?"

"Because why not? I don't know. Maybe because I thought he'd like somewhere different than normal."

"Oh, yes, that makes a ton of sense." Wynn couldn't help but grin. "And for the record, Nova and I are tight. Right, girl?"

The golden retriever lifted her head from the cushioned swing she had claimed, then set it back down and closed her eyes.

"Ha!" Ember balled up her napkin and tossed it at him. "We call that a rejection in the Bryant family!"

Kind of you like you rejected Seth's request to mentor Devin?

The thought sobered him up quick, and thankfully, the conversation was steered from him to church tomorrow and what the ladies were planning to wear. A topic that came up at least once every Saturday when they did this, either during prep, while eating, or afterward. And Wynn nearly always put in some comment about not agreeing to wearing a dress or skirt because it wasn't masculine enough for him, something Grandma always got a kick out of.

But not tonight. No, tonight he was feeling like a heel for telling Seth no. What kind of man did that? Not Grandpa. Certainly not Dad. Probably not even Marshall.

Apparently I would—I did.

"All right. Now that it's decided to wear floral dresses, ladies, let's get this place cleaned up," Dad said. He met Wynn's gaze. "Wynn, you want to help me with the dishes?"

In other words, *Son, I can tell you need to talk about something.*

"Uh, yeah, sure." The smile Wynn found was nowhere near genuine. He knew that much as he collected plates and glasses. Carried them into the kitchen and immediately started washing them.

It was kind of pathetic. He was thirty-one years old and trying to avoid a simple conversation with his father, the man standing quietly beside him. Giving him space he probably didn't deserve.

"What's going on, Wynn?" Dad finally asked several minutes into it, breaking the tense silence. "And don't even think of giving me the go-around, either. I know my son, and I know when things aren't right. Is it something with you and Marshall's company? Jenna's house? The Gardens?"

Wynn stared at the steaming water as it ran over his hands, creating a waterfall, until his father reached out and tapped the faucet to turn it off. Why was he so reluctant to tell Dad about this? He was best friends with his dad, always had been. He looked up to and admired him, even strived to be more like him. John Bryant, the star quarterback and homecoming king during his high school years, who'd gone on to become chief of police in his hometown. Who was now a God-fearing, brave, respected husband, father, and business owner.

"Seth asked me to mentor a kid," he said at length, unwilling—or maybe just unable—to meet Dad's gaze. "And I said no."

Sounded even worse spoken aloud than it did in his head. That was nice. Just...peachy.

A sour peach, maybe.

"And why did you say no?"

Sometimes Dad's calm, nonjudgmental demeanor came in handy. Other times, such as now, it was almost irritating. He *shouldn't* be so understanding. Not when Wynn was being selfish. It wasn't like Seth had asked him to foster or adopt the kid. *Just mentor him*, he'd said. *Show him about construction; let him help at The Gardens. He has school during the day for now, but afterward...that's the time that counts.*

"I don't know. Maybe because I'm selfish."

Dad released a humor-less laugh. "You? Selfish? Not exactly the word I'd use to describe a person who, rather than seeking out high-profile, wealthy clients, builds homes for the ones who need them. Sure, you've built a successful company by doing that and you have done work for some of the wealthier people, but you're humble about it. So no, I wouldn't call you selfish."

"Okay, then why did I say no? He asked me to work with the kid for an hour or two after school. And I turned him down."

"Wynn, look at me."

Call him scared, but he kept staring at his hands.

"Wynn."

Reluctantly, he looked up and met Dad's gaze—the same deep blue as Wynn's. His dad had aged, sure, but he was still a handsome man. His sandy brown hair had grayed at the temples, but his features were still sharp. His six-foot-two frame was still muscular, due to him helping Wynn and Marshall on jobsites and the workouts he did and whatever Mom had him do. He was probably more faithful to his gym membership than Wynn, and Dad was married, had four grown children, two grandchildren, and ran an inn.

Here Wynn was, single, with a good job, and unwilling to mentor someone with fairly little.

"What's this really about?" Dad asked. "Because I'm completely certain it's not because you're selfish."

Wynn blew out a slow breath. "I'm scared I won't know how to do it. How to…mentor him. You're a dad, so when you and Mom took on fostering Ember, you already knew what you were doing. But I haven't the slightest idea about simply mentoring someone. Someone who has, from my understanding, a deceased mother and a nearly absent father. And what about his sister? Seth said she's only seven, so where will she go when Devin's with me?"

"Well, knowing Seth, he probably has a plan. And if not, he's working on one. He may not realize it or acknowledge it, but he's not as closed off as he thinks. But that's a totally different topic." Dad leaned against the counter, smiling slightly. "You're wrong about Ember, though. Yes, we were already parents, but we'd never fostered and adopted a girl with a past like your sister. We had a whole new learning curve to face. And I get it. Even just mentoring a kid like that is scary. But, if there was anyone able to do it, I'd say you are. Not that you have to. You don't. But if you change your mind, trust me. You'd be a great mentor."

"You really think that?"

"Yeah. I do. And even if you're the one mentoring this…"

"Devin. Devin Clark."

"Even if you're the one mentoring this Devin, trust me, you won't be in it alone. For one thing, you and I both know your mother will be all pro-chef and cook up feast after feast, insisting that he eats with us. And Marshall, well, he'll teach the kid a few things that're probably unnecessary but mostly harmless. Your sisters…we won't even go there." Dad was fully smiling now, and he picked up his dish towel again. "And as for me, I'll be supportive of you no matter which way you decide to go. The best way to make a decision, though, is to pray. The best answers come from the Lord."

Wynn nodded, too grateful to speak, and turned back to the sink just as the French doors opened and both of his sisters walked in with Noelle and Jess, talking about what game they were going to dig out of the closet. Grandpa followed closely, regaling them with his extensive history of winning, Sadie skipping along beside him.

Noelle glanced at him as they passed him, and that shy expression from earlier at his place was back. What was up? She wasn't exactly the shyest of people, not from what he knew of her. And after her threatening him with a frying skillet, the way she'd presented her ideas to the mayor, and everything else, he'd gotten to know her fairly well in less than a week. Sure, their conversation earlier about the cottages had been cut off prematurely, but Ember's text had been much more urgent than the actual situation. He still planned to finish that conversation when they had a moment alone.

But as for her sudden shyness...he had no idea. Maybe it was his family. Their lack of timidity could easily be overwhelming to newcomers, and in her defense, she hadn't been around all of them at once prior to this. Or maybe she'd decided on a better judgement of him after hearing about what he'd done to Sarah's goldfish however many years ago. It was obvious from the way she'd, probably subconsciously, stroked Nova from time to time that she liked animals.

"I have a feeling that smile isn't for Devin or Seth," Dad whispered, bumping his shoulder against Wynn's. "It seems that a certain young blonde has caught my son's eye, yeah?"

Heat warmed his neck and he scoffed. "What? No. I was just...thinking about Goldie. That's all."

"Ah. Right." Dad shut the cupboard door with extra force and winked. "That smile isn't for a goldfish, dead or alive, either. I've been around long enough, son. I've been around long enough."

116

CHAPTER
Eighteen

A growly rumble of thunder startled Noelle from her dream, and for a moment she wasn't sure where she was or why her legs felt weighted to the queen-sized bed.

Then, after the scent of fresh sheets and something like pancakes wafted to her nose, it all came back. The flood at the inn. Wynn opening his home to her. Supper and games late into the evening with the whole Bryant clan. Nova insisting upon staying with Noelle last night, and Wynn's exaggerated sadness because of it.

She wiggled her legs out from under Nova and sat up as another boom made her jump. What time was it? Probably fairly early, judging by the lack of light coming in through the windows to the right of her bed. Well, her temporary bed. A very comfortable temporary bed that she'd basically melted into last night. Had she even moved?

Noelle grabbed her watch from its charger on the table next to her bed and powered it on, glancing around the room while she waited. It wasn't huge, by any means, but it had a lake-y cottage-y feel to it. The walls were light shades of white, with one accent wall of very pale blue. White base and crown molding, and white trim for the large window whose panes were rain-streaked this morning. A five-drawer dresser against the blue wall and the chest at the base of her bed both added cozy wood elements to the room, and a door led to what Ember had shown as the closet yesterday during her tour. Oh, and the two bedside tables with lamps on them were the same wood. Maybe Wynn had made them?

It was nine o' clock?

An unintentional but audible gasp slipped from Noelle's lips as she stared down at the flowered screen of her watch. The chalk-like letters may be flowy, but they were also readable. And they clearly read *9:03.*

No, no, no. Why had she slept so late? The ivory sheets and white comforter tangled around her bare legs as she tried to get out of the bed. She never slept this late. Why today of all days? She'd been invited to church with the Bryant family and they said they left by quarter to ten. Never mind getting dressed, doing her hair, going up to the inn for breakfast.

Bottom line was that today was not the day for sleeping in.

Hoping Wynn or at least Ember hadn't left yet, she snagged the thick gray cardigan she'd worn last night as dusk approached. She pulled it tightly around herself and stepped into the hallway. Cool wood floors under her feet and that doughy, delicious, irresistible aroma of—

She drew to an abrupt halt before emerging from the hallway, stunned speechless for the second time in five minutes. Only this time it wasn't an unwelcome shock. Not really. Not at all, to be honest.

Wynn stood at the four-burner stove with his back to her, wearing black slacks and a crisp white button up, his suit coat draped sort of haphazardly over the back of a barstool, humming. *Humming!* And she stood in the shadowed hallway wearing Nike cotton shorts that wavered on the side of baggy, a T-shirt that'd been for one of Carter Inc.'s fundraisers several years back, and a cardigan that hid both. It probably looked like she had nothing on, which made her cheeks hot as she realized how awkward it would be if he assumed she was wearing nothing. Maybe she should just go back to bed. For, like, one second, since she was already running behind.

Then Nova walked past her and Wynn glanced up and he was wearing those glasses from the other night. Why hadn't she gone back to bed? And why hadn't she remembered to process the fact that he wore glasses at a time when he wasn't standing *right* there?

"Morning," he said, spatula in hand. "Hungry? Hope you like pancakes. Ember ran up to the inn to grab some yogurt and granola—my fridge and cupboards are sadly pretty empty right now—and she should be getting back any minute. We certainly won't be sitting outside, unless you want to get wet. Feel free to take your pick of stools. I don't have a formal indoor dining table."

Noelle opened her mouth and closed it, unsure of how to respond. "I, um…"

"I hope Nova didn't bother you last night," he continued, turning off the burner and transferring a steaming pan to a waiting trivet on the island. "She tends to be a bed hog."

Still self conscious, Noelle timidly finger-combed her hair. *Like that's going to help it any.* "Oh, uh, no, she was fine." She hesitated, torn between wanting to sit down and scarf up the grits and pancakes he was plating or going back to her room to change first.

Then, wearing a soaked, unbuttoned yellow raincoat that looked three sizes too big over black cotton shorts and a T-shirt advertising Bryant Bros. Construction, Ember walked in the door, and Noelle suddenly felt a little less out of place. Especially because Ember was barefoot and her hair was all matted to her cheeks. As long as, of course, she didn't focus on the fact that Wynn's shoulders filled out his dress shirt very nicely, or the five o' clock shadow on his jaw. Or, obviously, the glasses. Case in point, as long as she didn't look at Wynn whatsoever, she would be fine.

Never mind that that was practically an impossible feat.

"Morning, Noelle." Ember padded, her feet making squelchy water sounds on the hardwood, over to the island and deposited the soggy canvas tote on it. "It's coming down out there. To be honest, I don't think I'll even try to fix my hair. Plus I'd have to dry it first, and I don't really feel like doing that."

Wynn offered Noelle a gray-ish plate that appeared to be crafted of hand spun clay, and *Bryant* was stamped into the shiny surface. "Go for whatever you want. There's plenty of food. And, Em, they make umbrellas for a reason."

"Yeah, but then your hair gets stuck in the top of it and you're stuck in the rain and you wouldn't know anything about that because you don't have long hair." Ember held her plate to her midsection and gestured towards the mini-buffet Wynn had set up. Yogurt, granola, pancakes and syrup, and grits. "Guests first. By the way, his grits are fantastic. Lots of buttery goodness."

Was anything about Wynn Bryant not fantastic? Not that it mattered or affected her. She would be leaving at the end of May. Something that was growing harder to picture with every day that passed here. Last night, with Wynn's family, she'd felt…included. And seeing how John and Jackie interacted with their children and grandchildren only heightened Noelle's awareness that, whenever she got married and had kids, she would bring no family to the table. Not even ones who lived in another state, like Sarah's husband had said of his parents and his brother's family, who still lived in South Carolina. She'd clued in on Chris's desire to be closer to his family in some ways, but he seemed to be right at ease with the family he'd married into. Maybe there was underlying family dynamics that'd made his move here easier—whatever it was, the only married Bryant sibling and her husband certainly set a standard for young married couples in this day and age.

Noelle's parents were most certainly in different states, come to think of it. She'd just never spoken to either of them, nor had any recollection of even her mother, considering her grandparents had prearranged the adoption before Noelle's birth. Grandpa and Grandma had never been fans of Mom pursuing acting, but Noelle knew they'd loved her despite of her choice. They'd even offered to tell Noelle about her, share pictures with her. But other than the one headshot of Annabelle Carter she had, Noelle hadn't wanted it. She'd been reluctant.

Which was why, even now with both grandparents gone, the cardboard box marked *Annabelle's Things* sat taped and unopened in Noelle's attic. Maybe some day she'd decide to open it. Maybe not.

But for right now, she was most certainly going to enjoy this breakfast. And after that, get dressed in something hopefully rain-conducive, since the storm had no interest in letting up.

"Noelle?" Ember waved a spoon in front of Noelle's face. "Are you there? You seem to have fazed out."

Shaking her head, Noelle smiled faintly and readied a bite of pancakes. "Oh, yes, I'm fine. Just thinking about last night and how cool your family is. You guys are really blessed."

"Coming from someone who didn't have this for nine years, I totally agree," Ember said. "What about you? Family, I mean. You're cool, so I assume your family is too."

"Ember," Wynn scolded, meeting Noelle's gaze. Behind his glasses, his eyes read apology. "She's a guest."

"Uh, one you, brother dear, invited to our family supper."

"Yes, but—" He shook his head. "Sometimes you just don't ask certain questions."

Ember turned silent then, and even though Noelle appreciated that Wynn was trying to protect her, it wasn't like Ember would go around gossiping about Noelle. And even if she did, so what? There was nothing about her upbringing to be ashamed of.

"My grandparents raised me," she said gently. "Other than when I was born, I've never met my mother, and I don't know my father's name."

This time it was Ember's gaze that met hers, and Noelle was instantly glad she'd spoken up. Something in the younger woman's brown eyes said that, even though she now had people who loved and appreciated her, it hadn't always been that way. A level of understanding few people had. Granted, Noelle *had* had love and appreciation. Just not by way of parents and siblings.

"I'm sorry," Ember said at length. "Like Wynn said, it's really none of my—"

"No, you're fine," Noelle interrupted. "Really, it's no big deal. My grandparents were good people. Did you know that my grandma—Estelle Carter—kept The Gardens up for twenty years?"

"What, really?" Whatever interest she'd had in the food must be gone, because Ember set her fork down and turned to give Noelle her full attention. "Estelle Carter was your grandmother?"

Noelle nodded. "Well, her maiden name was Richmond, but yes. That's part of the reason I really wanted to do this project, to be honest."

"That's crazy. Not crazy, but it is. I volunteer at the library a couple days a week, and when I found out Wynn and Marsh were restoring The Gardens, I found some books there on their history." She lowered her voice, sort of conspiratorially. "Balsam Falls has books on basically everything that's ever happened here. Anyway, I saw pictures and stuff of Estelle Richmond but I didn't put two and two together. There was even a wedding picture. Wait, is Annabelle Carter your mother? Oh, my gosh, you don't have to answer that," she added quickly. "It's none of my business."

Noelle didn't miss the little sigh Wynn released, nor the pang in her heart at the mention of her mom. "She is. Let me guess, you've seen her movies?" Even Noelle didn't know what her own mother acted in.

Ember shook her head. "No, a little too dramatic for me. I'm more of an HGTV girl, to be honest. Or sometimes Dad and I watch westerns, and even though those are dramatic, old black and white films aren't quite like modern day dramas."

So her mother acted in dramas. No wonder her grandparents had wanted Noelle to be raised differently. She found a smile. "So... I'd love to see those pictures, but should I wait till tomorrow or is the library open today?"

"It's not, but I have a key. Trust me, nobody will think anything of it if we go today."

CHAPTER
Nineteen

Later that evening Wynn found Noelle on his back patio, everything from the chin down burrowed into a blanket. A steaming mug of tea rested on the wooden arm of her Adirondack chair, and Nova lounged by her feet. The dog had certainly taken a liking to her.

Wynn couldn't say much differently at this point.

He cleared his throat. "Mind if I join you ladies?"

Noelle glanced up at him and, even in the fading light, he could see tears in her eyes. "Go ahead. I was just thinking. And actually, this is your patio so technically you shouldn't have to ask to sit on it."

"Yeah, well, I did." He sat in the chair next to hers, taking in the orange sun sinking down over the expansive lake. Frothy pinks and oranges met the deepening blue of the sky overhead. "This view never gets old. At least, it never has for me, and I've been seeing this exact one for twenty years of my life. Well, close enough. The inn has about the same view."

"It's beautiful," she agreed. "I'm not sure how my grandmother ever left. I mean, I know she and Grandpa really loved each other, but still. Something about this town is magical."

Wynn hadn't failed to notice the photo displayed on her phone—the one she'd taken of the photograph earlier at the library. "Was your mom ever here? In Balsam Falls, I mean."

She shrugged. "Maybe? I know the town at least knows about her, since they have a few pictures of her here. Who knows? She might've come here one summer and my dad could even be from here. He could walk up to me or walk by me and I wouldn't even know it."

"You might. Not even consciously, but there's a part of you that would just...know."

"Maybe." She glanced down at the photo and Wynn followed her gaze.

Annabelle Carter was built very much like her daughter—or vice versa—with that petite frame and long hair. Annabelle, however, had brown eyes and hair and a slightly more circular face as opposed to Noelle's more oval face and blue eyes. Those traits must've come from her father. Whoever he was. What would it be like to not even know your own dad's name? Even Ember knew her birth parents. She'd lived with them for nine years of her life. Admittedly the worst years, she'd probably say, but she wasn't left wondering. Other than her mother's name, Noelle had nothing to go on.

"I think I want to find her."

The words were so soft, so unsure, that Wynn wondered if he'd only imagined them.

"My mom, I mean," she continued, not as quietly. She turned her head to look at him, resting her cheek against the back of the chair. "My grandparents always left the door open. They said they'd tell me about her if I wanted that. But back then, I don't know. I was okay not knowing, I guess. I didn't want to mess up what I had. Now... I think I'm ready. I've been thinking about it ever since your sister asked me this morning. Both of my grandparents are gone, and I have a fairly strong foundation of faith and means in my life. After twenty-six years of not knowing virtually anything, I'm pretty sure I can handle it. Whatever *it* is."

Wynn studied the expression she wore, the uncertainty in her eyes. Vulnerability. Maybe even a need for validity. In her work, and more importantly, in her personal life. She didn't come off as needy—certainly not monetarily or professionally—but every person deserved to be loved. To be respected. Wynn couldn't imagine how he'd feel if nobody had supported his and Marshall's decision to start their own company. If nobody validated his passion for woodworking on evenings or mornings when he wasn't needed elsewhere.

Speaking of, he needed to make time to get back in the shop. It'd been a while since he'd done that. Just him, wood, and nobody needing anything from him for a couple hours.

"Have you looked your mom up on Google? She's an actress, right?"

Noelle nodded. "Yeah. And no, I haven't. Besides the tabloids probably not being accurate, I haven't wanted to know if she's...married. And if so, to whom and if they have any other kids. Or if she has any other kids or marriages. Granted, that'll probably be the best way to get the basics on her right now."

"That's understandable." He rubbed his chin, trying to think of whether or not his mother would have any resources. She'd worked in family law. Over thirty years ago, but she still kept in contact with some of her attorney friends. Maybe they could help. "Not to change the subject, but it appears Nova has decided she likes you better than me."

A fraction of amusement lit her eyes as she smiled, a signal of the Noelle he'd been introduced to nearly a week ago. "Oh, I doubt that. You're her daddy. I think most girls are more attached to their dads than they let on. Ember and Sarah, for instance, seem really tight with your dad."

"They are. Ember especially, because her biological dad was abusive to both her and her mother. Not that her mom was a saint, but that's not my story to tell." He debated on whether to voice his

125

next thoughts or not, but the words were too pressing. Too important to hold back. "She looks up to you, Noelle. Ember does. And I don't mean that in a bad way or a negative way, but she just tends to cover up everything with bubbly humor *all* the time. When someone can see both her more personal side and her witty side, they've earned a place on her best friend list. I think you've already inspired her in the time you've been here. And as her older brother, I know that means a lot to her. Probably more than you'll ever know."

She bit her lip but said nothing, then finally broke eye contact and looked out over the darkening lake. Did she realize how beautiful she was? Something he couldn't voice aloud, but she was stunning, both physically and otherwise. Her strength was admirable, and she probably didn't even realize just how inspiring she was to not only his sister, but other young women.

Maybe finding her mother would help her realize that. Maybe not. Something totally out of his control. But he could pray for her, and he would most certainly be doing that.

Along with the prayers he'd started to say about his response to Seth.

CHAPTER
Twenty

A week had passed since Seth asked Wynn to mentor Devin, and he still hadn't worked up the courage to revoke his initial *no*. It really wasn't difficult. All he had to do was call, text, or stop in at the station. He hadn't done any of those three options, nor brought it up any time he had seen Seth in the last seven days.

His team had, however, made progress on both projects they were currently working on. Jenna's house, where he was this morning, was actually ninety-nine percent done. Depending on Jenna and the kids' schedules, they'd have them moved in within the next week or two. The impending reveal was both Wynn's favorite part of his job and his most nerve-wracking. Not that it should be. Compared to her current place, this house was more efficient, safer, and much more "fixed up." Considering it was new construction, it most definitely should be all three of those and then some.

As far as The Gardens went, demo was done. Even though she'd resisted, Wynn had managed to wrangle his sister into designing the space. Once she got her sketches to him, they'd take them to Mayor Leo before continuing. Their plan was to get the inside done while the temps were still regularly fluctuating between fifty all the way to eighty, then tackle the outside. That part was going to be the most work. Other than demo and clearing the building, it wasn't in bad shape. Outdated, yes, but in decent condition. The outside was a different story.

For now, his focus was supposed to be on following Sally Darren through Jen's house to make sure all the design elements were correct. He, however, had a hard time concentrating on anything but two things on drastically different spectrums: Devin and Noelle.

Devin, because of the weight of saying no and wondering if he'd ever get the guts to talk to Seth about it again before it was too late.

Noelle, because... Well, mainly for reasons he had no right thinking about. Like how well she fit into his family last Saturday, and the fact that she'd been invited again tonight. The fact that she was with his sister at the library for the morning and helping his mom with meal prep this afternoon. The fact that he hadn't stopped thinking about her since she'd arrived nearly two weeks ago.

"...like how the herringbone pattern on the floor compliments the light fixture over the island," Sally was saying, her transparent clipboard tucked under her arm. "Wynn, are you listening to me?"

He shook his head to rid the Devin and Noelle thoughts. Or at least try to. "Sorry, yes. I am."

Sally's painted pink lips pursed, and her rigid posture said she didn't believe him. "Then everything in here is good and we can move on to the living room?"

"Yep. Looks great." It did—simple, cozy, and way more spacious than Jen's current kitchen. Something she would never complain about but deserved to have better. "I'm a personal fan of the herringbone pattern. Really compliments those lights over the island, you know what I'm saying?"

"Wynn Bryant, you're lucky you're so good looking or you'd be looking for another interior designer," Sally scolded, wagging her manicured white fingernail at him. Matched her white buttoned shirt with a starched collar and the bright coral capris she had on. "You will, however, need to be finding a new one anyhow, seeings as I'm retiring after this spring is over. Barry and I are planning to travel, now that the kids are grown and on their own, so to speak."

Wynn's eyebrows shot up as he followed her into the living room. "Oh, really? When did you plan to tell me? You've been doing projects for us for a decade. Practically designed all of Balsam Falls."

"Are you trying to remind me how old I am?" She winked at him, resting her hand on the back of the brown leather couch. "No, we decided a few weeks ago. Wanted to have some time to make sure, but I think we're both excited. Barry finally has the time now that he's retired from the marina, so we may as well get on with it. You never know what'll happen in the world these days. Crazy. Anyway, how about that sister of yours? She's got a knack for design, according to the ladies at my Bible study. She's going to be a nice little wife and mama some day, she will. We've already been ruling out men for her."

Ember would gag at the thought of the, while well-meaning, older church ladies setting her up. Wynn couldn't exactly blame her. They'd tried and failed for both him and Marshall. Probably were determined to set up at least one Bryant sibling before their days were over.

"You know, Betsy's granddaughter, Madison—"

"That subject is strictly off limits, Sally, as you and I well know." He walked around the room. Studied the white-washed brick fireplace and its wooden block mantle. Inspected the sofa and chairs. "This room looks good. On to the next one."

Sally clucked her tongue disapprovingly, something that didn't even faze him anymore, but they kept going. And miracle of miracles, had the whole place walked through within the sixty minutes of an hour. That was quite possibly a new record, considering Wynn usually blocked out at least three hours for this walk-through on other projects. Those hours weren't his most productive, but they were necessary.

"I'll make sure to get those last few things in by early next week, and we should be good." Sally unlocked her Jeep from where they stood on the porch. "This is a great house, Wynn. Some of your best work."

He dipped his chin. "Thank you. Still gonna be around for the Spring Fling? Ember's designing The Gardens. She'd never say it, but it'd mean a lot if Balsam Falls's most established designer was there to see it."

Sally repositioned the designer leather portfolio bag on her shoulder. "We will still be here. Barry's handling the fireworks. I'll make it a point to talk to Ember at some point during the event. See you next week."

Wynn nodded and tucked his hands in the front pockets of his jeans, taking a moment to breathe as he took in what would soon be Jen's front porch view. Short spikes of grass that had started filling in lined the freshly poured sidewalk that, in one direction, led to the driveway, and in another, to the street. It was a middle-class neighborhood as opposed to the low-income one she was currently in thanks to her ex's doing, and the neighboring houses were a little close for his taste but they were well-kept and owned by people who would be good for Jen. Other parents her age, children for Ella to play with now, and ones for Eli to play with down the road.

Just after Sally had pulled out of the driveway, a white Explorer pulled in. *Noelle's car.* Well, her rental. She and Ember and Sadie emerged, and Wynn lifted his hand in greeting. Tried to ignore how good Noelle looked in her fitted jeans and a billowy pink blouse, taupe heeled sandals matching the light jacket she wore. Definitely didn't notice her loose curls, the ones that she seemed to be irritated with as she pushed them over her shoulder. Since the new flooring for her room at the inn would take a week or two to arrive, she and Ember were still his houseguests, but he'd left before either of them were up this morning.

"Uncle Wynn!" Sadie ran up to him, her pigtails swinging. "I went to the library with Aunt Ember and Elle today. The library lady even let me stamp a book, and then I did one on my hand."

Wynn swung her into his arms, but her use of *Elle* had snagged part of his attention. "Oh, really? Does that mean you're due home by—" he picked up her hand "—the eighth of April? Your mom might not like that very much."

Sadie giggled. "*Nooo.* I didn't mean to do it, silly."

"Ah. I see." He glanced at his sister and Noelle. "Want to take a tour? Everything's almost done, so you'd get the gist of it. Marshall left when he heard Sally Darren was coming, and other than the movers, our crew is pretty much done. Nobody's here, though, since it's a Saturday. Move onto adding on to the Pearson's' house next. Anyway, you guys can come inside if you want."

"Actually, we came to tell you something we found today," Ember said, nudging Noelle in the side. "Go ahead. I promise I don't always steal everyone's thunder. Only when it counts."

Noelle pulled something from her pocket and handed it to him. "We found that in one of the history books. Tucked into the crease of the pages. Either nobody's found it before—which is kind of unrealistic—or they've just left it in there."

Shifting Sadie to his left arm, he unfolded the crinkled paper. A young woman stared back at him from a photograph in black and white, the quality marred by grain. But not so bad he didn't recognize that the woman was Noelle's mother. The setting was hard to tell, but it appeared to be Falls Lake behind her. Noelle's mom wore cutoff jean shorts and a striped tank top with an oversized white shirt unbuttoned and billowing around her. She was smiling and holding her hair back with her left hand, even though tendrils blew across her face.

"There's also a note on the back," Noelle said, her hands clasped in front of her. "Not sure what it means, but it's there."

Wynn turned the photograph around. *Today was a day I've only ever dreamed of, and yet it wasn't like a dream at all.* He squinted and read it over again, confused by the words.

"Nothing like a riddle, huh?" He passed it back to her. "I believe that was taken by Falls Lake, though. And either she asked a stranger to take the picture, or someone was with her."

"True, but the most interesting part is this." Ember held her phone up, the display zoomed in so far it was beyond pixelated. "Look! She has a ring on. A rock ring. Like, a rock as in an engagement ring rock."

"Mommy has a rock," Sadie exclaimed, leaning in as she clutched onto Wynn's shoulder. "Right, Uncle Wynn?"

Wynn took the phone to see it better and pressed a kiss to his niece's temple. "Yes, she does. And I kind of see it, but it's really blurry zoomed in that far. That said, hypothetically speaking, if she got engaged here, trust me. It wouldn't have been swept under the rug."

"Yeah, but from the little I've ever pieced together about my mom, she would've done everything in her power to keep it low profile," Noelle said, biting her lip. Not quite as bright pink as Sally's, but there was a glossy pink sheen to Noelle's. Why exactly was he looking at her lips? "So I don't know what happened, but this picture is the only thing we found, other than a couple headshots. There was a decent amount about my grandma, and a little about my grandpa. Maybe she was only here once. Don't know."

"Or maybe not," Wynn countered. "What if she came back with that photo in tow and tucked it in the book?"

"Then people would've noticed, and you would've heard about it," Noelle said. "How do you come up with these ideas, anyhow? Are you some sort of undercover detective?"

Ember snorted.

Wynn chuckled and let Sadie down, watching as she trotted to the other end of the porch to see the froggy bench they'd put there for the kids. "You already know how tight Jess and Marsh are, which means Seth hangs around a decent amount. One, because of that, and two, because he really admires my dad. Mainly because of dad's former role as chief of police. But anyway, the most interested he is in anything is his job…or Jenna." Wynn winked and tapped the wooden pillar supporting the porch roof. "But again, you didn't hear that from me. Shall we go on a tour now, ladies?"

CHAPTER
Twenty One

Jackie removed a measuring cup from the microwave filled nearly to the I cup mark with melted butter. "I'm sure there's other recipes that probably use less butter, but in this house, we like our potatoes well coated. And there's a lot of us, so that means there needs to be a lot of potatoes."

Noelle watched with fascination as Wynn's mother readied the bag to toss the potato quarters in. "So, you coat them in butter and then parmesan cheese and flour?"

"Well, you could probably do it that way, but I've always poured the butter over the top of them after they're coated." Jackie motioned to the four glass pans set out on the island. "How about I do two pans, then you can try it out for the other two? Trust me, it's hard to mess up this dish."

"Oh, no, it's fine. I can just watch."

Jackie shook her head. "You'll never learn something if you never try. Like I said, worst case scenario is you'll skimp on butter and have to answer to the men in this family. No biggie. They'll go easy on you."

"Don't be too sure about that. I know how willing they are to challenge somebody to do something." She held up her hand. "This bruise is from my attempt at using a hammer yesterday. Fortunately I didn't break anything, but I don't think I'll be swinging one of those again anytime soon. Not even for the promised cinnamon roll."

Jackie paused mid-shake of her parmesan-cheese-and-flour Ziploc bag. "Please tell me you still got the cinnamon roll."

"Oh, yes. Marshall was reluctant, but Wynn and Ember agreed that I had indeed swung the hammer. I think that's the best cinnamon roll I've ever had, to be honest."

"That's something I can agree with you on." Jackie arranged the coated potatoes in two of the pans. "Our town is lucky to have a coffee shop like Cozy & Grounds and a baker like Jess, especially because we don't have our own bakery. Luna and her husband, Ian, did a lot of work to get that place looking like it is these days. That building used to be the newspaper office and press. All right, come on over here. It's your turn."

Noelle hesitated, but something about Jackie's gentle smile persuaded her to roll up her sleeves and round the island. "You're sure you trust me to be in this beautiful kitchen? I know how to make, like, two things, but I think there's a reason Grandma preferred me being in the office with Grandpa."

"Well, that's how it still is with Ember—when she's not working, I usually send her to help her dad—but she's learning. First off, you drop the potatoes in the bag and seal it without releasing the air. Then shake them like your life depends on it. My personal preference is to dance around the kitchen Gangnam Style, but that's totally optional."

"Don't do it." Sarah walked into the kitchen, carrying two tote bags and still managing to look effortlessly stylish in her leggings, sandals, and oversized lightweight sweater, her dark blonde hair pulled into a thick braid. "It's a trap. Your best bet is to slowly, quietly, and peacefully retreat from the kitchen. Then run as fast as you possibly can as far as you possibly can. Or drive. Probably a better idea."

"Sarah Joy," Jackie scolded, swatting at her oldest daughter with an oven mitt. "Your brothers have influenced you too much. What did you bring in these?"

As mother and daughter interacted over something as simple as groceries, Noelle's thoughts ventured back to the picture she and Ember had uncovered earlier. The photo currently on the dresser in her temporary room at Wynn's. The one in which her mother was, quite clearly, sporting an engagement ring. One that wasn't huge but certainly wasn't tiny, either.

And it had been taken right here in Balsam Falls.

Had it been before Noelle? After? Why had her mother written what she did on the back? Who had taken the photo? And why was it tucked in the folds of a Balsam Falls history book between two pages about the groundbreaking for an undisclosed new building?

Questions piled up in Noelle's mind, sending her thoughts into a tailspin.

Then there was the mix of regret and guilt because she hadn't asked her grandparents about Mom at any point. Mom's choice had affected their lives just as much, if not more, than it had Noelle's. They were the ones who'd sacrificed the most. Not Noelle. And maybe it would've been therapeutic for them to talk about it. Which was now, obviously, an impossible feat. Other than prayer, which wasn't exactly the same as sitting down to have a conversation with someone here.

On the flip side, here she was with this wonderful family, something that both made her feel included and feel a little sad. Sad that her mother had created this whole big. . .mystery, whether or not that had been her intent. Sad because, come the end of May, she'd go back home to her regularly scheduled life. To life without Wynn and Ember and their entire family. To a life she'd been, almost unbeknownst to her, slowly detaching from. Ever since her grandfather's death last November, she'd become less social and less spontaneous. More work and more burying her emotions.

Just the mere thought of leaving was enough to make her want to cry. For as much as she'd detached from her life in Mississippi in the past months, she'd attached double to this town in two weeks. More specifically, this family and their wonderfulness.

Such as Ember inviting her to tag along to the library this morning. Between the three of them—Noelle, Ember, and Sadie—they'd probably caused the poor librarian several panic attacks. First, when they'd knocked over a stack of thick encyclopedias they'd been reshelving, causing a loud *boom* to reverberate through the ornate two-story structure. Then when Sadie had stamped not only her own hand but also directly on the page of the book—over the author's name. And finally, when Ember had discovered that photo of Mom. Their squeals had caused more than one head to turn, and not exactly in a positive way.

Or afterward, when Wynn had given all three of them a tour of the house he and Marshall were nearly done with. Though he probably hadn't realized it, he was so good with his very inquisitive niece. And he hadn't looked the least bit shabby with the four-year-old on his shoulders, his shirt pulled taught over his shoulders as he held onto her. There were just certain things that were attractive about certain men, and one interacting with a child was one of them. Especially a little girl who clearly adored her uncle Wynn.

Noelle was starting to adore him too.

And she had zero right to. She couldn't say she had no reason to, because really, that was untrue. There were a lot of traits to Wynn Bryant that merited adoration in some way, shape, or form.

Not that Noelle needed to let that adoration run much deeper than it already did. She didn't intend to leave Balsam Falls nursing a broken heart all because of herself. There might be a lot she still needed to learn, but guarding her heart was not on that list. She'd had a relationship end poorly a couple years ago, and she couldn't even place all the blame on the guy she'd been dating. No, he admittedly hadn't been as worthy of adoration as Wynn Bryant—Grandpa's distaste for Charles should've been her first clue—but she'd probably been lacking in some area of their relationship, too.

So yes, she knew how to keep a guard up. She just needed to make sure to not let it slip for foolish reasons.

For instance, he'd had ample time to bring up the cottages again, but he hadn't. Red flag number one.

"Noelle, dear, I believe the potatoes are coated quite well." Jackie's voice broke into Noelle's thoughts. "But you can toss them as much as you want to, long as they're ready to go in the oven by four."

Noelle's neck warmed as a flush undoubtedly started crawling into her cheeks. "Oh, yes. Sorry. I guess I kind of spaced out for a minute. Do I just put them in the pan now?"

Jackie nodded. "Just arrange them however they'll fit, and then you'll pour the butter over the top. Then we can move onto the meatloaf. Sarah, can you please get the meat out of the fridge? When are your brothers and Ember supposed to get here? Or where's your dad? I might need someone to run and get more parmesan cheese and lettuce."

"Chris can stop at the market when he and the kids come over." Sarah pulled two cookie sheets covered in raw ground beef out, kicked the fridge door shut with her foot, and carried them to the island. "Wow, those are heavy. Mom muscles must be a thing, because I've slacked in lifting any weights lately. At least my husband keeps me accountable to some form of exercise by giving me twenty 'kid-free' minutes to make sure I get my yoga in." She set her palms on the island countertop and leaned into them. "Otherwise my workout schedule would probably be nonexistent. What do you need help with, Mom?"

How come the words *Mom muscles, my husband,* and *Mom* stuck out to Noelle, she didn't know. Maybe because she wondered if she'd ever settle down and become a mom? Wondered if she'd ever have a daughter or son that would call her Mom, or any nieces and nephews to call her Aunt Noelle. Or maybe instead of Noelle, they'd call her Elle, like Sadie had taken to doing.

Yes, her best bet would be to stay unattached here.

Because no matter what her bank balance was, it would never be able to buy her out of the pain that'd come from attachment to something she'd just have to say goodbye to.

CHAPTER

Twenty Two

It took ten days for Wynn to work up the nerve to talk to Seth about mentoring Devin. Well, actually nine, because he'd texted him last night about meeting Tuesday morning at Cozy & Grounds.

Today was Tuesday morning, and Jess's frosting-smeared cinnamon rolls sat in front of both Wynn and Seth, the steam from them creating an aromatic vapor. One that did absolutely nothing to block the smug look on Seth's face. He was one year younger than Wynn and yet Wynn felt like a little kid who'd been wrongly accused of stealing his sibling's marker.

More than likely thanks to the uniform. Maybe it was like white coat syndrome for patients in a hospital. He'd coin it "blue uniform syndrome" and call it good.

"Are you planning to explain why we're here or just sit there and wish I didn't already know?" Seth broke the silence, using that droll tone he seemed to have mastered over the years. "Because yes, if you were wondering, I do know why we're here. And you talk about Ember being vague in texts. Have you looked at your own?"

Wynn shot him a look. "Then why are you just sitting there? You're head of the police department. You can take charge."

"You're head of your own business." Seth smirked and took a sip of his coffee. "What made you change your mind?"

That was the million dollar question, wasn't it? A valid question, but it was kind of hard to answer. He hadn't *not* wanted to do it when Seth initially brought it up, and yet that was difficult to explain since, yeah, he'd said no. And then changed his mind after a decent chunk of time.

"There wasn't really a reason, other than I took some time to think about it." Wynn shrugged, trying for nonchalance as he forked a bite of cinnamon roll into his mouth. "Plus, Jen's house will officially be done after tomorrow, so our biggest project is The Gardens. The addition at the Pearsons' is minuscule, and our next house build doesn't start until June. So I do have the advantage of more free time."

"Uh-huh." Seth said the words as if he didn't buy them. At all.

Wynn cleared his throat. "So how is this going to work? He has a younger sister, and from what you said, he does a lot of the household stuff. Where will she be when I'm with Devin? Or Devin's with me, I guess."

"About that. I may have omitted the tiny detail that she would probably need to hang out with you as well. But before you go all berserk on me, she's about the quietest and calmest little girl you'll meet. She won't cause any problems."

"Problems? Seth, I'm not worried about her causing problems. But Devin's thirteen—he'll be able to keep up if I need him to do something. I don't have eyes on the sides or back of my head to watch her while we're working. And what is a six year old girl supposed to do on a construction site?"

"Seven. Sophie is seven. And I don't know. Maybe that blonde that's helping you could be with her."

"Um, Noelle is here to work on The Gardens. Not babysit."

Seth arched a brow as he took a bite of his roll. "So, do tell. Is that why she was with you last weekend when you got back for the flood? Or why she was at Saturday supper the past *two* weeks in a row? Or, and this is the best one yet, why she's staying at your house?"

"Hey, Mom and Ember came up with the idea to have her stay at my place. Who was I to turn her down? Besides, Em's staying with me too. How do you even know about that? You're a cop, sure, but that definitely does not give you the right to know all of my business."

"I was standing right there when it was decided, remember? I believe the words were—"

Wynn held up a hand. "Save it. Don't need to hear any more. Back to Sophie, though. I can't ask Noelle to babysit her."

"Can't, or won't?" Seth flicked the salt packet before tearing the top off and sprinkling half over his remaining cinnamon roll. One of his very odd, very disturbing habits. "Because it surprises me that you skipped straight to moving in together. I mean, I'm not perfect, but it just doesn't seem like you to skip dating. Engagement. Marriage. *Then* moving in together. And trust me, Judge Warner Chapman would not be able to keep quiet about Wynn Bryant eloping in this town, so I know that didn't happen."

"Seth," Wynn warned, glaring at his friend. "I already explained it to you. Would you like to talk about you and Jenna? We can most certainly do that, since you appear to have all the time in the world this morning."

That shifted Seth's whole demeanor. Wynn may not be a cop, but he did know how to quiet the people he knew best. And considering he'd practically seen Seth every day for the past twenty years thanks to Marsh and Jess being inseparable, he'd learned exactly how to press the *Subject Change* button. Currently it was to bring up Jenna or Ella or Eli. In the past it had ranged from Seth's lack of waterskiing abilities to his high school graduation photo, where his hair stuck up like Alfalfa. In addition to Jess and Marshall's friendship, Wynn's mother had offered to homeschool Seth and Jess alongside her own children, but their aunt and uncle had been strictly against that. Instead, Seth and Jess had spent nearly every afternoon following school with the Bryants.

None of that was applicable to this conversation, but mentioning one of those sore spots would probably still get a rise out of him if push came to shove.

"You're sure Noelle wouldn't be willing to do it?" Seth asked. Only this time his tone didn't imply any trace of teasing. "Your relationship aside, I mean. She'd be at The Gardens anyway, so you wouldn't be asking too much of her."

Wynn hesitated. "I'll think about it. But temporarily, I guess she'll have to just hang out. I can grab some coloring stuff, otherwise. When do you want me to start this whole...mentoring thing?" The words still didn't sound right for him. How was he supposed to mentor a kid he knew virtually nothing about?

"Does that mean you're going to watch Sophie until you're done 'thinking about it'?" Seth's expression was downright mischievous all over again. What was with him this morning? "Because you do realize you don't have eyes on the sides and back of your head, right? That negates your whole—"

"Seth, I don't know what happened to you since I saw you last, but you're acting weird. And I am going to have to get to Jen's house soon. When is this mentor thing supposed to start?"

"All right, I'll stop now. For a little bit." Seth finished off his coffee, then pulled a piece of paper from his shirt pocket. "Here's a little bit of info on Devin, mainly their address, but I would rather you learn from Devin directly about other stuff. Part of my reasoning for this idea is to hopefully get him to open up more. I don't think his dad—Robert Clark—is physically abusing him or Sophie, but I need more information. Clark hits it pretty hard at the bar every night, so that coupled with the loss of his wife could spell out for disaster. I just can't do anything officially unless there's solid evidence. Nor will I. Clark, much as I dislike his choices, deserves a shot to prove himself."

Wynn's irritation with Seth dissolved some as he realized the weight of this situation. "So there's a possibility of abuse going on?"

142

"With alcoholics, there's always a chance of abuse. So yes, there is. And now that Devin's older, we need to monitor it more closely. He's a good kid for the most part. Rough around the edges for sure, but I would hate to see temptations get the best of him, and those are strongest between after school and suppertime. By him being with you, it'll minimize that opportunity by about one hundred percent. Plus, you're a trustworthy guy. He'll be able to confide in you."

"Well, I'll do my best. I can't say I'm experienced in this area."

"No, but look at how you've been to Ember. Same situation in some ways." Seth paused as a barista with curly red hair came to collet their empty mugs and plates. "Regarding when to start, could you pick the kids up from school tomorrow? Their dad works at the lumber yard till five, and he probably takes off for the bar by six. I need you to have the kids back to the address on that paper by ten till five. To be clear, Clark doesn't know about this, nor do I want him to. We don't need him acting on his best behavior. Defeats the whole purpose."

"Wait, Robert Clark from Dickies? That's Devin's father?"

Seth nodded. "Yes. Does that work for you?"

It hadn't ever occurred to him that the tall man with the obvious chip on his shoulder was Devin's *dad.* He'd been at Dickies Lumberyard for years, and Wynn had only talked to him once when nobody else had been around to take his order. But after the initial shock wore off, a resolve seemed to come forth. To make sure these kids were safe, they needed a stranger they could trust. Apparently he was that stranger.

"Sounds good to me."

--- ⁂ ---

CHAPTER

Twenty Three

"Paint colors aren't just important, they are the *most* important design decision," Ember said, balancing her paper plate on her bent knee. "Because, depending on paint color, you choose trim work. And design elements. And decorations. So you can see why I'm trying to get you to decide on your prominent color."

Noelle tried to hide her smile as she took a bite of hamburger pizza from Giorgi's. They'd been here all day getting walls rebuilt, sanding salvageable floors and, for the past hour, discussing paint colors. At some point, Jess and Seth had shown up, followed by pizza, and now they were scattered around the main room of The Gardens with paper plates and plastic Solo cups of Sprite. The only ones carrying on conversation right now were Ember and Marshall, with Wynn putting in a word here and there. Noelle, Jess, and Seth were simply enjoying the meal for the moment.

Previously, Jacks frozen pizza had been her go-to, but Giorgi's? Between the buttery crust, the zippy tomato sauce, and the cheesy, meaty toppings, it had claimed the number one slot on her favorite

144

pizza list. How she'd get it when she was back in Mississippi was yet to be determined.

"Okay, then if you don't like white, what color?" Marshall asked.

Ember dropped her chin to her chest. "No, no, *no*. I didn't ever once say I didn't like white. I just want to make sure whatever we go with is going to compliment the outdoor space too, and all white would have to be broken up by some kind of accent wall no matter what. That's just a design rule of thumb in my book."

"Hey, what if someone painted a mural on one of the walls?" Jess asked, visibly perking up at the idea. "The text could say *The Gardens* in a banner-like font over top, and then the muralist could paint flowers or a scene below that. It would be great for people to take pictures by, which they would then post to social media, so basically it would be free marketing for us. Or for The Gardens, I guess."

Seth grabbed another slice of pizza from the box on the sawhorse by him. It was sort of odd to see him in jeans and a hoodie as opposed to his uniform. "But the price to have a muralist do it wouldn't be free."

"No, but what about the wow factor?" Jess set her plate down and instructed for Nova to leave it, then motioned to the biggest wall across from the door. "I mean, imagine it. Walk in and boom! Bright, happy, *custom* mural. People'll be like, 'Wow! Hey, can you take my pic—"

"And I'll post it to social media," Marshall finished with a grin. "Yeah, we got that part. Who around here would even be able to do that sort of thing *if* we were to make it work?"

Wynn looked at Seth. "I believe you know someone, Seth."

"Who?" Jess's brows wrinkled. "My brother knows someone? This brother? Seth?"

Seth made a face. "Do you have another brother I don't know about?"

"What—No. Seth, what are you talking about? Or who, I should say."

"Name starts with *J* and ends with an *A*," Wynn said, taking a sip of his soda. "Hint, we're literally finishing a house for this person. If that doesn't tell you who—"

"Oh!" Jess clapped her hands together, causing Nova to lift her head. "Jenna! Yes! Why didn't I think of her?"

"Because I'm just that good," Wynn quipped.

"Oh, no." Seth shook his head. "Uh-uh. I can't ask her to do that. She works full time at Farm to Table, and has two kids to feed. No way."

"My brother has a thing for Jen," Jess explained as she sat back down next to Noelle. "Which he can't deny because of that pretty little flush in his cheeks right now."

"That says nothing about me having a crush on Jenna," Seth said wryly. "People always get squirmish when they're in the hot seat."

"Ironic of you to say that, since you put people in the hot seat all the time." Jess's sloppy bun flopped as she leaned back against the wall. "And I never said you have a crush on her. I said you have a thing for her. If you prefer me to use the word crush, I will do my utmost bestest to remember that."

Noelle tried not to laugh at the look Seth gave his sister. It was clear he wasn't a fan of this topic—nor would Jess or Marshall probably be, if what Wynn and Ember were whispering about was their relationship—but if Jenna could paint, maybe it was worth a shot. Jess had a point about a mural being a great touristy attraction, and since Balsam Falls didn't have one like that, why not add one? Not only that, but it may potentially help bring in people wanting to rent out the space, which would not only benefit the city but it would give them a reason for having had this restoration done. The business side of Noelle, something she'd honed from years of watching Grandpa work with clients, really liked that side of Jess's idea. And it wasn't exactly like they had no funds to work with. The city had given Wynn and Marshall a decent budget, making it clear the city was obviously not hurting at all. Even if most of their budget would go to the outside space, they could figure out how to get this done.

"She'd get paid for it, Seth," Jess was saying, clearly unwilling to give the idea up right away. Or maybe at all. "And as for the kids... I'll watch them. Ella probably has pre-school—"

"Not until next year," Seth said.

Jess's lips quirked. "Well, it's just dandy that you know *everything* about Jen, big brother. I'll just watch both of them, then. We can hang out here or at the inn or at Jen's house. I'm sure Joanna Crawford would let her have time to paint. Or at least a couple hours every day."

"We'd need to have it done within a few weeks, to tell the truth," Wynn said. "The mural would have to be done before any design elements or furniture comes in. We've basically got a month and a half to have everything—inside and out—finished, because then the decorations specifically for this event will need to be put up and all that. I do think it would be a good idea, but only if it can be done by mid-April. Possibly late April, but that may be pushing it."

"So that leaves two and a half to three weeks," Jess mused. "Seth? Will you at least talk to her? Like, tonight or tomorrow?"

Seth hesitated. "I don't know, Jess. She may not want her artwork on display for everyone to see."

"I'm meeting with Mayor Mason and Joanna Crawford tomorrow morning," Noelle said, glancing around the room. "I can bring it up to Jenna then? Before I'd even present the idea to Mayor Mason, so then nobody would have their hopes up. Would that work okay?"

All eyes turned to Seth, and Noelle had to hide her smile again. It was sweet how much Seth obviously cared about Jenna, even if he didn't want to let on that he did. She'd met Jenna yesterday at church, and both she and her kids were very sweet.

"Okay," Seth conceded. "Because—and *only* because—I trust Noelle not to hound her about it like Jess would."

This time Noelle couldn't help the laugh that squeaked out. Wynn glanced at her, amusement twinkling in those stunning blue eyes of his. Really, they could give the sparkling lake a run for its money.

"Finally I'm not the one being blamed for my 'exuberance'," Ember said, standing up. "Who's ready to decide on paint colors?"

CHAPTER
Twenty Four

"M iss Carter, it's good to see you again."
Noelle smiled and stood to shake the mayor's hand.
"Good morning, Mayor. How have you been?"

"Very well, very well." The mayor sat down across from Noelle at the table she'd picked along the windows looking out on Main Street. "Joanna will be with us shortly. Have you ordered yet? They have the best pancakes you'll ever taste here. Hands down."

Probably didn't compare to Wynn's from-scratch ones, but she decided against voicing that aloud. "I've already eaten, but I'll have to try them out sometime. Feel free to order, though. It won't bother me."

He reached for a menu stored in a metal paper holder. "I've been working on this new diet, you see, so that's been a challenge. They call it a see-food diet. Been working out well, but if I see too much food, I eat too much food."

Noelle chuckled, but Jenna Williams walked up to their table before Noelle could respond. The young mother was girl-next-door pretty with her blonde hair and hazel eyes. The hair tie holding her ponytail matched the pale green of her T-shirt today, and she wore an apron around her waist with Farm to Table's logo on the bottom right corner.

The restaurant itself had a freshly rustic atmosphere. The walls were covered in white-washed barnwood, and the floors were polished cement. A light up *Order Here* sign hung over the order counter with wavy refurbished metal on the side, and they'd used neat little Mason jars as light fixtures throughout the space. Though she'd yet to see the outside seating in person, there were pictures hanging on the wall and she'd put it on her Balsam Falls bucket list to sit out there at some point. Twinkle lights hung as a canopy over the entire patio outside, intertwined into the green vines that sheltered it even more. Wood plank flooring, galvanized pipe and wooden tables, and heaters gave the space a cozy feel. The fireplace on the inside of the building, constructed of neat sandstone style rock, was also on the exterior wall. And as for the rooftop dining Wynn had mentioned, well, that was just as pretty if not as fancy.

Balsam Falls really did have everything right there, minus big box stores, and if she were a citizen, Noelle would probably rarely leave. And she was here before all the summer activities started, like water fun, donuts on the dock—something all the Bryant siblings raved shamelessly about—s'mores by the shore, and whatever else went on in a touristy town like this. Another thing that appealed to her about the town was their obvious affinity for alliteration. Catchy, maybe a little corny, but very endearing.

"Hey, Jenna, before you go, could I talk to you about something?" Noelle glanced at the mayor as he started getting his papers out. "Actually, I think I'll take a look at your menu up front."

"I can bring one to you," Jenna offered, her brow furrowed.

Noelle stood up and shook her head. "Excuse me, Mayor. And no, I can walk. I haven't seen everything up close. It's so cool in here."

"Yeah, Jo and her husband did a lot of work but Wynn and Marshall helped too." Jenna set her hands on the countertop as she stepped behind it. "What did you want to talk to me about? Or did you just want to order something?"

The sweet scent of fresh roses filled the air, undoubtedly coming from the vase of roses with...wait, did that say *Estelle's Flower Shop* on the tag dangling from the twine around the jar's mouth? Noelle made a mental note to look that up later. Estelle wasn't a common name, but it was her grandmother's name. There was a very, very miniscule chance that a woman named Estelle owned the flower shop now. Like, that would be a little weird.

"Noelle?" Jenna prompted.

"Right, sorry." She smiled what she hoped was a warm smile. "We were talking about paint colors for The Gardens last night, and it got brought up to have a mural on one wall. Wynn mentioned that you're really good at painting... Would you be interested in painting it for us?"

Jenna's mouth formed an O, and her hazel eyes widened. "Me? I mean, yes, I like to paint, but I've never done anything like that before. It's just a hobby, and I have my job here."

"I know. But if we could work something out, we'd really love if you could do it. If not, that's totally okay."

"What kind of mural are you thinking?"

"Well, it would probably have The Gardens logo and then some kind of decorations. Maybe flowers or something like that. You would get paid, of course, and all the paint expenses would be covered. Our hope is for people to want to take pictures by it and of it, like a permanent photo op background. An attraction to town, even. Plus, it'll set the space apart."

Jenna bit her lip. "Can I think about it? When do you need to know by?"

"That's the thing. We'd need the mural done by the middle of April or maybe late April. So, yes, you can think about it, but it's a bit of a tight turnaround."

"Oh. That is kind of tight. I'll think it over and let you know by tonight, though, if that's okay?"

"Sounds fine to me. As for my order, I'll just take a side of bacon, please. It smells heavenly, and I'm not even that hungry."

Jenna laughed. "Sure thing. We'll have it out soon."

An hour later, Noelle's stomach was full of not just delicious bacon, but also the samples Joanna had provided: homemade tomato and cream cheese bruschetta, cornbread muffins, and fall-off-the-bone barbequed ribs. Possibly the best ones Noelle had tasted. She and the mayor had instantly wanted to go with them for the event, but then had to reconsider because of the change in event style. The bruschetta would be great, though.

"And how many people are you expecting?" Joanna poised her pen over her notepad, her nails painted the same pale pink as the leather notebook cover. She came across as a stylish and bubbly person, from her dark red hair and its wavy curls to her T-shirt advertising Farm to Table and her loose but still shapely jeans and Birkenstocks. "Probably, what, a hundred or so?"

Mayor Leo rubbed his graying handlebar mustache. "It's hard to tell, since this'll be the first time The Gardens are open in twenty years. We've already got several businesses interested in sponsoring the event. I'd say a minimum of one hundred. Probably on the upper end of two to two-fifty, but that's just a guess. What would be the easiest to cater for that?"

"Hmm. Maybe chicken fried steak?" Joanna pulled her leg up, hugging her knee to her chest. "No, scratch that. I want something sophisticated but also springy. And by spring, everyone is antsy to grill out, but that size of event would be pricey to do steak or anything like that."

"Steak, yes! Let's go with that. The city will cover the cost, as long as you can handle it."

Joanna's green eyes widened. "Leo, that's a lot of steak. A *lot* of steak. We can probably swing it, but—"

"No buts about it." The mayor swung his gaze to Noelle. "Does that fit in with your theme for the event? We could have some kind of potato with it, and then a salad."

"Oh, um, I think so. I mean, yes, but like Joanna said, that's a lot of steak."

"And we have a lot of people to feed," he spoke the words matter-of-factly. "Ones that are anticipating a nice, sit down meal. If we were in Maine, we'd do lobster. We're not. We're in Nebraska, so we'll do beef. Steak it is. Are there any other questions or decisions to be made here today?"

Noelle glanced at her list. They'd apparently decided on the main course and sides, but dessert would come later. Jenna would have an answer to her tonight, so there was no point in bringing that up now. And Mayor Leo had okayed their other developments, including a couple designs Ember had sent with Noelle this morning. Nothing else was on the list, which made Noelle happy. Checked off lists were always a good thing.

"No, I believe everything is covered," she said, sliding her pen into the spiral binding of her notebook. She was nearly out of pages in this one, meaning it was nearly time to buy a new one. Something she dreaded; she'd been planning parties in this particular notebook—a big, spiral bound one with bright splashy colors on the cover—for years now. "Unless either of you have anything, I'm good."

Mayor Leo shook his head. "Good here."

"I'll be getting an estimate here and get back to you," Joanna told him. "But otherwise, nothing more on my end."

"Wonderful. Then we're done here."

—⌒✑⌒—

CHAPTER
Twenty five

Was this how it felt to be a parent whose kids went to school? Wynn genuinely had no idea how it felt to be the child nor the parent, thanks to having been homeschooled, but he couldn't say he'd quite planned on sitting in a row of vehicles when Seth had asked him to pick up Devin and Sophie. Not to mention that his Silverado was out of place in the sea of minivans and SUVs. He himself probably looked like he was lost, but he was not, so there was that. Never mind if he was clueless of how this operation worked.

Finally, by closer to four than his original plan of three-thirty, he reached the front of the line. A man he recognized vaguely as the principal walked up to his window, wearing a reflective vest over his mustard colored dress shirt.

"You're new to our line up," he said, not the least bit animation in his tone. Monotony at its finest. "Though I don't think I'm the only one who noticed."

Yeah, well, Wynn wasn't here to notice the looks several minivan moms had sent his way as they'd driven by. "I'm here to pick up Devin and Sophie Clark, Mr...."

"Jeff Stanhoue," he said. "Why would you be here for those two? I don't recall ever seeing you here before. What's your name, anyhow? Wait, are you that Bryant boy? Ben, is it?"

Masking his irritation at the man's clearly preconceived view of his family—must be one of George Fleming's best buddies—Wynn grabbed the note Seth had scribbled yesterday before he'd left. Couldn't really argue a handwritten note from the chief of police in Wynn's favor, even though Seth had chicken scratch penmanship. Did they force him to type all his reports at the station?

"Wynn Bryant," he said evenly as he passed the note. "Direct instructions from Chief Johnson to pick up Devin and Sophie. If you just tell me how this works, I'll be getting out of the way for the others."

Mr. Stanhoue eyed the note warily. Good grief, did he think Wynn was lying? Trying to abduct the kids? Wynn understood security measures and all, but really? He'd probably balk if Seth verbally told him Wynn was supposed to be here. At this rate Wynn would no sooner have picked the kids up than he'd have to be taking them home. This schedule wasn't going to work long-term, but it was going to have to do for today. There was no way he was about to back out now, even if that's what Jeff Stanhoue would like.

"Give me a minute." The principal folded Seth's note and tucked it in his shirt pocket, then ambled—slowly—over to a tall woman wearing an even less friendly expression than Jeff.

Thank goodness Wynn didn't have to deal with this ridiculousness on a regular basis, because it wouldn't be going on if he had any say in it. Which he probably wouldn't, hence his desire to homeschool in the future.

Jeff Stanhoue disappeared into the entry of the school for a moment, then came back out with two African-American kids that could only be Devin and Sophie. Devin was lanky, and clearly

155

unhappy to be…well, probably living. He wore his jeans far too low for Wynn's liking, and his white T-shirt hung loose on his thin shoulders. The kid obviously needed more food, that much was clear.

Sophie, on the other hand, looked like the princess every little girl should be treated as. Her hair was pulled into two thick, dark braids with pink bows on each of the ends, and she wore a matching pink shirt with her much nicer fitting jeans. Her tennis shoes, though clearly worn, lit up with every bouncy step she took.

Wynn got out of his truck and rounded the cab, focusing on making a good first impression. Not on the principal—that was already null and void—but on the kids. He couldn't blow this. If he did, he'd have to answer to Seth, and it would just prove that his initial *no* hadn't been a mistake. Seth had, at least, said it was okay to use his name if push came to shove. Judging by Devin's rebellious glare, it would most certainly be coming. Sooner than later.

"Kids, this is Ben Bryant," the principal said, his previous monotony laced with something like a snobbish sneer. So be it. "Do you know him?"

"It's Wynn," Wynn said as evenly as he could manage. It wasn't often someone grated on his nerves, other than Ember, and that was nothing compared to this guy. "Wynn Bryant."

Mr. Stanhoue made no indication of apologizing. "Right. Do you know him, Devin?"

Devin's glare hadn't thawed any, that was for sure. "No. Never saw him."

The principal looked pleased that he'd, supposedly, been proven right. About what, Wynn wasn't sure. It was true—they'd never been introduced prior to now. But Wynn wasn't lying.

"Officer Johnson asked me to come get you guys," Wynn continued, undeterred by the principal's smirk nor by Devin's demeanor. "I'm going to take you to get a snack before taking you home. Would you prefer cinnamon rolls from the coffee house or muffins from Farm to Table?"

"Really?" Sophie's dark brown eyes sparkled with a guarded hope as she gazed up at him, her grin revealing that she was missing her two front teeth. Made Wynn's heart turn over at her enthusiasm for something so small. "We can do that?"

"Ye—"

"No," Devin cut in coldly, grabbing his sister's hand and giving it a tug. "Come on, Sophie. We need to go home so Dad doesn't wonder where we are."

Robert didn't get off till five, and then it would probably be another ten to fifteen minutes before he got home after that. There was no reason for Devin to want to rush "home." Unless he wasn't going straight there, which was part of Seth's concern.

"But he said…" Sophie's sentence trailed off when Devin shifted his glare in her direction.

"No, Sophie." He nodded to the principal before pulling his sister towards the sidewalk in the opposite direction.

Wynn darted out and planted himself in front of him. Devin may have cutting looks, but Wynn had height and strength on him. His heart twisted again at Sophie's crumpled expression. Did Devin care at all about her feelings?

"Listen, I know you don't know me, but you're my responsibility for the next hour," Wynn said, crossing his arms. "If you'd rather go to my office, fine, but Seth asked me to do this and I refuse to break promises. Ever."

"Seth doesn't have to babysit us. I'm thirteen now." The sun glinted off the earring in Devin's right earlobe. That was lovely—and all the more reason for Wynn to make good on his promise. Because no, thirteen was not even close to being able to make educated decisions when a child had no mother and a nearly absent father. "Tell him we're fine. Come on, Sophie. Hurry up."

Wynn opened his mouth as the kid continued, but a throat clearing stopped him. He gritted his teeth as he met Jeff Stanhoue's smug gaze. The man was downright infuriating, and Wynn had no reason to take it. No reason at all, now that the kids had left.

"I believe that's your cue to leave, Mr. Bryant," the principal said crisply. "Have a good evening."

Infuriating and, even if he had no reason to take it, Wynn couldn't do anything. They were on school property. Wynn didn't bother to respond—because, like Dad always said, no response was a response—as he brushed past the other man and got into his truck to leave.

Time for plan B. Whatever that was.

―⁓∽⁓―

CHAPTER
Twenty Six

At least Wynn wasn't the only one who was obviously none too pleased with Jeff Stanhoue's actions, considering Seth's less-than-pleased response to what had gone down yesterday afternoon at the school. But right now they seemed to have made a nonverbal agreement to put that on the backburner for the sake of what was happening this morning. In less than five minutes, Jen and the kids were supposed to arrive at their new house for the first time.

Wynn and Marshall had come over an hour ago, then Ember and Noelle thirty minutes later, and Seth had just pulled up in his cruiser. Apparently this was a big deal—which was kind of true, considering Jenna was getting to move into this house a month or so earlier than planned. Things would still need to be moved from her current place, but otherwise the house was complete. Thanks to many donors, generous volunteers, donated supplies, and their dedicated crew.

"You should really think of something clever like Chip and Jo from *Fixer Upper* have for their reveals," Ember observed, not for the first time, as they watched Jen's car park along the curb. "So then it would be a whole countdown and stuff instead of just *bam!* Here's your house, hope you like it. Oh, I think she's already crying."

Seth crossed the lawn to her vehicle and, since it took a couple minutes before she got out of the door he'd opened, Wynn would say she was definitely crying. Which was a much better reaction when it came to women than no emotion at all. They'd had one homeowner who'd just stared at the house without saying a word, without shedding a tear. Fortunately she'd grown to love it, no small thanks to her husband's urging, but Wynn would take tears any day over that.

Once the kids were both out, Wynn and Marshall crossed over to where they were standing, leaving Ember and Noelle chatting about the curb appeal of the house.

"Wynn, this is…" Jenna's chin trembled as she looked at him. "I don't… How did…"

"People care about you, Jenna," he said gently. "Welcome to your new home."

Jenna sniffed back tears as she hugged both him and Marshall, two times each. "Oh, my goodness. You guys… It's so beautiful. I love it. Oh, no, Eli, don't eat that."

Wynn chuckled as Seth scooped the boy off the ground and replaced the fistful of grass he'd pulled up with a sippy cup of what appeared to be water. If not for the presence of Jenna and uncharacteristically quiet Ella, Wynn would have a heyday with Seth's ease around the two-year-old. Did he carry sippy cups in his cruiser these days?

"What do you think, El?" Jenna squatted down beside her daughter, wrapping her arms around her in a hug. "This is our new house. Look, there's even a swing like we have at the other house, and this one has brand new handle ropes. Maybe we can play on it after Mr. Wynn and Mr. Marshall show us the inside. Would you like that?"

Ella cast a hesitant glance at the swing set peeking out from the backyard as she leaned into her mother. "Will I still have my princess castle?"

Jenna swept Ella's hair back as she stood, reaching for her daughter's hand. "Of course. We'll bring it over here, as well as your toys and books and clothes. And we'll bring Mommy's and Eli's stuff too. Maybe, if you say please, Officer Seth will even do that when he watches you for Mommy this evening."

"Please, Office Seth?" Ella tilted her head back to look up at him. "Will you bring my princess tent tonight? Mommy always reads to me before bed in it."

"I would love to do that, Ella." Seth winked at her. "Who wants to see the inside? I have it on good authority that Wynn and Marshall always have cinnamon rolls waiting for pretty girls …"

That was all the encouragement Ella needed. She let out a squeal before taking off for the door, her mother, Seth, and Eli trailing behind. Ember was already waiting, ready to open the door. Apparently she'd deemed herself the revelation queen today. Noelle was still standing on her own over to the side.

"I'll be in in a moment," Wynn told his brother. "Go ahead. Take a couple pictures, too, please."

Marshall nodded and started up towards the porch. Wynn tucked his hands into the pockets of his slacks—he and Marshall made it a point to dress nicely when it came to reveal day since they encouraged their clients to do so—and crossed back over to the driveway.

"You're welcome to come in," he told Noelle, who offered a small smile. "As you can see, it's kind of a free for all on who showed up today. Besides, Seth was right. We always provide cinnamon rolls on reveal day. Mainly for Marsh and I, but nobody needs to know that."

Her gaze wandered to Jenna's car, then the house, and back to him. "She's a really good mom to those kids. And she's even using a couple evenings plus three full days a week to do the mural at The Gardens."

With You I Am

Unsure of what exactly she meant by that, he nodded. "She is. She could've easily wanted to walk away from the kids when Pete left with most of their money. Or when he's refused to pay child support. Several times. But yes, she's a great mom."

"And Seth? He's obviously good with the kids. What's the story there?" Then, as if the words had come out unintentionally, she held up a hand. "Never mind. Sorry. I don't mean to pry."

Wynn shrugged. "It's fine. He and Jess were raised by their aunt and uncle after their mom died and their dad went into prison shortly after for several reasons, none of them related to his wife's death. Jess isn't quite as wounded by their dad's poor choices, probably because of the fact that she was only six, but Seth is just as scarred now as he was when they first came here twenty years ago. Pretty sure, contrary to the evidence, he thinks he'd end up like his dad if he ever had kids. Which is clearly not true, but you know how it goes."

"Yeah." She smiled. "Congrats on another successful reveal. Not that I've ever seen one of your other reveals, but I'd say this one was successful. Okay, I'm going to stop while I'm behind, because I'm obviously behind."

Wynn laughed, amazed at the way honesty just seeped right into her words. "I don't mind when you ramble. Matter of fact, it kind of takes me back to that first day when you tried to shove the door into me, then threatened to wallop me with a skillet."

Pink flushed her cheeks. "You just had to remind me, didn't you? In my defense, I thought you were some kind of burglar or abduction person. It would've been kind of sad to have not been prepared. Wow, that was a really confusing sentence and...and now I'm rambling again."

"To be clear, I like your rambling," he said quietly. "And I am very glad you chose not to clobber me with the skillet."

Noelle's gaze met his, and it was all he could do to not reach out and tuck her hair behind her ear or touch her cheek. For all the insecurities she'd both directly and indirectly confided in him

162

about, most of them concerning her mother, she had numerous other more courageous and noble traits to counter them.

"Noelle, I've been meaning to bring up the cottages," he began, and her eyes widened. "Our conversation got cut off last time and with everything, I haven't remembered to bring it up. I haven't forgotten about them either. I was wondering if you'd want to help plan a small party for my parents' thirty-fifth coming up, and we can discuss the cottage idea further at that time. No promises, but I would like to check into my options."

"For real?" Skepticism laced her words.

"Yes. Trust me, I wouldn't have brought it up otherwise."

Noelle squealed and before he could process it, she'd wrapped her arms around him in an enthusiastic hug. Once he got his bearings back, he laughed and hugged her back, doing his best to ignore how well she fit into his arms. How that coconut vanilla scent of hers embraced him. How her head rested below his chin on his chest, her hair tickling his skin, and her petite frame making him feel suddenly protective of her.

After a few seconds longer than a normal hug between friendly acquaintances, she moved back, her cheeks fully flushed as she pushed a thick section of blonde hair behind her ear. Her gaze was on Mrs. Daphne's house—one of the few older people in this neighborhood, something Wynn knew because she'd brought him and Marshall plenty of cookies during this build—behind him.

"I'm sorry," she said softly. "That was... Never mind. Um, yes. I'd love to help you plan something. Is there a time that works for you?"

"You don't have to apologize, Noelle. And let's play it by ear. Sometime in the next few days would be ideal. I'll talk to Sarah and Marsh and Ember to see what would work best."

She nodded. "Sounds great."

Then she turned and walked towards the porch, where Ember had just come out, leaving him standing there wondering what exactly had just happened between them.

Hugging Wynn had been a big, humongous mistake. Not because it was a bad hug. In fact, it was the direct opposite of that. She'd been embraced in the strength of those arms and held against his firm chest. He'd reciprocated her embrace, had even laughed. And not in an awkward, condescending way. No, the bottom line was that she'd enjoyed the hug *too* much. Something that completely clashed with her no attachments plan.

At least he hadn't brought it up at all the rest of the day, not even when they were alone in his truck to pick up the first order of painting supplies. Instead he'd explained in detail about how yesterday's attempt to pick up Devin and Sophie Clark from school had gone, and her distaste for anybody relating to George Fleming grew. How could a man treat people so badly? Worse, how could he make other people view a family as deserving of respect as the Bryants through such a jaded lens? Not only was it aggravating, it was just downright mean. Especially when that principal guy purposely called Wynn "Ben."

He was most definitely not a Ben.

Nor was that whole problem something she could do anything about.

The tray of swiss coffee colored paint on the floor in front of her, however, was something she could do something about. Somehow they'd trusted her with her own roller—one that, with its extender all the way out, practically doubled her height—to paint a wall in the main room. The biggest wall, aside from the one Jenna was planning to paint the mural on. Wynn and Marshall were each working in their own separate rooms, and had told her to holler if she needed anything. They might not have realized it, but they would probably be finished with their entire rooms by the time she worked up the nerve to put one roll onto the wall.

Sending up a silent prayer that she didn't mess this up, Noelle dipped her roller into the tray. The pale, creamy paint seeped into the foam as she coated the roller like Wynn had instructed her to. She'd never done this before, and it was both exhilarating and terrifying. What if the paint splattered onto the ceiling? Or got under the plastic cloth thing they'd taped over the trim and sanded down floors? Maybe this was a bad idea.

Noelle was about to set the roller down when there was a knock on the frame of the open door. She glanced up in time to see Seth usher in two African-American kids, and she could see his cruiser parked and running outside behind them. The girl, who must be Sophie, had an awestruck expression on her face and Noelle instantly liked her. The boy, Devin, looked as if he were a hornet who'd been riled up by an innocent child who'd been unknowingly playing by a hornets' nest.

"Hey, Seth—er, Officer Johnson." Noelle bent to set the roller handle down, unsure of how to address Seth in this situation. Should she have said Chief Joh—

She tripped over the paint roller's handle when she tried to step over it, causing the paint tray to topple over and splatter not only her, but the wall and... *Oops.* She'd speckled both the kids' clothes and Seth's navy blue uniform with dots of swiss coffee paint.

"Hey, Seth. What—" Wynn's sentence trailed off as he halted, his own jeans and T-shirt faded and painted on, but not with swiss coffee, so more than likely from previous projects. *Show-off.* "Well, nobody invited me to the painting party."

Noelle shot him a look that she partially hoped was a glare.

"Well, me either, but here's some extra sets of hands." Either unbothered or just too kind to say anything about the new decoration on his uniform, Seth nudged the Clark kids forward. "I'll leave you guys to it, since you've already met Wynn. I would come by to get them and take them home, but I have some paperwork to handle and then I'm heading to Jen's. She'll be here around six or so."

"I can do it," Wynn said, hands resting on his hips. How did he manage to look *so good* after painting for the past twenty minutes, and Noelle probably looked like a hippie hobo? A backwards cap had never looked so good on a man as it did on Wynn Bryant. "Sophie, would you like to help Noelle with, well, we'll figure something out. Devin, you can first start by getting

Noelle a new tray and pouring some paint into it. Then come with me. We're working on the back room."

Noelle thought about volunteering to get her own paint, but after the fumble from about three minutes ago, she probably shouldn't even be allowed near the paint. Period. She wished she could clean Seth's uniform, but what was she supposed to say? *Can you give me your uniform so I can get it dry cleaned for you? I'm so sorry I got paint on it.*

"Hi there, Sophie." She lowered to her knees in front of the girl instead, ignoring the way her jeans squished with paint on the plastic cloth underneath her. "My name's Noelle. I like your shoes."

Sophie glanced down at her feet where, thankfully, the glittery pink tennis shoes had been spared in the paint shower. "Thank you. They light up."

"Ooh, I wish mine did that." She motioned to her Brooks, which had not fared as well and were currently oozing swiss coffee. "But they don't, so yours are definitely cooler than mine. What would you like to do? We could have some crackers and then maybe try to paint? Or do you have something else in your backpack you want to do?"

Sophie cast an uncertain look over shoulder at Seth, who still stood in the doorway as if to tell Devin he had no other choice but to be here. Something that, after yesterday, was probably a wise move on his part.

"Go ahead," Seth urged with a smile for the girl. "I'll talk to you later, Wynn. And when I do, I expect to hear better news than yesterday, Devin."

That statement was met with a glare/scowl mix from the teen, who had yet to do as Wynn asked. Noelle wasn't the one mentoring him, but boy, would he be grating on her nerves right about now if she were. He was already doing so, and she hadn't even done anything to insult him. Maybe Wynn, as bad as it sounded, hadn't been wrong in wanting to turn down what Seth had asked. Clearly Devin had a problem with all of their very existences.

"See you later, Seth," Wynn said, lifting a hand in a wave as the police chief left. How was he so unfazed by Devin's cold, cold shoulder? "Devin, paint in the tray now, please. We've got work to do, and I don't deal well with dilly-dallying."

Okay, so he wasn't unfazed. Just way more controlled in how to respond to the angry teen. More controlled, but also more gracious in some ways. Noelle wasn't sure how her voice would come out. Probably far less authoritative than it sounded in her head.

Also, Wynn's no dilly-dallying rule must not apply to her because, hello, she'd just spent the past twenty minutes doing absolutely nothing except staring at the blank wall, too afraid to put paint on it.

With an obvious attitude, Devin let his backpack slide to the ground. He set to work on getting the paint stirred, with Wynn carefully watching his every move. Wynn looked like a hard core coach of some sort, the way he stood there with his arms folded over his broad chest, his expression non-forgiving. How did he make that stance so attractive?

"Okay, so how about it?" Noelle turned back to Sophie after what had been a really long lag in time. "Should we get some crackers?"

The little girl hesitated, but she took Noelle's hand. Noelle tried her best to hide her smile, even though it felt good to have one of the kids more willing, and she chose to glance over at Wynn on the way to the room they'd designated as the break room with snacks and a couple chairs.

Bad idea.

He was looking at her—what about Devin?—with a serious expression on his too-handsome face, his blue eyes intent. Why was he looking at her like that? Oh no. Was he remembering the hug she'd sprung on him earlier and trying to figure out how to bring it up?

Or, and she really, *really* shouldn't even wonder this, but was he actually looking at her with admiration? Not just the "great job out there!" kind of admiration like a teammate would another teammate, but the other one. The look… One Noelle wasn't sure she'd ever seen a man wear specially for her.

And then she tripped—on *air*—and his gaze shifted back to the sulking teen preparing the tray of paint for her, effectively forcing her to focus on finding the crackers she'd promised Sophie.

Not on Wynn Bryant's ridiculously blue eyes.

CHAPTER
Twenty Seven

"Well, that went better than I expected." Wynn's gaze followed Devin and Sophie until they disappeared into their trailer house, then he glanced across the cab. "Thanks for hanging out with Sophie. Seth had told me he was going to try to bring the kids by, but it wasn't a done deal so I didn't bring it up."

"Of course. She's a sweetheart. And you can see how well painting was going for me, so honestly, I was probably better off coloring with her. Sorry again about the mess. I'll pay you back for that paint I wasted."

Wynn navigated his truck from the trailer park entrance onto one of Balsam Falls's side streets. "Don't worry about it. I highly doubt Mayor Leo will have any qualms about you spilling a fourth of a can of paint. We've got plenty."

"Are you sure?"

"Yes."

Silence hovered between them, and he tried to come up with words to broach the topic he'd avoided since this morning. The longer he'd thought about it, the more he'd realized what a mistake he'd made by promising to talk about the cottages when they met up with his siblings to plan Mom and Dad's thirty-fifth. One, in case she decided to give him a hug all over again when he told her he was going to pursue the project—and if so, his siblings did *not* need to witness that. Especially because Ember may or may not have seen the one earlier today already. And two, because he couldn't bring it up when they were around. He'd tell his family, he would. Just not yet.

"Listen, Wynn, about that hug. I didn't mean anything by it." Noelle broke the silence, her words quiet. "I mean, I did, but not like *that.*"

Oh, it was tempting to ask her what "that" meant, but he refrained. "It's fine, Noelle. Like I said, you certainly don't need to apologize to me. I did mean to bring something up, though."

"Oh. Of course."

"About the cottages... When I said we'd talk about them when discussing the party with my siblings, that won't work. My goal is to have mostly everything worked out and *then* tell my family about them. So, that said, do you have a little bit of free time right now?"

"Um, yes—I mean I have nothing I'm doing. I am, but not. I don't have anything to do right now, if that's what you're asking."

This time he didn't bother trying to hide his smile. "Good. Since we have time before Jenna gets there, and Marshall is taking Jess to see her aunt and uncle, what do you say we pick up where we left off before Ember texted me about the flood?"

When he'd asked her about picking up where they left off, Noelle hadn't been sure of what he meant, but she'd never expected he would take her to eat at Farm to Table as an early "work" supper. Nor that they would sit outside under those twinkling Edison lights and that there would be a man wearing a Hawaiian shirt and khakis playing his guitar and singing on a small stage, his voice serenading them as they ate their meals. If she'd thought the ribs were good, she'd been underestimating Joanna's salmon and asparagus and green beans. Yet another thing that had separated her from other kids growing up—she'd loved vegetables, excluding broccoli. Maybe she hadn't ever loved them as much as she did right now, sitting at a table with Wynn, though.

She was almost glad their conversation had been cut off that Saturday morning.

"Color-wise, I'm sort of stumped." Wynn had pulled his sketchbook out after their plates were cleared away, and they'd just started talking about the exteriors of the cottages. "Especially because Ember said that paint color choice sets the stage for the whole project, and I kind of have to agree with her on that."

Noelle rested her chin in her palm as she studied his sketches, acutely aware of his masculine cologne or shaving cream or whatever it was and how close he was to her. "Well, it depends. I'm partial to blues and whites and yellows, but what are you going for? A beachy—no, make that lake-y feel? Or just regular cabins?"

"Definitely not just plain old regular cabins. That would be very dreary, based on the way you said it." He held up a hand, as if sensing her *"I didn't mean it that way"* coming. "And no, that's not the only reason. I'm torn, though, between wanting them to stand out or wanting to keep them more nondescript. Mainly because they're going on George Fleming's property."

"Yeah, but it won't be his property when these cottages are built on it." Her paint-coated jeans crackled as she bent to untie her shoes and slipped them off. The atmosphere was too cozy and inviting, even if it was still light outside, to not get a little more comfortable. "I mean, unless you want to go into business with the man. Maybe you could recruit that principal to help you with them. Aw, that'd give him something to do during the upcoming summer break."

Wynn gave her a look. "Yeah, right. That's exactly what I'm going to do. Name it Stanhoue and Fleming Estates."

"Oh, what a name. Let me guess, they'll be gated?"

He released a mock scoff. "Is there any other way? Absolutely, they will be. I'll probably even hire security to stand at the gates twenty-four-seven. Everyone who stays there will undergo total background checks and one, maybe two, in-person or phone call meetings to discuss why they even want to stay there. And then they *might* be granted permission, but for a pretty penny."

Noelle laughed. "Sounds like...something. I think I'll stick with the inn, thank you very much."

"Even when your room floods out?"

Especially then. "Even then. I like the food."

It was his turn to laugh. "I can't argue with you there. As far as colors, though, what would you do? For real?"

"Oh, boy. Um..." She scooted his notebook closer, taking in the surety of his sketches. Maybe he'd done them lightly to begin with and darkened the pencil strokes later, but either way, they exuded strength and stability. Just like Wynn himself. "To be honest, I think I'd do the exteriors a light gray, with yellow French doors as the front entry, and navy blue scoopy—I don't know the actual name for it, but you have them drawn here—shingles on top," she said, pointing at his drawing.

"Go on," he urged.

She hesitated, buying herself time by taking a sip of water before looking at the sketch again. "I guess I'd have plenty of big windows, of course, and have flower boxes—maybe green ones—under each of them. Then you could plant flowers in them for spring and summer, put haybales and bright fall-colored leaves in autumn, and Christmas and winter decorations for winter. And you could have a front porch, but who wants to stare at houses across the street? If you were gonna make them ADA compliant, put a ramp out front and focus your design efforts on the back. A nice deck, and maybe even fire pits for each cottage. That way they can enjoy the lake view, and from there you'd catch some of the sunrise and the sunset."

Wynn rose his eyebrows. "So, when you said the ideas on your phone weren't all of them, you weren't kidding."

"Um, no, I guess not." She bit her lip, but the ideas just kept coming. "Oh, and you could have the chimney be painted gray to match the exterior color, because let's face it, who doesn't like a fireplace? Even in the summer. It just adds a cozy element. And that way, if it was raining or something, they could still make their s'mores. It'd just have to be inside, is all."

"That's a very good point."

"Plus, you could do fencing around the front with individual gates for each property, but that kind of reminds me of a security gate and, to be honest, I don't really love picket fence. So scratch that, unless you actually like the idea. Then feel free to do it. I'm just tossing ideas out there. And I'll stop now."

The corners of his lips quirked. "I'm not a fan of picket fencing, either, so that idea can be nixed."

"Well, do you like that? The paint and stuff. This is your project, so it technically doesn't matter what I do or don't like."

"Oh, but it does." He scooted his chair back, and for one terrible second she thought he might be going to ask for the ticket. Meaning this impromptu supper that was romantic even though that wasn't at all what it was supposed to be would be over. Then, swiftly ending her premature panic, he stood and held out his hand. "Would you like to dance, Miss Carter?"

Her eyes widened as she stared at his hand, then looked up into his eyes. "Huh?"

"Would you like to dance?" he repeated. "It's a shame that Marshall and I put in this nice plank flooring out here and nobody even dances on it when they have live music. And besides, this guy is singing some good songs. Least we can do is encourage him a little. Unless you don't dance. In that case, well, I don't know what to say."

She knew how to dance. Loved it, actually. But with Wynn Bryant? She'd already been in his arms today and enjoyed it far too much. And that hadn't been in this beautiful, romantic setting with the singer performing an acoustic, stripped down version of Bob Dylan's classic *Make You Feel My Love*.

"Well?" His hand was still held out. "Maybe it'll give you even more of those ideas that, by the way, yes, I do like."

How could she say no to that? Short answer, she couldn't. Very aware of her paint stained jeans and T-shirt and her lack of shoes, she slid her hand into his larger, rougher one. He smiled and led her through the maze of tables to what must be the designated dance floor, twirling her once before he settled one hand on her waist, keeping hold of her other one.

"People are watching us," she whispered, suddenly in tune to all the eyes that had followed them all the way from their table. "Are we supposed to be dancing? Maybe we're not, and that's why nobody's dancing. Except us. We're dancing."

His eyes twinkled down at her as he led them in a slow two-step. "Relax, Noelle. Trust me, I wouldn't have asked you to dance if we weren't supposed to be. Joanna wouldn't have left this space table-free and hired this guy to sing if we weren't supposed to dance." He leaned down, his breath tickling her ear. "Let's be honest, the other people are just too scared to be out here. And now especially, considering I'm dancing with the prettiest girl here."

Noelle didn't have the chance to respond—not that she could even form words right now—because he twirled her out again after he said those words. And when he pulled her back in close, well, she couldn't really help but think this was the single most romantic place in all of Balsam Falls. Possibly in all of Nebraska. Maybe even the United States or the entire world.

While Wynn hadn't been planning to take Noelle to Farm to Table, much less ask her to dance, he didn't regret it one bit. Nor had he been able to resist asking her. Not when she'd looked as cute as she had with her paint-splattered clothes, bare feet, and obvious excitement to be sitting outside at the restaurant. He knew she liked the place—he'd overheard her telling Ember how cute it was after her meeting with Joanna Crawford and Mayor Leo yesterday—but the outdoor seating was a step up. And since it was protected, it was better than the rooftop seating for evenings like this when it still cooled off at night, plus the heaters distributed throughout the space helped.

That way they'd also had their stomachs full to go back to The Gardens while Jenna started on the mural. Devin had primed the mural wall earlier, and though he'd done it with a defiant set to his jaw, that had allowed Jen to start sketching out her design right away. She'd warned him that she would probably take the longest to sketch it, but as long as it was done in time, that was fine by him. Though in a different way than a painter, he understood how creativity worked—only when it wasn't forced did it come to a person.

While Jenna worked on that, he and Noelle had continued working on the walls, and they'd managed to get one coat of swiss coffee on all the walls it was supposed to be on. Tomorrow, they'd roll on a second coat. It would help to have Devin around again. For as angry as the kid clearly was, he really *was* a good worker. Definitely needed to work on the attitude, but he hadn't left right away. That was an improvement from yesterday.

After showering—a long, hot one to wash off all the grime and paint from the day—he pulled on shorts and a T-shirt, then padded out to his living room. Noelle and Nova were curled up on the sofa, Noelle's laptop open on the coffee table. Upon closer inspection, he realized that Noelle was not only laying on Nova, but she'd fallen asleep. His heart beat an extra time as he took in the way her messy bun blended in with Nova's golden fur, and how Noelle's lashes rested on her freckled cheeks. Her breathing was even as she slumbered, her one arm around Nova and the other dangling off the sofa. Fuzzy pink socks peeked out from the gray blanket she was snuggled under.

Ember had gone to bed before he took his shower, and he really didn't want to disturb Noelle when she looked that comfortable. He reached down to close her laptop so it wouldn't drain the battery, but the words on the screen caught his eye.

With You I Am

To: Catherine Sutton
Subject: My Mother
Even though he should just leave it alone, close it like he'd planned to, his eyes had a mind of their own as they wandered to the body of the email draft.

Dear Ms. Sutton,

My name is Noelle Carter—Annabelle Carter's daughter. This may seem odd, and I know you probably won't be able to gauge who would claim such a title, but it's me. My grandparents, Annabelle's parents, raised me. Now that they're both gone, I have decided to try reaching out to my mother. When I looked her up, I found your information, hence the reason I'm sending you this email.

I know you're just her agent or manager or whatever, but is there any way that I could somehow contact my mom? Annabelle, I mean. Google said she hasn't married or had any children, and that she lives in California. Like I mentioned already, this has to be odd for you, but I would really appreciate if you could at least give me something to go on. Or if you would show this to my

And that's where it ended, only a blinking curser left. Next to her laptop was the big, sort of falling-apart notebook she carried around with her, opened up to a bullet point list for The Gardens. She was nearly out of sheets left to use.

"Wynn?" Noelle's voice, sleepy as it was, caused him to spin around. "Did I fall asleep? Oh, no, I fell asleep."

Feeling like he'd been caught red-handed, Wynn simply didn't move. "It's fine. I was just going to close your laptop and...then I read your email."

"Oh. That." She pushed to a sitting position, reaching up to smooth her wayward hair. "I probably won't send it. I didn't even finish it, as you probably noticed. What time is it?"

"Almost eleven. And you should. If you managed to find this—" he glanced at the screen for reference "—Catherine Sutton, don't you think it's worth a shot?"

Noelle sighed and man, she looked equally as pretty as she had when they were dancing only hours before. "Maybe. Maybe not. But, as you also already know, she's not married. No other kids. According to Google, anyway." Yawning, she stood up, the top of her head barely reaching his chin. She closed her laptop and hugged that and her notebook to her chest, then met his gaze. "Thanks again for supper, Wynn. It was really good."

With that, she pressed up on her tiptoes and kissed his stubbled cheek, then turned and hurried down the hall before he could say a word in response. He touched the spot on his cheek where her lips had been only seconds ago, stunned for the second time in one day.

Maybe he'd underestimated Noelle Carter and what she could do to him.

No, that wasn't a maybe.

He had *definitely* underestimated Noelle Carter and what she could do to him.

CHAPTER
Twenty Eight

Even though painting had made Noelle's muscles way more sore than any workout she'd done in her life, it was a satisfying ache. One that reminded her of the fact that, against seemingly stacked odds, she'd learned a new skill: how to paint walls. She may never need it again, but hey, she could say she'd done it.

With that came the celebration that all of the walls, excluding Jenna's mural wall and the exterior of the building, were painted. And they looked really good, if she did say so herself. Next would be to paint the trim, which probably took more skill than she possessed, and then to stain the floors. At least Wynn and Marshall had family members and a crew who were more than willing to help out, and even Devin was helping without complaint. Not without attitude, but as long as Seth was the one to pick them up from school, so far there hadn't been any more problems. Yesterday, after everything had been painted over a second time, Noelle and Sophie had gone down to the coffee house to pick up smoothies and cinnamon rolls for everyone. The girl must be comfortable around Noelle, because she'd chattered on and on about what she was learning in school, unlike if Wynn or Marshall or John was around. Excluding Seth, she was more hesitant around men. Probably part of the reason Seth was concerned about her and Devin.

Today, Noelle's third Friday in Balsam Falls, she was planning to meet with Wynn and his siblings after the work day to talk about their parents' anniversary party, which was only supposed to be a couple weeks away. They probably should've started planning several weeks prior to now, but she wasn't about to tell them that. Not when Sarah was married with two little kids, Wynn and Marshall were running a successful business, and Ember not only volunteered at the library and worked at the inn but also worked part-time at Cozy & Grounds. Something Noelle hadn't known until last week. At least they were wanting to plan something to celebrate their parents. Some kids probably didn't even know when their parents' anniversary was.

If, that was, they had one.

Noelle had thought, every time her grandparents' June anniversary rolled around, that her parents didn't have one. They weren't married, after all. Or maybe they had been, if that photo was worth anything, and nobody had known. Maybe it had been a brief marriage. Maybe they'd only been engaged, her mom and whoever Noelle's dad was.

She rolled over in bed—her watch told her it was six-thirty—and snuggled back in, just to soak up this luxurious time for a few more minutes. She didn't hear any noises coming from the kitchen or living room, so Wynn had probably already left. Ember would more than likely venture out around seven, and if Noelle was still there, they'd eat their bowls of cereal together before going their separate ways. Talk about whatever came up, as if they were life-long best friends instead of just having met a few weeks ago. They'd settled into a routine over the past couple weeks, and Noelle had to admit she'd kind of miss it. The new flooring was being put in her room now, and John had promised to have her back to the inn by the end of Sunday. Which was a good thing. It was.

For the moment, in this quiet room with early morning light coming through the windows, Nova still snoozing on the foot of the bed, she simply lay there and took it all in. She'd been in Balsam Falls for not quite a month, and it had been nothing like she'd expected. She hadn't expected to grow attached to the people and places here at all, let alone in such a short amount of time. Courtesy of Carter, Inc., she'd flown to several cities in many states because a company wanted her to plan their event. But never had one of those trips made her wish she didn't have to go home. Maybe briefly, probably due to some awesome pool or spa or amenity, but not because of relationships.

Most definitely not because of Wynn Bryant.

She let out a muffled groan into her pillow. With every day that passed, her resolve to stay unattached was crumbling. It'd been happening all along, but Wednesday had just bumped it up to a landslide and she was helpless to even try rebuilding her lowering guard.

What if that supper and dancing had been presented as a date instead of a work supper? If she was wanting to stick to her plan, that could've never happened. And she never should've kissed his cheek, even if he had looked genuinely embarrassed that he read her email to Catherine Sutton, her mother's manager.

That was another thing. If she'd never come here, never seen the way the Bryant siblings interacted with their mother and vice versa, would she have ever decided to pursue trying to find her own mother? Or would she have just spent most of her life wondering, then one day *maybe* have the nerve to Google Annabelle Carter, only to find out it was too late?

If you managed to find this Catherine Sutton, don't you think it's worth a shot?

Wynn's words from less than forty-eight hours ago came back to her. She hadn't deleted the draft. In fact, she'd finished typing it and then left it sitting in her drafts folder.

She sat up, ignoring the way her muscles complained, and glanced at the laptop sitting on the small desk. Then, with what could only be a sudden wave of desire to find her mother, she got out of bed and opened it up. Once the laptop had powered on and connected to the wi-fi, she opened the email app.

"Here goes nothing," she whispered to the silence of the room.

Nova stuck her nose into Noelle's free palm, as if offering support when Noelle clicked the send button.

"Why are you even doing this?" Devin gestured to the room around them at The Gardens. "I mean, it's obvious that you have lots of money. So why would you waste your time 'mentoring' me? And don't even act like that's not what you're doing. Seth isn't as tricky as he thinks he is."

Wynn leaned back, his paintbrush dangling over the paint tray as he considered his answer. "First off, this project isn't happening because of my money. The city is responsible for everything you see happening here."

"That's a lie, and we both know it." Devin mirrored Wynn's position, but his brush dripped onto the drop cloth. "You've got a nice truck and Main Street business and yeah, I've noticed the tools you're using here. Those are definitely not all owned by the city."

"True. But if you think I was handed a successful Main Street business and a nice truck and tools, you're wrong. Started off by doing odd jobs here and there for my parents, and then eventually for other people to earn some money to begin buying tools and all that. It took many years before my brother and I were able to buy a building on Main Street—one that needed plenty of renovations, by the way—and the truck came years after *that*. Didn't happen without plenty of work on my part. Well, mine and Marshall's. We may have differences here and there, but we're a team, my brother and I."

Devin must've realized how much paint had started to puddle under his brush, because he rested it on the edge of his own paint tray. "That's another thing you have. A family."

"You've got Sophie and your dad. That's not nobody."

"Yeah, but—Actually, never mind." He picked the brush up again and turned back to the base trim they were working on.

"Does your dad abuse you or Sophie?"

Devin's hand slipped at the question, causing him to smear the freshly painted wall with the dark gray they were using on the trim. Before Wynn could say they'd go over it and not to worry about it, Devin turned a glare on him as he let the brush fall onto the floor. Dots of paint sprayed the wall from the force of it.

"That's all this is about, isn't it?" he spat, jerking to his feet. "Seth set this up so he could try to find a reason to take us away from Dad. But he can't. I won't let it happen."

Wynn set his brush down and stood, catching Devin by the arm before he could leave. "Devin, calm down. Your sister is out there with Noelle. Do you really want to upset her by storming out of here?"

The teen yanked his arm away from Wynn's grip, but to his credit he didn't leave. Not right away.

"And no, that's not all this is about," Wynn continued calmly, since Devin was clearly the opposite of that right now. "But if there's something going on at home, even verbally, then it would be important to tell me. And yes, I would tell Seth. Abuse of any kind is not okay. Not ever."

"Just because he drinks a lot doesn't mean he hurts us," Devin exclaimed, refusing to meet Wynn's eyes. "And we need to go. Because yeah, I also know that Dad doesn't know about this arrangement. So much for honesty, huh?"

Wynn sighed, but he nodded. There was no use in arguing with the kid today. He did need to get them home, he just wished it was on better speaking terms. Yesterday and Wednesday hadn't been perfect, but they hadn't been like this. If Wynn pushed it any harder question-wise, Devin would probably take Sophie and make her walk home with him. And more than likely wouldn't show up on Monday, even if Seth left him no other choice.

"And even if you 'worked' to get where you are, it's not like me," Devin continued, words hot with obvious pent-up anger.

"You've got a perfect family and a perfect girlfriend and a perfect life. So you shouldn't even try to make me see the similarities, because there are none."

Then Noelle appeared in the doorway, her expression troubled as she looked between them. "Uh, we might have a problem out here. No, we do have a problem. In the form of Sophie having scratched her knee, and I don't know where the Band-Aids are and I've also never fixed a crying child's scraped knee."

Under other circumstances, Wynn might've laughed at her stark worry over something that could be fixed with a dab of Neosporin and a bandage. Right now he felt like doing anything but. Brushing past Devin, he rested his hand on Noelle's back to guide her back towards the main room. "I'll grab the first aid kit. Give me just a minute."

Noelle's nod did little to relax her taut expression, but Wynn turned to get the kit and was met with a glare from Devin. The teen rolled his eyes as he stalked past Wynn and headed towards his sister.

Wynn closed his eyes briefly, reminding himself to not take Devin's icy demeanor personally. The kid was hurting for probably more than one reason, and if Wynn got worked up, that would only intensify the situation. He was wiser to stay calm and try his best to stay patient.

"You look like you wish that water was something a lot stronger," Ember said to Wynn as she sat down beside Noelle at Wynn's outdoor patio table. "Rough day at The Gardens?"

Wynn let out a less-than-amused laugh. "Yeah. Something like that. But it doesn't matter. We're here to talk about Mom and Dad's anniversary, not my day. Noelle, would you like to get us started, seeings how we're finally talking your language?"

While she appreciated his attempt to lighten the mood, Noelle had overheard the words Devin tossed at Wynn earlier, and she could tell it hurt him more than he wanted to let on. She had hoped to talk to him about it, tell him he was doing far better than she would be with Devin, but they hadn't had a moment alone. Maybe that was for the best.

"Well, first of all, what kind of party are you wanting?" she asked, forcing herself to not focus solely on the man directly across the table from her. Especially not the troubled expression in his eyes. "And how big? That'll give us a direction to start with. And if you have any other ideas, bring them on. I'm all for not coming up with everything on my own."

"Probably not super big," Sarah said, glancing at her siblings. "I mean, I know we wanted to invite some of Dad's old cop buddies and Mom's attorney friends, but that's still not a lot of people. Any of the extended family that can make it, which might be not much since this is such short notice. Anything beyond that, I have no idea. You guys have anything?"

Marshall took a sip of his water. "Nope. No offense, Noelle, but party planning has never been my thing. Probably why it's a good thing there's people like you who can do it. As long as there's food and dancing, count me in."

Dancing. As if of their own accord, Noelle's eyes darted in the direction of Wynn, who offered a wan smile—the first one she'd seen from him since Devin's painful words.

Ember cleared her throat, probably because she noticed the look between them, but thankfully she stayed quiet about it. "Dancing, yes, what a great idea." Okay, she kind of stayed away from the topic Noelle sincerely hoped didn't get brought up. "Should we hire a DJ or have live, *romantic* music?"

"Either way is fine with me," Wynn said, his voice normal. "Sarah? Marshall? Noelle?"

Her eyes widened. "Me? No, this is your party. Your parents' party, I guess. I'm just helping you plan it, is all."

"Right, but you're invited, so what do you prefer?"

Was he flirting with her? If she wore glasses—thank goodness he wasn't wearing his glasses right now—she imagined this would be where she nudged them up on the bridge of her nose.

"I, um," she said, realizing they were actually waiting on her answer. "I guess it depends. For an outdoor event, I'd recommend live music, especially if you have the lake as the backdrop. For indoor, either way would be okay. You could hire that guy from Farm to Table the other night. He sang lots of older love songs, which would be perfect for an event like..." Noelle trailed off, suddenly aware of the fact that none of Wynn's siblings had been informed about their supper out. A fact she had not known until now. But it made sense—he hadn't told them about the cottages, and that was their whole reason for going there.

"We could do that," Wynn said, showing no unease about the topic. "I can ask Joanna about him on Monday. Do we need to discuss decorations or colors or food or anything?"

"No, I personally would be much more interested in discussi—"

"We should most definitely talk about decorations and colors and foods," Sarah cut in, raising her eyebrows at Ember. "Considering that's what we're here for, and I've got a husband and kids waiting for me at home. Something none of my three siblings here have."

"Hey, I'm only nineteen," Ember said, holding her hands up, palms facing out. "Wynn and Marshall, well, they certainly aren't without options. Technically, there's not even a man around here I'd even be interested in. Not tall enough or good looking enough. And yet, both of my brothers just sit there and have—"

"Party planning, Ember," Wynn interrupted, though amusement hid in the quirk of his lips. "We're here to talk about party planning. Not our love lives."

"Or lack thereof," Ember mumbled.

She received looks from both of her brothers in return.

Noelle cleared her throat, willing away the flush in her cheeks. "Well, the traditional color for a thirty-fifth wedding anniversary is coral, or any kinds of reddish-pink. So we could go with that, or something totally different. And you could have someone cater or—Wait, where is the party going to be? I should've asked that right away."

"At the inn," all four siblings said in unison.

"Probably the backyard," Sarah added. "So long as the weather's nice. And coral would be kind of pretty. Ember and I could handle decorations, and Wynn and Marshall could take care of food. You could ask Jess to bake a cake, Marshall."

Marshall nodded. "I will. And as long as whatever I'd need to make can be grilled, I'm up for it. What about invites? Or are we just texting and calling, since it's such short notice?"

"If you give me names and addresses, I don't mind designing invites and sending them," Noelle volunteered. "They're just a more formal way. You could also text too, though."

Wynn nodded. "Good idea. I'll help you with them. Now, we just have to keep this a surprise—" he pointed a look at Ember "—from Mom and Dad. Nothing can be said around them, not even hand signals or mouthing words to each other. Are we clear?"

Ember mock saluted. "Sir, yes, Sir."

Too bad Noelle's feelings weren't nearly as clear as that agreement, especially when it was very clear Wynn's siblings had caught on that something was up.

Noelle just didn't know what that "something" was.

And she didn't even know if she wanted to know.

CHAPTER
Twenty Nine

This wasn't the first time Wynn had been in his wood shop—a renovated medium sized shed in his backyard—so late at night, but it was the first time in a long time. He couldn't remember the last time he'd even come out here last, let alone when it was going on eleven at night.

Water lapped at the bank of the lake as he twisted the doorknob, and not even a breeze stirred the trees. A perfectly peaceful night, as far as the weather was concerned. It was mild, too, meaning they'd probably have decent weather tomorrow. Maybe he'd be able to recruit Dad and Marshall to help him start in on the overgrown, practically-needing-to-be-demolished, outside of The Gardens. Then, come Monday, their crew wouldn't have as much to do.

Wynn flipped on the switch by the door and light flooded the shop. It had been so long and yet nothing had changed. His workbench still sat in the middle, sawdust and old junk wood he'd planned to use sitting on top. A wooden counter went all the way around the perimeter with storage underneath and tools evenly distributed where he liked them. Hand tools and corded tools hung on the pegboard background he'd installed, with outlet strips every here and there.

It smelled like sawdust, immediately transporting him back to when this was his passion. To a time when he and Marshall weren't hired to build homes for people, and Wynn was excited to just have something as small as a person wanting a shelf built for their living room.

Devin's words from earlier had hit him. Harder than he wanted to admit to anybody, himself included.

Had he been so focused on the success of Bryant Bros. that he'd forgotten what he had? The family who'd been there long before this business and other relationships. When had he let his life get so full with other things, mainly work-related, that he'd started missing out on even coming out to his shop? He and Dad and Marshall used to spend hours out here with the French doors open to the lake view as they drew up sketches and put together projects. He had his family to thank for the house he lived in too. It had come with the property back when Mom and Dad bought it, and they'd started tinkering around, fixing stuff that needed fixed as a project, after Dad's legs had healed. It had been a project for Dad and Wynn and Marshall to play around with; a way for them to learn about renovating.

Now it was Wynn's, and he still took it for granted. The house could've gone to Marshall, the son who still lived at home. The one who put in more hours than Wynn at the inn. Even though his dad had been through something as horrible as he had and they'd all walked through that dark valley together, Wynn *still* took things for granted. This shop. His business. His family.

Maybe, as painful as the words were, he'd needed to hear them in order to be able to mentor Devin how Seth wanted. How God wanted. After all, how could he preach something he himself wasn't fully living?

It wasn't like he didn't spend any time with his family or appreciate what he had, though, and that may be the key difference between him and Devin. Wynn wasn't so far gone that he couldn't, hopefully, get a grip on his shortcomings. Neither was Devin, and he was going to prove exactly that to the kid. It might take a lot of effort and some hurtful conversations, but Wynn had never been a quitter, and he wasn't about to start now.

What he really needed to know was what Devin was passionate about. Because while he was a solid worker, construction was clearly not his passion in life like it was Wynn's. And unfortunately, that may be the most difficult task of all.

Wynn smoothed his hand over the old barnwood sitting on top of his workbench, relishing the roughness on his palm. Yes, it had been far too long since he'd just messed around with a project out here.

As an idea, a tiny one, began to form in his mind, he crossed to the French doors on the opposite side of the shed and opened them. Cool night air ushered in the din of crickets and bullfrogs, moonlight spilling in and blending with the overhead lighting. The smooth surface of the lake reminded him of several years back when he and Dad had snuck out here late every Friday night, occasionally joined by Marshall, for several weeks. Dad had even convinced Sarah to come out and help them a time or two. Mom had probably known all along, looking back now and remembering her knowing expressions when Wynn would nearly fall asleep at breakfast Saturday morning, but she most certainly had not seen what was coming.

They'd built her a custom wooden rolling ladder for her library and given it to her on Mother's Day that year. Wynn would never forget his mom's expression when they revealed it to her. She'd cried, then kissed Dad and patted his cheeks as he laughed, then hugged all three of her children—Ember hadn't come along yet—and told them how much she loved it.

And while doing homes for people made his soul sing, he'd missed this. Not necessarily so late at night—depending on how long he stayed out here, morning would come way too soon—but he needed to not wait months and months to do it again.

He turned back to his work bench, gaze hitching on the doorway he'd just come in ten minutes ago. If it was someone else standing there, he might've given them a piece of his mind for approaching so quietly and making his heart nearly give out, but not Grandma. Margaret Watters may have been a wealthy woman and still retained plenty of funds, but she also had plenty of wealth by way of wisdom. And at this point, he probably needed all the wisdom he could get.

"Grandma," he said, hoping his smile hid the scare her presence had given him. "What are you doing up at this hour?"

"Are you suggesting I need beauty sleep?" Grandma moved into the shop, still wearing her coral cropped pants and matching blouse. "And, I think I'm the one who should be asking what you, my dear grandson, are doing up at this hour? As your grandma, I have that right, among others, but we won't go into that right now. What's troubling you?" She held up her left hand, where she still wore her large wedding ring despite her husband having been gone for over five years now. "Don't try to tell me there's nothing, because I'll know that's not true. I raised three sons, remember? Your mother was the easy child, but that's beside the point. Come on. I need a little excitement in my life, so bring it on."

Wynn chuckled as he leaned back against the countertop, tucking his hands into his pockets. "If you're looking for something exciting, I'm probably not it. You'd be better to go to Marshall. I'm sure you heard Jess is leaving at the end of this summer. That is…something. Probably not exactly exciting, but definitely interesting."

"Nah. I've already talked to him about it, but I'm sure he'll have another Granny chat here in the near future if he doesn't take the advice I gave him the first time." Grandma rose her eyebrows, eyeing him skeptically. "So, what's going on with you? Is it your business?"

"What—No. Why do people keep asking that? First Dad, then you."

"That boy is a good one, your daddy. You know, your grandpa and I didn't like him all that much to start with. We'd had no problem with the girls our sons brought home, but your dad... He was not what we expected for our Jacqueline."

Wynn nodded. "The cultured, beautiful attorney Jacqueline Watters decides to go out with the town chief of police John Bryant. Sounds like a conflict of interest to me for sure."

His grandmother rolled her eyes. "Not because of that, Wynn, and you know it. We had just pictured somebody with a less dangerous job. Well, less dangerous and more money than your dad's salary. But your mom got her father's stubborn streak, so any attempt to influence her against it was null and void."

"She got her father's stubborn streak?" Wynn laughed. "I don't think you're remembering your stubborn streak. And yeah, I do know you have one, so you cannot even try to deny it, my dear grandmother."

Grandma waggled her finger at him. "Who gave you the authority to throw my words back in my face? I think you're just doing it to defer from the topic we're here to discuss, and that includes but is certainly not limited to the pretty little blonde currently sleeping under your roof. I most certainly hope that you're in sep—"

"Okay, all right," he interrupted, holding up a hand. "That's enough of that. She is in her own room, Grandma, and there's no lying in that statement. And what do you mean? Noelle's in town to plan the Spring Fling." He pushed off the counter and started inspecting the boards that he'd brought out here years ago. "There's nothing going on between her and I, anyway."

"Oh, there's a spring fling going on, all right," she mused. "I suppose you two were slow dancing at Farm to Table the other night because there's nothing going on between you, hmm?"

Wynn spun to face her. "How do you know about that?"

"Oh, honey, you should never underestimate the power of a loving grandmother like myself. I have my ways." She picked up one of the smaller pieces of wood. "There's nothing wrong with liking someone, Wynn. You're well over twenty-one, and I most definitely don't want to leave this life without having more great-grandchildren. Noelle is a pretty young woman. You two would make a very spiffy couple. I might even venture to say that your children would be downright adorable."

"Grandma, she lives in Mississippi. If you think I'm interested in moving to Jackson, you are wrong. Unlike some people, I never had the urge to try and escape my hometown as soon as possible. Or ever, in this case. Since you're here, though, can you pass me that pair of safety goggles, please? And if you're staying, put a pair on too."

She slid on his more expensive pair, but didn't pass the other ones to him. "Just because she's from there doesn't mean you couldn't work something out. Your grandpa and I were from halfway across the US from each other and look how that turned out. We ended up where he was from. So that's something in your favor."

Wynn reached for the glasses, which she held out of his reach. "Can I please have those? It's late—"

"Yes, it is. And until you tell me what's really bothering you, I won't be giving you these glasses. Nor will either of us be leaving, and to be honest, I don't really feel like sleeping out here tonight when I have a warm, king-sized bed all to myself at my house. But since I care, I'd do it. Perks of having a grandma like me."

"I don't—"

"Wynn, no matter what you say, it will not change my mind, so your best bet is to just talk."

Pressing his lips together to withhold from groaning, he met her gaze. "I'm not sure what to do. Seth trusted me to mentor this Devin kid, and so far all I've managed to do is anger him even more. The first day—"

"Who? Seth or the kid?"

"The kid," Wynn said dryly. "As I was saying, he walked away from me the first day. Then there were two days of him helping without actually complaining or storming out. And today, any and all progress I thought I'd made went completely out the window.

He tossed words in my face about my perfect life and family and girlfriend. That last one isn't even true. None of it is. I mean, yes, it's close to perfect, but we've had our challenges. Dad's accident, for one thing, and whatever else along the way."

"I see. Well, I'm no wise sage, but I like to think I've learned some things in my eighty-nine years of living. And what I've found is that when someone is hurting, they are prone to take it out on someone else, even if they don't even intend to do that. And I don't know this Kevin, but if Seth—"

"His name is Devin."

"Kevin, Devin. Same difference. Anyhow, if Seth asked you to mentor him, he must believe you can give him the guidance he needs. The Lord wouldn't have let it happen if He didn't see that it was the best avenue for this Ke—Devin."

"Okay, but what if I can't?"

Grandma shrugged, his safety glasses still dangling from her finger. "Way I see it, that's a choice. You think you're gonna succeed, you're gonna succeed. You think you're gonna fail, you're gonna fail. It doesn't matter how the other person or persons feel when your mindset is to succeed. That's not how faith works."

"For not being a wise sage, you're pretty darn wise, Grandma." Even if it grated on his ego, she was right. He hugged her from the side. "I love you, by the way. I hope you have many more years left, too."

She smiled and patted his chest. "You're a little sucker-upper, Wynn David. And I hope so too, especially so I can love on those cute little great-grandbabies you're gonna give your favorite grandmother."

Sunday morning, Noelle's last morning at her temporary lodging, Noelle found herself taking extra care in how she styled her hair and what she chose to wear for church. Not for any reason in particular, but it felt good to dress up after so many days of wearing her paint-stained clothes for working inside and out at The

Gardens. They'd weed-eated the entire outside yesterday—and by they, she meant the Bryant men—and then Noelle and the Bryant ladies and Jess had walked the freshly pruned property and discussed what landscaping they could put where.

Slowly but surely the project was coming together.

After the last bobby pin was in place, Noelle carefully examined herself in the mirror of the bathroom across from her room. She'd chosen a light pink dress with loose sleeves that hit right above the knees and paired it with her taupe wedged sandals. For her hair, she'd washed it last night and let it air dry, then curled it this morning. She'd twisted a section from each side back and pinned it for a half up, half down look. It was simple and not all that time consuming, but it was elegant. Grandma had always reminded her that a lady was supposed to be elegant, and a gentleman to be dapper.

She smoothed her hands over her dress one more time before collecting her things and taking them back to her room. She grabbed her purse, spritzed herself with perfume, and headed down the hall to the kitchen. It didn't shock her like the first time, but Wynn in a suit would certainly never fail to impress her. He looked equally as good in jeans and a T-shirt, but considering she'd grown up with her grandfather wearing suits nearly every day, there was something about them that would always be special to her.

"Good mor—" Wynn's sentence was cut off when he glanced up from the griddle of pancakes he was standing over. His eyes widened as they swept down to her feet and back up to her eyes. At least his glasses were absent this morning, but his rolled sleeves exposed his tanned, muscled forearms, so she wasn't sure if that was any better. "Noelle, you look beautiful."

Her cheeks warmed under his scrutiny. "Thank you. Is Ember here yet?"

As had been the ritual every Sunday morning she'd been at Wynn's house, Ember made a quick run up to get some food from the inn. Always in her pajamas and always barefoot. The girl was unafraid of what people thought of her, Noelle had to give her that much.

"Not yet." He pulled the dish towel from his shoulder and nodded to the pan of oatmeal on the stove. "If you're hungry, there's food ready for you. She'll probably just get yogurt or fruit, I'm guessing. Hang on and I'll grab a spoon for the oatmeal."

"I can get one." After having been here long enough, she'd learned where several drawers and cupboards were located, especially the ones containing utensils and bowls. "Does this one work?"

He turned to face her, and she second-guessed asking him. The space, or lack of, between the stove and island was not very much when there were two people standing there. And even with her heels, he was still much taller than her. Tall, lean, and devastatingly handsome. She may lack culinary skills, but she was ninety-nine-percent sure that was a recipe for disaster.

"Perfect," he said. "Listen, Noelle, I wanted to talk to you about something. My grandma mentioned to me the other night that a person's success depends on their outlook. And the more I've thought about it, the more I'd like the cottages to succeed. So that said, I was won—"

"What cottages?"

Noelle and Wynn both jumped at the sound of Ember's voice, and the plastic serving spoon Noelle was holding fell, clattering noisily on the wood floors. *Oops.* So...now what? Should she pick it up, or just leave it?

"Well?" Unlike previous Sundays, Ember was already dressed in a long flowered dress and a jean jacket, her long dark hair curled. "Wynn? Hel-lo? Are you there?"

Wynn cleared his throat, bent to pick up the spoon, and grinned. "Hungry for pancakes, anyone?"

CHAPTER
Thirty

Being sandwiched between two Bryant siblings in church when one of them knew something the other didn't was…interesting. Noelle had felt like just as much of a deer-in-the-headlights as Wynn had looked when Ember walked in earlier, but since he'd somehow managed to get out of telling her at that moment, it meant sitting beside one sibling who pretended as if nothing was amiss and another who acted like everything was amiss. It wouldn't even be shocking if Ember went right on up to the pastor, "borrowed" his microphone, and tried that route to get Wynn to spill.

That would mean interrupting the pastor's sermon on friendship and how important relationships were, something that was making Noelle feel fidgety. His words on how people had so few people close to them made her balk. She had friends. Maybe she didn't have weekly dinner parties or see them much outside the office, but they were her friends. They'd drop whatever they were doing to help her if she needed it.

Wouldn't they?

Or was that just an image she'd concocted in her own mind to make up excuses for the lack of relationships in her life? Had she been so focused on her career and not wanting to get hurt by letting anybody in that she'd lied to herself? Worse, that she'd lied to God? The one she was supposed to be the most honest with, and yet she'd pushed Him the farthest away.

"We were not created to be in seclusion," the pastor—she remembered his name being Jason Quinn, but he'd told her to call him Jay—continued, his hands on either side of the collapsible music stand. The church itself wasn't new and fancy, but it wasn't old either. It was light, spacious in an inviting way, and modern enough to appeal to younger people but traditional enough to draw older folks too. "Relationships are not supposed to be optional, they're supposed to be optimal. Not one single person is born without there having been some kind of relationship. You have got to have parents—you're born to your mother and father, no matter what, for starters. And possibly to siblings. To…"

Tears stung Noelle's eyes as Pastor Jay continued, and his words grew more blurry as she came to the realization of what she'd been doing. Of how she'd been closing herself off. Not only to people, not only to herself, but to God. When was the last time she'd opened her Bible? That thought pained her nearly as much as the pastor's words about being born to parents, maybe even siblings. Because, looking around, she saw families. Young, probably just married or engaged couples. Couples with young children. Couples with teens.

The Bryant family, who took up two whole rows of chairs, with Jackie's mother and John's father and everyone in between sitting and listening to the sermon together.

It hurt because she didn't have that. Her parents had chosen worldly things over their own daughter. Or at least her mother had. She had no clue about her father, and she couldn't decide if she liked that better or worse.

But Even Jess and Seth, who had no parents, sat there in church together with their Bibles. Little Eli was on Seth's knee, with Ella separating Seth and Jenna. And Noelle had neglected not only her Bible, but also having a church to attend. People to gather with.

"Fathers are there to lead the home," Pastor Jay was saying, and he'd moved to the right side of the stage. "Dads, if you don't tell your children you love them, if you don't encourage them in their faith—not *your* faith, but *theirs*—then things are gonna have to go one way or another. And to be honest with you because I know that's what you're here for, things probably won't go real well. Mothers, it's the same for you, but in a different way. Men and women were created as two different people—my wife likes to remind me of that when I do something she doesn't understand— and as a mother, God very specifically designed you to fill that role. While some of you may not have the role models of parents for different reasons, there was someone who raised you. The parental role is not one to be taken lightly. Did you know that..."

Wynn leaned down, his voice soft and low near her ear. "You okay?"

She thought she might cry at the tenderness in his words. "I'm fine."

"There's a room outside the sanctuary if you need a moment. And if not, well, I'm here."

I'm here. How long had it been since she'd heard those simple, uncomplicated words from someone who meant them? Other than her grandparents, who had most definitely cared, had anyone ever said them like Wynn had just said them to her? In a quiet, not flashy for the whole world to hear, but truthful promise.

As a tear slipped down her cheek, Wynn reached for her hand and squeezed it. Then didn't let go. And Noelle found herself praying, perhaps not gracefully, but praying all the same. For God to guide her. To tell her what she was doing wrong and how to fix it. That she would have the courage to listen to Him, regardless of what His words were.

―∽⁰⊘⁾―

Wynn wasn't sure how he'd done it, but he'd managed to make it all the way through the service and fellowship afterward without Ember bringing up the conversation she'd walked in on that morning. But judging by the way she kept glancing his way across the table during lunch, it was a matter of minutes before he'd be presenting his plans to everyone in his family. Plus Jess and Seth, which wasn't shocking, but it still made him nervous. Other than Noelle, nobody knew about this. No one but him and God.

And he probably hadn't done all that well of keeping God informed on it, either.

"So, since we're all gathered together on this lovely spring day," Ember said once there was a lull in conversation about the upcoming tourist season, "I believe my brother has something he'd like to tell us about."

"Which one?" Grandma said, her expression that perfectly perfected Grandma look. The one that said she knew exactly which one, even if Wynn had no idea how that was actually possible. "Marshall, did you finally ask Jess out on a date?"

Marshall choked on the bite of food he'd just taken, and Jess's cheeks flushed a deep red. Oh, how Wynn wished that's what the topic was. But again, his grandmother knew exactly what she was doing.

Also, it was kind of unfair that she didn't receive a wrath from Marshall when she brought up his relationship with Jess. Marshall, after recovering, only kind of laughed it off and very clearly avoided Jess's gaze.

"No, Grandma, the other brother." Ember arched a brow as she looked at him. "What cottages were you talking about?"

Grandma made a sound. "Huh. Well, that wasn't even what I was thinking this was about. Carry on, dear."

He really, *really* did not want to do this right now. He wasn't prepared to give a speech on the cottages that had no solid plans yet. He hadn't even tried to contact George Fleming or whoever handled his real estate.

Then he met Noelle's eyes, and her slight nod gave him a welcome boost of, while hesitant, much-needed confidence. It also reminded him of how soft her skin had been against his when he'd held her hand earlier today, how much smaller her hand was than his.

"I would like to buy those empty lots George Fleming owns and put three cottages up on them," he said slowly, holding Noelle's gaze as he tried to ignore the doubt that nagged him. "They'd be used as vacation spots for families who can't afford a real vacation, and they could also be used as an extension of the inn. It's always got bookings however far out, so having that additional space would probably be a nice addition. And I don't know how I'd be able to swing it since it's not a hired project, which is why I hadn't told you guys yet, but that's what I want to do. I've had the idea for a while now. Noelle saw my sketches, and she prodded me until I realized how badly I did want to do this project. So that's all it is."

His proclamation was met with raised eyebrows and slack-jaws from everyone except Noelle and Dad. Noelle was looking at him with an expression that made his thoughts venture back to when Pastor Jay had been talking about parental relationships. He sensed it'd been a while since she'd had anybody care, and while he had no right to feel protective of her, he most certainly did feel protective of her. She wasn't only that feisty, skillet-wielding girl he'd met that reminded him of Rapunzel. She had layers, a depth that interested him more than any outward beauty. In fact, that probably did relate to Rapunzel in a sense that she'd been trapped and it hadn't been entirely her choice.

Of course, the fact that Noelle was so innocently pretty wasn't exactly a turn off.

Dad cleared his throat, and Wynn hesitantly glanced at him, surprised to see the look of fatherly pride on Dad's face. Why he'd expected anything less from his father he had no idea, but it still buoyed his confidence some. Especially because everyone else still looked like he'd just presented a very thorough presentation on something very...thorough.

"I wondered when something new would come along for you," Dad said with that easy smile of his. "Actually, I probably should've told you first that I think that's a wonderful idea, and your mother and I will help in any way we can. Then say that I'm happy you've come up with something new to do."

Mom glanced at Dad, her mouth still slightly ajar, then seemingly snapped out of it when she looked at Wynn. "Yes—Of course. Yes, we will do whatever you need. You know what, why don't I call my church ladies right now? We can start putting some ideas—"

"Honey, I think that can wait until after lunch." Dad smiled as he leaned over and kissed his wife's forehead, then stood with the pitcher in his hand. "I'm going to get some more lemonade. Don't make too many decisions about these cottages without me, all right?"

Then the onslaught of opinions came rushing in from most everyone around the table, inputting ideas about colors and textures and front porches and toilets—*why* were they talking about toilets?

It wasn't until he realized that Noelle hadn't said anything for a while that he glanced at her, only to find her chair empty. His brows furrowed. Where had she gone? She'd been here only a couple minutes ago when he'd told his family about the cottages. Hadn't she wanted him to do that? Why would she disappear when he'd finally, even if it'd been forced out of him, told them?

"Hey, what if we did a separate theme for each one," Ember said. "That way it wouldn't be the three identical little houses next to each other, because let's face it, that would just be plain bo— Wynn? Are you listening to me?"

Even though he wanted to go find Noelle—he probably *should* go find her—he found a small smile instead for his sister. "Yes. I'm listening."

"Great spot to clear your head, isn't it?"

Noelle jerked around, wiping her eyes and scrambling to her feet. "John, hi. Sorry, I was just...thinking for a few minutes."

John motioned to the chair she'd just jumped from. "Don't worry about it. You're fine. Everybody needs some time to think every once in a while. This spot has provided me plenty of thinking opportunities. A lot of times it was when my wife was having a time or in a tizzy and I just needed a little space away from...that."

She released a small laugh as she sat back down, her phone in her lap. "My grandpa had those instances. Grandma was a wonderful person, but she had her quirks. As all of us do, I guess."

"That we do. Mind if I join you?"

"Go ahead. Technically this is your property. Like I told Wynn about his patio, you shouldn't have to ask to sit on your own dock."

"Right, but you're our guest. And the Bible instructs us to serve others, which was part of the reason Jackie and I invested in this place." John sat down on the other rattan wooden chair next to hers, a smile playing at the corners of his lips. "I'm not so sure we knew what it would entail, but we're still here over twenty years later, so that must mean something."

"Wynn told me about your accident," she said softly. "That must've been a really difficult time for you guys."

John tilted his head back and forth, a trait she'd seen Wynn do several times. "It was, yes, but it was because of it that what really mattered came into focus. I was forced to reevaluate what meant the most to me. You have a lot of time to think when you're forced to be on a hospital bed, and I can tell you that, even with the pain, I wanted to do anything but think about things I knew needed to be addressed. I'd known it before the accident happened. And I was lucky to live. God could've decided that was it. I hadn't made the necessary changes, so He could've been like, 'All right, John, you've had about a million chances. Time for me to focus on the next person.' But that's not how He operates."

Noelle remained quiet. She took in the rippled lake in front of them, and how birds dipped and flew and zipped around in the deep blue sky. The puffy white clouds that drifted by slowly.

"I've found that one quote about God wrecking our plans when He sees they're gonna wreck us to be pretty accurate," he continued, also facing the lake. "And sometimes that hurts. The wreckage is painful. Often times, you feel buried under the rubble of it. It can even feel like He's not there. And while some people mistake those times for God's lack of presence, I like to think of it as His lack of presents as in the wrapped with a bow kind. Because as badly as we think a sugarcoated, pretty wrapped box is going to fix our problems, that's not what will. It's in those low, often painful, moments that we find the real gift, and that's the never-ending love of God. Once you choose to trust Him wholeheartedly and promise to leave behind what it was that was harming you, what caused you to hit rock bottom, you see the gifts that God has given us. The gift of His Son, the gift of our lives. The fact that we have breath to breathe is a gift in and of itself. One many of us, myself included, tend to take for granted more often than not."

A lump formed in her throat as she squeezed her eyes shut against the sting of tears. The way everyone had jumped on board to help with the cottages, seeing how Wynn's family supported him so lovingly, it had made her feel uncharacteristically jealous. And she didn't like it. Couldn't stand it, actually. Which was why she'd escaped before it could make her say or do something she'd end up regretting later. And then the email from Catherine Sutton had come through, only further stirring up her emotions.

"My children, Wynn in particular, have told me bits and pieces of your past," John said, and she could feel his gaze on her now. "It sounds like you're a far more courageous person than you give yourself credit for, Noelle."

Noelle wiped a tear from under her eye as she bit her lip, wondering if this was how it felt to have a father who cared about you. One who wanted to see you succeed. One who wanted to see you, period.

"I don't know about that," she said, swallowing as she looked at him. The resemblance to all of his children was there, but, and perhaps biasedly, she'd say Wynn had inherited the most of his father. Not only physically—though he'd most certainly gotten his blue eyes and chiseled features from him—but inwardly. "Just because my mom and dad were absent doesn't make me courageous. Certainly not as courageous as you. I can't even imagine being a cop."

"It's not the easiest job, that's for sure, but that didn't make me a man of courage. No job, no matter how dangerous it is, could do that. Trust me, I fall short in plenty of other areas. That's why the Lord gave men women—they tell you when you're doing something wrong, and until you fix it, you are nowhere close to heroic or courageous in her eyes." He paused and chuckled, shaking his head. Another trait Wynn had in common with his dad; how he injected humor into even the more challenging conversations. "The odds were not stacked in Jackie and I's favor in the beginning. We came from opposite sides of town, and sometimes, I'm amazed that I have a woman like her. But I'm not here to bore you with the stories or woes of my life."

Didn't he realize how much this meant to her? How much she craved this honesty and truth?

"My mom is an actress," she said after several minutes had passed, picking a piece of lint from her dress. "And even now she's made it clear that her career is more important than her only daughter. Her only child. I tried reaching out to her. It was rebuked. My dad—I don't even know his name. But I see you and Jackie and your kids, and I just see how wonderful your family is. You guys are so blessed."

John nodded. "We are. And we're blessed to have you in our lives. I don't think it's any coincidence that you're here now."

"You don't?"

"No. God doesn't do coincidences. He only does carefully organized miracles that, by some people's standards, are not miracles at all. But believe me, when you look back at this time some day, you'll realize it. I've realized that many times over about my accident. Probably not in the midst of what feels like a trial, but I can promise you that it will make sense one day, because God always keeps his promises. Even the ones we didn't know He made." His smile was gentle and fatherly as he rose, tucking his hands into the pockets of his slacks. "And Noelle?"

She shaded her eyes as she looked up at him. "Yes?"

"If you'd like to know the way to my son's heart, it's through honesty and truth. That said, a little ice cream never hurt anybody."

CHAPTER
Thirty One

Wynn set Noelle's phone down after he read the email response from Catherine Sutton, amazed in a twisted way that someone as important as a mother would instantly reject her adult daughter's attempt to reach out. What, did she think Noelle wanted money? Did she think she wanted a shoe in to Hollywood? Because unless he was just plain gullible or Noelle was really good at playing people, that was not the Noelle he knew.

In writing, Catherine Sutton had said that Annabelle had no interest in connecting. No wonder he'd seen such pain in Noelle's eyes around his family yesterday. If he would've known, he'd have said something to her. What he'd say, he had no idea. Here he was, standing in his own office with her while Marshall was on a call and he still had no clue about how to respond.

"So, that's that." Even though she looked more rested and less hurt than the day before, Noelle's dismissive words couldn't hide the emotions he knew she was feeling right now. "At least now I know. Just don't go there, because obviously I'm better off not knowing, whatever it was that happened."

"Okay, but you don't have to let her off the hook so easily. Maybe this Catherine Sutton is A, *not* your mother's manager; B, didn't even show your mom the email; or C, she's your mom under an alias."

Noelle's lips twitched. "Do you recall when you asked if I watch a lot of crime shows? Tables are turned. Do *you* watch a lot of crime shows?"

"No. I barely watch any TV, let alone crime shows. Usually just the occasional game or something." He motioned to her phone. "But seriously, it's not impossible. Actually, it's kind of clever, because you'd be reading the emails intended for your manager."

"Probably sums up Hollywood in a nutshell," she mumbled. "Lies and deceit. But like I said, it doesn't matter. She doesn't want to talk to me, clearly, so I'm not going to waste my efforts on it. What I do need to do is work on the outdoor space for The Gardens. It's April now. The event is less than two months away."

He grinned. "Astute observation."

Noelle let out a groan and dropped into the chair behind her. "Wynn, I'm serious. How are we supposed to have an event at The Gardens if there are no gardens?"

"Another as—"

"Don't even say it."

"Okay." He sat in his own chair, folding his hands on his desktop. "I won't."

"It's moments like these when I see some of the key differences between men and women."

"You might have to elaborate."

She made a face, her eyes narrowed and her lips pressed into a thin line. Kind of cute, if you subtracted the edge of annoyance to it. If this were a different scenario and he had the right to lean over and kiss that pretty little pout on her lips, he'd do it. He had Dad to thank for that sound logic. But this was this situation, and his thoughts should be on anything but kissing Noelle Carter.

Didn't matter that she'd kissed his cheek less than a week ago.

"Landscaping is kind of really important," she was saying. "We don't want people to show up expecting this gorgeous space and walk up to what it is now. That would be a very awful scenario. Think of it this way: if you revealed a house to someone and they just stood there—didn't say anything, didn't smile or laugh or cry—you'd feel like you failed on all accounts."

Wynn had a feeling she meant more to her "failing" scenario than just business, but he wasn't going to go there right now. "We've had that happen."

"Exactly. So you obviously—Wait, really?" Her eyebrows scrunched together, creating a groove between them. "Seriously?"

"Yep. Quite possibly the worst reveal of our decade in this business, but what fun would it be to have only success stories, right?"

She blinked at him. "Actually, a lot of fun. One time I was hired to plan an event for a tech company in Dallas—they flew me out and paid for my lodging and all that—and everything was great. The food we lined up, the guest list, the decorations; it was all perfect. And then it rained. On our *outdoor* event. And let me sum it up in one sentence for you: tech and rain and unhappy clients spell out for disaster with a capital D. Possibly all caps. Let's put it this way: they never invited me back."

Wynn did his best to keep his amusement stifled. "That's bad. But hey, it didn't stop you from planning events, so that's something."

"And that less-than-stellar reveal didn't stop you from building houses. I guess we both understand how to brush those mistakes off and try to do better next time, huh?"

Okay, that was most definitely not solely related to the work topic they were on, and he wasn't going to let this one slide. Not when it was clear that email had wounded her more than she wanted to let on. Like a wounded animal that hadn't taken a shot strong enough to kill, but it had caused unnecessary pain anyway. He didn't want to see Noelle wounded. He wanted to see her soaring.

"Wynn?" Noelle asked. "Why are you looking at me like that?"

Because I know you're hiding your pain and I want to help you. But that wasn't something he could say aloud. Or maybe he just wouldn't. Either way, now was not the time.

"Sorry. Spaced out for a minute." He offered a smile. "Should we start planning for what landscaping we want, Miss Carter?"

How come Wynn had texted her when she was literally within a hundred yards of him, Noelle had no idea. But he'd asked her to come over to his house later this evening to talk about the anniversary party again with his siblings, so she'd said she would. Marshall confirmed it when they were having lunch, and there wasn't anything stating they'd gotten everything settled last time. Even if she thought they had.

So, after she changed into leggings and a comfortable sweatshirt that evening, she got her notebook and laptop together, talked to Jackie and a nice, middle-aged guest by the name of Sandra for a few minutes, and left the inn. It was starting to get dark—why they'd wanted to wait until nine at night was beyond her—and only the streetlamps illuminated her way as she walked next door to Wynn's house.

Where was Sarah's SUV? Maybe, and this would be odd because Sarah had always been early, she was running late. Considering she had two kids and a handsome husband like she did, that was entirely possible. A little odd and uncharacteristic for simple, straight-laced Sarah, but not totally impossible.

She knocked, then clasped her hand around the worn fabric strap of the bag over her shoulder. The purse/tote had been a gift from her grandparents when she turned twenty-one, and she'd been using it ever since. The faded pinks and purples and blues and oranges were just a little too bright to be considered pastel, and she loved how happy it was. The fact that they'd had *Noelle Marie Carter* monogramed onto the front of it was another reason she loved it so much.

After several minutes had passed with no answer, she started to worry. What if something had happened? Maybe to Sarah or Wynn or any of them. But no. Jackie had been talking with her only minutes ago, so the likelihood of that was next to impossible. She tried knocking again. Nobody answered. She peered in the window to the right of the door, feeling like a spy, but could only see that there was a baseball game on the TV and it appeared there was a light on in the kitchen, though she couldn't actually see the whole kitchen from here. Apparently he was home, so why hadn't he answered? What if something had happened to him and nobody knew about it because no one was here?

Maybe she should just go in.

And then the thought came to her that he could possibly be in the shower and couldn't hear her knocking. It would be really awkward to walk in unannounced and… Yeah, she nixed that idea for the sake of both her and Wynn.

She was a few minutes early. She could just go around back and sit down at the table until the others arrived. It was possible one of them had texted her to let her know they were running late—Wynn and Marshall had still been working on demolishing the old water fountains when she and Jenna had left—and she hadn't seen the message because she hadn't looked at her phone for a while. She'd been catching up on emails from the office while she ate the grilled cheese she made in the kitchen at the inn.

Praying she was right and nothing had happened, she went down the porch steps and started around back. This way she could put her thoughts down on paper beforehand and not be—

Noelle stumbled to an abrupt halt as lights blazed to life in front of her, illuminating Wynn's backyard. Her mouth hung open as Wynn himself stepped forward, holding a box in his hands. Above him, twinkle lights were strewn from the edge of his house to the trees in the yard, and a big white sheet hung tautly between the two largest trees. Sprays of flowers were used to decorate the space, and pillows and blankets had been set up on the patio where the table usually was, and it was all so much to take in at once.

"Wynn, what is this?" she whispered as he approached her, looking impossibly handsome in something as casual as sweats and a gray T-shirt advertising Bryant Bros. and his glasses. Oh, his glasses. "What is all this?"

He stopped in front of her, a tender expression on his face. "This is a movie night. And in this box—Well, you'll have to open it to find out."

Tears sprang to her eyes, and she blinked furiously to try and keep them at bay as he handed her the little wooden box. Carefully, she released the springy lock and opened the lid, laughter mixing with her tears to create a terrible bubbly sound.

Resting on a bed of pale pink tissue paper was bug spray and a note was tied around the bottle's neck. She swallowed and glanced up at Wynn, who only smiled, before she pulled the note out.

I figured this may come in handy for this evening, if the bugs around here find you to be as sweet as I do. And if they don't, well, that's good for you but they don't know what they're missing out on. – Wynn

Noelle's lips trembled as she closed her eyes and wondered how in the world he'd come up with this crazy idea. Or, better yet, why had he done this for her? Especially on a weeknight—a Monday night. After a day of hard, physical work, he'd done this?

"Wynn, I don't..." Opening her eyes, she didn't hesitate as she stepped into the embrace he had waiting for her. "Why did you do this? I thought—I thought we were talking about your parents' anniversary."

His arms tightened around her, securing her into the safe haven of his strong embrace. "You deserve to be cared for too, Noelle. You give and give and give and expect nothing in return, even though you deserve everything in return. So I present you with a movie night under the twinkle lights Mom and Ember found downstairs. I hope you like the movie *Tangled.* Figured these lights could compare to those floating lanterns in the movie. Could've gone out on the lake, I guess, but electricity and water don't really mesh well."

Another watery laugh bubbled up and she straightened. "As it so happens, I love that movie."

Two hours later, Wynn was the only one still awake as the movie faded and the credits started rolling on the screen in front of them. He had Dad to thank for that—he'd been the one to find the projector and a big white sheet—and his mom and Ember to thank for the rest.

And even though it was late on a weeknight, Wynn had no regrets about doing this. The awe alone on Noelle's face when she'd finally come around back had been all he needed, but having her nestled into his side right now wasn't unwelcome in the least. Nova, as he'd come to expect, had chosen to curl up beside Noelle instead of him, and both girls had fallen asleep when they were only halfway into the movie.

Wynn hadn't had the heart to move either one of them, but now that the movie was over and it had become noticeably cooler outside, he probably should. Noelle wouldn't feel so great if she woke up the next morning with knots in her neck from sleeping on the hard ground.

He glanced down at her, smiling at the way her head burrowed into the hollow below his shoulder and her right hand rested on his chest. She'd pulled the fuzzy pink blanket—that was Ember's—all the way up to her chin initially, but it had since slipped down some, which was probably part of the reason she'd moved so close to him.

Whatever the cause, he didn't mind it at all.

Even if only for the moment, he had her in his arms, and he was grateful for that much. After reading that email earlier, he'd racked his brain on what he could do to show her someone cared. He'd considered taking her out to eat, but that would mean being out in public, and perhaps selfishly, he'd wanted anything but that. He'd wanted her to feel comfortable, and dressing up to go out didn't sound all that comfortable. Not to mention it would've been a lot harder to figure out how to invite her to a fancy supper compared to inviting her for a so-called anniversary planning party.

After he soaked in a few extra minutes of this peaceful moment, he touched her arm. "Noelle, you probably don't want to sleep here the whole night. Your muscles might not thank you tomorrow."

Slowly, she stirred and blinked her eyes open, an adorably confused rumple in her brow as she sat up—partially. She was clearly still dazed, meaning it must have been a good nap. Apparently she'd needed the extra rest. If her sleeping patterns recently had been anything like his, that nap had been much needed. Between The Gardens and Devin and the cottages and, yes, Noelle, his sleep time seemed to be decreasing night by night.

"I fell asleep on you again." Pink stole into her cheeks as she swiped at her hair. "Well, this time it was on you. Last time it was on your dog on your couch. But that's not what I meant. I mean— Never mind."

Wynn chuckled and stood, stretching his neck before he offered his hand. "I get what you were saying. And don't worry, Nova skipped out on me too. I finished the movie all by my lonesome self. After seeing it to refresh my memory, these lights pale in comparison. But I'd rather you fall asleep here than on a rickety wooden boat on the lake at night."

Noelle let him pull her up, and she stood there looking at him, making him wonder for the second time in one day what it would be like to kiss her. Wondering how soft her hair was. Wishing he could pull her into his arms and simply hold her like he had earlier, even if he didn't kiss her.

"Thank you for the movie night," she whispered, her eyes wide and so very blue under the twinkling lights. "Even if I did fall asleep."

"You're welcome." He found a smile as he leaned down and pressed a kiss to her forehead, lingering for a moment or two longer than necessary. "Good night, Noelle."

He couldn't be sure, but that really did look like a blush in her cheeks as she smiled shyly and turned, her bag looped over her shoulder.

"Hey, Noelle?"

She turned back around.

"Don't ever forget how special you are."

She smiled at him, and he was pretty sure that warmed him more than anything else ever had.

CHAPTER
Thirty Two

Of all places to run into George Fleming, Falls Market was the last one Wynn would've expected. And yet there he was, studying Wynn, Noelle, Devin, and Sophie like they were outsiders. Which, considering none of them were a part of his inner circle of friends, they probably could be classified as outsiders to him. And Wynn didn't mind that at all, no matter how much he disliked that smug expression on the older man's face. Fleming wasn't even all that old—maybe sixty-five?—and he already looked another five years older than that.

"Wynn Bryant." The words weren't said in a friendly tone.

Wynn didn't miss how Devin clenched his fists, and he noticed Noelle clasp Sophie's little hand. He hadn't had a chance to talk to her alone after Monday night, but that was okay. Devin hadn't shown up on Monday, so when he and Sophie had come the next day without Seth, Wynn had been shocked. Nearly fell dead over when Devin apologized. Not in a totally accepting way, but it was a start.

So today, Thursday, they had decided to take the kids to get a donut from the grocery market, and now their mission had been interrupted by George Fleming. Lovely.

"Mr. Fleming," Wynn said evenly. "How are you doing?"

George narrowed his eyes—a shade of blue Wynn would describe as a stormy sea, not at all like Noelle's beautiful sunny blue eyes. "I've been fine. We're putting up a new resort on the west side of the lake. Planning to have it open for next summer. Going to have plenty of fancy amenities that nobody would expect in a small town like Balsam Falls."

In other words, they wanted to give tourists everything they couldn't get at Wynn's parents' inn. Though it wasn't surprising, it made Wynn's blood heat. His family had made a good living off the inn, but a new resort that probably had a fancy indoor waterpark? They'd take a hit, and Fleming was well aware of it.

Besides, who needed a waterpark when you had a beautiful lake and plenty of activities or shopping in town already?

George shifted his grocery basket to his other arm, his grin broadening in the most conniving way. "Hired that Smith kid's company to oversee the project. It's going to be real nice once it's done. You and your...little friends here will have to come by some time."

That lit a fire in Devin, but to his credit, he didn't use those tightly bunched fists. "Do you realize that you're talking to the owner of a construction company you clearly didn't choose to hire? Not that he'd even want your money or approval with the way you treat everyone you think isn't good enough for you. My dad included."

Wynn wasn't sure he could've said it any better himself, and he was feeling just about as heated as Devin sounded, but he did everything he could to restrain from saying or doing something he'd only regret.

"I see you've set up a little cheering squad for yourself, Bryant." George's expression didn't falter. In fact, it may have become even more smug. "If that's what you need to make you feel good about how you've treated me, good for you."

"The way *he's* treated you—"

"It's not worth it, Devin," Wynn interrupted calmly, though his teeth were gritted. "Have a good day, Mr. Fleming. Come on, guys, we've got to find those donuts, huh?"

Noelle glanced up at him, a blend of worry and questions in her eyes, but he only smiled at her and guided their crew away from Fleming. Sophie clung tightly to Noelle's hand, even as they each selected a donut from the case the market bakery had, and Devin looked downright convicted. Of what, Wynn wasn't sure. He hadn't missed the glare Fleming had shot both Devin and Sophie, but prior to now, that wouldn't have bothered Devin. Not even the other day when he'd apologized. There had still been some kind of barrier between them.

Once everyone had chosen their donuts—Wynn and Devin went for chocolate glazed, Noelle a blueberry cake, and Sophie a white glazed long John with sprinkles—Wynn paid for them and they emerged into the fresh April sunshine. Falls Market was on a corner of Main Street, and one could catch a glimpse of the sparkling lake across the street and behind the shopping emporium.

He and Noelle had picked the kids up from school, much to Jeff Stanhoue's disapproval, and come directly here. Work could be done later. Right now it was more important to spend a little bit of quality time with the kids, and Noelle seemed to have picked up on that.

"What if we drove up to the outlook of The Falls to eat our donuts?" she suggested as they buckled into his truck.

Sophie, who had already taken a bite, stared at them from her booster seat in the back—a purchase Wynn had made in hopes of exactly this. "Uh-oh."

"Don't worry, you've got plenty of donut left," Wynn assured her, sliding his sunglasses on. "Everyone else up for it? I think it sounds like a great idea. Devin?"

The teen met his gaze in the rearview mirror and for the first time, Wynn saw a sliver of respect in his eyes. "Let's go for it."

"Can you hold my donut, please?" Sophie leaned forward, holding her donut between the front seats. "'Cause I might eat it 'fore we get there, otherwise."

Wynn smiled as he took the pastry and set it on the parchment paper in the cupholder beside his. "Well, we wouldn't want that, would we? Everybody buckled up and ready to go?"

When everyone nodded, he turned the key in the ignition and backed out of the parking stall, thanking God for this second chance with Devin.

And praying he didn't blow it.

"I think this is my prettiest view I've saw," Sophie said as she sat on Wynn's shoulders, one hand clutching her nearly-eaten donut and the other holding onto his hair. "It's so pretty."

Though her sentence wasn't grammatically correct, Noelle smiled at the girl's enthusiasm. According to Devin, they'd never been to see The Falls and they'd lived in town since Sophie was two. And considering she was seven now—nearly eight, she always made sure to add—that was a decent chunk of time.

Noelle had still yet to fully process what Wynn had done for her Monday night. Other than her grandparents, she'd never had anyone go to such great lengths simply for her. It was hard to know how to accept it, she was learning, because it was so very unexpected. And while they hadn't spoken specifically about that, the week had only improved from there. Mostly due to Devin seemingly setting aside his own pride and coming back to apologize. Whether or not Wynn ever vocalized it, she could tell it meant a lot to him.

"Did you know that, when it's summertime and all you want to do is lay on the floor with a ceiling fan blowing on you, it's not quite as hot right here?" Wynn said, both his hands holding onto Sophie's legs to prevent her from falling. The view of The Falls was gorgeous, sure, but it paled in comparison to Wynn and Sophie and the image they made, standing there at the railing like father and daughter. Not even their differing skin colors could make them look less like such. "Because of the power of the water and how much water there is, the mist you feel right now will always be cooler than the air. Which is why it has the nickname the 'Cool Overlook.' It's kind of like those misters they have at the zoo in Omaha, only this one is natural."

Even Devin, on Wynn's other side at the railing, looked impressed. "Let me guess, it's always packed up here on those hot days?"

"What's a zoo?" Sophie asked.

Wynn hesitated for a moment before continuing, taking Sophie's question in stride even though the girl had clearly not retained knowledge of a zoo from school nor from actually being at one. "A zoo is a place with lots of animals in it. And correct, it is always packed up here when it's hot. But today's an exception because it's barely spring and most people are working." He grinned up at Sophie. "Which means we have the place all to ourselves. One time my mom rented out this place—the whole Cool Overlook—for my birthday, which is in July. And then, much to our disappointment it rained all day. So instead of wasting the opportunity altogether, we played in the rain puddles. I was only eight at the time, and to me that was the best present ever. The only downside was that the cupcakes got ruined, because even under the shelter over there, rain slanted in."

Sophie giggled. "Mr. Wynn loves to have 'ventures. Tell us another story."

"Another one? Oh, boy, let's see here. Well, one time—Hold on, are you a fan of goldfish, Sophie?"

"Dad doesn't like any pets," Devin said quietly, eyes focused forward.

Wynn somehow didn't miss a beat. "Okay, well, let me think of a good story to tell. Ah, yes. Maybe it could be one about the time…"

For several minutes, Noelle simply listened to Wynn's probably exaggerated tales of when he and Marshall had built a tree house or when they'd scared Sarah by putting a toy mouse in her bed, but then she noticed Devin had wandered over to one of the tables under the picnic shelter. Wynn turned, but she touched his arm to let him know she'd handle this one.

She also tried to ignore the solid forearm muscle under her hand that, she'd learned, came from day after day of physically demanding work.

"Mind if I join you?" She stayed a few feet away, not wanting to crowd Devin's space. A circle of grace, as her grandmother had always said.

He shook his head no.

Noelle sat on the bench beside him, quietly wondering how it would be best to open a conversation. Maybe she should've let Wynn handle it. After all, Seth hadn't asked *her* to mentor the teen. In fact, she often wondered if he still frequently remembered how she'd slammed straight into him that first day. Or when, only last week, she'd speckled his uniform with dots of swiss coffee paint. Had he gotten the paint out? Either yes, he had, or the uniform she'd seen him in lately was a different one. Seth, as she'd learned, was far too kind to say anything about it.

It still didn't sit all that well with her.

"Sophie really likes it up here."

Okay, well, that made it easy. Devin had started a conversation instead of her, which was much nicer than her starting one by saying the wrong thing. "Do you like it up here?"

Devin didn't look at her. "Yes. But mostly because she does. I guess I tend to forget that she's only seven."

"You're only thirteen," Noelle pointed out, hoping that it wasn't taken the wrong way.

"And?"

Was that question actually meant to be answered or...? "And you shouldn't have to be like an adult because of that."

"Maybe not, but somebody has to do it. And when your dad is at work for eight hours a day, then at the bar for at least four, it's kind of hard to expect him to fill that role. Sophie doesn't

220

necessarily realize that, nor do I want her to. That's part of the reason I didn't like this whole arrangement. She's already too attached to Seth as it is."

Noelle's brows creased. "What do you mean?"

Devin shot her a look, then gestured to Wynn and Sophie, who hadn't moved from their spot at the railing. "Come on. You can't tell me you haven't noticed how much she likes you and Wynn. I don't want her to get attached and then just be abandoned after a while."

Noelle couldn't speak for Wynn, but she was fairly sure he'd want anything but that to happen. As for her, well, that was a tough one. She couldn't promise to prevent that from happening. Not when she would be leaving in less than two months. Oh, how she wished she could promise to stay. But staying wasn't possible, no matter how much wishing she did. Carter, Inc. depended on her being in Jackson, and Balsam Falls was a fifteen hour drive away. Too far for weekend visits, or even just a day or two here and there.

"Has that happened before? Her getting attached and then being abandoned."

Devin's nod was almost so slight she wasn't sure it was a nod. "Yes. And it's my responsibility to protect her from letting it happen again."

Noelle was torn between bringing up her and Devin's conversation, one that hadn't gone any farther than Devin saying Sophie's protection was his responsibility, to Wynn or not. He hadn't asked, even though he probably wanted to, but somehow it felt wrong to tell him about it. She felt like Devin had trusted her enough to confide in her, and she didn't want to ruin that. But she also didn't want to keep it from Wynn.

And so she weighed both options for the rest of the afternoon and into the evening before deciding to bring it up. The idea of keeping something that might be vital to Wynn or Seth was enough to make her forget about doubting her choice. She'd do it when they were alone, even though the thought of being alone with Wynn for practically the first time since Monday unnerved her some. Not because he'd do anything inappropriate—that was the last thing Wynn Bryant would do—but because she was scared she was falling in love with him. And there may not be anything she could do about it. But Devin was more important than her fears, so she pushed them aside.

Following supper—John had grilled burgers for all the guests, which included Noelle, a middle-aged couple, and two younger couples right now—Noelle found Wynn in the kitchen washing dishes. Since they'd used plastic silverware and paper plates there weren't many, but she grabbed a towel to dry anyhow. Grandma had always praised her on her dishwashing and drying skills, a compliment Noelle had taken to heart because of her lack of culinary talent.

"I can take care of these," Wynn said, glancing down at her. "I mean, unless you want to help. If that's the case, you won't find me complaining."

Noelle laughed as she started drying the pan he set on the drying mat. "I'm not very handy when it comes to cooking, but I'm not entirely useless in the kitchen. I've been told I'm a very good dish washer, and that was by my grandma, so yes, I did take it as a compliment."

"I see. Well, it's never too late to expand your kitchen talents to something like preparing a meal."

"Grilled cheese is my current specialty, but I can whip up a killer frozen pizza if someone really wants me to show off."

Wynn chuckled, his arm brushing hers as he set a salad bowl on the mat. "I'll have to remember that when I'm craving grilled cheese or pizza."

As nice and easy as it would be to stay on this topic, that's not why she'd come in here. "Hey, Wynn?"

"Yes?"

"Earlier at the lookout of The Falls when I talked to Devin, he told me that part of the reason he was worried about your arrangement with Seth is because he doesn't want Sophie to get attached. And then later be abandoned. He also said that his dad is gone at work for eight hours, and usually spends at least four hours at the bar."

"I figured so. What do you mean about the other?"

Noelle shrugged, her focus on her hands. "I don't know. He just said that, so then I asked him if it had happened before and he said yes, then didn't say anything more."

Wynn's hands stilled, and the extended pause all but forced her to look up at him. "He didn't say who he'd been abandoned by?"

She shook her head, wishing she had a better answer. "No. I didn't want to pry, but I could have—"

"You're fine, Noelle," he interrupted, his smile doing very little to lessen the unease in her tummy. Or maybe she'd mistaken fluttery butterfly feelings for unease, considering she was standing very close to him and he was looking at her just like he had on Monday. "The fact that he told you that much is enough for now. What's going to be will be."

Oh, how easy it would be to rely on those sensitive eyes. To lean on his solid faith when it felt like everything in her life was up in the air. To get so used to his warm, strong hugs that she never wanted to leave town.

"Hey, Noelle?"

She blinked. "Yes?"

"Thank you for telling me. Knowing you, you probably debated whether or not to, and I appreciate you being honest with me."

Noelle smiled and nodded, not yet trusting her voice to function. Not when he was looking at her like he was, with that serious expression, his blue eyes intent. She swallowed as her heartbeat pounded against her chest, and she sincerely hoped he couldn't hear it.

Was he going to kiss her? Because if so, she wasn't ready for it. But at the same time, she was.

At this moment, she would surrender the fear of falling if he kissed her, because she couldn't seem to think of a reason not to. Not when she knew how wonderful and courageous and amazing

Wynn Bryant was, and somehow that was overpowering her desire to flee from any and all attachment right now.

As if reading her thoughts, Wynn leaned toward—

"Wynn?" *Ember's voice.*

Noelle jumped away from him just in time for his little sister to walk into the kitchen carrying a pan of what appeared to be brownies, hoping beyond hope that she had not witnessed that moment. Whatever *that moment* had been. Because it had most certainly set the stage for something more than whatever they had now, which she wasn't even certain had a label. A business relationship? A friendship? A friendship business partnership?

"Hey, sis." Wynn's voice was perfectly normal as he smiled at his sister. How did he manage that?

Ember's smug gaze traveled back and forth between them— Noelle had put at least two feet of physical space between her and Wynn. "Hey, big bro. Once you guys are finished with the kisses— I mean, dishes, you can come out back for some dessert."

Heat flared up in Noelle's cheeks, and she avoided Wynn's gaze at all costs. Seth was right: people always got squirmish when they were in the hot seat.

CHAPTER
Thirty Three

A girls' shopping day was the perfect way to forget about last night's interrupted...moment with Wynn. Or it should be, but Noelle was struggling to put it out of her mind when it just insisted on playing over and over again. And then she'd wonder if she'd misread the whole situation, because she'd never exactly been in one like that. Yes, she'd been on many dates and been kissed, but she hadn't ever felt towards another man what she felt towards Wynn.

Which was why she'd jumped—perhaps too enthusiastically—at the opportunity to go shopping with Jackie, Sarah, Ember, and Jess when they'd brought it up last night while having dessert. It had sounded like a good idea to put some space between her and Wynn.

She hadn't factored in that physical distance did nothing to dissuade thoughts of him.

"Ooh, look at this one," Sarah said, lifting the edge of a floor-length, pale green dress.

It also hadn't escaped Noelle that they were standing in a shop called Happily Ever After, a bridal store in downtown Balsam Falls.

Not that it should matter.

Jackie glanced at her daughter's find. "That's beautiful. It would be really pretty on you. Or Ember, with her darker hair. More of a contrast."

"On me?" Ember peeked out from a clearance rack, her expression disgusted. "No way. I am not wearing a booger green dress to the Spring Fling, thank you very much."

Noelle tried to hide her laugh.

"It's not booger green, Ember," Jackie said with a shake of her head and an apologetic glance at the sales lady. "It's sage green, and I think it's pretty. You should try it on, Sarah, since your sister seems to be too picky this morning."

Ember's focus was back on the rack of brightly colored marked down dresses. "I'm not too picky. Just saying what I don't like. If a girl is gonna spend money on a dress like this, she ought to really love it."

"She has a point," Jess said, holding up a pretty pink gown with sparkles adorning the fitted bodice. "What are you thinking, Noelle? You haven't really looked much. There's a lot of dresses here."

I haven't, but only because I can't get a certain tall, handsome, and charming contractor out of my mind. A problem she'd never had—not being able to get someone out of her mind. She'd never been so…whatever this was that she couldn't concentrate on anything else. And it was partially exciting but partially irritating. Did Wynn have any idea what he was doing to her heart?

She had a feeling the answer would be yes. Maybe Marshall could let remarks about Jess or even his own feelings he had for her roll off his shoulders, but Wynn didn't work like that. He knew what he was doing, even if it was driving her absolutely crazy. Because it was doing exactly that, so if that was his goal, he was succeeding with flying colors.

"Do you not like any of these?" Jackie asked, her dark brows scrunched. Wynn's mother always looked so pretty and feminine, with her dark, shoulder length hair and the simple yet elegant dresses or blouses and jeans she wore. Very much like a devoted wife, loving mother, and respectable businesswoman all in one. "We can always try a different place if you'd like. There's several options in town."

Noelle smiled. "No, no, this is fine. I was just thinking and seeing what you guys liked. It's been a while since I've been shopping for dresses like these. Most of my formal events are more, let's see, black dress and black suit, if that's a thing. They don't really groove on color."

"Well then, you've come to the right place," Ember said, gesturing to the dresses around them. "Balsam Falls loves color. A lot. Personally, I think light pink or lavender would look amazing on you. Your dress that you wore to church was so pretty. That color works really well on you."

"Thank you. I think I've always liked it because it's pale enough to fit into the corporate world." She looked at a navy blue dress with a pretty neckline, but it was many sizes too big. "Otherwise my closet consists of lots of whites and grays and blacks as far as work clothes go. Not a lot of color."

"It's probably way more organized than mine, though," Ember said. She held up a hand. "Please don't comment on that, Mom. I am trying to—*Oh*. That is the most stunning dress I've seen today."

Noelle glanced up from the pale yellow dress she'd just pulled out. "This one? Then try it on. It would look amazing on you."

The younger girl hesitated, then grinned as she took the dress and the assistant lady—had she said her name was Jane?—led her over to a fitting room. Jackie mouthed a *thank you* to Noelle as she followed her youngest daughter, and Noelle smiled. Wynn wasn't the sole reason she'd fallen in love with this town—possibly the biggest reason why, but not all. His family and the town itself had sucked her right in. Made her feel like she was one of them, instead of just a guest.

If only her own mother would feel that way.

Noelle pushed the thought away as soon as it entered her mind. She'd barely thought about her mother's rejection since Monday, and yet there it was. A big, glaring reminder that, even now, her mother wasn't like Jackie Bryant. She hadn't ever wanted to be, and it was foolish to think that would magically change now that Noelle was old enough to fully understand what little she did know about her mother. Some things were best left in the past where they belonged.

Since she hadn't found a dress she really loved, she ventured over to the seating area where Jackie and Jess were sitting, waiting for Sarah and Ember to try on their dresses. The bridal shop wasn't huge, but it was cute and chic. White trim lined the base of the pale pink walls and the furniture matched the trim, gleaming under the pretty chandelier-style light fixtures. A gray and white and pink rug had been rolled out underneath the furniture, contrasting the dark wooden floors. Beautiful framed photos of brides hung on the walls, and thick but silk ivory-colored curtains separated the fitting rooms from the main room. A step up led to a semicircle of mirrors for a girl to look at herself in. They even had a small selection of men's tuxes, and Jackie mentioned that she wanted her husband and sons to visit in case they could find something for the event.

"So, you leave for Paris at the end of the summer, right?" Jackie asked Jess. "And you'll be there for how long? Two years?"

Jess nodded, her hands clasped around her purse in her lap. "Yes. Well, maybe. That was my initial plan, but depending how it goes, it might be extended to four years. I might be able to come back for a break or two, maybe in the summer. My classes don't start until September, but I'm flying out in August so I can get a little bit acquainted beforehand. I've never been outside of the States, so I'm kind of nervous."

"I'm sure it will be a wonderful experience for you," Jackie said with a warm smile. "And then you could come back and open up a bakery in town. Isn't that something? We have all these eating establishments and a wonderful coffee house, but no bakery."

"That would be really awesome," Jess said softly, and Noelle could sense that she had more she wanted to say, but Ember chose that moment to announce herself.

"Are you ready?" Wynn's younger sister asked, the curtain hiding her.

Jackie shook her head with a small laugh. "Yes, dear. We're ready."

"Ta-da!" Ember emerged from behind the curtain, Jane carrying a pin cushion behind her. Poor lady looked a little overwhelmed. "What do you think?"

"It's stunning, honey," Jackie said, pulling her phone out. "Here, let me send a picture to your dad and brothers. Get up there on the step with the mirrors around you."

"No, don't send them a picture," Ember said. "They can't see it until Spring Fling."

"But—"

"Mom, that's just the rule. We seem to be in a drought of weddings, so they can handle waiting a little over a month." She stepped up onto the step. "Oh. Does it make me look fat in my stomach? Sarah, does that booger one make your stomach look fat?"

Noelle laughed at Ember's lack of more gentle terminology. The poor employee just stood there with her pin cushion, a pen stuck into her low bun, and looked like she had no idea how to handle the situation.

"Um, no." Sarah walked out of her changing room, holding the extra long skirt of the dress off the ground. "But it's about a mile too long."

Jackie slipped her phone back into her purse. "Well, that can be fixed. I think you both look beautiful. Can you have these altered by May twenty-seventh?" she asked the employee.

Noelle's own phone vibrated, and she opened the text from Wynn to find a selfie they'd taken with Devin and Sophie yesterday at Cool Overlook with the message *Thought you might like to have this keepsake. How's the dress shopping going?*

On their own accord, her lips lifted into a smile as she typed out a response, only to find everyone looking at her when she glanced up. "What?"

The ever-knowing Ember grinned. "That was Wynn, wasn't it? What did he say? Don't tell him about my dress."

Noelle blinked innocently. "I have no idea what you're talking about."

"Oh, plea—" Ember's gaze swung to Jane. "Jane, let's see your best wedding dresses."

"I have a whole new appreciation for landscapers." Devin groaned as he pushed his shovel into the dirt. "And for machinery. Don't you guys have some kind of equipment that can do this instead of torturing ourselves?"

Wynn stuck the point of his own shovel into the ground and leaned on the handle. "We do, yes, but this is more fun, isn't it?"

The teen frowned—no, scowled—and hauled a load of broken up dirt and ceramic into the wheelbarrow.

"I'll take that as a no. How about we take a break and get something to drink? Trust me, it's much easier when you're hydrated. And this work will help bulk up your muscles without going to the gym."

Devin rolled his eyes, but he willingly followed Wynn over to the cooler and grabbed a bottle of Gatorade. "Maybe I prefer the gym. At least nobody is telling me how many reps I have to do, even if Seth has to be there because I'm so—" he made air quotes "—'young.'"

They sat down in the sparse shade of a tree that had only started filling out for the season, both facing the lake. "Yeah, well, you are. And you've done a good job of being the adult in the house, but you still deserve to be a kid, too."

"Let me guess, Noelle told you about what I told her?" Devin took a long drink of his electrolyte-infused water, then squinted up at Wynn despite the shady spot they were sitting in. "And don't try to pretend you magically knew. You might be older than me, but I'm smart enough to know better."

"Yeah, she told me. Your dad do anything at home other than sleep?"

"Pays the bills. More than I can say for myself."

"Devin, you're thirteen."

"And Sophie's seven, meaning she needs somebody to care for her. I'm her brother. That's my responsibility." He took another pull from his Gatorade. "You've got sisters, so you should know what I'm talking about."

"I do, but it shouldn't be your sole responsibility. I didn't raise my sisters. Helped out, sure, but didn't raise them. Certainly didn't make sure they were fed and clothed properly, nor did I make all the meals. Big difference."

Devin lifted his shoulder and let it drop. "You didn't have no mom and an alcoholic father. Big difference. Way I see it, there's no other way. Sophie needs to be taken care of, and I'm able to get that done. It's not a bad thing."

"Never said it was, but if you're taking care of your sister and the house, something has to give." Wynn unscrewed his own Gatorade but didn't lift it to his lips. "How are your grades?"

Another half shrug. "Good enough to pass."

Wynn sighed, feeling like he wasn't getting anywhere. At least Devin had been saying more when he was upset instead of obviously trying to cover up whatever it was he wanted to cover up. And Wynn wasn't naïve enough to believe there was nothing. If Seth was as concerned as he was—he sent a text faithfully every evening or spoke to Wynn in person to see how it was going—then somebody wasn't saying something. For Seth to go to as drastic of measures as asking Wynn to get answers and purposely keeping Devin's dad out of the loop, there was something going on.

"You like her, don't you?"

Wynn frowned. "What?"

"Noelle. You like her."

"We're not here to talk about who I do or don't like."

Devin snorted. "Then what are we here for?"

"I believe you know the answer to that question." Wynn glanced at the teen, who still kept his gaze forward. "Who abandoned you?"

Devin's jaw tightened. "That's not important."

"Maybe it is to me."

"Why?"

"Because I care, whether you believe that or not. And you might not realize it, but my life is not perfect. Close to it in some areas, but definitely not perfect. And if you think it's always been *easy*, you're wrong on that too. My dad was in an accident when I was nine. He could've died. He's very fortunate to be walking."

Devin finally looked over at him. "How'd that happen?"

"The accident?" At Devin's nod, Wynn continued. "He was a cop for twenty years, and chief of police for fifteen of those. Patrolling one day, and someone ran a red light, running into the passenger side of my dad's cruiser, causing his vehicle to slam into a pole. Could've been it for him. His legs were crushed, but he was *really* lucky nothing else had been damaged. Doctors told him he wouldn't walk again. Six months in and after several surgeries, he left the hospital, determined to get better on his own. Took another six months, but he did it."

Devin swallowed, facing forward again.

"Who abandoned you guys, Devin?"

Devin stayed mute, his jaw locked and his eyes glossy.

Wynn sighed, but it wasn't worth pushing him too hard. He'd done that once before, and that had nearly ended things. As badly as he wanted to know whatever it is that Devin was hiding, it was going to have to come out whenever Devin was willing.

Wynn could only pray that day was sooner than later.

CHAPTER
Thirty Four

After having met George Fleming in person, it felt even more like trespassing to be standing on his empty lots. Especially with Wynn and several of his family members, including Marshall, John, and Ember. Contrary to the way the weather had been going, today was overcast, damp, and breezy. A perfect day to curl up with a book or, better yet, to catch up on some emails, even if it was the weekend.

But no, here she stood in her jeans and recently purchased rainboots and Wynn's flannel shirt again, shivering as the guys talked about roof pitches and foundations.

In other words, they were speaking a language entirely of their own.

"Well, if we went with the higher pitch you'd be less concerned about rain and snow piling onto it," Wynn said, hands on his hips. He appeared to be cool as a cucumber in his jeans, cowboy boots and his unbuttoned flannel jacket over his gray T-shirt. "So if we went with five-twelfths or six-twelfths, that would be the best option. What do you think, Dad?"

John chuckled and held his hands up. "Don't look at me. I'm not the contractor of this bunch. But I will say that I can see why you would want to build here. It's about the best view a person could ask for of the lake."

"Maybe I'll move into one of the cottages once they're built," Marshall said. "You willing to sell me one?"

"Depends what your budget would be. As long as it wouldn't take either of us down, then yes, we could work something out. I think it would be too much to put four in, wouldn't it?"

Marshall rose his brows. "Seriously? What if, because I'll obviously be helping with them, I could…"

"I think they've forgotten we're even here," Ember said as she stood beside Noelle, a hoodie bunched around her face. Kind of looked like Mikey from *Monsters Inc.* considering her sweatshirt was green. "Tends to happen when they get in the zone."

Noelle pulled the flannel tighter around her as a breeze slipped by them. "The zone?"

"Yep. The construction zone. My dad says he's not the contractor, which is all fine and good and true, but don't let him fool you." Ember's eyebrows rose as far as her sweatshirt allowed. "He knows his way around tools and wood and…" She waved her hands emphatically. "And roof pitches. He just likes it when us kids figure it out—or at least try to—on our own before he helps. Perks of having a retired chief of police homeschool dad."

"Gotcha. Well, excluding the whole cop part and dad thing, I was homeschooled, so I sort of get what you mean. But hey, at least that means they have faith in us."

"That, or they really don't and they're testing us to see how long it takes for us to realize that they were right all along. But your way was more optimistic, so we can go with that option."

Noelle laughed. "Does this happen regularly? These little brainstorming sessions?"

"Every time they're going to start a new project, yes." Ember crossed her arms over the Under Armour logo on the chest of her sweatshirt. "And usually I'm the lone soul tagging along, so it's nice to have someone else with me. I've picked up on some construction jargon because I have two contractor brothers, but I think I've tuned most of it out."

"Well, until I came here, I had never even swung a hammer, nor had I torn down a wall. While I can't say I would be able to do it all on my own, it's kind of fun. You can take all your frustrations out on that poor wall and not worry about how you're breaking it."

Ember nodded. "That's very true. Honestly, this is probably the biggest reno project they've done in quite a while. They'll do smaller ones in between other jobs, but nothing on this scale. I think it's kind of good for my brothers, Wynn especially."

"Just Wynn?"

"No, but him in particular." Ember's grin gave away her reasoning before she even said it. " *You've* been good for him. I haven't seen my brother so lovey dovey in a long time. Actually, he's never really been serious about anyone since I've known him, so that alone is something. He really likes you."

"Nothing has even—We aren't *together.*" Noelle put extra emphasis on the word, as if that would make it true in Ember's mind. "We're just working together, is all."

Ember snorted. "Okay. You tell yourself that, but trust me, I have been told I'm brilliant. And I have an extensive history on knowing about love."

"Oh, really?" Another gust of wind blew Noelle's hair across her cheeks, and yet the men still seemed unbothered—now talking about the scale of the build or something. "And how do you figure that?"

"Multiple reasons. One, I quite clearly witnessed how a spouse should *not* treat their spouse, and now I have amazing parents that show me exactly how they're supposed to treat each other. My dad is one of the most romantic guys I've ever met—he still brings Mom flowers every week and usually cooks supper at least twice a week. Two, I was the maid of honor at Sarah's wedding, and let me tell you, a girl learns a lot by filling that role. Third, books. I have a whole collection of romance novels—Christian ones, obviously—in my mother's library, and here's this: the bar for my future husband has been set high. And both of my brothers meet those standards, but obviously not for me, because that's just—no. But for you…" Ember's eyes sparkled, even with her tightly bunched sweatshirt. "How old are you?"

"Twenty-six." Because really, would she get away without answering? "I turn twenty-seven in June."

Ember nodded slowly, thoughtfully. "Uh-huh. Wynn will be thirty-two in July, so that would work nicely. My dad's four years older than Mom, so that's pretty close. Here's the real question, though. Do you like butter pecan ice cream?"

"My personal favorite is strawberry, but yes, I do. I like pretty much all types of ice cream, so there's that. But I live in Mississippi, Em. And yes, your brother—both of them, but Wynn in particular—is a great man. I just don't want you to get your hopes up for something that wouldn't work out."

"Oh, yes, of course. And that's why you're wearing his shirt, right?"

"Em—"

"What are you discussing over here, ladies?" Wynn's blue eyes sparkled, and was it only her or was he standing extra close to her? "Let me guess, what roof pitch would be best for the cottages?"

Ember patted her brother's chest and shook her head. "Oh, my dear brother, you wish that's what we were talking about. Since Noelle's not alone anymore, I'm going to go give my two cents on these cottages to Marshmello and Daddio."

Wynn's brows rose and he stared after his sister, then let out a low whistle as he turned back to Noelle. "She's in rare form today, huh?"

"Or natural form." Noelle really tried not to let them, but her teeth chattered. And probably not because she was cold because she wasn't *that* cold. It was nearly seventy degrees out here. "Marshmallow?"

"Are you cold?"

"Huh? Oh. No. I mean, not really. I'm fine."

"Uh-huh. Right." Still, he stepped into a spot where the wind would have to go through him to get to her, and the odds of that happening were quite slim. "And about the Marshmello, it's not the kind you've probably got in your mind. Ever heard of the rapper guy?"

Noelle squinted. "Maybe?"

"Well, for a while, Jess has called Marshall 'Marshmello' and he calls her 'Jessie J' because her name is Jessica Johnson. So sometimes we'll bring them out, but that's more Ember's thing than mine or Sarah's. Marshall and Ember have a lot in common personality-wise. Sometimes it's a little scary just how much. If it weren't for their age difference, I would seriously wonder if they were twins separated at birth."

She let out a little laugh. "I could see that."

"So, what were you guys really talking about?" The smirk he wore so effortlessly was downright mischievous. "And don't say it was actually roof pitch, because even my sister hasn't come to understand what that means. Let me guess, it was about me?"

"What? No." *Be nonchalant, Noelle, nonchalant.* She gestured to their surroundings, but her planned speech went out the window when a shiny black SUV drove by slowly. "Wynn, who was that?"

His expression hardened and he released a sigh. "George Fleming. Or one of his sons, probably. He's divorced, but he has two sons and they're both about as lovely as he is. Don't worry about it. We're not trespassing, so he can't do anything except what he just did."

"The other day at the market, he said something about how you treated him." Noelle searched Wynn's eyes. "What was that about?"

"That's just something he tells everyone who doesn't kiss up to him," Wynn said dismissively, though he looked anything but that. "So, if you were talking about roof pitches, what'd you figure out would be best for these cottages?"

Noelle hesitated, resisting the urge to glance over her shoulder in hopes of catching another glance of the vehicle. "Oh, um, well... Probably five-twelfths."

He smiled, but it didn't fully reach his eyes, and that trace of unease came back. Only this time because of the fact that there was more to the story than anybody was saying out loud, and not because she was standing next to Wynn doing dishes.

Wynn had to hand it to Jess—the mural was going to make The Gardens' event space stand out. Jenna had been working on it for at least two hours every day, some days more, and she'd finally settled on her design. That meant, come Monday, the sketch would be transformed into a colorful wall of what would be the focal point when a person walked in.

After Jenna left for the night, Wynn gathered his things and closed up The Gardens, then went home. His mother had apparently brought food over at some point, so he took a quick shower and ate before taking Nova out for a walk. The evenings were starting to lengthen by this time of year, and that made it much nicer for days like today when he put in a few extra work hours. It'd cleared off from the morning's doom and gloom, leaving behind a gorgeous sunset over the smooth lake.

They'd made progress from a pre-construction standpoint on the cottages today, thanks to Marshall and Dad's help. Once they had everything budgeted, Wynn would be able to go to the bank and, hopefully, get the process moving along. If they could close on the property sale by the end of May—aka, Fleming didn't play dirty pool or try to blindside him—they'd have no problem getting these cottages up by this fall. Or next spring, depending on how things panned out with other jobs and life's responsibilities.

And for as much as he'd dreaded telling his family without first having a game plan, it turned out to be extremely useful to have their advice to make that plan. He just hoped he hadn't gotten anybody's hopes set too high, considering they were planning on buying land from George Fleming. A man who would probably rather come face-to-face with a grizzly than any of Wynn's family.

His little drive-by that morning had only reminded Wynn of the fact that the man refused to let go of the past.

Wynn took Nova for a longer walk tonight, inhaling the fresh air as they strolled through downtown Balsam Falls. Even though it wasn't even official tourist season yet, downtown was humming with activity. Lights glowed from all the quaint but welcoming shops lining the cobblestone street, and patrons went in and out, carrying shopping bags on their wrists and wearing smiles as they conversed with friends. There was a certain feel to Wynn's hometown that couldn't be compared to any other place, even though he'd barely traveled enough to know that for certain.

Locals would stop him to say hello and ask about how his family was doing, so he'd do the same for them, savoring the people who *did* respect his family. He understood that respect was earned, not just given, but some people had that backwards.

Tourists, on the other hand, wanted to stop him to pet Nova. The dog lapped up the attention, often rolling onto her back so her tongue lolled out the side of her mouth as they gave her a belly scratch. Then she'd grin up at him after as if to say, 'They love me, Dad, can't you tell?' And, of course, business owners would only boost her ego further by offering her a treat which, after two, Wynn had to start declining.

The setting sun bathed the town in golden-orange light, and it was warm on Wynn's skin. As he often felt after the winter months, Wynn was excited for the promise of the upcoming summer season. Especially because this year may be his family's last year before Fleming's fancy new resort stole customers. Sure, there were other lodging options currently available, but nothing like what the man was planning to build.

Just as he was on his way by the inn, Noelle appeared from the opposite direction. She smiled when she saw him and waved. Considering she wore leggings, a T-shirt, and tennis shoes, she'd probably gone for a walk of her own.

He ignored the little voice that taunted him about how easily she could pick up a date when she looked like she did.

"Hey," he said as Nova closed the gap between them. "Out for a walk?"

Noelle squatted down and rubbed the golden's ears, but her smile was directed up at him. "Yeah. Well, I almost stayed in, but it was too nice to skip out. Ember was going to join me, but she and Jess are doing some project for the library or something."

Too bad they hadn't left at the same time. He would've willingly invited her to go along with him, even though she'd obviously taken a different route.

"A library project, huh?" Wynn asked. "I'm surprised Jess is interested. She tends to want to be in the kitchen rather than a library, but she and Em are pretty close, so it's not all that shocking."

"How is the mural coming?"

"Really good. Jen said she was going to be starting in with actual paint on Monday, so it should move pretty quickly from there."

Noelle stood, her hands on her hips. "That's so exciting. I wonder how long it'll be before she has clients wanting their own murals."

Wynn chuckled. "Knowing Balsam Falls, probably not very long at all. Hey, um, I wanted to talk to you about this morning and the whole George Fleming thing. Do you want to come over to my shop for a few minutes?"

Her eyes widened, but she quickly masked her shock with a nod. "Sure."

"My dad and George Fleming were never best friends or anything, but there was a time when they knew each other well enough to have a friendly conversation or say hello in passing," Wynn said, leaning against the island thing in the middle of his shop. Probably had an actual name, but Noelle didn't know what that would be. "And then the day came that any and all friendliness was severed because of my father's accident."

Noelle leaned against the cabinets directly in front of him, puzzled at what he was saying. "Because your dad decided to leave the hospital?"

"No. Because George was the one who ran the red light and ran into my dad's vehicle that day."

"Wynn." The word was hardly louder than a whisper, and Noelle had to refrain from stepping forward to hug him.

"My dad didn't stay angry—in fact, I'm not sure he ever was angry because he's not that kind of person—but from that day forward, there's been a divide between our family and him. No matter how many times my dad has tried to reach out, George won't hear of it. And as you've seen, certain people have been influenced by that. I'm not sure what George's side of the story is, but apparently it's not honest, because there's evidence and there were witnesses, so he must have them fooled somehow. Not once has he apologized to my father."

"But I don't understand... Was he injured?"

Wynn's jaw tightened. "Not seriously. A few bumps and bruises. Dad's problem was that his vehicle slid and ran into that light pole. Otherwise, his injuries might not have been as serious."

"I'm sorry, Wynn. That must be hard, knowing your family has only tried to make things right and your attempts are rebuffed."

"Yeah, well, it happens." He shrugged and turned, but his hands were braced on the edges of his work island. "Can't do much about it."

Noelle didn't respond. She knew how it felt to be rejected, and while George Fleming wasn't related to Wynn and his family, he was an influential member of their hometown. And it had to cut deep when someone wouldn't apologize for something that had happened over twenty years ago. Something that the person who'd been seriously injured had put behind him.

"That's why you were so hesitant about the cottages." The words came out only seconds after the realization of it dawned. "Wynn, I'm so sorry. I never should've tried to pressure you into wanting to do the project. Not when I didn't have a clue about the history there and how—"

"Noelle, you're fi—"

"—much it had impacted your family. Oh, my goodness, why didn't you *say* something to me? I never would've—"

And then it happened.

The kiss.

Noelle wasn't sure how it had gone from her apologizing to Wynn kissing her, but it had and it was and she was acutely aware of Wynn's hands on her cheeks, his lips on hers. She had one brief thought that this wasn't at all what was supposed to be happening—she had been apologizing, right?—but as she got lost in his kiss and his embrace, she couldn't bring herself to move away.

She melted against his solid chest, her hands resting on his muscled back, the warmth of his skin seeping through his T-shirt.

And she felt like she was floating. In a wonderful, happy world where there were no George Fleming's to steal her joy. Where there was no rejection from her mother. Where only she and Wynn existed in a downright magical bubble.

After what felt like forever, and yet very little time at all, Wynn eased back. But only slightly. He rested his forehead against hers, his strong hands resting on her back now, his breath warm on her cheek.

Wynn Bryant had kissed her. Her! He had kissed her, and he seemed to have done it on purpose and...and it had been wonderful.

"I've been wanting to do that for a while now," he murmured, his low voice huskier than normal. "And since you wouldn't stop talking, it was the perfect opportunity. Especially because every other time we've been interrupted."

Noelle thought she might fall over, but he seemed to be steady, so she simply leaned into his arms and released a shaky laugh. "A while, huh? We haven't known each other that long."

"Long enough." He lifted his head and a rush of cool air filled the space, even though his expression was anything but cold. Something new burned in his eyes, almost so intense it stole her breath, but also so tender it made her realize the magnitude of this moment. "For the record, this means we won't be able to go back to where we were before. Contrary to how it may seem, I'm not the guy who goes around kissing women and forgetting about them."

"Does that mean I'm unforgettable?"

Wynn's eyes crinkled as he smiled. "Very unforgettable. And another thing, this probably won't be kept a secret for long. I wouldn't be surprised if Ember was looking through the window right now, to be honest with you."

Noelle jerked away, her gaze sweeping the plethora of windows on his shop. Who had so many windows on what appeared to be a remodeled shed? French doors, windows on every wall, windows in the door—

He laughed and pulled her back into his arms, dropping another kiss on her lips before resting his chin on her head. "Yes about the secret. No about Ember. Trust me, she's not *that* good."

"You're sure?" And really, did she care? Probably not, considering she had yet to come down off cloud nine.

"About ninety-nine percent sure, but I refuse to say a hundred percent because I'd hate to lie to you right off the bat." He released her, his grin laidback and charming, then grabbed a piece of wood. "How would you like to learn to make a floating shelf?"

Noelle's lips twitched at the word *floating*, considering she still felt like she was doing exactly that. "You're gonna trust me with your tools? These fancy ones?"

He let out a soft laugh, his eyes sparkling. "Yeah, but I hope you realize that you're going to have to trust yourself too, because I can only guide you so far."

"Maybe I should just watch."

"Oh, no, you won't." He motioned for her to come over to where a tool with a big round blade was sitting. "First, you're going to learn how to cut wood."

Her eyes widened. "Uh…"

"Just kidding. We're going to sand a board I've already got cut." He flashed her a smile that made her relive the kiss from only moments ago all over again. "You'll do great. Trust me."

Trust me. Prior to now, she might've balked at anyone excluding her grandparents who said those words to her, but at this moment, she couldn't bring herself to want to do anything other than trust Wynn. Not in this cozy little shop with Nova lounging near the open French doors, locusts and crickets singing in the background, and the wonderful knowledge that she hadn't been imagining the connection between her and Wynn.

No, that wasn't her response anymore. She had no idea how this was going to work or what would happen when her allotted time in Balsam Falls was up, but for now and possibly for the first time in her life, she was going to surrender it to God and let Him guide her with the details.

CHAPTER
Thirty five

Wynn really had not been planning to kiss Noelle, but since words weren't cutting it, that seemed like his best option at the time. And now, a little over an hour later, he had no regrets about it. His only problem was how to tell his family without getting "I told you so's" from all of them. Not that Marshall had any ground to stand on, because he absolutely did not. The others, well, unfortunately, they did.

"Am I doing this correctly?" Noelle glanced up at him from the board she was staining. "I'm probably not doing this correctly."

"No, you're fine," he said. "Just try to keep from having any streaks, and since you're using a T-shirt, you shouldn't have to worry about that. We'll let it dry overnight and then put a second coat on it tomorrow."

"And then put the rope through it?"

"Not quite." At her visible disappointment, he only smiled. "Trust me, it takes just as long for everyone. After the second coat of stain, you put a layer of poly. Then you can do one of two things.

Either sand it and put one more coat of poly, or just do the one and then put the rope through. Whichever you prefer."

She bit her lip, and Wynn refrained from kissing that befuddled expression. He was planning to take things slowly, which meant he probably should've asked her out before kissing her, but he couldn't turn back now. Nor did he want to.

"Would it be impatient of me to just skip the second coat of what was it? Poly?"

"Polyurethane, yes. And no. The shelf will still be just as pretty as you are."

His compliment caused her cheeks to flush and she turned back to what she was doing. Wynn leaned against the workbench while she worked, marveling at the fact that Noelle liked *him*. She probably had plenty of hotshot business associates or bigwig lawyers or doctors jockeying for her and yet she'd chosen him. At least he assumed as much, considering she hadn't negated his statement about no turning back.

As far as kisses went, the obvious attraction had far exceeded any other kiss he'd had. He wouldn't change anything about it, not even how it'd happened. If he'd continued to wait for the "perfect" moment, he may very well still be waiting when he went to his grave. Life had many perfect moments, but usually a person had to initiate them somehow. That had been a prime example of doing just that.

"Does this really look okay?" Noelle asked.

Forcing his thoughts away from the woman staining the board to the board itself, he nodded. "Looks great. It'll dry and then be ready for more stain tomorrow. How about that? Your first wood project, and it looks awesome."

She stripped the stain-coated gloves from her hands and grimaced. "Don't say that yet. There's still about a hundred steps left, and I could easily mess up any number of them. I think demo is more up my alley because I'm supposed to break things while doing that. And even if this turns out okay, that doesn't mean you should ever trust me with those big tools. You probably shouldn't. *I* wouldn't trust myself with them."

Wynn laughed and tugged her close to him. "Like I already said, the shelf looks beautiful. Trust me, it will turn out perfectly, even with the steps you've still got to do."

"You really think so?"

"Yeah, I do." Unable to resist, he leaned down and kissed her softly. "So, since we're here, should we discuss when our first date should be? Or do you have a thing against being seen in public with me, because not only will my family pick up on it rather quickly, but—" he lowered his voice, fighting to keep a straight face "—so will the church ladies. And they will run like crazy with the knowledge that I'm seeing someone. Honestly, I wouldn't be surprised if they ran a feature in the *Balsam Falls Gazette*. Headline would be something like 'Bad-Boy Bryant Ends Up with Classy City CEO.'"

Noelle made a face. "You are not a bad boy. Unless there's something I don't know about your past that I should?"

"Nope. Well, there would be, but you've already heard about when I flushed Sarah's fish down the toilet."

"Yeah. That was sad."

"Well, I'd say he lived, but he probably didn't."

She gave his chest a playful shove. "Wynn! That's so mean."

"You have to admit that it was funny. C'mon. You know you want to."

"Not really."

He arched a brow. "So… About that date. Are you free tomorrow evening?"

"I might have to check my schedule. See, there's this party that's coming up next Saturday and there's people who have RSVP'd and we still have to decide on food for sure. And figure out how to decorate the space because the people who the party is for live at the event location, so that might not work out, since it's supposed to be a surprise party. Wow. Um, so yeah, I might actually have to take a raincheck."

"A raincheck, huh?"

She nodded.

"Fine, but I'm not going to stop asking. How about Monday night?"

Her laughter in response was about the sweetest thing he'd heard in his life.

Happiness should never be contingent on a specific person or place, but Noelle wasn't sure she'd ever felt as happy as she did sitting in the row of chairs between Ember and Wynn as she did at that moment. Only a week ago had Pastor Jay been talking about relationships and she'd been hesitant to allow anyone close to her.

Last night's kiss and the woodworking and the joy she'd felt as she'd drifted to sleep at the inn with thoughts of the evening had completely changed all of that. Had totally upended all her reservations about relationships and, judging by John's knowing expression, he hadn't forgotten about their little chat from last Sunday. Honesty and truth. She hadn't gotten to the ice cream part yet, but she'd been honest with Wynn from day one, and she had no intentions of doing this any other way. Nor did he, from what she gathered.

Today's message was on praying for what you were wanting, even if you didn't know how you were going to achieve it. Pastor Jay wasn't old, probably somewhere around fifty, and Noelle liked his style of preaching. It wasn't in-your-face, but he also didn't sugarcoat things. He explained it according to the Bible, then gave ways of how he'd seen those things in his own life. Such as when he and his wife had been praying on how to go forward after deciding to resign from a church that hadn't aligned with their beliefs fully. At the same time, this church had just had their pastor resign, and been looking for a new head pastor. There were probably other details that he didn't disclose, but it was still a story of how God tended to work in mysterious ways.

Such as the letter that Mayor Leo had sent, which had started the chain of events that had ultimately led to where she was today.

"Is that smile for the sermon or for me?" Wynn leaned down, his voice quiet. "Because as much as I enjoy Pastor Jay's sermons, I kind of selfishly hope it's for me."

"No talking during church sermons," Ember whispered from Noelle's other side, her grin saying she knew that something had changed between them. "Don't be a bad influence on her, Windy."

Noelle frowned. "Windy?"

"Long story." Ember faced forward again. "I'll tell you later. You know, when we catch up on, oh, the past twenty-four hours."

Wynn shook his head, but he reached over and folded Noelle's hand into his, giving it a slight squeeze.

Noelle really, really tried not to let her cheeks flush as Wynn's grandmother leaned around her grandson and used both thumbs to...what? Give them her approval? Probably. At least Ember didn't say anything further as they listened to the rest of the sermon, then one of the associate pastors led them in prayer before dismissing them.

Everyone rose from their chairs, filling the sanctuary with conversations—most of them centered around who was having what for lunch afterward—as they gathered their purses and kids' stuff. Noelle looped her purse over her shoulder, waiting until the rest of the Bryants were ready to go.

"Be prepared for the church ladies," Wynn murmured as he guided her towards the church lobby with a hand on her back, both his and her Bible in his other hand. "Trust me, they have some kind of sixth sense. They appear out of—"

"Oh, my, you must be Noelle."

"Nowhere," Wynn finished, then turned as a short, gray-haired African-American woman who appeared to be at least eighty-five approached them. Her flowered skirt swished around her calves, and her heels click-clacked on the tile flooring. "Mrs. Lilah Carson. I haven't seen you for a while."

"Oh, I was out with that nasty flu for a couple weeks." Lilah waved her hand dismissively, her brown eyes instantly honing in on

Wynn's hand, still resting on Noelle's lower back. She met Noelle's gaze, her purple-rimmed glasses punctuating her enthusiasm. "You are a very pretty young lady, and our Wynn here is such a good catch. I heard about you from my friends—we've been trying to set this boy up for a long time now. How did you two meet?"

Noelle glanced up at Wynn, who looked like he'd rather be chewing on nails than talking to this Lilah. "Well, I was asked to plan the Spring Fling at The Gardens, and the fact that my grandma used to tend to them made me very intrigued, so I took the job. And on my first day here, I was checking everything out at the building there on the property when I locked myself into a room. So I was virtually stuck, which is when Wynn showed up and...and saved the day."

Lilah clasped her hands under her chin. "Oh, that sounds just like our Wynn. Always such a hero, this one is. Like I said, we tried to set him up—"

"Okay, Mrs. Carson," Wynn cut in with a little laugh. Was he actually nervous? "As nice as it was to talk to—"

"Hold on a second, did you say your grandma tended to The Gardens?" Lilah's brows scrunched together. "What is your last name again, dear?"

"Carter. My grandmother's name was Estelle Richmond, until she married William Carter."

"I'll be go to heaven," Lilah exclaimed, and Noelle felt Wynn flinch. Poor man wasn't sure how to act around older women. "I can't believe I didn't realize that sooner. I'm Lilah Carson, used to be Lilah Potter, and I own the flower shop in town. Your grandma and I were the best of friends, and we kept in loose contact for a little while after she and your grandpa got married and left. Oh, do I have some stories for you!"

"Wait, did you name the flower shop after my grandma?" Noelle's heart raced and she glanced up at Wynn, who smiled. "You knew her?"

"Honey, your grandma and I were some of the most hip people around back in the day," Lilah said, her own face lit up. "We used to dream of owning a flower shop together, and we'd spend our days in those gardens after school. I really did love them, but your grandma… They were her *life* until your grandpa came along. You know what, do you have any plans for this afternoon? Why don't you and your handsome beau come over to my house and I'll make some tea and we can talk? I've got pictures and stories for you galore."

She looked at Wynn again and he nodded, even though she knew he'd probably rather do something else entirely than going to Lilah Carson's house. "I would love to, Mrs. Carson."

Though spending the afternoon in Lilah Carson's living room had been the second unplanned thing to happen in the past twenty-four hours—kissing Noelle definitely ranked above all else—he got to be with Noelle while she learned about her grandmother's earlier days, and because that meant something to her, it meant something to him. He hadn't missed the way she'd perked up earlier in church when Lilah mentioned her friendship to Estelle, and he'd wanted to do whatever was going to prolong that happiness. Even if it meant choking down the older woman's too-sweet tea. Had she poured the whole jar of honey into his cup only, or was Noelle just better at pretending the liquid wasn't threatening to close her throat in?

"I can't believe she did that," Noelle said. "My grandmother snuck into the community pool? For real?"

Lilah nodded, her rose petal teacup resting on its saucer on her lap. "We did a few things we probably shouldn't have, but we weren't actually trying to cause any harm. Just wanted to give the town a little excitement. Never mind that we got in trouble, but that's how we got started with The Gardens, which is why I brought it up. The judge decided to give us each community service hours, and it was probably because they desperately needed help at The Gardens, but obviously they wouldn't frame it that way."

Noelle's brows drew together. "Wait, how old were you guys?"

251

"When that happened? We were only seventeen. Good golly, that seems like a long time ago. Is your grandma...?"

"She passed away almost five years ago," Noelle said softly. "And my grandpa died last November."

Wynn took that opportunity to set his tea on the coffee table and reach for her hand, giving it a squeeze. She hadn't told him a whole lot, but judging by the way she said it, her grandfather's death had been unexpected. And since that had been the last family member who wanted to acknowledge her, he could only imagine how hard it must've been.

"Oh, honey, I'm so sorry," Lilah said. "One of my greatest regrets is not keeping in touch with her. She told me when she was expecting, which was a year or so after she and your grandpa got married, but that was right at the time I was getting ready to get married, and our letters got more and more sparse from there until we weren't sending them at all. I never even heard what gender the baby was or what its name was, but it must've been a boy, since you have your grandparents' last name."

Noelle swallowed, and he could tell her smile was forced. "No, it was a girl. Annabelle Carter. My mom is an actress, and she wasn't married when she had me. But I have never really met her. My grandparents adopted me right after I was born. Well, the adoption was finalized beforehand, but they raised me from day one. Mom wasn't interested in the responsibility of a child, I guess."

Wynn sensed she had to refrain from adding *and she isn't now, either* to that statement.

Now Lilah was the one to set her tea on the coffee table. "Oh, my heavens. I had no idea. I'm sorry—I never would've asked if I'd known that."

"No, you're fine," Noelle said with a smile. One that wasn't fake, but Wynn could tell there was a certain degree of sadness to it. "My mom had her reasons, I'm sure, and my grandparents were wonderful. They were always there for me, even though they didn't have to step in like they did."

Lilah shook her head. "You are a very gracious girl, Noelle. And Wynn Bryant." She cut her gaze at him, and he felt like he was a soldier standing at attention to his commanding officer. "You ought to treat this girl like the treasure she is. You got that?"

Wynn nodded. "Yes, ma'am."

"And if you really want to show me that you are doing that, you ought to get her flowers and chocolate. Every girl loves to get that, and trust me, it is the best way to get her to love you even more. My husband used to go into my flower shop when I wasn't the one working to get me bouquets of flowers, and he was so proud of himself." The older woman's brown eyes crinkled as she smiled, as if recalling precious memories. "Love can be one of the best things you'll ever experience in your life. But if you want any relationship to work, remember that God has *got* to be at the center of it. No way around that one. If He's not at the center, trust me, it will not be anything like the movies that leave that part out promise it to be. They tend to forget the Jesus when they're promoting the happily ever after. And as great as it is to have someone who is good looking and smooth talking—yes, I am looking at you, Wynn— what is on the inside is what really matters. And it's not that happily ever afters don't exist—they most certainly do, and it can be the most wonderful adventure of your life, but you have to remember God. If you do that, then happily ever after is more than promised to you."

CHAPTER
Thirty Six

Estelle's Flower Shoppe turned out to be a cute little place that was equally as colorful on the outside as the inside, and Noelle's grandmother would've loved it. The shop's exterior was painted a pale teal color with a bright yellow door and a pale pink bicycle had been propped up with flowers in its basket. A wooden bench sat under the window opposite the bike that had a window decal reading *Estelle's Flower Shoppe* in flowy letters.

Noelle found herself hanging out in the shop whenever her help wasn't needed at The Gardens or if Wynn and Marshall were working on their other project throughout the week. Lilah had a couple little tables set up near the front windows, allowing lots of natural light to pour in. Noelle worked on what to list on the updated website for The Gardens, took care of some things Lucy sent her way, and finalized details for Saturday's anniversary party.

She and Wynn had mailed out invitations only a couple days after that first meeting about the party, and he'd told her about half had RSVP'd. He and Marshall were going to grill burgers and have a few different salads for the food, Ember and Sarah were in charge of decorating and distracting their parents somehow, and Noelle had talked to Joanna Crawford about the singer who'd been performing that evening, and since he'd had a cancellation, he was going to perform at the party.

And when she wasn't working or spending her free time with Wynn, she listened to Lilah tell stories about Grandma and their adventures growing up. They'd lived next door to each other, and while their childhood homes weren't there anymore, she said they'd both been right on the lake. They'd dug holes to find gold in their backyards or gone swimming in the lake or spun stories of how they'd always be best friends. Noelle soaked up the details and in some ways, it made her miss her grandmother even more. In others, she realized just how full of a life her grandma had lived in her eighty years. Lilah also showed her pictures, some that were framed and hung on the wall and others in a box she kept in her back office, of Grandma. There was one of the two of them holding garden trowels with floppy sun hats and polka dot dresses on, and another of them standing behind a table set up as a flower stand.

Noelle and Lilah, unbeknownst to Wynn and his siblings, also worked on a few special floral arrangements for the party. They used a colorful array of bluebells, peonies, zinnias, and daisies in a variety of colors ranging from pinks to purples to blues. Noelle couldn't say she was extremely talented in the arranging of flowers, but Lilah was excellent at sketching the idea out on paper, and she'd get the bouquets ready tomorrow for the event tomorrow evening.

Wynn had tried to make it work for them to go on an actual date, but both their weeks had filled up. Instead, they spent their lunch breaks together, she helped with what landscaping she could, they spent time with his family and, her favorite, they hung out in his wood shop. Even though she enjoyed getting dressed up and going out, there was something to say for all the little moments. Not only had she gotten to know Wynn better through their more personal and meaningful conversations following The Kiss—the one that could not be topped, though the ones that followed it couldn't be sweeter—but she shared about her own past. About growing up in Jackson. About what she loved to do when she wasn't working. About how she'd closed herself off and hadn't really realized it until coming here.

Which was why she was so shocked when Wynn walked into the flower shop just after five Friday evening, wearing tan khakis and a light blue polo that both hugged his biceps and highlighted his eyes and announced to her that they were going to go out to eat.

Noelle glanced at Lilah, who only grinned, then at her plain T-shirt dress and Converse before looking up at him. "Now? But I've been working all day and my hair is a mess and—"

"And you look absolutely gorgeous to me," he interrupted, leaning down to kiss the top of her head. "I need to talk to Lilah for a minute, if you want to get your things together. And we're not going to Farm to Table, but we will be walking to our destination. You can put your bag in my truck, if you don't want to carry it. On second thought, would you mind waiting in my truck while I talk to Lilah?"

"Wynn, we really don't have to go out tonight," she said, even as she started picking her stuff up. Lilah would be closing soon. "You've been working all day, and I'm sure you want to relax. Trust me, it's very sweet of you, but I don't expect to be taken out to eat all the time."

"Maybe not, but I've already got arrangements made. Lilah can back me up."

Noelle's gaze darted to the older woman, who nodded vigorously. "Trust me, honey," Lilah said. "When a man who looks like your man does wants to take you out, you don't turn him down. Go! You've been working your little booty off all week. Have fun and try to put work out of your mind for the night."

Noelle hesitated, but she nodded and got her things organized just so in her bag, her mind concocting ideas of where they were going to go. She'd only really eaten homecooked meals and Farm to Table and Giorgi's since she'd been here, but there were lots of eateries listed on the page in the *Balsam Falls Guide* in her room at the inn. From Mexican to Italian to American to Chinese, there was pretty much some restaurant here to satisfy whatever hunger a person had.

As had been asked, she went out to Wynn's unlocked truck to wait, doing her best to not look into the flower shop's windows. Lilah had the space much more modern than Noelle had expected her to. The interior brick walls had been painted white, with the flower shop's logo in a splashy teal on one wall. The checkout counter was to the back of the space, and floral arrangements were artfully placed on shelves and stands around the shop, broken up by displays of inspirational signs and jewelry and whatever else Lilah seemed to think went well with flowers. Then, at the end of the day, Lilah put all the flowers into a refrigerated room in the back to keep them good. Noelle imagined that the natural light during the day kept the flowers perky and happy.

Then Wynn walked out of the shop emptyhanded and, against her will, Noelle felt a twinge of disappointment. She shouldn't— she literally just told him she didn't need to be taken out or anything—but she supposed that was what happened when a girl set her expectations too high.

"I hope you know that I was extremely tempted to kiss you when you were rambling on in there, but I refrained," Wynn told her once he opened her door. "It went well the first time I interrupted you, but there wasn't a Lilah Carson watching us."

Noelle made a face as she stepped down from the truck with his assistance, finding the brief disappointment to be gone as he smiled down at her. "Is that a thing now? To interrupt my ramblings by kissing me? Because as I recall, you told me you like it when I ramble."

"Yeah, well, that was before I had the right to kiss you." His grin caused her belly to flip-flop as he rested his hands on her waist. "So, now I like it even better because yes, I do plan to do kiss you whenever it's appropriate when you're rambling."

"How many words count as rambling, because that may—"

"That many," he interrupted with a smirk before his lips met hers.

A little zing of elation shimmied up her spine, and she wound her arms up and around his neck, her fingers brushing the hair at the nape of his neck. This man and his wonderful kisses would never get old. Nor would she ever fail to remember how good it felt to let go of the fears that had been tethering her to the ground for too long now.

"Noelle Carter, you are amazing," he murmured as he stepped back, enfolding her hand in his. "Simply amazing."

Yeah, well, he was too. She just wasn't quite as handy with words right after he kissed her like that, so she merely smiled what must be a cheesy smile and leaned into his side as they stepped onto the sidewalk.

Wynn couldn't recall the last time he'd felt so content in his life. Or maybe that wasn't the right word to describe how it felt to walk down the street with Noelle, hand in hand, nothing but this moment on his mind. Maybe, prior to now, he'd been *too* content, and that probably meant he'd been too stuck and comfortable to take a step out in faith.

He was pretty sure he'd been taking nothing but steps—or maybe leaps—of faith ever since Noelle Carter had walked into his life a month and a half ago. It felt like he'd known her so much longer than that, and yet it also felt like time was going by fast. Too fast, some days.

"Where are we going?" she asked, breaking the easy silence. "Because it appears to be that you're leading me on a wild goose chase. Is that what you're doing? Maybe Libby would be a better companion for that."

Wynn pressed the crosswalk button. "Libby is a rooster, not a goose. And no, I know exactly where we're going."

"Why is her rooster named Libby? I mean, isn't it more of a girl name?"

"Probably, but Ember has a very deep and sacred bond with creamed corn, so she named her rooster off a brand of that." The walk signal appeared, and he led her across the street. "One of the many quirks of my sister. However, it does come in handy if you want to get on her good side, because let me tell you, there is no better way to do so than to buy her a can of creamed corn."

"Note taken. As for you, it's butter pecan ice cream, right?"

Wynn glanced down at her. "How did you know that?"

"Um, not important. I mean, it's obviously true, so that's all I need to know."

"Ember told you, didn't she?"

"What? No." Her grin gave her away. "Okay, so, she might've said so, but your dad was actually the one who told me ice cream is the way to your heart. And then Ember took it a step further by saying butter pecan is your favorite ice cream."

Wynn rose his brows. "You were talking to my dad about the way to my heart? Ember's not surprising, but *Dad?*"

"Well, technically, that wasn't the bulk of the conversation, but yes. He mentioned it. Ember said your dad's a romantic. I think you're just as much of one."

"Oh, you do, huh?" He smiled as he stopped them in front of Giorgi's. "And we have arrived at our destination. I figured you'd like to sit outside, so I reserved a special spot for us behind here. And I know how much you like their pizza, so here we are. Told you it wasn't going to be fancy."

Noelle wrapped her arms around him in a hug, her head resting on his chest. "I love it, Wynn. It's perfect."

What was perfect was how she fit in his arms, her hold surprisingly strong as she hugged him. Or how it made him feel when she trusted him like she did. Too bad things couldn't stay this way, even if he wanted them to. He wasn't oblivious to the reality that her life—her *real* life—was elsewhere and that her time in his town was limited. But he also didn't want to let that reality prevent him from wanting to pursue what was happening between them. Because it was something special, something no other woman he'd dated in the past could compare to. And he wouldn't, no matter what happened, allow worldly things to come between them, including distance like there was between here and Jackson. There would be a solution to that, Wynn was sure. If this was God's will—and it most certainly felt like it was—then He would make whatever necessary steps along the way known to them.

"How is Devin doing?" Noelle asked, wiping her mouth with the brown paper napkin. The sun glinted off the lake behind her, silhouetting her profile. "Has he said anything about the abandonment thing? I'm sorry I haven't been as much help with Sophie this week."

Wynn shook his head, wishing he had a different answer for her. "You're fine. Ember and Mom have been helping me out. And as for Devin, no. He'll talk to me about school and how he can't stand some of his teachers, or how Sophie loves to try and stay up past her bedtime, but when it comes to anything about that or his dad, he goes mute. I've asked Seth about it, but he doesn't know anything more than we do, and he wouldn't lie to me. Besides, if he knew the answers already, he wouldn't have even had a reason to ask me to do this whole thing."

"You said his mom died, right?" Noelle leaned back on her hands, her legs extended out in front of her as she relaxed on the blanket he'd laid out prior to going to the flower shop. "If that's the case, then it wasn't her."

"Yeah. It's not her. I double-checked." He finished off the last of his lemonade, then rested his arm on his bent knee. "There's an obituary from six years ago. Sophie was only one when her mom died. Pretty sure that's what led to Robert's alcoholism. That was before they moved to town. They lived in Colorado before."

"Did it say how she died?"

"Car accident. Drunk driver."

Noelle let out a little gasp. "Seriously?"

"Yep. Ironic that her husband turned to the very thing that took his wife's life, huh?" He released a breath. "I'll never understand the choices some people make. I mean, I can't imagine losing a spouse, but to become an alcoholic after a drunk driver killed your wife? It just makes me sad for those kids. Sophie may only be seven, but she's smart. Sooner or later, she's going to know just as much as Devin does. And that's only going to make it harder for Devin, because he's not going to be able to protect her forever."

"You can't let that get to you, though, Wynn," she said softly. "You can't control Robert or Devin or even Sophie. You can try to guide the kids, try to help Devin, but you can't make any of them change. Only God can do that, if the person is willing."

"You're a wise woman, you know that?" He smiled and motioned with his hands. "Come over here. Is it just me, or is it a little chilly out here?"

Noelle scooted over so her back was to his chest, her head resting against his shoulder. "It's still plenty warm out, but nice try. Thanks for supper. I think my assumptions were correct. You are most certainly a romantic like your dad."

Wynn wrapped his arms around her shoulders, his chin resting on her head. "Yeah, well, it's kind of easy when you deserve this and then some. How are things with your office in Jackson? We've talked about me and my family and my work and blah, blah, blah, but your life is important too. Although they're probably missing you, and if that's the case, well, you're here for another month and a half and I've got the paperwork to prove it."

She laughed. "It's good. They technically have everything under control, but I'm glad I'm not off the grid. They may make the problems a little bigger as it is, however, if I was unreachable, you'd probably be hearing about wildfires originating from Carter, Inc. on the news. And it'd spread real fast, considering you never hear of wildfires coming from the city. But anyway, you get my point." She let out a little huff. "Basically, it's going great. Awesome. Amazing."

Wynn chuckled. "I'm glad to hear it. Hey, have I officially asked you to go to my parents' anniversary party as my date? I don't think I have."

"Twice."

"Seriously?"

She tilted her head back to look at him. "You're quite the jokester this evening."

Wynn grinned, and she rolled her eyes.

"Yes, I did remember. But they say the third time's the charm, so could you say it once more? Just to be sure."

"Yes, Wynn Bryant, I will absolutely go with you to your parents' anniversary party." She smiled up at him, her pretty blue eyes sparkling "There. That make you happy?"

He leaned down and kissed her. "Happier than any butter pecan ice cream ever could."

A knock on the door woke Noelle from her sleep, and oh, how she would've liked to stay in bed. After last night's pizza date, they'd gone for a walk downtown and gotten ice cream at the Dairy Dock before Wynn brought her back to the inn. Rather than working anymore, she'd helped Ember reorganize her books—which translated to sharing as much as she was willing to about their date—and then taken a long, hot bath, enjoyed a cup of tea, and crawled into bed to read a little bit before snuggling under the covers. Sleep had come quickly, accompanied with dreams of the Spring Fling and Wynn and…and then the knocking interrupted all of that.

Noelle stared at the door, hoping that would prevent the person from knocking anymore. It was seven-fifteen, though, so she should probably—

Another knock.

"Okay, okay, I'm coming."

She fumbled to push the covers back and crawl out of bed, then grabbed her trusty gray cardigan and wrapped it around herself, slipped her fuzzy slippers on, and crossed to the door.

Nobody was there.

Frowning, she poked her head out. The hallway was empty. What in the world? She was about to close the door and seriously examine her brain to see if she'd actually heard knocking when something on the floor just outside her room caught her eye.

Flowers.

Noelle covered her mouth with her hand as she squatted down and inhaled the fresh scent of pink roses and white carnations and whatever other flowers the bouquet consisted of. They were arranged in a glass vase with a pale pink ribbon tied around its neck. Next to the vase sat a big, spiral bound notebook with a pair of flower earrings and a note on top.

"Wynn, you little romantic," she whispered as she picked up the gifts and took them into her room.

She unfolded the note, unable to keep the smile from widening as tears pricked her eyes.

In case you were under the impression that I simply wanted to talk to Lilah—even if she was your grandmother's best friend once upon a time, she is still one of the "church ladies"—that was not the case.

I hope you enjoy these flowers that aren't nearly as beautiful as you, and the new notebook. I noticed you were running out of pages in your old one, and even though I'm not sure if this is the "right" kind, I hope it is. I thought you'd like the colors.

And last but not least, the earrings. They caught my eye, which reminded me of the pretty lady who caught my eye during that March snowstorm. Maybe, if they won't clash with your outfit (I know that happens, I grew up with Mom, Sarah, and Ember) you can wear them to the party tonight.

Oh, and good morning, beautiful.

Love, Wynn

263

Noelle reread the note about three times, taking in the shape of his letters. They reminded her of the way he'd drawn up those cottages: strong and steady and sure.

Regardless of any grudges held against the Bryants by George Fleming—even ones that weren't valid, considering George had been the cause of the accident—or any tension with Devin, that was exactly who Wynn was. A strong, steady, and dependable man. One who would, in a heartbeat, lay down his life for those he loved.

And how Noelle had been as incredibly blessed as to be the woman whose heart he was pursuing, she had no clue. But she did know that she wanted to be the best version of herself that she could, because like Lilah had said last Sunday, a relationship couldn't be based on looks or physical attraction only. It required the inner beauty and strength that came from God alone.

Filled with determination, Noelle pinned the note to the corkboard she'd hung over the desk—perks of driving instead of flying: she got to bring her corkboard, and there had been a picture there already, so she'd temporarily replaced it—and then grabbed the Bible she'd brought with her from her nightstand.

The best way to achieve that goal was to go directly to the source of where God's answers were found, and right now, she was going to do exactly that.

CHAPTER
Thirty Seven

Mom and Dad will never in a million years guess what we planned for them," Ember said as she walked into Noelle's room carrying a duffel bag later that afternoon. Wynn's little sister looked fresh and youthful in her sporty outfit of shorts and a T-shirt, her dark hair gathered back into a long ponytail. "Sarah has them totally thinking that our gift to them is solely the supper out. But little do they know who and what will be waiting for them when they get back. Eek! I'm so excited."

Noelle smiled as she closed the door behind Ember, relieved to hear that John and Jackie hadn't suspected anything when they were told they were being treated to a supper out. It had been Sarah's idea, and even though there would be food at the party, it was the only feasible way to get them out of the house for part of the later afternoon and early evening. Little did they know there would be around twenty-five people outside of family when they got back, and that the guests they had for the night included people they hadn't seen for years. Ember had decided to put fake names into the reservation system, otherwise their parents would've noticed.

265

Right now, though, Noelle had promised Ember they could get ready together. Ember, however, had discovered the bouquet and earrings and notebook Noelle had left on the desk when she'd left this morning to work on The Gardens for a while.

"What. Is. This?!" Ember pivoted around, her brows raised. "I mean, I know he really likes you, but wow. He must really, *really* like you."

Noelle only smiled and touched the petal of one of the roses. "I like him too. And yes, you can take some of the credit for calling that earlier than I did."

Ember giggled. "No, you knew it. You just didn't want to admit it. And did I really sound surprised about the flowers just now? Because—and Wynn technically didn't want me to tell you, but oh well—he had all that delivered this morning and had me put it outside your door for him since he had to get going early. Was my knocking super annoying?"

"You were the insistent knocker?" Noelle shook her head. "I'll admit, I really did not want to get out of bed, but the surprise was worth it. Thanks for being the little courier pigeon."

Wynn's sister let out a snort as she plopped her duffel on the cushioned bench at the foot of the bed. "I've never had the privilege of being called that, so you're welcome. Okay, we can talk while we're working, but we should probably start getting ready. Sarah will be on my case if we're not ready in time. And let's face it, knowing me, I won't be ready in time. What are you thinking for your hair?"

"I'll probably just curl it. I'm planning to wear this dress." She held up the pink-coral dress she'd brought along but had yet to wear it. "It just so happens to kind of match the color scheme of the party, even if it is a little more pink than coral."

"Oh, my goodness, I love that," Ember exclaimed. She unzipped the duffel and proceeded to pull out a flat iron, a curling iron, a hairbrush, hairspray, two different dresses, and a pair of flats. "I decided on these two dresses, even though I can obviously only wear one. What one do you like the best?"

Noelle studied them—one was about calf-length, pale green with tiny pink and white flowers, and short flowy sleeves; the other was navy blue, same length, and had orange and pink and white flowers. "Hmm. I think I like the green one better."

"Oh, thank goodness." Ember stuffed the navy one back into the duffel and set the other one on the bed. "That blue one is pretty, but I was hoping you'd say that. Also, I was wondering…would you want to do each other's hair? You don't have to want to. I'll be fine. Me and Sarah do it sometimes, but since she's got Sadie we usually just do our own in the same room or something, but she couldn't make it work today. But anyway, you don't—"

"I'd love to," Noelle interrupted. "I obviously don't have a sister, and I've never really had any super close friends to do it with, so that sounds like a lot of fun."

"Really?"

"Really."

Ember beamed and let out a little squeal as she gave Noelle a hug. "Well then, I'll get the curling iron plugged in. Thank you, by the way. It means a lot to me."

Noelle smiled and hugged the younger girl back. "Trust me, it means just as much to me."

"You scared or something?"

Wynn glanced over his shoulder as Marshall approached where he was standing under the pergola behind the inn. "I just hope they're surprised. It's not exactly the easiest thing to do, planning a surprise party for your parents. Especially when it takes place on their own property."

"Yeah, well, look around." Marshall gestured to the five round tables they'd set up where friends and family were already waiting, talking amongst themselves as Benji, the hired musician, played lightly in the background. The girls had placed pale coral tablecloths over each table, and *someone* had sent flowers to use as centerpieces. "We've got everything ready. All we need now is Mom and Dad, and they'll be arriving in about ten minutes. Just relax."

"Where are the girls at?"

Marshall rose his brows. "Missing your girly friend, are you? We just saw her this morning."

"I asked about the *girls*," Wynn said, eyes narrowed. "Girls, plural. Our sisters and Jess and Noelle included. And you can't give me any grief, because you still haven't asked Jess out. Time's ticking, bro. She's going to leave in August, and you'll probably still be dragging your feet."

"It's not that simple, Wynn," Marshall said quietly. "She was hurt in the past by men. She won't even drive. I refuse to hurt her even more."

"Marshall, how do you—"

"Five minutes until showtime," Ember exclaimed as she walked out of the inn's back door, Noelle and Sarah's family and Jess trailing behind. "Wow. You two actually look...good. I'm impressed by the coral ties. Is everyone here?"

"Yes, ma'am." Wynn slipped his arm around Noelle and kissed her forehead. "Who gave you permission to look so pretty?"

Noelle's cheeks pinkened, but she grinned. "You look pretty handsome yourself. Wow. Everything looks amazing, guys. And even though I don't know any of those people, it looks like everyone showed up, right?"

"You guys are so cute," Ember said with a sigh, looping her arm through Marshall's and leaning her head against his bicep. "Some day, there is going to be a man in my life that makes me smile like that."

"Not for a long, long time," Marshall said. "I'm not ready to have my little sister be on her little love island yet. And for the record, Wynn and I will be just as instrumental as Dad is when it comes to okaying your future man."

Sarah, wearing a long pink dress that matched Sadie's, smiled as she cradled Will to her chest. "Whoever he is, he'll be a very lucky man for our Ember. But right now, Em, Mom and Dad are probably pulling up and you should—"

"I'm going!" Ember disappeared back into the house.

"Here goes nothing," Marshall said.

Wynn glanced down at Noelle, who wrapped her arms around his waist. She looked beyond beautiful in a pinkish dress that hit just below her knees with buttons all the way down its front. Her blonde hair had been curled, and it fell in loose waves over her bare shoulders. Whatever perfume she'd used was just as sweet as her.

"Oh, they're coming," Sarah hissed, motioning for everyone to be quiet. "On the count of three. One, two, three!"

"Surprise!"

Mom and Dad halted in their tracks as soon as they stepped outside, and both of them wore equal expressions of shock. After a moment, Dad set his hand on his wife's back and guided her out, and Mom covered her mouth as she reached out to embrace each of her children, mumbling words of amazement and gratitude and surprise.

"You guys!" Tears glistened in her eyes, making her words watery. "How did you do all of this without us knowing? And my brothers and our friends and—How did you do it?"

Wynn hugged his mother tightly. "We have our ways, Mom. It happened to be that we also had an event planner on hand, so as much as the four of us would like to, we can't take all the credit."

"Oh, my babies." Mom hugged him again, then moved onto Noelle. "Thank you so much. You guys! I can't believe you did this."

Dad came next, and though his emotions weren't as forthcoming as Mom's, his voice was choked up as he hugged Wynn. "Thank you, son. All of you, I guess. It's not real often that kids get to surprise their parents like this. I'm impressed. And blessed. So very blessed."

"Go talk to your friends, guys," Ember said, nudging their parents towards the tables of waiting people. "Some of them traveled to get here, and they want to talk to you. Marsh and Wynn made the food, me and Sarah did décor, and Noelle got music, which will start after the speech. But go and have fun, party people. Tonight is your night completely off from the inn and any and all..." Her voice drifted off as she led their parents away.

"Mommy, can we get food?" Sadie stood up on the toes of her shiny pink flats. "I'm hungry, Mommy. Daddy, can we get food?"

Sarah passed Will to her husband, then took her daughter's hand. "Well, it just so happens that I'm hungry too. Let's go see what Uncle Wynn and Uncle Marshall made, shall we?"

"If it's not good, Wynn made everything," Marshall called after them. He winked at Jess. "Shall we get some food, Jessie J?"

Jess smiled and nodded, and Marshall brought up something about the cake she had made as they followed the others, leaving Wynn and Noelle alone under the pergola.

"Hey, you pulled it off," Noelle said, reaching up to straighten his tie. "And the food smells amazing. I have to admit, though, I'm most excited about dessert. Sorry."

Wynn made a mock pouty face. "That's fine. I'm fine. I'll be fine. Don't worry about me. I'll just eat my hamburger while you eat the cake. It's fine."

Noelle laughed and pressed onto her tiptoes to kiss his cheek. "You're cute, Wynn Bryant."

He grinned as he let her lead him by the hand to the buffet style table filled to overflowing with food.

"Over the years, I've learned a lot from my parents," Wynn said into the microphone, his hands tucked into the pockets of his black dress slacks. "And while I like to think they thought of me as the angel growing up, my siblings may not appreciate that very much."

Noelle laughed along with everyone else, and tears came to her eyes as she glanced around. Because of the love this one couple shared, they were all here today. The lake sat as a beautiful backdrop, and Benji strummed lightly on the guitar as Wynn gave the speech he'd prepared. One he hadn't allowed anybody to read beforehand, even when Noelle had offered to get him a container of butter pecan ice cream just for him.

"But I think the real angel of our family is my mother," he continued after the laughter had died down. "Heaven knows the four of us were anything but angels growing up, and my mom still treated us with love and tenderness and respect. I remember one time in particular when we were just having one of those days. You know the ones where everyone is just moody for no apparent reason? It was one of those. I think Sarah was about sixteen, I was thirteen, and Marshall was nine. We didn't have Ember yet. It was hot out and the AC wasn't working, so we had guests who were hot and we were hot—and I think you get what I'm saying. We were all irritated, which, in the hospitality business, is a bad deal. So the day wore on, and then the final straw was drawn when we were having supper and Marshall decided to dump his water on me.

"And even though she probably wanted to, Mom didn't get mad. In fact, she just smiled real calmly and continued eating. Let me tell you, that was absolutely worse than her yelling or screaming at us. Then Dad walked in—he'd still been trying to fix the AC—took one look at me and Marshall, and asked, 'Why didn't you wait for me to play in the water?'"

Another round of laughter, but this time Jackie reached over and rubbed her husband's shoulder and Marshall's cheeks had turned bright red.

"Later, I asked Mom about it," Wynn went on. "And she told me that there are some things in life that'll upset you. Make you mad, even. But it's usually not worth wasting your time on those things. Confront them when necessary, she told me, but don't let the little mix-ups get in the way of the bigger plan. And while I'm nowhere *close* to as good as Mom of doing that, she sets the stage for how everyone should be. And then there's my dad."

Noelle swallowed as Wynn paused, his gaze searching out his father. She knew the bond between father and son was deep, but based on the apparent tears in both of their eyes, it was even deeper yet.

"As everyone here knows, Dad had a pretty bad accident twenty or so years ago," Wynn said. "And even though I could talk about that, about his drive and his comeback, that's not what I wrote down to say tonight. It's not what I'm going to share with you. Just recently, I was asked to do something that, quite frankly, scared me to death. Mostly because it meant stepping outside of my comfort zone, and I'm not huge into that sort of thing. But anyway, Dad being the Dad he is told me this: 'The best way to make a decision is to pray. The best answers come from the Lord.' And I'm certainly no pastor—why my siblings even decided to put me behind this mic, I have absolutely no idea—but my dad has never, *ever* failed to lead my mom, my siblings, and I to God. His answers, as he often told us, weren't his but they were God's. He used that reasoning mostly when he was telling us no about something we wanted, but that's beside the point. What I'm trying to say is that my father has shown me many, many times how to be a man. And not only that, but a man of God. I'm not saying he's perfect, but in my eyes, he's pretty close to it. I love you, Mom and Dad. Happy thirty-fifth wedding anniversary!"

Noelle smiled as she clapped along with everyone else, blinking back tears as Wynn came back to the table and hugged both of his parents. He looked more handsome than ever in his slacks and a white dress shirt with his coral tie, and as he hugged his dad, the resemblance between the two was uncanny.

"Your speech was amazing," she told Wynn as he sat back down next to her. "It was really sweet."

Wynn rested his hand on her shoulder and released a breath. "If I never have to do that again—be on a figurative stage—I won't. But thank you."

"Were you just *trying* to make me cry?" Jackie wiped the corner of her eye, her tender expression purely maternal as she looked at her oldest son. "Because if so, you did very well."

"Maybe I should've done the speech," Marshall teased. "Then my mama would look at me like that."

Ember rolled her eyes. "She already looks at you like that, Marsh, and you know it. But yeah, good job, Wynn."

John stood and held out his hand. "May I have this dance, Jackie Bryant? I believe our song is playing."

"I would love nothing more," Jackie replied, her smile radiant as ever as her husband—equally as handsome as both of his sons in a charcoal suit and baby blue shirt—led her over to the dance floor. Jackie's light yellow dress fluttered around her calves as John twirled her around and into his arms, then she laughed as he leaned down and whispered something to her.

Wynn cleared his throat, then stood and held out his own hand. "Well, we wouldn't want them to be all alone out there. Would you like to dance, Miss Carter?"

Smiling, Noelle slipped her hand into his. "I would love to."

CHAPTER
Thirty Eight

"Out of all the parties I've done, I think this one is my favorite," Noelle said, her hands resting on Wynn's chest as they danced. "Mainly because of your parents. They're just so…in love. I guess that's inspiring to me."

Wynn's face was soft in the dim light of the Edison bulbs Sarah and Ember had strung overhead. "They are. And they always have been, but their relationship deepened after the accident. Which is understandable. I've taken things for granted, I still do, but that reminder always gives me a swift kick in the rear. Especially when it comes to people. Not so much for belongings."

"How could it not, though? I mean, I'm amazed at your family's strength. And your dad…" She shook her head. "I'm just amazed. That's all."

"Some days, I wonder how in the world my parents were able to do what they did in their pasts. I mean, Mom became an attorney and practiced family law for several years, and Dad was a cop. Pretty sure I'd flunk out in both professions. And the fact that they both, in their own time, gave up those jobs to open an inn and homeschool their children…sometimes it makes sense why people are weirded out by us."

Noelle laughed. "Maybe they can think you're weird, but that doesn't mean they should treat you like some of them do. The fact that your parents went so much against the grain is inspiring in its own way. My grandparents did that by homeschooling me and allowing me to work my way up in the company rather than going to college."

"True." He grinned. "I'm sort of happy they did, and I'm really happy your grandmother was from here, because otherwise we might not be here today. And that would just be plain sad."

"It would, huh? And why is that?"

Wynn smirked, his arms tightening around her. "Oh, let's see here. Because there's a good chance our mayor wouldn't have asked you to plan the Spring Fling, meaning you would have never had a reason to come here, and that means we never would've met."

"Oh, but we could've. What if I'd…been in the mood to come stay at a cute inn on a lake in this cute little town?"

"Not impossible, but doubtful."

"Or maybe you would've decided to come to Jackson because you wanted to see a whole different part of the country."

"Okay, that one's pretty unlikely. Unless it was for you, I can't say I have a reason to go to Jackson. I'm not much of a city guy, to be honest with you."

She feigned a pout. "Does that mean you wouldn't want to visit LA? I heard they have this super neat construction expo every year, and they show you how to build skyscrapers. Maybe you could start a skyline in Balsam Falls, and that would probably get far more tourism than The Gardens ever will, because—"

"Not interested," Wynn mumbled as he leaned down and kissed her. "And yeah, in case you were wondering, that was definitely rambling."

Noelle smiled as he kissed her again. "Maybe I was rambling on purpose. And there might be, but I've never heard of a construction expo in LA, so that was a lie."

"Feeling sneaky tonight, huh?" Wynn lifted his head, crinkles fanning from the corners of his eyes. "Did my sisters give you a pep talk or something on dating their brother? I mean, I'm not complaining, but I would like to know for future reference. You know, for whenever some dude comes in and Ember thinks he's all wrong for her and then he's not and I get proven right. I'd also love to be proven right about Marshall and Jess, but I'm not sure about those two."

"Maybe you should be." She nodded towards where Marshall and Jess were dancing. "They look pretty close to me."

Wynn glanced over his shoulder, his brows raised when he turned back to her. "Well, we can only hope they come to their senses. Marshall's known to be the more outgoing and laidback brother to most, but around Jess that tends to change. Not entirely. He still jokes and teases and all that, but he's scared of hurting her. Which is great, but it's a little unnecessary. I can't be the only one who sees the connection between them. I *know* I'm not the only one."

"Oh, I think they see it," Noelle said. "But, and I'm speaking from experience here, I know that it can be kind of really scary to put yourself out there. I was terrified when I realized how much I liked you, but it kind of didn't matter because you kissed me and then it was all over."

He chuckled and took her hand to twirl her around once before pulling her over to the cake table where Jess had cut pieces and put them on little plates for anyone's convenience. "Good. It accomplished what I hoped it would. Are you hungry? This cake doesn't deserve to just sit here like this, and all that dancing... I'm just hungry."

"How many pieces have you already had?"

Wynn glanced at her. "Two. Like I said, dancing makes a guy hungry."

"Slow dancing hardly takes any energy at all, Wynn."

"Well then, I have no excuse. Would you like a piece?"

She hesitated, but grabbed a paper plate with a slice of Jess's chocolate cake on it and took it back to the table. The air had cooled off considerably as the evening wore on, clouds gathering over the lake, and she pulled her cardigan from her purse to put it on. Was it going to storm tonight?

"Here, let me help you." Wynn set his fork down and helped her into the sweater, brushing her hair away from her shoulder. "Nice earrings, by the way. Whoever gave those to you has impeccable taste."

"Oh, he does. He also sent me this beautiful bouquet of flowers and this notebook and this love note. It was a wonderful gift to wake up to this morning."

Wynn rose his eyebrows. "A love note, huh? You must really like this guy. What, does he plan parties too? Work in a corner office overlooking a city skyline with a downtown penthouse?"

"No, no, but he does use plans for his jobs that he does. They're far more extensive than *my* plans, that much is for sure."

"Oh, so he's...a Lego master dude? You know, the ones who get paid to come up with the design booklet things with their own brains?"

"Ah, yes. He's very thin and wiry, with glasses and wears hoodies and Converse day in and day out. A geeky kind of guy."

"Wiry?" Wynn made a face. "Really?"

"Yes, really. My vocabulary has been expanded to more impressive adjectives since I've been reading one of the books Ember lent me from her collection."

Wynn groaned. "She didn't get you hooked on those too, did she? Please tell me you didn't get hooked on them. Because I cannot possibly measure up to them, and that alone sets the stage for a failed relationship."

"Excuse me?" Ember herself walked up to the table carrying two cake plates. "Have you read them, Wynn? They don't set the stage for a failed relationship. And both you and Marshall are perfectly suitable to be heroes in books."

"Are both of those pieces for you?" Wynn asked.

Ember sat down at the table and grinned. "Maybe. But that's beside the point. You are a great guy. I mean, any man who takes a girl out for pizza and ice cream and gets her flowers is a total keeper in my book. Pun totally intended."

Noelle giggled at Wynn's exasperated expression. "She's right. You are definitely along the lines of being a perfect hero. You want to know your one fault?"

"Oh, I can't wait to hear this." Wynn's voice dripped with sarcasm, even though he was smiling.

"Um, it's, uh, that you have yet to show me any of your...other projects." Noelle wrinkled her nose. "Sorry. I tried to come up with something clever. That's what I got."

Wynn laughed, stretching his arm around her shoulders. "If that's my only fault, then I guess I'm doing better than I thought I was."

"Way to go," Ember mumbled, her mouth full of cake. "You just inflated his ego. Thanks, Noelle."

Noelle only smiled shyly, but it was the truth—she had yet to discover a fatal flaw to Wynn. Sure, there were certain things about him that were probably considered flaws, just like every human being, but not one that was going to deter her from liking him. Not one that was going to turn her off. And certainly not one that would knock him off the list to be eligible as a hero in one of Ember's love stories.

Loud, insistent knocking paired with a growl of thunder forced Wynn from his otherwise peaceful sleep. He squinted as he tried to get his bearings. What time was it? His fingers were still sleepy and lackadaisical, apparently, because he fumbled to grab his glasses and slide them on as the knocking intensified. Who was banging on his door at—he tapped the top of his alarm clock—two in the morning when it was raining and thundering and lightning?

When whoever it was failed to stop, he groaned and rolled out of bed, pulling on his T-shirt from the night before on his way out the door. Nova trailed behind him, her own growl more menacing than most people expected from a sweet girl like her. Lightning flashed, illuminating a short-ish person on his porch through one of the glass panes on the side of his front door. He hoped Ember hadn't decided she wanted to have a chat in the middle of a rainy night—that had happened before, which was what concerned him.

But really? They'd been at the party until a little after ten, then torn everything down when the clouds got too dark and stormy looking, so did tonight have to be the night for it? He'd see his sister in only a few hours for church, lunch, and whatever came after that. Couldn't she wait?

Wynn motioned for Nova to stay back, then pulled open his door. "Ember, if you—"

It wasn't Ember.

Devin and Sophie stood on his porch, and Devin's hand was raised as if to knock again.

"Devin?" Wynn frowned as he moved aside to let them in and closed the door. "What are you doing here? Let me get you guys some towels. Hang on just a sec."

The shock of seeing the kids on his porch slowly started to subside as he crossed to the hall and pulled two towels from the closet, but it was quickly followed up by a deluge of questions. What were they doing at his house at two in the morning? Why had they come here? Had something happened? Had their dad not come home?

"Here, let's get you two dried off," he said gently. Devin took the towel and dried himself off, but Wynn knelt down to help Sophie. The little girl was wearing pajamas with princesses on them, and she looked partially ready to cry, partially ready to fall asleep right there in his entryway. "Dev, what happened? Why are you here at two in the morn—Did you *walk* all the way here?"

The teen nodded, and the expression on his face was so pained that it made Wynn stand up and pull both kids into his arms, regardless of whether Devin was going to like it or not. Something was wrong, and he needed to find out what, but he couldn't do that when they were wet and cold and clearly shaken up.

"Come on, let's get you guys warmed up," he said softly, guiding them towards the bathroom. He grabbed his phone from the kitchen island and powered it on. "We'll get dried off, and then you can tell me what happened, okay?"

An hour later the kids were clean and in dry clothes—Mom had some of Sadie's clothes that, while a little small, fit Sophie well enough, and Devin wore a pair of Wynn's shorts and a T-shirt, even though he swam in both—and they were seated in Wynn's living room with some saltine crackers. Wynn had called Seth first, who'd fortunately been on duty and come over, then Noelle and his mom. Mom had already gone back to the inn, but Noelle and Seth were still here, and the storm still raged outside.

"When did your dad leave?" Seth asked, seated on the chair next to Wynn's, his notepad open. No part of him was relaxed tonight, from his intense expression to his rigid posture. "Tonight? Or last night, I guess."

Devin nodded. "He c-came home from Johnny's and-and then he got all mad because he found out that w-we had been at The Gardens and he got mad and t-then he left."

Noelle glanced at Wynn from where she sat on the sofa beside Sophie, and her eyes spoke of sadness.

"Did he hurt you guys?" Wynn asked.

Devin shook his head, but his voice trembled as he spoke. "No. B-But I thought he would come back and he didn't and-and then I came here because I didn't know what else to do."

"What time did he leave?" Seth asked. "And thank you for not staying home. That was a good idea, but you could've called me. It's storming outside, Devin. Or called Wynn, I guess."

"He left about eleven," Devin said. His gaze remained glued to the floor. "I'm scared, Seth. What if he—"

Seth held up a hand. "Don't go there, Dev. We don't know what happened. Johnny's is closed now, but he may be at another bar in the area. We'll start there. Did he take the car?"

Devin nodded, his miserable expression saying he knew the repercussions his dad was going to face just for drunk driving alone. He'd said that he always walked to and from the bar, which was how come he hadn't already been picked up.

"And when you say he found out you were at The Gardens, do you mean today or what?"

"He heard from some person at work that I'd been going to hang out with the Bryant brothers all the time," Devin said quietly. "But I don't think it was an employee, 'cause he said the guy ordered a lot of lumber."

Wynn's heart dropped as Seth met his eyes. If it wasn't someone who worked at Dickies, it was probably a client. And the only client who'd be getting a bulk order of lumber that'd tell Robert was George Fleming. Wynn should've known the man would do something after seeing them at Falls Market that day.

"Did he say a name or anything?" Seth's calm inquisition was too polite.

Devin shook his head. "No, but you're smart enough to guess. Or at least I think that's who it would be."

"Yeah, that's what I was afraid of." Seth sighed and slid his pen into its slot on his vest, then glanced at Wynn. "I'm going to take a look around town and, if he's not here, get in contact with some area agencies. I'll keep you posted. Are you okay with the kids staying here until we have more information?"

Wynn stood and gestured to the door. "Yes. Before you go, can I talk to you for a minute? If Noelle doesn't mind being with the kids."

"Go ahead," Noelle said. "We'll be fine."

Seth touched Devin's shoulder before he followed Wynn out onto the porch, and it was clear the pair had a deeper bond than either wanted to admit.

"You don't think he left for good, do you?" Wynn asked, even though he'd rather not know.

"No, but if he was at Johnny's like Devin said he was, he's already had plenty of booze," Seth said, hands on his belt. "Which means he's driving under the influence, and that alone is a big problem. I don't want to know what he's thinking by driving like that, but I'm going to find out. Maybe you could ask Noelle to stay here? Sophie seems to be pretty close to her, and it might help out. Plus, you two are chummy now, and no, I don't want any details."

Wynn let out a soft laugh and rubbed his hands down his cheeks. "You sure?"

"Do I look unsure?"

"Maybe."

Seth gave him a dark look.

"Fine, I'll refrain. And yes, I'll ask her. Any tips on how to handle Devin?"

"Nah. You've got it under control." Seth clapped Wynn's shoulder. "Thanks, Wynn. This helps a lot. I'll let you know if and when I know something more."

Wynn nodded, then sent up a silent prayer for protection over everyone as Seth walked down the steps into the rain.

CHAPTER
Thirty Nine

Somewhere around four Seth sent a message to let Wynn know there were no new updates on Robert's whereabouts, and Wynn relayed the message to Devin. Noelle and Sophie had both fallen asleep curled up on the sofa, but Wynn wasn't even close to being able to do so, and neither was Devin. Very little conversation had been exchanged since Seth left, but Wynn could tell there was something more Devin wanted to say. He only hoped it wasn't that his father had been abusive in some way, shape, or form.

"Wynn?"

Wynn straightened in his chair, meeting Devin's tired gaze. "Yes?"

"It was my brother," the teen said quietly. "The one who abandoned us."

Shock rippled through Wynn, and he did his best to not let it show on his face as he tried to come up with a response. Devin and Sophie had another sibling?

With You I Am

"My dad was married before, and he had a son with her before they got divorced," Devin went on, his eyes glued to the floor now. "He's ten years older than me. We hardly look alike though. His mom is white."

"And he abandoned you?" Wynn was struggling to piece it together.

"He left when he turned eighteen to go into the military and he never came home. He *promised* me he would always be there. He promised!"

Wynn closed his eyes, wishing he could take away the pain Devin was feeling. He wished he could lift it from his thin shoulders, relieve him of the heavy burden. But he couldn't. Not really.

"Devin. . ." He cleared his throat. "I'm sorry."

Because really, what else could he say?

"He didn't die, if that's what you think. Or at least we never heard that he did. He just never came back." A tear rolled down Devin's cheek, and he wiped it away quickly. "He left after Mom died when he promised me he'd never leave me—leave *us*, but he did. And if you try to find a reason for my dad to be locked up, I won't let it happen. I won't leave Sophie. Not ever."

"I get that, Devin, but if your dad is doing something he—"

"He's not!" Devin's thunderous words were punctuated by him jerking to his feet and running out the back door.

Wynn let out a weighty sigh, thankful the girls were still asleep, and stood, his muscles protesting the movement from the previous morning's work and the dancing last night. He adjusted the blanket over Sophie and Noelle, then leaned down and kissed Noelle's head before he took a deep breath and went outside, praying Devin hadn't taken off. The last thing they needed right now was to have Robert and his son missing. The circumstances were dire enough as it was.

Great, he'd used the word dire. Maybe he was more fit for those romance novels of Ember's than he thought he was.

284

But Devin hadn't run off. He was sitting on the top step of Wynn's back deck, his elbows propped on his knees and his head in his hands. The rain had mostly subsided, but water dripped from the eaves and the trees. It also pooled on the wooden deck, but Wynn wasn't nearly as concerned about getting his clothing wet as he was about Devin, so he sat down beside the teen. He rested his own elbows on his knees and clasped his hands, not saying anything. He had a feeling Devin needed to be the one to speak up first, even if it was challenging to not ask questions or try to offer up advice.

"Justin was who I looked up to when I was little," Devin finally said, his voice hoarser than normal as he lifted his head. "Even though he was so much older than me, he always hung out with me and did stuff and even would teach me stuff when Mom and Dad were at work and we were home from school. We used to sing together and we'd record songs on his phone, and he'd teach me the piano, 'cause his mom had taught him when he was young. And then he enlisted and we haven't seen him since."

"What branch did he go into? Marines, Army...?"

"Marines." Devin met Wynn's gaze then, and even in the dim lighting, Wynn could tell they were bloodshot from crying and a lack of sleep. "My dad won't even talk about him anymore, but I know it broke his heart just as much as Mom dying did. And I don't know how to help him. I don't want to lose my dad too, Wynn. I can't lose him!"

Regardless of what Devin would think, Wynn reached out and pulled him into a hug again, holding him tightly as the teen's thin body shook, his tears soaking Wynn's shirt. Tears came to Wynn's own eyes and he squeezed them shut, praying that God would prevent Robert from making any foolish decisions tonight. Praying that He would give Wynn the words to say to the hurting boy in his arms. Praying for the older brother who, in the midst of his own pain, had chosen to abandon the ones who had needed him most.

"What if he crashes or he does something that he can't fix or he—"

With You I Am

"Devin, don't go there," Wynn interrupted, his voice firm. "Do *not* go there. It's not worth it. Whatever happens, it's going to be okay. God's got this, okay? He's got you, He's got Sophie, He's got your brother, and He's got your dad."

"Then where has He been all this time? Why does He let my dad keep going to the bar if He really cares?"

Wynn pursed his lips, pondering the right words. "He's there, Dev. But your dad may not be letting Him in, which always makes it seem like He's not around. You promise me your dad doesn't abuse you and Sophie?"

His question was met with silence.

"Devin?"

"He's never laid a hand on either of us," Devin whispered, moving out of Wynn's embrace. "His words...they hurt sometimes. I always try to not say very much and then it doesn't last long because I know he's drunk and he won't really remember it. But when he came home last night." He shook his head, his cheeks tear-streaked. "I've never seen him that mad. 'Course, he left before it could get real heated."

"Part of that is my responsibility," Wynn said. "We shouldn't have kept it from him. I'll give him that much."

Devin shook his head. "Trust me, that really has nothing to do with it. Kind of, but not really. We hardly see him during the day, Wynn. To be honest, within the past month we've spent more time with you than with our own dad. We see him for about an hour or so every day. You spending time with me and Sophie... I didn't ever want to admit it, but I liked it too much. And that's why I was scared. For Sophie, but only because I know how it feels to be abandoned, and I don't want to see her go through that. She was only two when Justin left. It was right before we came to town, and ever since then..."

"Your dad's been practically absent," Wynn finished. "Right?"

Devin nodded. "But Seth didn't really start noticing us or him until a few months before he introduced us to you. Sophie got really attached to him in that short amount of time."

286

"Well, even though I know where you're coming from, I'm not going anywhere. So long as you're around, I'll be here. And I'm sure you've thought about what's going to happen when Noelle leaves. Believe me, I'm in the same boat. But we may not know that until the time comes. Which means we have to trust that——"

"Let me guess: God's got it?" A flicker of humor flashed in Devin's dark eyes.

Wynn bumped his shoulder against Devin's. "Ha. So funny. Listen, Dev, I don't know what Seth will find out, but I want you to be prepared for the reality that he won't be letting him get off with driving under the influence. So if you need some space or time alone, just say the word and I'll give that to you."

His statement, like the question earlier, was met with silence.

Wynn offered an understanding smile, then started to stand, but Devin's words stopped him.

"Will you pray with me? I don't really know how, but maybe you can help me."

Masking his surprise with a nod, Wynn sat back down and held out his hands. Devin placed his in them, and they both bowed their heads as the first hesitant rays of dawn began to rise in the east.

Noelle's first thought upon waking up was actually a question. When had her warm, comfortable bed become so…uncomfortable? She blinked, rolling her neck as she sat up. Where was she? Light immediately assaulted her and she slammed her eyes shut as she tried to figure out the answer to that question.

Then she heard Wynn's and Seth's voices, and all the events from the wee hours of the morning came rushing back to her in record speed. The party. The thunderstorm. Wynn's phone call. Devin saying that his dad had left hours before. Curling up on the sofa with Sophie. If anything else had happened, she didn't know about it. How had she fallen asleep? She'd been wide awake when Wynn woke her up with the news that Devin and Sophie had shown up on his doorstep.

Careful not to disturb the still-sleeping Sophie, Noelle eased out from under the blanket as her eyes slowly adjusted to the sunlight coming in through the windows. She wrapped her cardigan around herself and crossed to the entryway. Wynn wore shorts and a T-shirt, but Seth was still in his uniform. Had he been working all night?

Also, her hair must look terrible. All that leftover hairspray—because Ember had used a *lot* of it—paired with that terrible sleeping position? Not exactly a good combination.

"Hey, Noelle," Seth said with a tight smile. "I'm glad to see that you guys got some shut eye."

Wynn slipped his arm around her waist, his presence warm and solid and familiar. "Devin is sleeping in the room across from mine. Did you sleep okay?"

"Aside from my position, yes," she said, yawning. Even with having that kink in her neck, she must've slept pretty hard. "Are there any updates? Did you find Robert?"

Seth nodded. "Yes. He'd driven about a mile and a half out of town and parked off on the side of a dirt road off the highway. I have no idea how he managed to stay on the road that long, because he had plenty of alcohol in his bloodstream, but he did. He was out cold when they found him. I doubt he'll be feeling real good when he wakes up. He was feeling *too* good when they brought him in to me."

Noelle released a breath she felt like she'd been holding since Wynn had called her. "Oh, thank God."

"But that doesn't mean we're out of the woods," Seth continued. "We're most definitely not. I have more than enough evidence, which means that Clark will not be released anytime soon. And that means that I get to notify CPS. I have to, legally."

Wynn stiffened beside her, and the muscle in his arm tightened. "They aren't going to take the kids, are they? I'll keep them until...whenever. You can't make them go into CPS."

"Believe me, I would rather not, but that's part of my job. If I don't report it, I'm going to get in trouble. Not to mention that

Clark has left the kids alone for prolonged periods of time between when they were in school and when he got home from work, then again when he went to the bar. Since they were with you, I let that go for the time being. But the DUI…I just can't let this one slip. I wish I could just snap my fingers to make it all better, but that's impossible."

"Then what do I need to do to get temporary guardianship or whatever it is? I won't let them go into the system, Seth. I won't."

Seth released a heavy sigh. "I admire your—"

"Did you find my daddy?"

All three of them jerked at the sound of Sophie's sleepy voice, and Noelle squatted down as the little girl ran over to her for a hug. Even if she had a knot in her neck, she didn't regret sleeping on the sofa. Not when she'd had Sophie snuggled up next to her, sleeping soundly after what had been a turbulent night.

After a moment, she stood but she kept her hand on the girl's shoulder as Sophie clung to her leg.

"Well?" Devin appeared next, his expression hopeful and a little more rested than earlier. "Are you going to answer her question?"

Seth shifted, his own face completely void of emotion. "Yes, we found him. But right now, I need you guys to stay with Wynn, okay? Are you all right with that, Sophie?"

Sophie nodded, her grip on Noelle's leg tightening. "Uh-huh."

"Good." Seth nodded towards the door. "Devin and Wynn, can I have a word on the porch, please?"

It shouldn't be, but the main thing on his mind as Wynn stepped out and closed the door behind him was just how maternal Noelle looked standing there with Sophie. She'd welcomed her so naturally it was as if she'd grown up with the best motherly role model a person could have. But she hadn't. And yet, she hadn't hesitated at all when Sophie came running towards her.

"He's in trouble, isn't he?" Devin asked, bringing Wynn back to the present.

Seth rested his hands on his belt. "Yeah. He is."

"Is he okay? Physically, I mean."

"Other than being hammered, yes, he's physically unharmed and nobody else was harmed." Seth filled Devin in on what he'd told Wynn and Noelle only minutes ago. "...and I have to report it to CPS. There's no way to get around it."

Devin's eyebrows drew together. "Can't we just stay here? If Wynn will let us, I guess. I don't want Sophie to be taken away from me. I won't let her go through what I did when my brother left me."

Seth's surprised gaze swung to Wynn, then he looked at Devin. "Your brother?"

Okay, so maybe Wynn should've filled him in on that as soon as Devin had told him, but they'd prayed and then he'd settled Devin into bed and he'd hardly made it to his own bed before falling asleep. And that had been less than three hours ago. In his defense, Seth hadn't told Wynn right away that they'd found Robert Clark, so there was that.

"Devin?" Seth prompted.

With a quick glance at Wynn, Devin cautiously explained a shorter version of what he'd told Wynn earlier. It still hadn't fully processed that Devin and Sophie had another sibling, but Wynn blamed that on lack of sleep and too much going on to have retained full thinking capacity.

"So you have no way of contacting him?" Seth had taken out his notebook and was writing something down.

Devin shook his head. "I haven't seen him for five years, Seth. What, do you think I have him on Facebook or something?"

"No. Do you actually have Facebook?"

"Ew. No." The teen wrinkled his nose, arms crossed over his chest. "Facebook is for old people who want to talk about recipes and weather and politics."

Seth shot him a look. "It can also be useful in obtaining certain information, Devin. Your brother's full name is Justin Clark?"

"Yes. You never answered *my* question. Can we stay with Wynn?"

"Dev—"

"*Please* let us stay here," Devin pleaded. "I'll do whatever I have to. But just let us stay here. That's all I'm asking."

There was an extended pause, but Seth finally sighed and tucked his notebook away. "I'll see what I can work out. And that is *not* a promise. Are we clear about that?"

Devin nodded. "Yes."

"All right. Then I'll...talk to you guys later, when I have an update."

After Seth had left, Devin turned and hugged Wynn. All on his own accord. Surprised, it took a minute for Wynn to reciprocate, but as he did, he found himself praying yet again.

CHAPTER
forty

The rest of the day felt like it went by in a blur. Wynn had meant it when he said the kids could stay with him, even if he hadn't considered the fact that it would be a longer process than simply keeping them indefinitely. Since he wasn't a family member and Robert was still their biological father, it could be tricky. But Wynn would do whatever it was going to take if it meant the kids wouldn't go into the foster system.

And the first step, according to a reluctant Seth, was to meet with a social worker. So, as Wynn got dressed Monday morning, he went through what he could possibly say to come across as he genuinely cared—because that was the truth. He did care. A lot.

But the foster system wasn't one that revolved around feelings alone, and he also knew that. Which was why he'd cleaned the house and made sure everything was tidy after the kids had gone to bed last night. Noelle had helped him, and they'd had a little while to talk before she'd gone back to the inn. Seth had mentioned that, if Noelle was planning to be any help with the kids, Noelle should be there during the meeting, so she'd promised to arrive before the social worker was due at nine.

"You're kind of jumpy," Devin said around a mouthful of Lucky Charms. "Are you always that way when you're nervous?"

Wynn adjusted his shirt collar again. "Jumpy? I'm not jumpy. And who said I was nervous?"

"I did," Devin said.

"I think the muffins are burning," Sophie observed.

Wynn spun around and yanked a dish towel from the handle of the oven before he pulled it open. A plume of heat and smoke went straight into his face and he waved it away before grabbing the pan. Hopefully this social worker didn't mind crispy muffins, because the edges were clearly that. And then some.

"I think they're eatable." Wynn set the pan on a cooling rack, closed the oven door, and glanced at the kids. "They don't look too bad, right?"

Devin rose an eyebrow but he merely took another bite of his cereal.

"Well, it's too late to make a new batch." Wynn gathered Sophie's empty bowl and rinsed it out. "Can you go brush your teeth please, Sophie? Seth and the social worker will be getting here in about fifteen minutes."

Sophie slid down from the barstool, but she didn't move. "Noelle's coming, right? She told me she was gonna come."

Wynn knelt down in front of her and smiled. He'd learned that Sophie was far less intimidated by men when they were near her height. "She's coming, sweetheart. Any minute now, actually. I'll bet that, if you go brush your teeth, she'll be here when you come back out."

"What if she's not?"

Oh, the inquisitive nature of kids. "If not, then she'll get here right after. Sound good?"

Sophie nodded, hesitated a moment, then took off for the bathroom. Wynn's mother had gone to the store and bought kids' toothbrushes and Seth had swung by their house to get some clothing yesterday. He'd also called the school to notify them that the kids wouldn't be there Monday, which was today. And even though Wynn had skipped on church for the kids' sakes yesterday, he didn't think he'd ever felt as close to God as he had when Devin had asked him to pray with him.

"I probably should've asked you if we could stay here before telling Seth that," Devin said, his cereal gone. "Sorry."

"I had already told him you could—that I wanted you to. So actually, by you saying that, I think there's a better chance." Wynn shrugged. "Not that I know anything about these kinds of situations. I really don't. But right now, can you rinse your bowl out and put it in the dishwasher, then go and brush your teeth for me?"

Devin, to Wynn's amazement, didn't complain as he did what Wynn had asked him to. At least they'd cleared the whole trust hurdle. If they hadn't, Wynn doubted he'd have a fighting chance of becoming the kids' temporary guardian. As it was, him being a single man who had no familial tie to the kids meant it would be a process. He couldn't recall everything Seth had told him yesterday, but he had little doubt the social worker would refrain from laying it all out there. Probably more than once.

At seven to nine, there was a knock on the door before Noelle walked in. She wore a pink sundress with a cardigan and sandals, and her hair was pulled into a loose braid.

"Good morning." Wynn leaned down to kiss her. "Sleep well?"

Noelle smiled. "Honestly, not really. I was too anxious for today. You?"

He let her go before him into the kitchen. "Same. But as far as I know, the kids slept well. I got up early to make a batch of muffins and, well, my intentions were good, but they got a little burnt."

"Oh, I'm sure they'll taste great. Better than mine would." Noelle's face lit up as Sophie ran down the hall and straight into Noelle's open arms. "Good morning, Soph. No running in the house though, okay?"

Sophie glanced up at Wynn with a shy but ornery smile, then grinned up at Noelle. "My teeth are all clean now. Can you see?"

"Oh, wow." Noelle held a hand over her eyes. "Soph, those are so bright I can't even look at them. What kind of toothpaste did Wynn get you?"

Wynn wiped the island off before draping the washcloth over the sink divider. "Don't look at me. Mom got it for me."

"Does this look okay?" Devin emerged from the hall, his face unsure as he gestured to his khakis and a blue polo. "The pants are kind of short, but it's all I've got."

"It looks very respectable, Dev," Wynn said just as there was a knock on the door. His pulse quickened. "All right, guys. Just be yourselves and *please* be honest, okay?"

Both kids nodded, and Noelle smiled as she stood with a hand on each of their shoulders. Wynn took a deep breath, then found what he hoped was a friendly smile as he pulled the door open. Seth stood there in uniform, and a middle-aged woman with a tighter than tight bun on her head, a no-nonsense expression on her face, and wearing a gray pencil skirt and jacket stood beside him. She had a leather bag looped over one shoulder-padded shoulder, and her eyes were serious behind her thin glasses.

"Deborah Hunter, this is Wynn Bryant," Seth said. "Wynn, Deborah Hunter."

Wynn held out his hand and the woman took it. Hesitantly. "Nice to meet you, Mrs. Hunter."

"Miss," Deborah corrected, withdrawing her hand. He had the strong feeling she wished she could squirt some hand sanitizer on it from the way she brushed it off on her clothing.

Okay. "Yes, of course. Please, come in." He stepped aside to allow them in, and Seth shot him an apologetic look before he quickly switched back to his trademark Seth expression. Wynn gestured to the kids and Noelle. "Miss Hunter, this is Devin, Sophie, and Noelle. Everyone, this is Deborah Hunter."

The social worker nodded stiffly, but Wynn didn't miss how her gaze roamed around his house and he was suddenly very relieved he'd been able to clean. His house was never messy—not even when his family descended on it for the evening or day or whatever—but he had a feeling Deborah Hunter would judge him based on a throw pillow out of place.

Fortunately, he knew how to style throw pillows. But only because of the houses he and Marshall had done, and thanks to his mom and sisters.

"While I don't have a formal dining table, we can sit in the living room or on the back deck," Wynn said, hoping to fill the lag in conversation. "I have some lemonade and muffins made up. Excuse the little bit of..." He trailed off at Seth's slight shake of his head. "Anyway, whatever you prefer. Just let me know."

Deborah peered up at him—not through the lenses of her glasses. "I would prefer to take a look at your house before we talk."

"Yes. Right. Of course." *God, a little help here?* "Do you want me to show you to the rooms? Or you're welcome to just look around on your own."

"No, thank you. I'll ask if I need something. Do you have a basement in this house, Mr. Bryant?"

Wynn shook his head. "Not a full one. Only a storm cellar and a small storage room. That's the last door at the end of the hall to your right."

Deborah nodded curtly and her heels clicked on the floor as she disappeared down the hallway.

"She's a barrel of fun," Devin whispered after the woman had disappeared, smirking.

Seth shot him a look—one that did little to hide his own amusement. "Yeah, well, you'd best be on good behavior if you want this to work out."

Devin held up his hands. "I'm just saying."

Wynn exchanged a look with Noelle, but he did his best to stay neutral a few minutes later as Deborah came back out and continued to the other hallway.

Whatever happened, he would know he tried.

Noelle didn't particularly like Deborah Hunter's demeanor, but she supposed it took a pretty strong personality to be a social worker. There were a lot of different situations, different levels of intensity, but none of them were exactly pretty. Even in this case, who knew how long it would be before Robert was allowed to see his kids and vice versa. Nobody but God, she guessed. Unless Robert made some drastically different choices, it wouldn't be anytime soon.

But sitting between Wynn and Sophie at the outdoor table on Wynn's deck, she felt like she was being scrutinized. Every move, every cautious but honest word.

"So, let me get this straight," Deborah said evenly, her pen poised over her notebook. "You've been 'babysitting' these kids, and now that their father is in jail, you just want to have them come live with you? You're not married, and you don't have a foster license."

"Correct," Wynn said, his voice ever so calm. Too bad looks couldn't influence Deborah, because Wynn looked great. Clean-shaven, clear-eyed, and well dressed. And if they went there, Noelle doubted the social worker could match his evident physical strength. Her puffy shoulder pads paled in comparison to Wynn's noticeable biceps and broad shoulders. "I would rather them stay with someone they know and trust than possibly be separated and placed elsewhere. This way they'll be able to stay in school, Officer Johnson can monitor the situation, and they'll be together."

Deborah seemed to think about that for a moment. "How long have you known these children?"

"About a month or so," Wynn answered without hesitation. "We're restoring a city property, and Devin has been a huge helper with painting and landscape work and whatever else my brother and I need help with. And Sophie loves to hang out while we're working with my mom or sister or Noelle. While that project will be done in a month or so, we would still be able to have a similar schedule. My parents fostered and then adopted my youngest sister."

"And how long ago was that? Have they kept their foster license up?"

Wynn shook his head. "It was ten years ago, and no, they haven't."

"I see." Deborah took a note, then turned her attention to Devin. "Officer Johnson told me you want to stay here. Why is that?"

Devin glanced uncertainly at Wynn, who nodded, then met the social worker's gaze. "Because I trust him. He listens to me, he never has tried to raise his voice or hurt me or Sophie, and I know that we would be safe here."

Noelle couldn't prevent the little burst of happiness she felt at Devin's explanation, especially because she remembered the day he'd walked out of The Gardens with Sophie and Wynn hadn't expected him to come back. Now here they were, Wynn selflessly opening his home to these kids. Not to mention the fact that Devin had decided to come *here* to Wynn's house rather than go somewhere else. He could've gone to the police station or not even decided to tell anybody that their dad had left.

"...and your relationship with Mr. Bryant is?"

Noelle blinked, trying to process the question that was obviously directed at her. "Oh, um. Sorry. We're...dating."

"So there's no engagement or marriage?"

Hadn't they already covered that? "No," Wynn answered. Still as calm and collected as Noelle wished she could be. "There's not. But according to my research, it's not a requirement to be married. Correct?"

"Well, yes, but—Never mind." Deborah tidied her already tidy papers and directed her gaze in Sophie's direction. "And you? Would you like to stay here?"

Sophie's head bobbed up and down. "Uh-huh. Mr. Wynn makes yummy food. I like his cereal. It has marshmallows."

A bowl of Lucky Charms probably didn't constitute as making food, but aside from the blackened muffins in the middle of the table, Wynn was an excellent cook. Prior to this chain of events, he'd promised to give Noelle a few cooking lessons.

Those weren't anywhere near the importance level of this.

"So you trust him, then?" Deborah pressed.

Sophie looked up at Noelle, her gaze worried as she slowly nodded. "Uh-huh. He takes good care of us, and helps Devin lots."

"I see," Deborah said for what seemed like the hundredth time. "Officer Johnson, do you trust him? Mr. Bryant, that is."

Seth nodded. "Absolutely. He would never do anything to harm the children, and I trust that he can meet their needs financially and emotionally. If it's possible, I would rather see them stay here than go into the foster system, like Wynn mentioned before."

There was a stretch of silence while Deborah scribbled away on her notepad. What she could possibly have to write down, Noelle had no clue, but she wrote fast. And tiny, from the looks of it. How did she have so much to put on paper?

Sophie tugged on Noelle's arm. "Did I do okay?"

Aware of the fact that Deborah's hand had stopped moving, Noelle smiled at the little girl. "You told the truth, right?"

"Uh-huh."

"Then yes." Noelle put her arm around Sophie's shoulders. "You answered perfectly, honey."

Sophie beamed at her.

Deborah cleared her throat. "All right, then. I'll do what I need to and then drop by in the next day or two to go over with what you will need to do, Mr. Bryant. Is there a specific time that works best for you?"

Noelle could hardly contain her excitement, but she stayed quiet and sat still as Wynn and the social worker discussed a time to meet. Then Deborah collected her things and said she would see herself to the door.

"Well, there you have it." Seth clapped Wynn's shoulder as they all stood. "Don't forget that meeting, by the way, and be prepared for unexpected visits from here on out."

Wynn nodded, his hands resting on each of the kids' shoulders. "Got it. Thank you, Seth. I appreciate it."

"Of course," Seth replied "I'll see myself out."

"So we get to stay here?" Sophie asked, gazing up at Wynn.

Noelle thought her heart might burst from the adoration in the seven-year-old's eyes.

"Yes, Sophie, you are going to stay here," he replied, his smile gentle. "You're sure you're okay with that?"

Sophie's nod was enthusiastic. "Uh-huh. Can we have a snack now? I get hungry when there's nervous people around."

Wynn laughed and gestured to the door, his gaze catching Noelle's. "Let's go find a snack, and then we'll talk about how the days are gonna go."

———

CHAPTER

Forty One

"Do you ever actually get mad?"

Noelle glanced up from the stack of books she was sorting. "What do you mean?"

"Do you get mad?" Ember repeated, her brow furrowed. A pen stuck out from the messy bun on top of her head. "I mean, you've never even gotten upset in the whole time I've known you."

"Neither have you," Noelle pointed out, unsure of where this conversation was going. They were each sorting returned books, previously in easy silence, to put back on the shelves at the library. "But yes, I guess I do sometimes. I think everyone has their moments here and there. Why?"

Ember hopped up on the library counter, her legs dangling over the edge, and sighed. "I don't know. Well, I do. But I also don't."

Noelle bit her lip. "You might have to give me a little more information than that, Em."

"It's just... I don't know what I want to do." Ember rubbed her hands down her cheeks. "I mean, I see Sarah and she's a stay at home mom with a ridiculously awesome husband who's a

301

successful marketing guy, and Wynn's a successful construction guy who's now taking care of two kids and Marshall's co-owner of that successful construction business and Mom and Dad run an awesome inn and I'm just...here." She blew out what had to be a much-needed breath and picked up one of the books on a sorted pile. One that had a freaky looking snake with a sword on the cover and big block letters for the title. "I volunteer at the library, work part-time at the coffee house, work at my parents' inn and still live with my parents. Nothing stellar there."

"Hey, you're still young. And I lived with my grandparents until just last November. Well, with Grandpa, I guess. If he was still alive, I would probably still be there. Or we would've found a different place together. Plus, you have really awesome parents."

"I know. And I love them. I do. But you know how everyone always asks you what you want to be when you grow up? Well, now I'm technically grown up and here I still don't know. Pathetic, I know, but I...I just don't want to disappoint my parents."

"Not at all what I was thinking, Em," Noelle said. "Do you realize that you've overcome a lot more in your nineteen years than some people in longer than that? I think disappointing your parents is the *last* thing you would have to be concerned about."

Ember rose a brow. "And do you have an example to back up that whole overcoming thing?"

"Well, I mean... No, not actually, but you have. Wynn told me your birth parents were less-than-stellar. He didn't give me details, and this isn't me asking for them. I'm simply telling you that exactly what you're doing is just as important as somebody who has a supposedly lucrative job."

"Less-than-stellar is one way of putting it," Ember mumbled. "And thanks. I know that, I guess. I just wish I had some kind of plan. That I'd know when something will finally click into place and I'll have a passion to wake up and pursue every day. Like you— you get up, excited to plan parties."

Actually, over the past few days of seeing Wynn step selflessly into the role of temporary guardian, a new dream had started forming in her heart. One that she'd thought of briefly in the past, but had never known if she'd make a very good wife or mother. Her grandparents had shared a wonderful marriage and had been wonderful parental figures to her growing up, yes.

But that did not mean she was cut out for it. She'd been born outside of marriage, not to mention that her father nor mother had even tried to have some kind of relationship with her. She was sure her grandparents would've allowed that. Right? They'd never talked about their daughter much—never had they talked about Noelle's dad—but they'd left the door open for the possibility to talk about it. They surely would have worked with Mom to have some kind of arrangement if Mom wanted it.

Ember cleared her throat as she hopped off the counter. "How could I forget to add to Wynn's very *stellar* life that his girlfriend is a party planner and she's clearly as in love with him as he is with her? Huh. I can't believe I forgot that part. Geez, Ember, you're slacking."

Heat flushed Noelle's cheeks and she shook her head. "Who said anything about love? We're taking things slow. Now he's got the kids, and Spring Fling is only a month away. Which means I'll be leaving."

"Have you talked to Wynn about that? I mean, I could be wrong, but I think you like him way more than you're letting on. And I know he likes you, because I know my brother. He isn't the kind of man to be in a 'casual' relationship. I mean, sometimes he's seriously clueless, but you're the only woman who's made him...like this. He's so happy. And that is not because winter's over or because of their business or anything like that. It's because of you."

Noelle couldn't help but doubt the words, even if she knew they were true—that's exactly how she felt. And certainly not because of her work or because of her mom or her dad.

"Yep, you're a goner." Ember grinned as she moved a nonfiction book on football, followed by baseball and basketball ones to a new stack. "See, somebody who checked these books out must be really into sports. And by you just blushing like that, I can tell you're really into Wynn. That's not something that requires any form of rocket science to figure out."

"Did you just compare Wynn and I's relationship to a sports enthusiast? I'm willing to bet you're not even into sports."

Ember shot her a look. "Oh, really? You haven't been around the Bryant family during football season."

"Wait, are you guys actually that into it?"

Ember snorted. "No. But I'm glad I made you think so. The only thing I know about football is that I can't run the length of the field without feeling hyperventilate-y and that there's a quarterback and what the ball looks like. Okay, we should probably get to work. Even though, yes, I know it's my fault for stalling. Thanks again for helping me today. I appreciate it. And Cynthia doesn't mind. I've even had Marsh help me, so trust me, you're a lot better here than him. I'm pretty sure Cynthia only let him stay because she liked staring at his face."

Noelle let out a little laugh.

"And she's probably eighty, so there's that." Ember stacked several piles of books on the cart and glanced at Noelle. "You want to keep sorting or put these away?"

"This place is *huge*," Sophie exclaimed with wide eyes as they walked into Farm to Table. "It goes on forever and ever. And there's green stuff on the wall."

Wynn glanced down at her and smiled, amazed at the trust the little girl had in him. "Those are some of the herbs Joanna uses to cook food here. Where should we sit? Inside, on the roof, or outside?"

"Green stuff, huh?" Devin said quietly. "What kind of operation is going on here?"

Wynn shot him a look and guided the four of them up to the counter. "We'll take a table for four on the rooftop, please."

"No, can we sit out there?" Sophie pointed to the doors leading to the outdoor seating. "Please?"

"I stand corrected," Wynn said. "We'll take a table on the outdoor patio."

The young hostess nodded, grabbed menus, and led them outside. She seated them at a table close to the stage and Benji waved to them. They settled around the table, Wynn in between Devin and Sophie with Noelle across from him. Wynn had hesitated about taking the kids out to eat—it had only been a handful of days since Robert had been caught and Wynn had volunteered to keep the kids temporarily. And though Deborah was clearly not his biggest fan, she'd provided all the necessary documents and classes and resources, and he'd promised to do whatever it took and to keep them as long as he needed to.

So even though a few people gave them odd looks, Wynn didn't care. They'd all had a heck of a week—parenting was nowhere near as easy as Mom and Dad or Sarah and Chris made it out to be— and they deserved a nice meal.

Tonight was not the night for Wynn to prepare that meal, which meant they were going out.

"What is fill-it mig-on?" Sophie's brow drew together, her brown eyes confused.

"Filet mignon?" Wynn repeated, leaning over to see where she was pointing on the menu. "Ah, yes. That's a fancy piece of steak. I myself prefer ribeye, but that's just me."

"Maybe you should find something cheaper, Soph," Devin said quietly, his own gaze on the menu. "That's really expensive."

"Actually, tonight, you each get to order whatever you'd like. So long as you will want to eat it and enjoy it," Wynn said. "My parents always taught me the importance of using money wisely, but they did their best to cut the word 'cheap' from all our vocabularies. They told us that, if a person works hard to earn his money, then he should be able to enjoy what it can buy—as long as it's for good—because everyone else could work just as hard to get there, but they have to do it. And as my dad said, if you have a cheap mindset, you'll have a cheap life. If you have a more-than-enough mindset, and do the work, you'll have a more-than-enough life."

"Your mom and dad are so cool," Sophie exclaimed. "I like them a lot. Your mom showed me how to make cookies today and that was lots of fun. I wish my daddy was like you, Mr. Wynn."

Her words knocked into Wynn with the force of a steam engine, and he offered a weak smile as he nodded to the menu. It was a cop-out, making her look over the menu without responding, but what did he say to that? Robert could be a good man, and he had been before alcohol had taken him over, according to Devin. But Wynn refused to make empty promises on a particular happily ever after. Not when there was no telling whether Robert would decide to change or not.

And if he didn't, then what?

Wynn had a healthy bank account, yes, but to adopt these kids? He would do it in a heartbeat, but money was not the sole factor. There were parental rights and CPS and a mile-long list of other details to consider. Devin, for one thing. Just because he'd wanted to stay with Wynn now didn't mean he'd want that permanently.

After they'd placed their orders and handed the menus back to their waiter, Noelle filled the air with conversation by asking both kids about their school day. She must've sensed that Wynn was trying to process Sophie's words, and that unspoken understanding was only one of the many reasons he was falling for her.

Then there was that. He was falling hard for a woman who, come the end of May, would be leaving. And while they both knew it, they were also both avoiding the conversation where they talked about it. Something that Wynn was more aware of with every day that passed. With every kiss and smile and touch and laugh, he was more aware that this would be coming to an end. His life was here, and Noelle's was in Jackson. He wouldn't ask her to move, and he would seriously consider doing it, but he couldn't. He couldn't move away from the business he and Marshall had built, nor from his family. And not from these kids.

But this moment wasn't for dwelling on what he couldn't change. So he pushed his thoughts to the back of his mind and focused on the present conversation that revolved around Mom and Sophie's cookie baking adventure from this afternoon.

Bellies fully, everyone pushed their plates away and leaned back in their chairs. Noelle probably could've ordered something a little lighter, but everyone else had ordered steak, so who was she to break the chain?

"That was the bestest food ever!" Sophie knelt on her chair, her dress fanning out around her. Wynn had certainly made the evening memorable for the kids by having everyone dress up. Devin and Wynn both wore khakis and polos, and Noelle and Sophie wore sundresses. "I love this place!"

Wynn chuckled and pushed back from the table, setting his cloth napkin on his plate. "I'm glad, Soph. Before we go, I have a question for you, Miss Sophie."

Sophie giggled as she looked up at him. "What is it?"

"Would you like to dance?"

The little girl's eyes widened, but she nodded excitedly and Noelle helped her get her chair back from the table and get down. And then Noelle's heart melted as Wynn picked Sophie up, his left arm supporting her weight as he guided her to put her left hand in his right one. Just like the time she and Wynn had danced here, the dance floor was otherwise empty. Also just like that time, Wynn didn't seem to care. Both his and Sophie's smiles were pure and real and happy. So very happy.

"Hey, Dev, while they're dancing, I'm going to go talk to Joanna for a minute about the food for Spring Fling," Noelle said, forcing her gaze from Wynn and Sophie. "You okay for a few minutes?"

Devin gave her a look. "I'm ten feet from Wynn and Sophie. I'll be fine."

Noelle made a face, but she got up and headed into the restaurant, which was nearly as full as the outdoor dining space.

Conversations hummed in the evening air and tantalizing aromas mingled with the din of voices.

"So I see the rumors are true."

The familiar yet unwelcome voice stopped Noelle in her tracks and she spun around. "What rumors?"

George Fleming sat at a table with what must be one of his sons, his expression as carefully and connivingly articulated as the masterpiece of the elegant entrée on the white plate in front of him. "About Wynn and those kids. He think he can play hero to everyone or what? Reality will set in once you leave and the fairytale is all over."

Whatever warm fuzzies she'd felt only moments ago watching Wynn and Sophie were all but gone, and Noelle refrained from fisting her hands. "He's not 'playing the hero,' Mr. Fleming, and we're very aware of reality. There's no fairytale to be had." Wynn's tender kisses and steady presence certainly made him fairytale-hero material, but that was strictly beside the point.

And even if it wasn't, there was no way on God's green earth that she'd say as much to George Fleming.

"I see." George swirled the whiskey in his glass, an icy glint to his blue eyes. "Oh, my bad. I apologize for not introducing you sooner. This is my son, Trevor. Trevor, this is Noelle Carter."

Noelle didn't care to be introduced to the sly-looking younger man, nor did she like how he looked at her. A look that was nothing like the respectful and loving ones Wynn gave her, and if she never had to run into either of these men again, she would have no hard feelings about it.

"Nice to meet you," she forced out, as cordially as possible. "Have a good evening, gentlemen."

With that, she turned, willing her heart to calm down.

"I know Bryant's eyeballing my land, Miss Carter. And I'll see to it that business is conducted fairly."

The *nerve* of the man! This time, Noelle just kept walking—straight back out to the patio and back to their table. She couldn't recall exactly what she'd wanted to discuss with Joanna, and right now, she just needed to calm down before she had the urge to stomp back in there and give the man a piece of her mind, something that would be very uncharacteristic of her.

It would also be satisfying.

So very satisfying.

CHAPTER
Forty Two

Here they were again, sitting at the two person table near the front window of Cozy & Grounds with Jess's steaming cinnamon rolls before them. Only this time Seth wasn't the only one interested in a woman, nor the only one with two kids who were attached to him.

Wynn was just more willing to admit it than Seth was.

"So it's been going well?" Seth asked as he sprinkled salt over his roll, the early morning sun glaring off his chest badge. "With the kids. I still don't want details on you and Noelle."

"Yeah, it has been. I admit, being a 'dad' is nowhere as easy as I thought, but in some ways it is." Wynn shrugged and cut off a bite. "But you would understand that. How are Jen and the kids?"

Seth glared. "Just because I don't want details of your relationship with Noelle doesn't mean I'm willing to talk about Jenna. The kids are loving the new house. I'll tell you that much."

"Good. I'm glad to hear it. The mural is awesome. Has Jenna picked up any clients yet?"

"Wynn, first of all, nobody's seen the mural yet, and two, you're still fishing for details. I'm not gonna bite." He took a sip of coffee. "I would like to hear exactly how the kids are doing, though. School and all that going okay? No fights or anything?"

Wynn rose his eyebrows. "Fights?"

"Devin is practically a target for bullying right now. I just want to make sure there's none of that going on."

"To my knowledge, no. I will say that the amount of homework even Sophie has is ridiculous. My mom is too nice. She helps them with it when I can't, but even I can hardly figure some of it out."

"Yeah, well, welcome to the educational system. Other than school, how's it going? Any surprise visits from Deborah?"

Wynn let out a breath. "Ha, no. Not yet. That woman scares me. I get having a certain level of professionalism, but yikes. She'd need something stronger than fire to thaw her out."

Seth laughed. "That's true. I felt kind of bad having her assign—"

"No you didn't. Don't lie to me like that."

"Actually, I did. She's…tough to connect with, I'll give you that much. But you passed her tests and she's letting you keep the kids at this time, so that's something."

"True." Wynn took a bite of his cinnamon roll. "As far as other things, we're doing well. No raised voices or real high emotions, so that's a win. You found anything out on their brother?"

Seth shook his head. "Not yet. His tour was probably up last year, so that means he could be anywhere. I checked social media and came up empty. But we'll keep working on that. All we can do."

"You don't think he did die or anything, right?"

"Couldn't be sure, but I doubt it. The family would've been notified. Like I said, we'll keep looking." Seth leaned back in his chair. "Robert has asked about the kids. I haven't given him much information, but I told him they're safe. This is probably the longest he's been sober in about five years."

Wynn nodded. "Bet he's enjoying that, huh?"

"Not quite. Pretty sure reality is setting in. Couldn't say I'd want to be in his shoes. I've been in Devin's before. That's hard enough. My biggest concern is that, if he'd get released, he'd just go running back to the bottle. But if someone comes along with the money..." He shrugged. "Can't do anything to stop them from bailing him out."

The comparison was accurate, only Seth's dad had failed to make different choices, meaning his parental rights had been terminated and custody had been awarded to Elias and Meredith Johnson, their father's brother and sister-in-law. Their dad's choices over the years, from the little Seth or Jess had said, had landed him behind bars over and over. Wynn didn't envy the life Seth had in that sense. He did wish his friend would realize that he was not his father, though. Wynn had his shortcomings, as did Seth, but compassion was not one of them. At least Wynn didn't think so, especially considering Seth's compassion lurking under the surface for even Robert Clark. A man who'd practically set his own trap and been foolish enough to fall into it.

"I've laid out a few options for him," Seth said. "We'll see how he decides to proceed. His best bet would be to get himself into rehab. Told him I'd line it up, but I can't make him do it. Till he decides or I have to decide for him, I can't have the kids see him. I wish it could be different, but that would most likely cause Devin to get angry and Sophie might get confused. Do they talk about their dad at all?"

Wynn tilted his head back and forth. "Very little. Mostly Sophie when she says something about what we did—basically she compares his shortcomings to me, and I try not to encourage her, but I don't want to hurt her. I also don't want to make their dad out to be the bad guy. He's still their father."

"He is, but Sophie hasn't really had the side of her father that Devin saw before his mom died, so this is probably new and exciting to her. What's an example of how she compared him to you?"

"We went out to eat at Farm to Table last Friday—Noelle and the kids and I—and she was saying how she'd baked with my mom and loved my parents and she said she wished her dad was like me. Other than that, it's been things like how I'll cook this food or play that game and she wishes her dad did too. Like I said, it's fine with me, but I don't know if I should encourage it."

"You don't necessarily have to encourage it, but don't try to discourage her either. It's good for her to have a standard set. Actually, it might help if and when Robert would be allowed to see the kids. Just because Sophie's only seven doesn't mean she can't know right from wrong. And right now, Robert's in the wrong. There's no way around that." Seth took the last swig of his coffee. "How'd they like the restaurant?"

"Loved it. Hesitant at first, Devin especially. But I'm glad I took them. For the most part, anyway."

Seth rose a brow. "What do you mean?"

"Oh, Noelle went in to talk to Joanna about Spring Fling, and George and Trevor Fleming were there. I think George stops there about every night for a drink, since he's too good for the bar. Anyway, I guess Trevor gave her a look that wasn't the most respectable, and his dad said I was trying to play the hero and he knew I was looking at his land and that business would be conducted fairly." Wynn released a humor-less laugh and shook his head. "I swear the man doesn't know when to quit. On the upside, Noelle told me she thought about giving him a piece of her mind, and that was a new side of her that I hadn't ever seen. She didn't, but she was not happy about it."

"He needs to watch his mouth is what he needs to do," Seth said, his tone laced with disgust. "And I doubt Trevor's any harm, but I don't personally have much respect for either of them. Nor for Garrett, but he's not even around anymore. Last I knew he was somewhere in Colorado. Probably don't want to know why."

Wynn chuckled. "Actually, that reminds me. We walked into Farm to Table and Sophie immediately pointed out the 'green stuff' on the wall, so I guess I can't blame anyone for questioning my role as a guardian."

"I'd like to see those doubters step into your shoes," Seth said wryly. "Bet they'd change their minds real quick."

"Does make you wonder, huh?"

Seth nodded. "Yep. Well, unless there's anything else, I guess I better get back to the Monday grind. How's it going at The Gardens?"

Wynn scooted back from the table. "We're about three-fourths done. And I think most of the party plans are done, so it's kind of a hurry up and wait thing. The mural is all done, though, and Jen did an amazing job."

"Good. I'm excited to see the finished product." Seth pulled his wallet out and opened it. "I'll cover your tab today."

"Aw, who knew Seth Johnson was such a soft-hearted friend?"

Seth grinned. "Very few people, and I'd like to keep it that way, thank you."

"Come on, Sophie, we're almost there," Noelle encouraged as Sophie got ready to toss the beanbag. "Just three more points, and we beat the guys."

Marshall shook his head. "Not necessarily. Devin could still cancel it out."

"Can I throw it?" Sophie asked.

"Go for it," Noelle said.

Sophie swung her arm back, then forward, then back, and then she released it. The beanbag sailed through the air and—and right into the hole of the cornhole board. Noelle let out a squeal, but she quickly muffled it and refrained from shouting to the rooftops that they'd won.

She didn't have to wait long, because Devin narrowly avoided being able to cancel their winning score.

"We did it, Soph," Noelle exclaimed, turning to shake Marshall's hand. "Good game, though."

Marshall made a face, but he shook her hand. "Uh-huh. We'll get you next time. Mark my words. It's beginner's luck."

"Oh, right." Noelle laughed as Sophie ran up, her hands held up for high fives. "Good job. Did you tell Wynn yet?"

Sophie shook her head. "He told me he was gonna go get s'more stuff and then we get to make a fire. I've never had a s'more before, but he said there's chocolate and I love chocolate, so I think I'll like it."

"Oh, I think you will too. Look, I think he's got everything. Why don't you go tell him about our victory?"

Sophie's face lit up just like her tennis shoes as she raced over to where Wynn and his dad and Chris were getting the fire ready to go. Noelle smiled and crossed from where the cornhole had been set up in Wynn's backyard to the deck. Jackie, Sarah, Sadie, Ember, and Jess were still sitting at the table, and they waved Noelle in.

"Come on," Ember said, gesturing to the empty chair beside her. "We were just talking about you and Wynn."

"Ember Lauren," Jackie scolded with a shake of her head. "Don't listen to her, Noelle. She doesn't always have the best filter on her. I thank her dad for that one."

Ember frowned. "Hey, it's better than being too filtered. And don't tell me that's not a thing. It's definitely a thing. I would rather tell people the truth than tell them something that may sound better or stroke their ego but isn't actually true."

"Yeah, but that wasn't true, Em," Sarah said, handing Sadie a different crayon. "Well, not totally. We were talking about Wynn and the kids. Not you and him."

Noelle waved her hand. "I don't mind. Sophie and I beat Marshall and Devin, so right now I'm pretty excited about that. She mentioned something about s'mores?"

"Wait, have you not had Bryant style s'mores yet?" Ember's eyes widened, and she continued before Noelle could even try to answer. "Oh, my goodness, you haven't, have you? You're in for a treat."

"They have toppings to put on them," Jess explained, probably picking up on Noelle's cluelessness. "Like strawberry and banana slices, caramel and chocolate syrups, etcetera. And you don't have to use graham crackers for the, well, bread of the sandwich. You have the option of waffle cone pieces or chocolate chip cookies or whatever they have."

Noelle's eyes widened.

"John had a s'more bar for me on our first date," Jackie added, her smile sentimental. "So it's been a tradition in the Bryant household ever since then. It's also why we try to space it out and not have them too terribly often."

"Wow," Noelle said, the idea of a s'more feast still not fully processed. "That sounds amazing."

"Grandpa makes the best one," Sadie said. "He puts *everything* on it."

Sarah chuckled. "Not quite everything, Sadie bug, but he puts a lot on his. And that is why you don't leave children unattended with my dad. He'll put them on a sugar high before sending them back to you. I can't believe Mom lets him get away with it, actually."

"Honey, there's some things about your father that I just can't fix," Jackie said with a shrug. "That's one of them. Are Grandma and Grandpa coming? I thought my mom would've been here by now."

"She probably has a hot date or something." Wynn's voice came from behind Noelle, and he set his hands on her shoulders. His warm, calloused palms felt so very good, especially when he started giving her a shoulder rub. She hadn't realized how tight her muscles had become—probably from sitting at her laptop too much. "And Grandpa...Well, I have nothing for him."

"Well, aren't you two little cutie pies?" As if she'd heard them, Wynn's grandmother walked out of his house carrying a beach bag, her grin directed at Noelle and Wynn. She glanced at Jess. "Has Marshall taken my advice yet, young lady?"

Jess raised her eyebrows. "And what advice would that be, Mrs. Watters?"

Margie's patterned pink and white silk scarf fluttered as she waved her hand. "Oh, never mind. I'll have to talk to him again.

Are we ready to have s'mores yet? And where are those kids, Wynn? I brought them something."

"Oh, boy." Humor laced Wynn's words as he gave Noelle's shoulders one last squeeze before offering his arm to his grandmother. "Can't wait to see this. And the s'mores are almost ready. Marsh and Devin are getting chairs for everyone."

Noelle couldn't help but smile as Wynn led his talkative grandmother down the steps to the waiting firepit, and Sophie demonstrated how she could do a pirouette, to which Wynn clapped and Margie bent to tell the girl something. If there was any part of Wynn that wasn't cut out for fatherhood, it must be minuscule or nonexistent, because he'd been filling that role for nine days now, and she'd yet to see something he couldn't do. He'd cooked for her and the kids, played board games, told stories about whatever princess he and Sophie dreamt up, tossed around a baseball with Devin in the backyard, and a whole list of other things.

That only made Noelle more reluctant to leave. Even though this wasn't a permanent arrangement—Wynn taking care of these children—she'd fallen in love with Wynn and the kids, and no distance or time apart would lessen the magnitude of her feelings.

Which scared her, because she had less than a month left here. She had responsibilities at home. Had a company to run, for goodness sake.

But even that knowledge could do nothing to squelch the desire she had to stay right here in this town forever. Regardless of what happened with Devin and Sophie and their dad, she couldn't simply brush off what she felt for Wynn. Couldn't shove her love for him in a box and place it in a closet, then open it whenever she missed him. Whenever she missed this place.

"Noelle?" Jackie's soft voice broke into her thoughts. "Are you okay?"

Noelle blinked and realized that the table had been vacated except for her and Jackie. "Yes. Sorry—I'm fine. Just space trucking, I guess."

Jackie didn't look convinced, but she smiled and nodded, then carried her sleeping grandson down to where everyone was waiting in a laughing, happy, loving circle around the fire.

Noelle forced her thoughts away and followed.

— ❦ —

CHAPTER

Forty Three

A simple shrimp alfredo was easy to prepare. Right? How hard could it be? The recipe Noelle had pulled up on her phone said it only took twenty-five minutes to prepare, and the groceries had been easy enough to find at the market.

"Okay, Sophie, are we ready to do this?" Noelle perched her hands on her hips, trying to ignore the rapid pace of her heartbeat. Just because she'd never done something like this and she was doing it in Wynn's beautiful kitchen with Sophie was no reason to sweat it. "Our aprons make us look professional, right?"

Sophie, standing on a chair Noelle had brought in from the back deck and set on a towel so it wouldn't scratch the floor, mirrored Noelle's position. "Uh-huh. Miss Noelle, have you ever done this before?"

Ha, wasn't that the question? Noelle offered a tight smile. "No, I haven't, but I can't imagine it's too hard. All we gotta do is cook the pasta and shrimp, then mix up the sauce in the same pan as the shrimp. So I guess the first step is to find the right pans to use, and it says we need one bigger and one medium."

"The pans are in that cupboard." Sophie pointed. "I've seen Mr. Wynn get them out of there before."

Noelle found two pans that closely resembled the ones in the recipe pictures on her phone and set them each on a burner. "Does it say to cook the pasta or the shrimp first? And do we need to get measuring spoons out?"

"They're right by the stove in that drawer," Sophie said, obviously trying to stifle her giggles. "And we gotta boil the pasta first."

"Oh, which means water would be useful to put in the pan, huh?" Noelle probably should have started with something easier…or just stuck with grilled cheese. But it was too late to turn back now. "Okay, we just need to take a deep breath and start all over. Well, not all over, all over, but you get what I mean."

Sophie's giggles escaped, and as the seven-year-old got swept up by a tide of laughter, Noelle couldn't help but get sucked in. What had started as a simple meal to have ready for when Devin and Wynn got home from working at The Gardens had turned into a fit of giggles.

"Maybe…we shouldn't…do this," Sophie exclaimed in between gasps of laughter, holding her side as she doubled over. "We might…burn Mr. Wynn's…kitchen!"

For some reason, that only made Noelle laugh even harder. She gripped the edge of the island counter, and gave up any resolve to try and stop the giggles. After the past couple weeks and what was currently weighing on her mind, it felt good to just…laugh. To not worry about anything for a few minutes and simply be there, in Wynn's kitchen, with Sophie.

"Well, boys, it's looking pretty good around here." Marshall stood facing the lake with his hands on his hips by Wynn's truck. "Hard to believe this place was basically too overgrown to see how pretty it is now."

Wynn had to agree with his brother on that one. They'd completely flipped the inside, yes, but the outside had the biggest transformation—and it wasn't even finished. Instead of crumbling flower pots and gnarly, overgrown weeds, there was fresh sod in some areas. No more shaggy green vines just waiting to trip someone on the sidewalk that wound around the property. Places where the new flower pots would go had been marked with spray paint. New water fountains that had sort of an old-world charm were being installed. And, possibly Wynn's favorite part, the tables they'd made out of cement and crushed tiles from the old fountains to preserve that piece of history in a newer, safer way.

Everything was coming together perfectly for the event in only a few weeks. As long as the weather held and they had a good turnout, The Gardens would be exactly the right venue for the town celebration.

"Proof that something beautiful can come out of something not-so-beautiful," Devin said quietly. "Thanks for letting me be a part of this, guys."

"We're not done yet, kid," Marshall teased, clapping Devin on the shoulder. "Still got plenty to do, so you might not be thanking us when it's all said and done. But it looks great, and I'm ready to get out of these clothes and get something to eat. See you guys tomorrow?"

Wynn pulled his keys from the pocket of his jeans. "Yep. Bright and early for me, Dev after school. Tell the parents hi for me."

Marshall nodded and started in the opposite direction towards his own truck. Wynn rounded the Chevy's cab and got in, Devin doing the same on the passenger side.

Today had been one of those really good days. He'd had breakfast with the kids and dropped them off at school, checked in with Seth, then had a short but sweet coffee date with Noelle before she headed to the flower shop and he to The Gardens. Following school, Noelle had taken Sophie and Devin had come to work with the crew. And even though every day since Robert's arrest had been similar to this, today just felt different. Lighter, maybe, even though Wynn wasn't sure why.

"Hey, Wynn?"

Wynn glanced across the cab at Devin as he turned onto his street. "Yes?"

"I meant what I said back there. I really am grateful for you guys letting me help you. It's really fun, and you were kind of right. It's better than the gym. Except Seth probably misses me whooping his butt on our reps."

"Ha. I bet he's crushed." Wynn chuckled. "And I'm glad. I like having you help out, and you've done a lot. You should be proud of yourself."

There was a pause, then, "Do you think my dad would be proud?"

Wynn felt a pang of sadness for the boy, but he nodded. "I know he would be. Listen, I wanted to talk to you about…" His sentence trailed off as he pulled up to his house.

"Why is Noelle dancing around your yard with a—" Devin leaned forward, seatbelt straining, and squinted "—pan in her hands?"

"Took the words right out of my mouth." Wynn shifted into Park, shut his truck off, and got out. "Noelle? Honey, what are you doing?"

She spun around, and Wynn tried not to laugh. What must've been a brand new apron with pink and white polka dots was blackened, and her hair had mostly fallen out of what appeared to be a braid. She held a skillet by the handle, wrapped in a towel, and her expression was part embarrassment and part fear.

It made him want to kiss her and ask her to stay right here with him.

Which, of course, he wasn't going to do. Not with Sophie standing in the doorway—her polka dot apron was clean—and Devin standing there trying not to laugh.

"I nearly burned your house down, that's what happened." Noelle's starched words were every bit as staccato as an uptight college professor. "And I did ruin your pan."

Wynn fought against the smile threatening to bloom and glanced at Devin. "Can you take Sophie inside and get changed? I think we'll go have pizza tonight, if everyone's okay with that."

"Pizza!" Sophie cheered as her brother guided her into the house.

After the door was shut, Wynn turned back to Noelle. "How did this happen?"

Tears welled in her eyes. "I was going to cook this shrimp alfredo pasta thing—me and Sophie got the groceries and everything—and have it ready for when you guys got home, but then I put the oil in the pan and turned it on and forgot about it and...and I ruined your pan. It's all black and burnt and—Wynn, I'm so sorry."

Wynn took the pan and made sure it was cool enough before setting it on the yard, then took her hands in his. "Sweetheart, I'm not worried about the pan as long as you and Sophie are okay. And shrimp alfredo? Why not something easier?"

"Easier?" Her voice went up an octave as a tear slipped down her cheek. Okay, that had been the wrong question. "The recipe said it was easy. It was only supposed to take twenty-five minutes and use only two pans and it looked so pretty in the picture. Even Sophie said so. But now there's a mess in your kitchen and I probably look like I stuck my finger in a light socket."

"You look beautiful, and my kitchen has seen some big messes before." He lifted her hands to his lips and pressed a kiss to her knuckles. "I appreciate you trying to cook for us. I really do. But a skillet? Really? I guess I should be grateful that you weren't threatening to whack me over the head with it this time."

That made her smile, and a watery laugh bubbled out of her. "I'm surprised you don't want to whack *me* upside the head with it."

Wynn chuckled and bent to retrieve the burnt pan, then pulled her close to his side. They were starting towards the house when the door burst open.

"The garlic toast is smoking," Sophie shouted.

Beside him, Noelle groaned.

Later that evening Noelle sat on Wynn's back deck, cleanly clothed and with her laptop open in front of her. The blank cursor on the equally as blank email draft stared at her, daring her to type what had been on her mind for several days now. Actually, it had been forming ever since she'd started helping Wynn with the kids consistently nearly two weeks ago. Ever since she'd realized, on a small-ish scale, what motherhood actually entailed.

She'd considered shoving the words aside, putting the idea out of her mind, but then Wynn had asked her to talk after he got Sophie in bed and Devin working on his homework, so she'd decided to bring her laptop out and at least get the words out of her.

So far, not even that had happened.

"Come on, Noelle," she whispered, taking a deep breath. "Just type it. Then you can decide if you want to send it."

With a deep breath, a smile from Nova, who was lounging by Noelle's feet, and a silent prayer, she rested her fingertips on the keyboard and started typing.

Dear Ms. Sutton,

While I'm aware of the response to my last email, I have something else I'd like to say to my mother, so would you please pass this on to her? Whether or not she responds, I just need her to read it.

Pausing, she flexed her fingers over the keyboard before diving into the body of the email—or rather the heart of it.

Over the past couple weeks, I've been able to experience motherhood in a very small way. I won't go into detail for privacy's sake, but it has made me realize some things. It's helped me to appreciate more than I ever have how much mothers sacrifice, how they love, and how strong they are.

So maybe it's because Mother's Day is coming soon or because of what I've learned, but I wanted to reach out to you, Mom, and tell you that I thank you for letting my grandparents raise me if you didn't feel adequate to do it. Thank you for sacrificing like you did, even if I wish I knew why you chose to do it. I guess I'm just saying that I respect your decision, regardless of how I would handle a situation if I was in one similar to yours—whatever that was.

And I suppose this is where it gets tricky for me. I guess I kind of debated whether to put this part in here, but then I felt it was necessary, so here goes. I love you, Mom. Whether I ever "know" you or not, you gave me life and for that I will always love you. Another lesson I've learned recently is one on love, and not solely romantic love. In a gentle way that isn't like a grand "salvation" story, I've deepened my relationship with God. I never doubted Him, exactly, but I was also never real close to Him. I've also grown to love some people, who have shown me just how wonderful love can be.

So, that said, I love you. I always will.
Sincerely,
Your daughter Noelle

As she typed the last characters, tears ran down her cheeks and she buried her face in her hands as she gave into the emotions. Every word she'd typed of that email had been true—she wouldn't have written it if she hadn't meant it. But it still left her with a myriad of emotions, and she refused to bottle them up.

"Noelle? Sweetheart, are you okay?"

Her head jerked up at the sound of Wynn's voice—how had she not heard him come out?—and she wiped her eyes. This was the second time she'd been teary-eyed with him today, and she had little doubt it was because of the words she'd just put into the email currently staring at her.

Wynn sat down in the chair beside her, his blue eyes concerned. "You're not crying about the meal again, are you? Seriously, Noelle, if you're worried about the pan, I am *not* concerned about it. There are plenty more like it."

She couldn't help but laugh as she wiped her eyes and shook her head, not yet able to form words. Not ones that would be complete or understandable sentences.

"Okay, then what is it?"

Noelle pointed to the laptop.

Wynn's brows knit together as he looked at it, then his expression softened with understanding as he read through the words. There were probably typos due to the tears that had blurred her vision as she typed, but oh well.

Instead, she soaked this up by studying Wynn's profile. The faint five o' clock shadow on his firm jaw. The concentrated slant to his eyebrows as he read. His blue eyes and borderline dark hair. It wasn't light-colored by any means, but it wasn't dark brown like his mother's either. His broad shoulders and obvious physical strength. And beyond that, his Godly heart and gentle soul and caring spirit.

Then he turned back to her, and she was fairly sure he had tears in his own eyes. "Wow...I just—I don't think I'd be able to do that if I were in your shoes. It's beautiful, Noelle, just like the girl who wrote it."

Noelle smiled, clasping her hands in her lap. "You really think so?"

"No, I know so." He gave her a tender smile. "Are you going to send it?"

"Um, I don't know. Maybe? I haven't decided." She shrugged. "I just needed to put the words down, at least, you know?"

Wynn reached out and tucked her hair behind her ear, then leaned forward and kissed her forehead. "I love you," he whispered simply, his lips warm on her skin.

The words rocked her, but not so much that she didn't realize that she loved Wynn, unlike she had any other man in the past. How she already knew that, she had no idea, but she just did.

"I love you too." Her words hardly qualified as a whisper, but he must've heard them, because he pulled her into a hug that felt exactly like the home she'd always wanted.

— ✺ —

CHAPTER
forty four

Whether or not Noelle ever got a response from Catherine Sutton or from her mother, that was what it was. She'd said the things God had encouraged her to and, with a prayer, she'd ended up clicking Send.

Considering that had been two weeks ago and she'd yet to hear anything, it was doubtful she would. But that was okay. She loved her mother, just like she said, but maybe it was best to love her from a distance.

Wynn, however, she didn't like the idea of loving from a distance, but if they didn't talk about it soon, she had no clue how she'd prevent it. She'd racked her brain for ideas on how she could be here and keep Carter, Inc. going.

She hadn't been extremely successful.

Then there was the guilt for wanting to stay here when her grandparents had entrusted their carefully built company to her. One that was based in Jackson and relied on her. They'd done well enough in her absence, but that wouldn't be a permanent solution. Lucy had told her multiple times that clients wanted *her*—Noelle

Carter, the sole granddaughter of Estelle and William Carter—to plan their events.

So why did none of the big city glitz and glamour appeal to her like it used to? When had her thoughts shifted to dreaming up ideas of a husband and children and possibly a smaller event planning business in this little lake town? Had she forgotten about the responsibility and trust that Grandpa had placed in her hands when he'd passed the title of CEO to her last November?

"You seem to be in deep thought."

Noelle jumped, glancing up as Jackie approached the outdoor table behind the inn. "Oh. Hey. Yeah, I guess you could say that."

"Do you want to talk about it?" Jackie motioned to the lake. "If not, I usually find many answers by simply taking in this view too, so I understand."

"I'm just..." She searched for the right word. "Confused?"

Jackie sat down in the chair next to her, crossing one leg over the other. "What are you confused about?"

"I...I was given the title of CEO very unexpectedly when my grandpa died of a heart attack last November," Noelle said slowly. "And only days before he died, he came to my office and told me that maybe it was time to try something new. Then, all those months later, Mayor Leo invited me to plan an event that's totally outside of what I normally do. And now that I have done it..."

"You enjoyed it more than you expected to?" Jackie offered.

Noelle nodded, meeting her gaze. "That, and I fell in love. With this town, with your family and this inn and..." She felt her cheeks warm. "And with your son."

Jackie only smiled. "I, as Wynn's mother, could not have picked a more beautiful, wonderful girl for my son to fall for. Trust me, he's had a couple duds in the past."

"Well, thank you, but I'm supposed to leave. Then what?"

"Have you talked to Wynn about this?"

Noelle shook her head.

"Then I recommend doing that before going to anyone else. Except God; He always come first. But come with me for a moment, if you don't mind leaving your things here. The crime rate at the inn is very low. Sometimes we have cookie thieves, though, so I can't say it's at zero."

"Oh dear," Noelle said with a laugh as she stood. "Let me guess, it's Marshall and Wynn?"

Jackie allowed her in the door first. "Yes, sometimes, but my husband is the real thief. He may be an upstanding citizen otherwise, but cookies are his one weakness. Fortunately, I know that and I keep the cookies in a hidden space most of the time."

"I can't believe he would do such a thing."

"Stick around for Christmas and you'll notice we have to put Santa's cookies and milk in a safe." Jackie winked as she led Noelle upstairs and down the hall to the library. "No, I love my husband. I just know of his weak spots, and do my best to help him."

Noelle smiled, clasping her hands as Wynn's mother pulled a drawer open on the desk. This room was like the rest of the inn: simple and airy, bright but cozy. A blue and white rug rested in the center of the room on the hardwood floors, and white bookshelves filled with books lined two of the walls. A cushioned window seat with books stored underneath and sheer curtains reaching down to the floor was situated facing the lake under the windows. Above the desk, framed photos had been hung neatly. Some of them were of the Bryant family, others of sunsets over the lake, and others ones of guests.

Jackie removed the lid from the box she'd gotten out and picked up a leather-bound journal. One that was filled so full it was nearly falling apart, and pages stuck out from odd angles.

"Ever since the kids were born—well, Ember since we started fostering her—I've been keeping a journal for each of them," Jackie explained, gaze tender. "I've written letters to them for milestones like their first steps, their first word, each birthday, graduation, dating, marriage—all the way to grandchildren. But I also wrote notes for the smaller things, and letters to their future husband or wife, depending on the child."

Noelle swallowed as she sat down on the window bench beside Jackie.

"I wanted my children's names to have meaning," Jackie continued. "For Sarah, her name means joy and princess. And we did consider doing all biblical names for our children, but when I was pregnant with Wynn, I discovered the *Canadian West* book series by Janette Oke. We still have that collection right over there. And though I certainly didn't picture my son to be a Canadian mounted policeman, I was married to one respectful police officer and reading about another. His name was Wynn Delaney in the book, and he was a gentleman. He had his flaws like all of us, but he was dutiful, strong, respectful and above all, Godly. When he and the heroine, Elizabeth, fell in love, he loved her and only her. And that's how John and I decided to name our first son Wynn David Bryant. You may have heard his siblings call him Wynn-Dee?"

Noelle nodded.

"That was a part of the books, a funnier one, and we didn't want to name him Wynn Delaney Bryant, so we chose a biblical name that started with a *D* so we could give him that nickname." She opened the notebook, thumbed through it for several moments, then pulled out a pink floral piece of stationary. "This is the letter I wrote years ago to Wynn's special someone. I'd like you to take it and read it, then return it to me whenever you're ready to."

"Oh, Jackie, I can't—"

"Yes, you can." She smiled and pressed the paper into Noelle's hands. "It's not something to pressure you or anything like that. You're welcome to share it with Wynn or copy parts of it down— whatever. But my hope is that it can help you, even if it's in a small way. I didn't have anybody to guide me when it came to real life like this, and I know that you've never been close to your parents. While my mother and I are close now, it wasn't until long after I was married with my own children that we became that way, and I was never close with my father. Not really. So however this can help you, God will see to that."

Noelle blinked back tears. "Can I give you a hug?"

Jackie laughed softly, but she reached out and embraced Noelle. "I love hugs. And trust me. God will make the path clear for you if you let Him."

With The Gardens complete—aside from special decorations specifically for Spring Fling—Wynn felt both happy and sad. He was thrilled to see the project turn out even better than they'd planned, but also sad because it signaled the end of a very special project.

The one that had been the reason for Noelle Carter coming into his life. The one Devin had helped with, where they'd ultimately started their unlikely friendship. One that had led to where they were today, Wynn being Devin and Sophie's guardian.

And with the completion of the project, Wynn knew it was time to have The Conversation. The one with Noelle about what was going to happen after the event was over this Saturday.

He carried two bowls of ice cream—strawberry for her, butter pecan for him—out onto his back deck after the kids were both asleep. Only two weeks ago he'd told Noelle he loved her in this exact spot. And he'd meant it. He *did* love her. Far more than he'd thought possible in only three months' time. Actually, it hadn't even been that long.

"Woah, what is this?" Noelle closed her notebook and moved it out of the way as he set the bowl in front of her. "You even put real strawberries with chocolate with it?"

Wynn grinned. "Hey, you should never underestimate the lengths I will go to for ice cream. Especially for a pretty girl like you."

Noelle leaned over to peer into his bowl. "Darn. I thought maybe you put slices of butter in yours. That would've been kind of gross though, sorry."

He laughed and kissed her forehead. "Have I told you that I love you? Even the odd food combinations and all."

"Actually, yes, but you can say it as often as you want to and I won't complain." Her eyes sparkled as she pulled away and readied a bite of ice cream.

For several minutes, Wynn didn't say anything as they ate. He didn't want to ever forget this moment. Not anything about it—the color of the sunset in the background over the lake, the birds chirping and, most importantly, the woman beside him. Some instances were better off without words, and this was one of them.

But he couldn't avoid the topic forever, especially if he wanted more moments like these, so he cleared his throat after they finished eating. "As much as I'd love to simply sit here with you, we need to talk."

She met his gaze. "Yeah. We do."

Wynn turned his chair to face her and held out his hands, palms up. "Look, Noelle, as much as I want this to continue, I can't be the one who holds you back. Your job—what your grandparents built—is in Jackson, and I know how much that means to you. I can't hold you back. I *won't* hold you back."

"Even if I said I didn't want to go back?"

His brows raised. "What?"

"Wynn, I love this town. I love its quirky characters and stunning views and your family's inn. I love your family and what they stand for. I love *you*." Uncertainty swam in her eyes. "And I've been praying really hard about this lately, and then earlier your mom shared something with me. I've been thinking, Wynn. What if I open an event planning business here? I could even ask Mayor Leo about maybe contracting to plan the city's events, and I could probably get other clients like, I don't know, graduations or birthdays or plenty of other events. I don't know how it would even work, really, but I'm willing to try."

"Noelle, honey, I don't want to discourage you, but is that what you really want? I refuse to be the reason you give up your grandparents' company."

"Who says I have to give it up?" Her brow furrowed. "I mean, I could always name it after them or something, but I could still work remotely for the Jackson location if I wanted to. People do that all the time, and I could even make a trip or two down there every year." A smile pulled up the corners of her lips. "You could come with me sometime. See where I grew up. But yes, honestly, the city life doesn't fully appeal to me anymore. The shine was already wearing off before I came here. I mean, if you'll have me, obviously."

He felt his own smile form as he stood and pulled her up with him. "If I'll have you? Really?"

"Well, I don't want you to not want me here. I mean, you're not the only reason I want to do this, but a big part of it. The way you are with those kids..." She shook her head, her hands resting on his shoulders. "It made me love you even more. So yes, Wynn Bryant, I do want to stay in Balsam Falls. And I guess God will have to take it from there."

"How about we both focus on Spring Fling, and then revisit it after that's successfully over? Take some time to pray about it." He slipped his arms around her. "If, that is, you're willing to extend your stay. And by the way, I happen to know the family who owns the inn pretty well, so I could probably arrange something for you."

She made a face. "That was a dirty trick, Wynn Bryant."

"Like calling me by my full name, do you?"

"Your full name is Wynn David Bryant."

He frowned. "How do you know that?"

"I don't know, how do I?"

"You, Noelle Carter, have been spending too much time around my sister. I think we'll need to discuss how to proceed with this new development and how we're going to minimize your—"

His words were cut off when she pressed up on tiptoe and kissed him. Wynn's eyebrows rose, but the surprise quickly wore off as he pulled her more tightly to him.

"Mr. Wynn?"

Sophie's voice had him jumping back, and he caught Noelle's flushed cheeks in his peripheral vision as he turned around. "Sophie."

The seven-year-old stood in the open doorway in those princess pajamas of hers, clutching her stuffed bear to her chest. "I had a scary dream that we got taken away from you and I thought it was real."

"Oh, sweetheart." He lifted her off the ground and smoothed her dark hair from her forehead. "Sophie, that's not going to happen, okay? I'm not going anywhere. I know that dreams can seem real sometimes, but that one wasn't real at all."

She nodded and wrapped her little arms around his neck, then rested her head on his shoulder. Wynn wasn't sure how things were going to pan out, but he did know that God was doing something. What, exactly, he had no idea. But it would be good.

God's plans were always good.

CHAPTER

forty five

I have to admit, I don't really understand why they named them party favors." Wynn used his pocket knife to slice open the bag of brightly colored confetti. "Did they think they were doing us a favor when they made them? Whoever they were. I mean, unless that's it, it just doesn't really make sense to me."

Noelle glanced up from where she and Sophie were cutting out paper flowers. "I have no idea, but they made it so we have lots of party decorations and don't have to make them all, so I'm glad about that."

"Says the person making her own decorations," Wynn teased.

"That's true, though I might have to Google the inventor. Okay, what am I supposed to do with this?"

"Make it rain?" Devin took a couple handfuls and held it over his head. "I bet all the guests would love it if they got tiny pieces of paper dumped on them when they walk in the door. Like in *Parent Trap*, but those were feathers."

Noelle shot him a look. "Yeah, or not. We're going to fill those plastic vases we picked out with that paper. There'll be one for each table and then a vase of flowers, too. I figured the paper pieces could pass as flower petals, because otherwise we'd need a lot of real or fake ones, and Lilah was already overwhelmed just with the other floral arrangements. Plus we have a variety of colors this way."

"What do I do with this?" Sophie held up a lopsided paper flower. "Does it look good? Yours are prettier than mine, Miss Noelle."

"Sophie, look how terrible my first one was." Noelle held up a very choppy looking flower. "You did a great job. And we're going to make a garland out of all the ones we cut out, so let's keep going. Hey, Dev, how about you put that confetti back and help us cut flowers? Maybe, if we get these decorations done, we can even convince Wynn to let us get ice cream at the Dairy Dock."

Sophie's eyes widened. "Can we? Please, Mr. Wynn?"

"If that flower garland gets done in the next hour and I get these vases filled, then yes. But—" he held up a hand "—you cannot rush. Work efficiently, not quickly."

"Count me in," Devin said, kneeling down beside his sister. "But I don't know how to cut flowers out. Are you going to time us, Wynn?"

Wynn nodded. "Yep."

"Here, let me show you." Noelle uncapped her marker and grabbed the stencil. "Maybe this is cheating, but we've been drawing out the flowers we like and then cutting them out. You just have to pick a sheet of colored paper, then…"

As she helped both kids with the flowers, Wynn couldn't help but be amazed at the fact that a girl like Noelle Carter wanted to give up her big city life for…this. For sitting on the newly refinished floors of an old but renovated building to help two kids cut out flowers. To stay for *him.*

He still wasn't sure he was comfortable with her giving up her other life—what if the shine of this place wore off eventually?—but he did know that he would support her. He'd scouted out a few empty buildings that, while they weren't on Main Street, could be a nice office space for her. He'd offer for her to use his and Marshall's space temporarily before any of the others, but not yet. Not until after Spring Fling was over, just like he'd suggested.

For now, he was going to soak up this Wednesday afternoon of decorating, and then enjoy each day after that, no matter what they held.

Shopping in general wasn't Noelle's strong suit—not when it came to clothing—but shopping for a little girl? The stores had plenty of cute things, yes, but how was she supposed to know what Sophie would or wouldn't like?

She probably should have brought Sophie along. Then the little girl could've said what she did or didn't like, and Noelle wouldn't be second-guessing everything she picked out. But she'd wanted to surprise Sophie, and that would've been impossible if she brought her.

Noelle studied a pink dress that had a flowy skirt, gathered waist, and a modest but pretty neckline. Would Sophie like that? She loved pink—her pajamas and tennis shoes and favorite shirt were all various shades of the color—but this dress was also kind of plain. Pretty, but plain.

Finally, she decided to call Wynn. He and Marshall had started on a new project that consisted of expanding a standing house in town, and though she missed working on The Gardens together, this was fun too. They'd settled into a routine over the past month, her and Wynn and the kids.

"Hey, pretty lady."

How was it that the mere sound of Wynn's voice could smooth her frazzled nerves? "Hey. I have a question, but if you're busy, I can ask you later."

Not really. She just wasn't going to say that.

"I've always got time for you. Unless you would've called about twenty minutes ago when we were putting a beam in. Then I probably would've had to call you back." Amusement underlined his voice. "Anyway, what's up?"

"Okay, so I wanted this to be a surprise, but I want to get Sophie a dress for Saturday evening. But I'm looking at all these dresses and I have no idea what she'd even like."

There was a short pause, then, "Well...I'm probably not a lot of help. Mom or Sarah or even Ember might be more helpful than me. What kind of dress are you thinking?"

"I don't know. Not something too fancy so she could wear it again, but I want it to be special."

"Hmm. Well, what are you wearing?"

The sneak. "Nice try, Wynn, but you already know that you're not allowed to know until Saturday. You've only got two days to go."

His sigh vibrated against her ear. "I still don't understand that rule. It's not like a wedding. This wasn't even supposed to be a formal event in the first place, until this little southern event planner came along and shook everything up. I'm still a little miffed that she wanted the fireworks."

"You are not," she said with a laugh as she fingered a yellow sundress. Too bland, though the color was pretty. "They'll be pretty, and you know it. Do you think Sophie would like a pink dress?"

"Probably. Depends what style it is. I know she really likes flowers. Must've gotten that from cutting all of them out the other day."

"That was a lot of flowers, but it was worth it." Noelle tucked her phone between her ear and her shoulder. "Okay, so pink with flowers. Do you think a longer one or a shorter one?"

"How short are we talking here?"

She rolled her eyes. "Knee-length or longer, Wynn. But probably longer, since we're all wearing long ones."

"Oh, so your dress is a long one, huh?"

"Shoot. Why'd I say that? Okay, I have what I need. Thanks. Love you!"

She ended the call before he could say anything more, but then her screen lit up with a text. From Wynn. In all caps.

I LOVE YOU.

Another text beeped through with a whole bubble of pink hearts.

Noelle couldn't help but smile as she replied about getting back to work with a heart and slipped her phone into her purse.

Ah, the lovely school parking lot.

A person would think Wynn would've gotten used to this place after having been here so many times in the past couple months, but that was not the case. And even though he was fairly certain the whole town was aware of his relationship status—from the good old fashioned town grapevine and not from a social media post— he still got looks from those minivan moms. The ones who were, more than likely, married. It was downright unnerving sometimes.

The minivan moms, however, paled in comparison to Jeff Stanhoue's scowl every time. Which didn't affect Wynn. Dislike for his family because of whatever twisted story George Fleming spun couldn't come against the fact that, against a few unlikely odds, Wynn had temporary guardianship of these kids. The school principal could glare all he wanted to as far as Wynn was concerned. Wouldn't change anything.

He'd grown accustomed to the fact that the line didn't move particularly quickly and made sure to have plenty of time for this errand every weekday. Something that always paid off when Sophie came running out with stories about her favorite teacher, Mrs. Jeffries, or how they'd learned this or what they'd done in art class, usually accompanied by a drawing for him. His fridge had never been so decorated in the seven years he'd had his house. Devin, on the other hand, let Sophie talk initially, but he always filled Wynn in on his day after they were home. Sometimes while they got supper ready or occasionally after dishes were done.

Wynn's phone lit up with an incoming call from Seth.

"Hey," he answered, easing forward behind a white Toyota.

"Are you at the school?"

The hushed anxiousness underlining Seth's words made Wynn's pulse quicken. "Yes. Why?"

"A woman by the name of Anita Clark showed up at the station about ten minutes ago, claiming to be Robert's ex-wife." Seth's voice was low. "And she has enough money to bail him out. More than enough."

Wynn's spirits fell in one swift drop.

"I don't want to go back," Sophie said, her worried gaze traveling between Wynn and Seth. "Don't make us, Mr. Wynn!"

Noelle's heart constricted at the pained expression Wynn wore. How could they know this Anita was really Robert's ex? And how had she magically shown up in town with plenty of money to bail her former husband out of jail? And why was everything Wynn had worked to get—endless paperwork, hours of training videos, the effort he'd put into caring for these kids—slipping through his fingers? She understood Seth had a job to do, and he wouldn't have brought it up if it wasn't true, but really?

Devin wordlessly set his hand on his sister's shoulder, wearing his own raw emotions on his face.

"I know, Sophie," Seth said quietly. Even stoic, non-emotional Seth looked worse for the wear, his hands clasped on the outdoor table and fatigue clinging to his otherwise handsome features. "But he's your father, and he still has his rights as such."

Sophie shook her head. "But I want to stay here! Mr. Wynn doesn't get loud and he's always home and he reads to me and plays with me and he loves me. Right, Mr. Wynn?"

Noelle swallowed, aware of how difficult of a position Wynn was in. Yes, he did love these kids. She knew that much from the past month of him caring for them. But Wynn's love—something she herself was absolutely gratified to be on the receiving end of—couldn't prevent Anita Clark from paying the posted bond to release her ex. To add to that unfortunate reality, Robert still retained all parental rights.

"Yes, Sophie," he said, his words slow, his voice rough. "I do love you. Both of you. But that means I want what is best for you guys. And I'm not going anywhere. I'll still be right here."

"But we won't be." Tears streaked Sophie's dark cheeks, and she got down from the table and ran inside.

Wynn closed his eyes and rubbed his forehead, the creases seemingly unceasing. "I should proba—"

"Do you mind if I talk to her?" Noelle glanced at Seth. "If that's okay."

Seth nodded. "Fine by me."

Noelle touched Wynn's shoulder as she passed him on the way into his house. She found Sophie in the room Ember had occupied back when Noelle's room at the inn flooded, sitting on the bed cross-legged with her teddy bear. Late afternoon sunshine streamed in through the window and dappled the room in light.

"Mind if I come in?"

Sophie shrugged indifferently but she didn't meet Noelle's gaze.

Noelle crossed to the bed and sat down, trying to think of the right words. Maybe she should've allowed Wynn to come in. Or even Seth. How was she supposed to know what to say?

"They can't take us away from here," Sophie cried, her brows drawn together. "I don't wanna go back. Mr. Wynn promised me he wouldn't go anywhere."

Noelle reached out to clasp the little girl's hand. "I know, sweetie. But like Wynn said, he's not actually going anywhere, and neither am I. Officer Seth will make it so that we can still see you, and I'm sure he'll make sure nothing happens to either of you. Remember that Bible verse we read the other night before bed?"

Sophie shook her head miserably. A sob shook her dainty frame.

"It said that we can't be discouraged. God wants us to be strong and courageous, and you are exactly that."

"I am?" Sophie looked up, eyes filled with tears.

Noelle nodded. "You are far braver than I have ever been. And I don't know what God's doing—sometimes He has really funny plans that don't make any sense to us—but *He* knows what He's doing. And you want to know what the bravest thing you can do is?"

"Go with my dad like I have to?"

"No, honey. While you do need to respect your dad—even if you don't agree with what he's done before—the bravest thing you can do is pray. It doesn't have to be any fancy prayer, but just talk to God. He's our wonderful heavenly father, and He loves you so much. Can you do that for me?"

Sophie scooted over into Noelle's arms, snuggling against her chest. "I love you, Noelle."

Noelle squeezed the little girl, praying God would reveal exactly what His purpose for this trial was soon. "I love you too, Sophie. So very much."

CHAPTER
Forty Six

Forty-eight hours.

That's the window of time Wynn had left with the kids before Robert got them back, and he'd already used nearly twenty-four of them up. Seth had worked out the agreement that they could attend the Spring Fling with Wynn and his family and Noelle as planned and spend Sunday with them, but come seven p.m. on Sunday, they would go back to their father. And his former wife.

Wynn didn't know why he didn't want to trust this Anita Clark—Seth had run an extensive background check on her, and nothing other than a speeding ticket or two had come up—but he just didn't. From what Seth had said, she was a nice enough person. Lived in Denver, worked at a trustworthy marketing firm, was clearly stable.

His feelings couldn't stop this, though, so there was no use wishing they could. Right now he needed to focus on the time he did have and use it wisely. And at the moment, it meant getting ready for the event that was going to start in only an hour. Noelle had worked too hard on this, as well as Devin, to not enjoy it.

All the girls, Sophie included, had gathered at the inn to beautify themselves, and the guys were congregated at Wynn's. Wynn wasn't sure if the girls were lacking in conversation like they were here, but he had little doubt it was thanks to the heavy cloud hanging overhead. Not actually—the day outside was warm and sunny and perfect for Spring Fling—but emotionally? He wasn't sure any physical cloud could ever compare.

"For the women who think us men aren't able to do technical stuff, I think they ought to try tying a tie," Marshall muttered as he stood in front of the microwave. "Maybe I would be better off with one of those adjustable neck ones with the knot that doesn't come untied."

Dad chuckled and motioned for his youngest son to face him. "Part of me is shocked you don't know how to tie your tie, but the fact that you're using a microwave for a mirror probably doesn't help."

"Actually, you'd be amazed how crisp the reflection is." Marshall propped his hands on his hips as their dad tied the black tie to match his suit. "Besides, Seth is too busy admiring his face in the only available mirror since Dev's in the other bathroom."

"Am not," Seth called indignantly.

Wynn had opted for a bowtie, and this one happened to be an adjustable one that came tied already. Maybe at any other time he'd tease his brother about it, but his mood didn't have the capacity to do that right now. Even Seth was in better spirits than him, and that was nearly unheard of. Probably because he was able to attend the event in an unofficial capacity, and Jenna and the kids would be there. Either way, Seth's happy-go-lucky demeanor was weird. Unnerving. Annoying, even.

A minute later, Devin strode out of the bathroom, looking uncertain.

Chris let out a low whistle. "Wow, kid. You look sharp. If my son dresses like that when he's older, I'd be a proud father."

Though his brother-in-law's intent hadn't been to rub salt on Wynn's currently open wound and the comment did make Devin grin, it stung. Wynn had never thought he was a replacement for Robert. But now that the kids were being swept out from under him just like that, he realized he'd grown way more attached to them than he wanted to admit.

Devin did look good. Really good. Per Wynn's mother's nudging, they'd visited a bridal store downtown to see about renting tuxes, and Devin's fit him perfectly. The teen had become noticeably healthier-looking since he'd been under Wynn's care, and his shoulders filled out the black tuxedo coat. His shiny black shoes were a perfect contrast to the crisp white shirt, and Devin had shown all of them up by going for the pink bowtie.

And it was too much for Wynn's emotions right now.

"I'll be right back," Wynn said. The air felt too thick, and he needed a moment to regroup, needed a breath of fresh air.

He went outside and stood in his backyard facing the lake, trying to calm the turbulent emotions rolling around inside him. It was like when a tornado formed—he had cold and hot feelings towards Robert Clark, and they were blending together to create a storm within him.

"You all right?"

Wynn didn't turn as his dad came to stand beside him. "I'm fine. Just needed a moment. Some fresh air."

"Ah." Dad tucked his hands into the pockets of his black slacks. "Because you don't look fine, and considering I've known you for nearly thirty-two years, yes, I do know when you're not fine."

"I don't understand it, Dad. Why did God let me get temporary guardianship of those kids just to take them away from me a month later?"

"Maybe they needed this time. Maybe Robert Clark learned something while he was sitting behind those bars. I know it hurts right now, but it will make sense some day. It may take time. It probably *will* take time, but He'll give you an answer. Let me ask you this: you went into it knowing it was temporary, so why do you think it didn't become permanent? Did you think temporary was going to magically translate into permanent?"

Emotions flared up within Wynn, and his words came out harsher than he intended. "Of course I didn't. I'm not naïve. But what if Robert just goes back to neglecting the kids? What if this was all a set up between him and his ex?"

"If that's the case, he'll have to pay for the consequences of his actions." Dad's calm voice only grated harder on Wynn's nerves. "That may or may not have been what happened. Only God, Robert, and Anita know the truth right now. But nobody walks away from their mistakes without consequences. Jesus forgives you, but He doesn't condone wrongdoings. And until a person recognizes his or her sins and decides to change them, He can't do much. He'll be there, He'll give them signs. But He can not change a person on His own."

"Then why did George Fleming walk away from your accident unharmed and you ended up with the crushed legs?" Wynn spun to face his father, the heel of his dress shoe twisting in the soft ground, vaguely aware that his words were fueled by his emotions. "Far as I can tell, he's doing just fine, and he doesn't seem to have repented. He's certainly never apologized to you, so I highly doubt he's apologized to God. No, he didn't get away with what he did without legal action, but he's fine now."

"He may be fine monetarily and physically, but not emotionally. He has one son who ran off to Colorado, another who doesn't have a clue what it's like to lift a finger, and yeah, he has a big house and nice vehicles and all the physical belongings, but there's not love there. And maybe he'll apologize someday. Maybe he won't. *I* have made peace with the situation, Wynn. And I know it hurts. But you can either let go and let God, or you can try to cling to the things you wish you could control." His father lifted a shoulder and let it drop. "Can't have it both ways, son."

Wynn clenched his jaw as Dad squeezed his shoulder before he left, leaving Wynn to stand there as tears he didn't feel like crying welled in his eyes. He pressed his fingertips to his stinging eyes, trying and failing to let go like Dad had said.

Wynn was extra emotional today, and Noelle couldn't blame him. She herself had her own scattered emotions, but he'd been even closer to the kids than she had been. He'd cared for them day in and day out for a month now. Bandaged scraped knees and calmed rattled emotions. Made meals and kept their grades up and cared for them not only physically, but spiritually and emotionally too.

So, as they sat at their table at the transformed, magical Gardens while Mayor Leo gave an introductory speech, she simply held Wynn's hand. Even if they were alone right now, she didn't know that she'd have the words to say to him.

"Everything here is pretty much brand new," the mayor was saying into the mic. "Back in March, the city came together and decided to restore this property. For the most part, this town has kept up its appearance, but for twenty years this place was neglected. Forgotten about. And then Noelle Carter, the granddaughter of Balsam Falls's own Estelle Richmond Carter, agreed to help coordinate this very event. She came all the way from Jackson, Mississippi, to work with brothers Wynn and Marshall Bryant to bring this property back to life. And folks, I believe they did an amazing job of doing so. Because some of you don't know what this place looked like before, we created a video of the restoration project. Thanks for coming out tonight, and enjoy."

Tears sprung to Noelle's eyes as Mayor Leo exited the makeshift stage and a video started rolling out on the big white projector screen behind where he'd been talking. Photos and video clips had accumulated over the past months, and everyone had put them onto an SD card for someone at the city to compile into this one video.

Images from when there were still boxes on the floor, from when the old windows were still there, and from when she and Ember were discussing design elements flashed across the screen.

Video clips of them laughing so hard they were doubling over as they attempted to paint and of Marshall trying to balance a paint roller on one palm.

Tears rolled down Noelle's cheeks the whole time. Every picture and video, the emotion-provoking song they'd put with it, caused her to relive all those wonderful times all over again. If only she'd taken the time to really, *really* immerse herself in all those moments when they weren't just memories.

But often that was how it went, wasn't it? Until one watched a video or saw a picture, they didn't realize how often time passed them by without taking the time to cherish every single precious moment. And by then, they couldn't turn around to try and soak it up more fully. All they could do was vow to do better in the future.

The last video—aerial drone footage of the freshly restored Gardens—faded to black. A photo of Noelle's grandmother appeared. Noelle bit her lip, still managing to read the text under the photograph, even with the tears in her eyes. *In Loving Memory of Estelle Carter, who once said this: "May we never be so consumed with the past and the future that we forget about the now."*

Wynn squeezed her hand and leaned over to kiss her forehead. The gentle smile he gave her was one that she would never forget, even though she didn't have a picture to preserve it.

The Gardens and this event could not have turned out any better if Wynn tried to picture them differently. Everything from the guests and food to the music and decorations was perfect. Other than the numbing knowledge that his hours with Devin and Sophie were passing by with every minute, tonight was better than he'd imagined.

It was hard to believe the place had been a dump only months earlier. Now, with its groomed sidewalks, charming fountains, and carefully pruned flowerbeds, The Gardens looked like they were glowing. Coupling the lake view with the rope lights neatly lining the pathway around the property, plus the Edison bulbs over the dance floor, it was nearly as magical as Lilah Carson said it had been back in the day. The inside was just as clean and welcoming, no small thanks to Jenna's gorgeous mural and Ember's clever design elements, which Sally Darren had praised her for.

Noelle had not only picked the perfect dress for Sophie, but she'd chosen a beyond perfect one for herself. Its pale pink color complimented her slender figure and delicate features, and the whole thing was covered in a thin layer of tulle or whatever that was called. It nipped at her waist, reaching down to the ground in a long, flowy skirt that swished whenever she took a step. The same tulle reached up and crossed elegantly around her neck, leaving her shoulders exposed. It was soft and feminine, just like the woman who wore it.

As the sun began its slow descent in the darkening cobalt sky, Wynn gathered Noelle close to him on the dance floor. Devin danced with Ember nearby, and Sophie with Dad. Mom was dancing with Marshall, and Sarah and Chris had formed a circle with Sadie, Chris holding Will, to dance as a family. Even the uncharacteristically happy Seth was dancing with Jenna and the kids while Jess talked to someone about her desserts and, more than likely, her upcoming trip to Paris.

Wynn estimated that an upward of close to two-hundred people had shown up, and though everyone was now scattered— some dancing, others conversing at their tables, some exploring the property and taking photos in front of Jenna's mural—he felt connected to his hometown in a whole new way. Even though it was a formal event, it wasn't stiff and awkward. It was somehow intimate and special. Healing, maybe.

"We pulled it off," he murmured into Noelle's ear, tucking their joined hands over his heart. "Your grandma and grandpa would be insanely proud of you, Noelle. *I'm* proud of you. Look at this place. It's glowing, and not only because of the lights."

She leaned back far enough to meet his gaze, and she smiled. "I didn't do it on my own. People might've wanted to flee if the renovation had been left up to me alone."

"Oh, I wouldn't be so sure. I saw how you can paint walls and swing a sledgehammer. If the event planning gig doesn't pan out, you could consider a career in renovations."

Noelle laughed, and the sound was like a balm to his battered emotions. "Do you remember how I got paint on Seth's uniform and my clothes? Or how terrible I am at swinging a normal hammer? The only reason the sledgehammer worked out is because I was actually supposed to put a hole in the wall."

"They say to focus on what you can do, not what you can't do."

"Yeah, well, the renovations you speak of are probably better left to you and Marshall." Her eyes sparkled, and her fingers played with the hair at the nape of his neck. "Are you doing okay? The kids seem to be having a good time. At least they still got to come to this."

Wynn exhaled slowly. "Yeah. I'm okay. And yes, I'm glad about that. I just wish it hadn't been so unexpected. It would've been different if Robert had gotten some kind of counseling or rehab and proven his desire to change, but he hasn't. I've seen Dev and Sophie flourishing lately, Noelle. And I don't want that to change. Devin's been able to be a kid for basically the first time since he was Sophie's age."

"I know. But we can't do anything. We can pray, though, and that's one of the most powerful tools. If not the most powerful one."

"That's true. You know what, I need to talk to my dad for a minute. Do you mind?"

"Go ahead—"

Noelle stiffened in his arms, her gaze locked behind him.

He frowned. "Noelle? Honey, are you okay? You look like you've seen a ghost."

When she didn't respond, her eyes still glued to something behind him, Wynn turned.

There, fifteen feet from them on the edge of the dance floor, stood Annabelle Carter.

CHAPTER

Forty Seven

None of the times she'd dreamt of seeing her mother, none of the what if moments, compared to the real thing. Instead of the elation she'd expected to feel, Noelle only felt paralyzed in place. She was vaguely able to hear Wynn's voice and feel him supporting her, but she felt like she was in a bubble.

Her mother was standing there, only a handful of yards away from her, and Noelle couldn't even respond to Wynn. A man she knew better than her own mother.

Mom looked…older than Noelle expected her to. She was a couple inches taller than Noelle, and fairly thin. Maybe too thin, but her loose white pants and dressy pink scoop neck top tucked into them made it hard to tell for sure. Her dark hair had grayed some, and her expression was serious.

Intent.

Focused directly on Noelle.

And then it felt like the bubble had popped and Noelle was all too aware of the music, of all the people around her. The fact that Annabelle Carter was here.

Annabelle Carter, my mother.

"Noelle, how about you sit down for a moment?" Wynn's low voice near her ear. His steady, protective hand on her arm.

My mother is here.

She let Wynn lead her back to the table, where he pulled out her chair for her. But shouldn't she go to her mother? How was this supposed to work? What would she even say?

Wynn motioned to her glass of water, then tucked his hands in the pockets of his slacks and wove around their neighboring table. Walked straight up to Noelle's mother. Mom was definitely too thin, and Wynn only looked taller and more commanding next to her. His black tuxedo jacket emphasized his broad shoulders, and his white shirt brought out the iciness of his blue eyes.

Okay, well, she hadn't seen him wear such a hard expression…well, ever.

She pulled her water glass up to her lips, the ice cold liquid cool and very welcome against her dry throat.

Though she couldn't hear their conversation, Wynn didn't stay over there long, nor did he look angry. Not happy, either, but definitely not angry. He nodded curtly, then came back over to the table and squatted down next to Noelle's chair.

"Feel better?" he asked, his face softening. Slightly.

She nodded. "D-Did she say why she's here? I-I never heard back from her. How did she know about this?"

"I know you didn't. She asked to talk to you, and I told her I'd ask if you wanted to. I don't want to get in the middle of it, but I want you to be okay."

Did she want to talk to her mother? Yes. And no. But which answer was the more prominent one?

She darted a glance over to find her mother staring at her, Mom's expression mostly unreadable. But she looked…sad. And it made Noelle's decision for her.

"Yes," she said as firmly as she could muster. "I do."

"Okay." Wynn's smile was tender, and he tucked a curl behind her ear. "You probably want somewhere more quiet. More private. Do you want to go to my house? The inn?"

"Kind of, but I also don't want to be so...secluded." It sounded silly. A grown woman didn't want to be alone with her own mother.

Never mind that she'd never even met her mother, other than for a couple hours following her birth.

"I understand. Farm to Table is open, if you want to go there. Do you want to be alone?"

So many questions and what felt like so little time. "Um...yes? I don't know. I don't want you to be taken from Devin and Sophie and the fireworks haven't started yet and I—"

"Noelle, take a deep breath," he instructed, setting his hand on hers. "Don't worry about all that. Do what you would like to do. You're more than capable of choosing."

She did as suggested, closing her eyes on the exhale. When she opened them, she mustered up all the strength she could find.

"I...I think I want to go alone."

"Okay." He stood and pulled her to her feet, gathering her into his arms for a strong, empowering embrace. "I believe in you, my love. Go get the answers you deserve. I'll be here whenever you're ready."

By the time Noelle arrived at Farm to Table and found a table in the corner near the windows, her nerves had become so prominent her teeth were nearly chattering. Her first words to her mother had been to meet at this restaurant and they'd been stilted. Formal. Nervous.

But she was here, and she could do this. She'd be twenty-seven next month. Wasn't it about time she got some answers?

She declined ordering anything when the polite young waitress approached her table, and only a couple minutes later, Mom walked in the door. Though thin and somewhat aged, she was still beautiful. She moved with grace and elegance, just like Grandma always had. It was no wonder she'd made it in Hollywood, with her lithe frame and striking features.

Mom was directed to Noelle's table and she crossed the restaurant, her hesitancy to sit obvious in the way she stood there motionless. Then, finally, she claimed the chair across from Noelle. For several seconds, neither of them said a word, as if sizing one another up. But Noelle had already done that. She was ready to get the answers she craved. Even if she didn't like them.

"You look just like your grandmother." Mom's first words were a hushed whisper, and her eyes filled with tears.

Noelle refused to let her own tears fall. Not yet. "How did you know to come here? You didn't even respond to my email. Neither of them, actually."

Pain tightened her mother's features, but not the physical kind that came from a wound. It was the emotional pain, the one that was a window to a person's deepest hurt. Their buried regrets.

"Actually, I did. Catherine Sutton is an alias. But you're right. I didn't respond to the second. But you have to know that I wanted to. Oh, Noelle, I wanted to reach out to you so badly." Mom swallowed. "But you've established yourself. Become successful. I also didn't want to ruin all that for you."

So Wynn had been right. Those words—the raw ones that Noelle had written—had gone straight to her mother's inbox. "What do you mean? And you didn't answer me—how did you know I was here?"

"After I received your second email, I called the office in Jackson to inquire about an event, but they said you were out of town on a job in Nebraska. I went out on a limb and looked up Balsam Falls, only to find that you were in town. And I thought about calling or emailing, but I just needed to see you. I didn't even intend for you to see me. Not really. But then you did, and I couldn't make myself leave."

"Wait, you wanted me to plan an event for you?" Noelle wasn't piecing the puzzle together.

"No. Well, not really. I wanted to get in touch with you in a way that wasn't over email, and I figured that was the place to start. Nobody knew it was me calling."

Noelle couldn't believe it. Her mother hadn't responded to that email, but she'd tried to locate her? Tried to contact her...indirectly?

"Why?" The question rolled off Noelle's tongue, and she couldn't help but finish it. "*Why* didn't you want me?"

Mom closed her eyes and took a deep breath, then met Noelle's gaze. "I came to Balsam Falls one summer when I was in between movie contracts. Mom had always talked about her hometown like it was some kind of vacation destination, and of course I never believed her. At that point I hadn't talked to either of my parents for a couple years, even though my mother sent me a letter every month. Always had a check with it. But anyway, I came to town and that's when I met your father.

"Tommy and I fell in love...quickly. Perhaps too quickly. By the time we'd been dating for two months and I only had a couple weeks left, he asked me to marry him." Mom's voice thickened with emotion, and she covered her mouth with her hand. "I told him yes."

The picture. She and Ember hadn't been hallucinating—there really had been a ring on Mom's finger in that photograph.

Mom drew in a shaky breath. "But when I told my manager I wanted to stay and marry him, he was furious. He told me I either went back to LA and left Tommy, or I stayed in Balsam Falls and could count on having no more contracts waiting for me. Ever. I tried to work out something so that I could do both, but there was no compromising. And when I told Tommy, we...we took our relationship farther than we should have outside of marriage because we were so caught up in our emotions. It wasn't until weeks after I'd left, after I'd broken off the engagement, that I realized I was pregnant. By then it was too late to change anything, so I didn't try. I didn't try to contact Tommy, and I sure didn't try to get my agent to understand.

"Once I was showing more, I found a way to get out of booking any more roles for the rest of my pregnancy. And I went home." There was a pause, and Noelle fought to keep her emotions at bay.

"My parents…they welcomed me with open arms even after everything I'd done. All the awful, naïve choices I'd made, they still let me in. But I couldn't keep you. I was scared and too caught up in the flashy, fake promises of Hollywood—basically because everyone wondered where Annabelle Carter had gone—and I caved to the pressure." Mom wiped a tear from her cheek, biting her lip. "There hasn't been a single day since I asked your grandparents to adopt you that I haven't wondered what it would've been like if I wouldn't have chickened out. That I haven't thought about you. I'm so sorry, Noelle. So, so sorry."

Noelle didn't know how to respond. She didn't know if she *could* respond. Part of her was still uncertain of putting any trust in Annabelle Carter, but she also didn't see why her mother would spin such a story if it wasn't true. None of it sounded untrue. Not that Noelle knew firsthand about Hollywood, but she'd witnessed plenty of cutthroat business people's tactics and how they utilized their power. Could not stand it. She doubted it was any different in her mother's career of choice.

"At that time, when I had you, I wasn't a faithful person either," Mom continued softly. "And for years following that, I didn't change. I kept God at arms' distance. Probably noticeable in the roles I played. And then one day a couple years ago one of my best friends died. Left behind her husband and two college-aged daughters. I realized then that I needed to change, and as badly as I wanted to reach out to you then, I wasn't ready yet. I…I contacted my dad last November, and I told him that I had changed. He wanted me to prove it. I had planned to fly out to see him and to see you and then…he died. I never got the chance to apologize to my dad, Noelle, and I will always regret not being closer to my parents. But I'll also understand if you don't have the desire to talk to me or see me again. I just need you to know that I am sorry. And I love you. I may not have been there for you, and I regret that more than you know, but I love you. I am so proud of the young woman you've become, and your grandparents did an amazing job of raising you."

Noelle opened her mouth to say something—what that something was, she had no clue—but her mother's face blanched as her gaze landed somewhere behind Noelle.

"Tommy?" The whispered word fell from Mom's lips.

Wait, what?

"Annabelle?"

Tommy? What? Noelle spun around in her chair.

"For a party that was planned in a short amount of time, this was pretty good," Marshall said as they sat at their table, waiting for the firework show to start. "I mean, unless you go all *Yogi Bear* on us with the fireworks. Then I'd have to knock a couple stars off my rating. For safety's sake, obviously."

"I think that would actually be pretty cool," Devin said, taking a sip of his punch. "It'd clear out the people."

Ember's brow furrowed. "Why would we want to clear the people out? Unless it's so I could have more cake. Then that would be fine with me. What have you *done* to me, Jess? This cake...I can't stop eating it."

Even though he appreciated everyone's attempt to lighten the mood, Wynn wasn't able to shake his worry. He knew Noelle's mother wouldn't hurt her physically—she'd told him that by her body language and soft voice—but still. He didn't like being kept in the dark, didn't like not being there.

Had he turned clingy?

He released a soft grunt at the thought.

Feeling antsy, he excused himself from the table and wandered over to where Dad was talking to Mayor Leo and his wife Charlotte. The mayor once again applauded Wynn on a job well done and said he had some other ideas to collaborate on and told him he'd be in contact soon. He must've sensed that Wynn had something to say to his father, though, because Leo wrapped up the conversation and moved on to talk to a city reporter covering the event. Probably be on the front cover in Tuesday's edition.

"Heard anything from Noelle?" Dad asked, keeping his voice low.

Wynn shook his head, barely resisting the urge to check his phone again. It was set to vibrate—he'd know when a text or call came in.

"Well, hopefully that's a good thing. Maybe there will be some healing that comes out of it." Dad slipped his hands in his slacks pockets, pulling his white dress shirt taut over his shoulders. Over sixty and he still had his physique intact. "But that's not what you want to talk about, is it?"

Wynn blew out a breath. "No, it's not. Listen, Dad. About earlier. I'm sorry. I was upset and I let my emotions get the best of me. The way I spoke to you—you didn't deserve that. If anything, I—"

"Wynn!" Marshall's hurried voice interrupted Wynn's apology. "This is just in. Those lots of Fleming's? They sold."

"What?" Wynn's eyebrows drew together as he read the text one of Marshall's buddies had sent, as he looked at the attached photo of a *SOLD* sign. "But I met with the bank and put in an offer. Haven't heard back yet. And they're sold?"

Marshall didn't get the chance to respond, because Wynn's own phone vibrated. He pulled it from his pocket, took in Noelle's clipped text.

I need to talk to you.

———

CHAPTER

Forty Eight

ifferent levels of shock, sadness, anger, and what seemed like a hundred other feelings jockeyed for Noelle's attention as she watched Wynn's truck pull into his driveway, the headlights temporarily blinding her.

Just like my mother showing up one minute, and my father the next.

Noelle had left Farm to Table sort of haphazardly, functioning in a haze of shock, and she'd texted Wynn and driven to his house. She'd lowered onto his cushioned porch swing as tears blurred her vision and realization started to dawn. She'd hugged her knees to her chest as if to help stop the shaky feeling she couldn't get rid of.

All the while, her head played a continuous loop of denial. *No, no, no* on repeat as if it could make it true.

But it couldn't.

The truth was the truth, and there was no way to get around it.

Wynn took the four porch steps in two and crossed to her with those long, easy strides of his. Everything about him was solid and sure. Unlike her life, which had had very little stability in the past six months. And when it had just started to feel like she was moving forward, just as she was making plans, her foundation had been ripped out from under her once again.

Just like when Grandpa died last November.

"Noelle?" Wynn sat down beside her, the swing shifting under his weight. "You wanted to talk? Please tell me your mother didn't hurt you."

"What? No." Not really. At least not physically. Maybe emotionally. Make that definitely on the emotional part. "Wynn, I need to tell you something. A couple things, actually."

His gaze held hers, his brows ever so slightly furrowed. "Okay...?"

"My mom... She was here and she did get engaged that summer, just like we figured after we found that photo." She pulled in a wavering breath. "And then circumstances caused her to break off the engagement and flee and all that. But that's—Wynn, I'm so sorry."

"Sorry for what?" Confusion huddled in his words, and he reached for her hand, his calloused palm warm against her cool skin. He must've noticed, because he shrugged out of his black tux jacket and draped it over her shoulders. "Noelle, if you're worried that my view of you is going to change because of your mom's choices, the way you were conceived, put those thoughts out of—"

"George Fleming is my father."

There.

She'd said it.

And just like she'd feared since turning to look up at the man back at the restaurant, since he'd shown her no affection, Wynn's mouth hung open as he probably tried to process exactly what Noelle had just said.

But even if she expected this reaction, it only confirmed her decision that she couldn't do this. She would not stay here, with Wynn and his amazing family, when she'd just be a walking reminder of the man who'd nearly stolen John Bryant's life over twenty years ago.

Even in her foggy state of mind, she'd been able to come to that conclusion. Especially when George looked at her no differently knowing she was his daughter. When her mother was sitting right there, a somewhat changed woman, and he spoke to her in somewhat cordial terms but completely ignored Noelle. Her own father had completely ignored her. Said that he'd sold the lots Wynn wanted, as if he hadn't just been introduced to the daughter he didn't even know he had.

That's why she had to go back to Jackson. Back to where people didn't know her story. Where they didn't know anything beyond the business front she presented.

Where she didn't get attached.

"Noelle, I'm not sure I understand... Fleming is your father?"

She nodded. Felt the weight of his gaze. "My mom...she called him Tommy because his middle name is Thomas or something, but then he walked up behind me and...and like I already said. I'm sorry."

"Why? Why are you sorry? That doesn't change anything. Not to me, not to my dad, and not to anyone else."

"But it does for me, Wynn." Before she could cry, before she caved and fell back on the surety of his words, she stood and paced to the other side of the porch. Wynn's masculine cologne embraced her like the jacket draped over her shoulders. "I can't stay here, Wynn. Not when—Not when I'll only be a reminder of the man who nearly took your dad's life. The man who has never apologized. I won't do it."

"That's not—Noelle, look at me."

She couldn't do that either. Not when her heart felt like it was being stomped on, and there was nothing Wynn could say to change reality. Just like the words she'd thrown at her parents— *how could you*, to be exact—she wasn't about to let her choice be changed because of a fantasy Wynn drew up that wouldn't work.

Because it was true. And denying it would only deepen the pain. Better to rip off the Band-Aid quickly than delay it. Even if it hurt like nothing she'd ever experienced before.

"Noelle, don't do this." Wynn was standing behind her now, and his deep voice was firm. A tear slipped down her cheek. *No.* "Don't push me away now. If you need to process, fine. But don't do this. You are *not* George Fleming, regardless of whatever messed up scenario you've got drawn up. I love *you*, Noelle, and your father is not going to change that."

Another tear she didn't want to cry escaped, and she swiped it away roughly. Mom's words came back to her. *We fell in love quickly...perhaps too quickly.* Yeah, well, maybe that's what had happened here too. Maybe Carter women had a habit of falling in love too quickly. Difference was that Wynn Bryant was exactly the opposite of George Fleming, and he deserved someone the direct opposite of Noelle. Someone with less baggage. Someone who could step into his lifestyle and not be an object of interest because of her mother's choices.

"I can't, Wynn. It's too fast, and I didn't—I can't do this. I have to go back. I'm supposed to go back—I have to."

Wynn's hand closed around her arm and he turned her to face him. "Noelle, stop. Your emotions are running high and you need some time to process them. Don't break this off right now. What we—" he gestured between them with a firm hand "—have is something special. Don't throw it away for the fear of something that you don't even know is true. That you know is *not* true."

But it was true. Eventually, maybe not tonight or tomorrow, Wynn would realize it was true. And then this, the inevitable chasm between them, would form.

Which was why she just needed to end it now.

Get it over with before they ever got to the point of engagement. Marriage.

"Don't do it," he said again, his voice low and those blue eyes of his pleading. "We'll get through this. I don't care what George Fleming thinks of my family, and I sure don't care if he's your father. He's not you!"

Pain flashed through her at the intensity of his words, and she couldn't stand that her voice trembled when she spoke. "I care, Wynn! Can't you see that? Maybe you can brush stuff off and pretend like it doesn't affect you, but I will not stay here with the knowledge of my birth father's wrongdoings. And besides that, he's my father. How can you think I'll be fine staying here when my dad holds plenty of influential cards in this town? He's going to make your life miserable, Wynn." Her voice cracked. "If I stay, he will make you and your family's life miserable. And I refuse to do that to you. I—I love you too much to do that."

Wynn's clean-shaven jaw clenched and his eyes darkened. "It doesn't have to be that way. Just hold off on doing this. Wait until your emotions have calmed down. Give me that much, Noelle. Please."

Oh, how she wished she could. She reached up and cradled one side of his jaw in her hand, her own jaw trembling as he closed his eyes. As he leaned into her touch.

"You are an amazing man, Wynn Bryant," she whispered as she rubbed her thumb over his cheek. "With you I am a better person. With you I've felt alive and loved and cherished. But I have to go now, Wynn. You deserve someone who won't wreak havoc on your family. Can you please understand that for me?"

She could tell he wanted to protest again as she leaned up to kiss his cheek, then stepped back. His fingers brushed hers as she passed his jacket back to him, and his eyes filled with tears as she stepped around him. But he didn't say anything, and tears clung to her lashes as she hurried down the steps.

Away from the man who deserved far more than what her presence would bring about.

Regardless of how much she loved him.

Wynn couldn't have been in a worse mood if someone tried to make him be.

He'd barely strung together enough sentences to form a short paragraph since his parents dropped the kids off for their last night at his house, and apparently the kids had picked up on his bearish mood, because they were quiet as they got ready for bed. Kept their prayers brief. Sophie didn't even ask for a story before bed, even though they hadn't gone a single night without reading one since the kids had been sleeping under his roof. He managed to squeeze out the "I love you" and "sleep tight" that had been customary for the past weeks, but that was about it.

Scratch that thought on his mood not being able to worsen. Come seven tomorrow evening when Robert took the kids back, he had a feeling nobody would want to be around him. He probably wouldn't want to be around himself.

At the moment, his mood was so dark not because of losing Noelle—not *solely,* anyway—but because of her reasoning. So what if George Fleming was her father? Even if he had certainly not seen that one coming, it didn't change his view of her and it never would. Couldn't Noelle see that he would never think of the woman he'd fallen in love with as the man who, as Dad said, had no love? Yes, he could see why she'd be shaken up, concerned even, but why couldn't they work through this together?

After he'd tossed and turned for several hours, he rolled out of bed, fumbled with his glasses, and padded out to the kitchen, Nova trailing behind him. Too bad it wasn't thundering or raining. It'd compliment his mood nicely.

He checked on both kids, kind of wishing he could be sleeping soundly like they were, then walked out onto his back deck. And, unwelcomed, thoughts of Noelle came rushing in.

She'd snuggled up to him and fallen asleep right there in his arms on this very deck while watching *Tangled* that Monday night. He'd kissed her for the first time in the wood shop only yards from where he stood now, and they'd stayed up late. Talking. Stealing kisses. Building her shelf. And, only weeks ago, they'd sat at the very table next to him and told each other they loved one another. *Loved!* Wynn did not take that word lightly, and yet it hadn't been enough for Noelle. It hadn't made her see that, no matter what the circumstances were, his love for her ran deeper.

And now all those moments were memories. History. Because of a worldly thing, Wynn had lost the woman he loved, just like he promised himself he wasn't going to allow.

But then, he'd tried. He'd done everything he could to salvage the splintering relationship they'd built so carefully. There was nothing that would change her mind. No words or promises or gestures that would prove the depth of his feelings.

And maybe that was what hurt the most.

Noelle's eyes were red and puffy from a night of very little sleep as she took one last look around the room. Absorbed the place she'd grown to love for what would be the last time. She'd packed up her things last night and had them all ready to go, hoping it would help her get to sleep.

It hadn't, nor had it erased the stark pain on Wynn's face from her memory. The feel of his cheek against her lips as she kissed him goodbye. Just the mere thought raised unwelcome goosebumps on her skin.

Right now, she clenched her jaw as she saw the flowers she'd laid out on parchment paper from the kitchen to dry. They were lined up on the desk, wilted, but preserved. If only she could preserve the good memories she had here, of the stunning view out her window. Of the warm, comfortable bed with its soft sheets and embracing comforter. Of getting ready with Ember for John and Jackie's anniversary party. The laughter and smiles.

But before she could give in to more tears, she looped her canvas purse over her shoulder, pulled the handle of her suitcase up, and exited the room. The door clicked shut behind her, and she genuinely hoped she could slip out unannounced, put the short note and number to reach her office if they needed more payment info on the desk.

She was wholly unprepared for the greeting committee in the entryway.

No, make that farewell committee.

"We're sad to see you leave, but know you're always welcome here," Jackie said softly as she smiled sadly.

"Have a safe trip home, Noelle." John's low voice held a note of melancholy.

How Wynn's entire family knew about her departure, she had no clue, but she could only nod. A lump formed in her throat as she looked at Jackie, then John. A teary-eyed Ember. Marshall. Sarah. *Wynn.* He captured her gaze as he rested one hand on Devin's shoulder, hugging Sophie to himself with his other arm.

And for one weak moment, she thought about changing her mind.

Then the memory of George Fleming telling her the lots had been sold—even with her mother standing right there—and his emotionless response to her being his daughter flashed through her mind and she steeled herself.

"Don't forget us," Ember said as she threw her arms around Noelle, squeezing tightly. "Promise me you'll never forget us, okay?"

Noelle's lips trembled, but she nodded. "I promise. You don't ever lose your charming personality, Em."

Ember moved back, biting her lip as a bittersweet smile creased her lips, but she didn't say anything further.

"Travel safe." Marshall's strong arms wrapped around her in a brotherly bear hug. *God, I love these people so much.* "And don't forget you know how to paint *and* break walls now. Just don't recommend working in the kitchen."

A teary smile came to her lips. "I'm going to miss you, Marshall. Don't ever lose that...well, charming personality of yours either, okay?"

Sarah laughed as she hugged Noelle. "I doubt there's any danger of that. We're going to miss you around here, you know."

"I know," Noelle said quietly, aware of Sophie's tearful gaze as she knelt in front of the girl. "Oh, Sophie."

The seven-year-old lunged into her arms and clung to her for several gut wrenching moments. Noelle buried her face in the girl's hair, praying Robert took good care of the kids. Praying Wynn would be okay after the kids were taken away from him tonight. Noelle blinked back her salty tears, then set the girl back.

"Be brave, Sophie," she whispered, framing the girl's dark face. "Okay?"

Sophie nodded tearfully.

Noelle swallowed as she stood and hugged Devin. Though the teen didn't say a word, his strong embrace and sad eyes spoke volumes, and she offered him a small smile.

And then she was standing in front of Wynn, trying to memorize every detail of his achingly handsome face. Those pained blue eyes. Tousled brown hair, probably from the same sleepless night as her. Firm, tightened jaw.

Then he leaned forward and pressed the softest, most tender kiss to her forehead. "I love you, Noelle," he whispered.

Noelle clenched her own jaw as he pulled away, and she managed to get through a hug from him too before she took one last look around at the family. The ones she loved too much to put into words.

Then she walked out of the Serendipity Inn's door for the last time.

CHAPTER

Forty Nine

"You know, bro, heartbreak doesn't look all that great on you."

Wynn wasn't sure what the purpose of that comment was, but he didn't turn from the stove to look at his sister. "Gee, thanks."

"I'm just saying. I don't get why you didn't try harder." Ember's words were perfectly innocent—or so she wished. "You guys were so perfect together. I mean, I was ready to ship you two off to be cast as leads in a Hallmark movie or something, but then this happened. Remind me why you didn't try harder to keep your relationship?"

"Believe me, I did." He turned the burner off and moved the pan of browned hamburger to the back burner. Just like his dreams for the cottages and for the future he'd naively envisioned with Noelle. "If you just came over to bother me about Noelle, please don't."

Ember snorted. "That's not the only reason I'm here. I also came for the food, obviously."

"Not funny." He shot her a glare over his shoulder.

"Woah. Cool off, bro." Ember held up her hands as she slipped off the barstool and came around the island. Broke off a piece of crescent roll dough to roll it between her fingers. "I'm just trying to lighten the mood a little. You've been like a walking storm cloud all week."

Well, she wasn't going to allow him to sulk in his stormy mood like he wanted to. It'd been five days since Noelle left. Five days since Robert had taken the kids back. Five days since Wynn had felt like doing anything other than work, question God, and sleep.

"You're right." He buttered the casserole dish, then dropped the dough in and fit it to the bottom. "I am a walking storm cloud. Can you grab that bag of cabbage from the fridge, please?"

The fridge. Still, Sophie's drawings hung on the stainless steel appliance. For what reason, Wynn didn't know. To torture himself, more than likely. Since it already felt like there was a hole where his heart was supposed to be, why not add to the anguish? Why try to make himself happier when he could wallow in this dark pain?

"At least you didn't forget your manners." Ember handed him the bag of cabbage to put in the runza casserole, then leaned against the counter beside him. "But still. I miss my brother. You hardly laugh or smile anymore. And you hardly talk. I mean, you've never been big on talking, but this is a new record for you. I think you've said, like, a thousand words total since Noelle left. And even though that sounds like a lot, it's not. A typical book chapter has about twenty-five hundred to three thousand. You haven't even said enough words to write a whole *one chapter.* I mean, I know I said I agreed with Noelle about how few words you..."

She must've realized that he wasn't interested in the topic of conversation, because she fizzled out. Wynn knew he was being uncharacteristically moody and it wasn't fair to Ember, but he couldn't just snap his fingers to shake his mood. It was dark and it prevented the truthful light from shining in.

Great, now he sounded cynical.

He dumped the cream of celery soup into the hamburger, then released a sigh as he set the can down and braced his hands on the countertop. "What have I done, Em?"

"Um... Do you really want me to answer that?"

Wynn glanced at her, what felt like the first smile since last Saturday pulling at his lips. "No. Probably not."

"But you did ask. I'm pretty sure that gives me the right to tell you."

"Fine. Tell me."

Ember cleared her throat, making Wynn regret his allowance before she'd even said a word. "You blew it. You had a shot at quite possibly the greatest love story ever—until mine, obviously—and you blew it. Poof! Went up in big orange flames and thick, crippling smoke. Choked that dream to death. Thanks to you, it died a harsh, painful death that not only crushed your dreams, but also—"

"Exaggerate much?"

She narrowed her eyes. "Not really. I mean, I don't see you floating around in your fairytale bubble anymore, so I'd say my assessment is pretty true. Adjectives just make it seem more colorful."

"He was right," Wynn muttered. He moved the emptied can to the sink.

"Who was right?"

Did she hear everything? "Of all people, George Fleming. He told Noelle the fairytale would end when she left." He dumped the second can in and pulled a spatula from the drawer, his laugh cryptic to his own ears. "And he was right, according to you."

"Oh. I didn't—You know what I'd like to do? I'd like to march into George Fleming's bank and straight into his office and tell him what a first rate *jerk* he is for doing what he did." Ember let out a huff as she gestured with her hands. "What kind of man doesn't even acknowledge their daughter is their daughter? He's the reason Noelle's even alive!"

Wynn chose to stay mute, quietly grinding pepper and sprinkling salt over the meat mixture. Hints of comforting aromas mingled in the steam drifting upwards.

"Oh, and another thing. The fact that he sold that land to someone after you made a perfectly fair offer just boils my blood. The nerve of the man!" His sister turned, paced to the other end of the kitchen, and stalked back. "I mean, fine, if he was going with the highest bidder, but Jeff Stanpoo is *not* a good...Oh, shoot, I wasn't supposed to say that."

Wynn's hand paused mid-stir. "Jeff Stanhoue bought the lots?"

"Um... Yes. And, uh, I wasn't supposed to say that, because Jess heard it from Seth and I have no clue how he knows but... Sorry."

Well, wasn't that just rich? Or maybe rigged. The man who'd treated Wynn so poorly when he dropped Devin and Sophie off *early* every morning for school and when he picked them up afterward was the one who'd bought the lots Wynn had been eyeballing.

Just as well. It wasn't like Wynn even wanted to be in any sort of negotiation with George Fleming. If he never saw the man again it would be too soon.

"Wynn, I'm sorry. I never should've—"

"It's fine." It wasn't, but he shot his sister a brief smile. "You want to get the other crescent rolls open? I have a funny feeling you won't be the only family member at supper tonight."

Her kitchen wasn't built for cooking. That must be a fact, because every time Noelle tried to make herself go in there, to cook something in it, she couldn't. It was like God Almighty simply said *No. You may not cook here.*

Not that she had a clue of what God was saying these days.

Ever since her arrival back in Jackson on Monday all she'd done was work. She went to the office early, came home late, and even filled up any spare hours by going over finalized plans or whatever work-related projects she could. That way she had no room for other potential thoughts to creep in.

Like Wynn.

Or her mother.

Or the fact that George Fleming was her father.

But mostly Wynn.

She tried so very hard to shove the memories of her time in Balsam Falls away. To forget about Wynn and his handsome face and heart-pounding kisses and culinary skills and dancing and— and none of it was supposed to be invading her thoughts at all.

Noelle grabbed the leftover sandwich from the sandwich shop on Carter, Inc.'s block, put it on a plate with some chips, and took that and her water bottle out back. She did her very best to ignore that her little city backyard most definitely did not look out over a glittering blue lake. Unless a person counted the Watsons' brown brick house to be one.

Since she knew what one actually looked like, no, a brown brick house was not comparable to a glittering lake. Not even close.

Too bad she couldn't have brought Nova back with her. It was as if she'd gone from having so many people, so much to look forward to, to nothing. Even work felt like it dragged by. She was pretty sure she would be fired by now for her lack of enthusiasm in the office, and she'd even considered firing herself. Probably the easiest termination she'd ever make. But then what would she do? Forage in the wild? Eventually her bank account would start dwindling, that much was inevitable. Which was why she'd be better off to stay, hope she dug herself out of this pity party hole soon, and put Balsam Falls in the rearview mirror.

And since she was rehashing all this for the millionth time, there was a pattern that hadn't escaped her.

Grandma had left town for love.

Mom had left town for love.

Noelle had left town for love.

Too bad Grandma's love had been the only one to come with her. The tradition hadn't carried through to the following generations of Carter women, apparently.

Noelle took a bite of the club sandwich and chewed it, resting her head against the back of her sun-warmed Adirondack chair. She hadn't even come out here since she'd been home. Hadn't really had the heart to, because it just reminded her, despite the lack of the lake, of sitting on Wynn's back deck. Or the inn's. Or anywhere downtown Balsam Falls that had a view of Falls Lake. Which was virtually anywhere.

She did feel kind of bad for leaving her mother like she had after Mom had opened up to her, but the fact that George Fleming was her father tainted the whole story. How could Mom have fallen for that man? Sure, that'd been years before the accident and he could've been different back then, but really?

Made Noelle shudder just thinking about it.

"Noelle Carter, it's been far too long."

Noelle's eyes opened as Lily walked over from her backyard, still as eccentric as she always was. This evening she wore an ankle length pink sundress, her bracelets still stacked up on her small wrist.

"Hey, Lily." Did Noelle sound as down and out as she thought she did? She tried for a smile. "I wondered if you were still kicking."

Lily's eyes narrowed as she claimed her usual chair. "What happened to you? I noticed lights on in your house all week, but I haven't even seen you. I was about to come on over here and see if someone new hadn't moved in."

"Oh, I've just been working a little harder to make up for all the time I've been gone. No biggie."

"Uh-huh." Lily grabbed a chip from Noelle's plate and munched on it. Loudly. "You're not telling me something, because I know you and you don't use words like 'biggie'. Let me guess. You fell in love."

Just the word *love* caused Wynn's face to flash to mind, and Noelle blinked away tears. Clearly not quickly enough, because Lily nodded slowly and made a clucking noise. Sounded like a chicken. Or like Libby. Noelle's heart squeezed even at the thought of a rooster. A *rooster* made her heart splinter yet again.

She was pathetic. Who in their right mind could start crying over a mere *rooster?*

"What's his name?"

Noelle really had no desire to say it out loud, but she knew Lily wouldn't let her get off the hook so easily. "Wynn. Wynn Bryant."

"Ooh. What a handsome name."

Yeah, well, it wasn't half as handsome as the man himself.

"So, what happened?"

Noelle groaned as she let her head fall back against the chair. "More like what *didn't* happen?"

"Uh, you're gonna have to explain that one."

"Yes. I fell in love, but not only with Wynn. And that's not even the half of it."

Lily's eyes widened. "Okay, now you've got me one part worried and two parts intrigued. You fell in love with more than one man? Hold on, is one named Wynn and the other named Bryant?"

"What?" Noelle shot the older woman an incredulous look. "No, I didn't fall in love with more than one man, and no, that's not two different men's names. I fell in love with Wynn Bryant *and* his family *and* the town. But again, that's only part of it."

Lily snagged another chip. "Well then, tell me the other part of it. You can't say something like that and then not spill, Noelle. You should know that."

And then, like a dam giving way, everything tumbled out in what were probably incomplete sentences. From the first day in Balsam Falls and how Wynn had figuratively come to her rescue to how she'd fallen down the steps at the inn. She told Lily about what John Bryant had overcome and how incredible the Bryant family was as a whole. Described her favorite parts of town— including but not limited to Farm to Table, Cozy & Grounds, Dairy Dock, Giorgi's, the inn, and obviously, The Gardens—and detailed the renovation. Explained Wynn's dream to build cottages for lower-income families to vacation at or disabled kids or just people in general.

She shared about how romantic Wynn was and his flowers and his notebook and how wonderful of a man he was. Didn't include that his kisses were sweeter than apple pie, but Lily probably gathered that from the flush Noelle felt in her cheeks.

But then she got to the whole Mom-showing-up and George-Fleming-being-her-father part, and it got a little trickier. It still heated her blood, and tomorrow would mark a whole week since everything had come crashing down.

She wondered if Robert had truly taken the kids back. If Wynn was as miserable as her. If life was just marching on calmly there, unlike in her heart.

"…and then I left," she finished, keeping her gaze on the sandwich. It kind of grossed her out, but it beat looking into Lily's eyes. "So that's that."

"Well, here I thought I'd had an interesting few months because of *my* new man."

Noelle's gaze jerked up then. "You have a new man?"

"Don't sound so surprised, young lady. Just because I've got wrinkles on my face don't mean I can't have me a new man." Lily tsked, shaking her head. "But that's not near as important as this. It sounds like this Wynn wasn't going to let you be worried about your father, and you still left him?"

"Lily, my father would make Wynn and his family's life awful if I stayed there. Maybe Wynn thought we'd be fine, but trust me, it would eventually end up just like this. It's better off to have broken it off before I got even more attached."

"Maybe you think so, but honey, what about Wynn?" Lily leaned forward in her chair. "Did you ever consider that he really won't be affected by who your father is or isn't? That he really didn't want to see things end?"

Noelle looked away. "Yes. And I get it, maybe it was kind of selfish, but I love him too much to put him through any possibility of my father's actions. He's already seen enough of them."

"You can tell yourself that, Noelle, but do you remember what I told you that evening before you ever left?'

Noelle swallowed.

"After you said that you were doing a renovation project, I said the work you would be doing would probably not be solely physical. That you wouldn't only be tearing down physical walls, but emotional ones too. That you were doing some soul-searching by stepping into such uncharted territory. And you did that, but now you need to ask yourself: Did you learn anything from it?"

CHAPTER

fifty

Wynn wasn't sure he believed the saying about time healing all wounds. Because he'd had ample time— nearly two and a half weeks—and he still felt wounded. Still hadn't recovered from the blow that'd been delivered on his front porch.

Sure, he'd somehow pulled out of his doom and gloom enough to somewhat enjoy work and time with his family a little more, but none of it was the same. Mayor Leo had asked him and Marshall about some other projects that were in the works to contract out. They'd finished the renovation job and moved on to meeting with a young couple to start drawing up plans for their new house. One that would be big enough to accommodate for the family of six they said they wanted, and one child was already on the way.

Wynn had envisioned something like that with Noelle. Maybe not a new house, but he'd thought about marriage. Thought about how wonderful Noelle would be as a mom. She'd proven that by how she cared about Devin and Sophie.

Devin and Sophie. Though Seth had been monitoring the situation, Wynn hadn't seen the kids since Robert had come to get them that Sunday night. He trusted Seth, he did, but at the same time, having two blows within twenty-four hours had been…difficult.

One saying he could get behind was the one about when it rained, it poured. For the lack of actual rain they'd had lately, it'd certainly poured back at the end of May in those whirlwind twenty-four hours. He'd been working on accepting that Robert was going to get the kids back, sure, but all acceptance he'd built up had gone out the window when Annabelle Carter had shown up.

And then everything snowballed from there.

Somehow it had led him here. Standing in front of George Fleming's modern day mansion on the east side of Falls Lake, pondering why he'd taken any advice from his brother in the first place.

Maybe you don't know the whole story, Marshall had said yesterday after the Chandler couple left. *You could talk to Fleming. You're a big boy. And yeah, I'm mostly suggesting this for my sake. It's no fun working with you these days. Probably rather have Ember, and that's a scary thought.*

Even though Marshall had only been teasing about wishing Ember was there instead—or at least Wynn hoped so—it had made him wonder. He knew how Fleming worked. Part of the reason his family didn't bank at Falls National. Though none of it had been brought to light, Wynn was willing to bet there were some less-than-legal business transactions that went through the massive stone structure. Didn't have evidence, but sometimes a person just knew.

That, however, wasn't why Wynn was here though. No, he was here because of some hopeless part of him that longed for Noelle to come back. To know why she'd taken everything they'd built together and thrown it out just like that.

And maybe to ask a few questions that he could only hope helped George Fleming think about his actions a little more than he ever had.

For what reason Mom had insisted on sending oatmeal raisin cookies along, Wynn wasn't sure, but he balanced the plate on one hand and knocked with the other. He tried not to think about the fact that he was about to confront the man who'd caused his father's accident, yes, but also the man who'd fathered the woman Wynn loved.

The door opened and Wynn was greeted by a surprised-looking Trevor. The kid was probably close to a decade younger than Wynn, and his clothing showed it—loose T-shirt, narrow light wash jeans, and those white shoes that didn't tie. Vans, were they?

"What are you doing here?" he asked.

Don't. React. "I'm here to talk to your dad for a few minutes, if that's okay."

Trevor's surprised expression morphed into a cocky grin—a trait he'd gotten from his dad. "Oh, you are, huh? He's on the phone right now, so sorry, but that's not doable. Have a good—"

"Then I'll wait," Wynn interrupted. "Got plenty of time. So, how's your brother doing lately? Heard he's in Colorado, right?'

These are Noelle's brothers, you do realize, right?

Oomph. He hadn't thought about that one.

Trevor shifted uncomfortably, hand still on the side of the door like he wanted to close it in Wynn's face. "I, uh, I'll go see when Dad will be done. Don't...touch anything."

Wynn had to bite back his laughter as he stepped inside and Trevor disappeared down a hallway with an aquarium overhead. A hammerhead shark followed him from above. For all the extravagance of the exterior, the interior wasn't lacking either. Marble floors and an open concept layout with a floating stainless steel staircase leading up to the second story. Straight ahead was a living room with white furniture and huge floor to ceiling windows facing the lake. Wynn could see part of the kitchen, and it was just as expansive as the rest of the rambling ten-thousand square foot home. A fact he knew from the complimentary luxury homes boat tour the inn provided for guests in the summer.

The word rambling just made him think of Noelle and those kisses they'd shared.

Personally, Wynn preferred the simple but airy design of the inn compared to this. To each their own, though, he supposed. Something about this, the minimalistic but industrial design that was so in right now felt...almost cold and unwelcoming.

"What do you want, Bryant?" The question was barked.

Ah, maybe that's why the house felt so cold. Wynn turned as Fleming ambled from the hallway, no sign of his son with him.

"Well?" The older man's beady eyes drilled into him. "You just gonna stand there and stare? If so, I've got better things to do."

Wynn cleared his throat. "Would you like a cookie? Mom just baked them this afternoon. They're oatmeal raisin."

"For the love of—I'm allergic to raisins. No." Fleming's face hardened and he turned. "I trust you can see yourself out, Bryant."

Ohh. That's why Mom had sent them. So much for her status as Balsam Falls Sweetheart—a title Dad often referred to her as. Wynn stifled his chuckle, reminding himself why he was here. "What did you say to her, Fleming?"

The man paused, and Wynn refused to shrink under the tension stretching between them. So taut a circus tightrope walker could probably carry a stick of fire across it and not fall.

"I don't know what you're talking about," he snapped.

Fine. He wanted to do this the hard way, Wynn would do it the hard way. But also the Christian way, because he wouldn't be surprised if the church ladies—who might've taken the breakup harder than him, and that was saying something—were listening in right now, his grandmother leading the pack. They'd probably wired some sort of camera onto him.

Which was awkward.

Wynn moved to stand in front of Noelle's father, using the several inches of height he had on the man to his advantage. "What did you say to her?"

"I told her the lots were sold," Fleming said with a shrug. "What else was I supposed to tell her? Annabelle didn't bother to tell me I had a daughter, and believe me, she knew where to find me. So, if you'll excuse me, I have work to get done."

"Fine. Then why'd you tell Robert Clark that his kids were hanging around—" he made air quotes with his available hand "—'those Bryant brothers'? Do you *realize* what that caused?"

George's blue eyes narrowed. As it turned out, they were the same as Noelle's, unlike Wynn had thought that day at Falls Market. But they also weren't, because Noelle would never look at a person the way her father was looking at Wynn right now. That said, there was resemblance between the two. The oval face. Stubborn jaw. While George was good looking in a harsh, unforgiving way, he was still a distinguished man. Sandy but grayed hair. Lean, average height and build. Blue eyes.

No, it didn't come as a shock to Wynn that Annabelle had fallen in love with him once upon a time. Ember had provided him with a couple books from the library, and George's smile and easy charm back in the day had been nothing like the deep scowl and world weariness etching lines into George's face at this time.

"Why *wouldn't* I tell him? Don't you think a man ought to know who his kids are hanging around?"

"What, positive influences? People who care about them?"

The older man only shook his head and made to go around Wynn.

Wynn stepped in front of him again. "I'm not here to cause even more of a rift between our families, and I think you know that. I am here to get some answers I think I deserve to have, considering you haven't treated my family with an ounce of respect since the accident. The one, let me remind you, was caused because you—"

"I've heard enough." Fleming held up a hand. "I might remind you that you're on my property. And while you might be buddy-buddy with Seth Johnson, that doesn't mean anything when it comes to the law. I know what you think of Robert Clark, but have you ever stopped to think about yourself?"

A surge of heat flooded through Wynn, and he barely resisted pivoting to leave this mansion he found himself standing in. Or throwing a punch. Which was very unchristian for one thing, and very unlike the way his mother had raised him for another.

"You took those kids from their father instead of finding the money I know you have to bail him out. What does that say about you?"

Oh, God help him, because he was mad. And he didn't want to do something he'd regret. Nor did he want to walk out now, leaving that smug expression on Fleming's face.

Instead of using physical strength, he chose to use the power of his words. And prayed they came out as he hoped.

"Mr. Fleming, while I understand that Noelle's mother could've contacted you—should have, even—that doesn't make it Noelle's fault," Wynn said evenly. "She's your daughter, and she deserves more respect than what you're giving her. Whether or not you think it does, your influence *does* matter to her. I know it firsthand. So I don't care what you think of my family, even if it's based on false reality. But I do care what you think of your daughter. Whether or not you care, well, I can't control that. Have a good day."

Wynn set the plate of cookies on the modern work of art that was apparently an entryway table, then turned and didn't stop walking until he reached his truck. He backed out of the driveway, drove a couple blocks around to the now sold lots, and pulled alongside the curb. He wouldn't get out, wouldn't demand an answer from God, but he did sit there.

He did allow the memories to come to mind like he expected them to. That first day he'd brought Noelle here, her shivering in his shirt and worried about trespassing and Ember's emergency text that interrupted it all. The second time, when he'd brought Dad and Marshall and Ember too. He hadn't mentioned it, but he'd overheard the very end of Ember and Noelle's conversation before interrupting them. The time he'd "continued" from where they left off after Ember's text and taken Noelle to eat at Farm To Table and danced with her, paint splattered clothes and all.

And for some reason, instead of making him want to yell at God, he found himself smiling as he rested his wrist on the steering wheel. He took in the still-empty lots. Tried to make peace with the *SOLD* sign staked in the dry ground.

And then he pulled away, sending up a prayer that God would convict the wrongdoers, regardless of whether they ever admitted to it. Whether he ever saw Noelle again, he had a sense of peace. No, the hurt wasn't gone, and he doubted he'd ever stop loving her, but he could move forward knowing he'd done everything he needed to. Everything he could do.

The rest was up to God.

"Carter, Inc., this is Noelle Carter."

Propping the phone between her ear and her shoulder, Noelle grabbed a sticky note and a pen from the organizer on the corner of her desk. She wrote down the potential client's name as well as what kind of event they were looking for and promised to have a quote to them within twenty-four hours.

The quote, though, wouldn't come from her. She'd pass it along to Lucy, who'd do that part of it, just like she had been since they'd stepped into these roles last November.

Late June sunshine poured in through the windows of her office, and she stood, phone still to her ear as Mr. Donovan of— what had he said? Tech Enterprises?—drilled her with questions.

"Yes, Mr. Donovan, I have handled events with a guest list of well over three hundred people before." Traffic bustled by on the busy street below, in a hurry as always. *Unlike Balsam Falls and their foot or bicycle traffic.* She pushed the thought away. "Like I said, we'll get a quote to you in the next twenty-four hours, then we can go from there. Does that sound doable?" She paused. "Good. I look forward to working with you, Mr. Donovan. Have a good evening."

After the call ended, Noelle wrapped her arms around herself, the crisp fabric of her gray business dress nothing like the sundresses and paint-splattered jeans she'd become comfortable with in Balsam Falls. It'd been nearly a month since she'd left, and she hadn't gone a single day without thinking of the town. Of the inn. Of the Bryants. Of Wynn.

Lily's words came back to her about if she'd learned anything in her time there, if she'd actually allowed her emotional walls to come down, but, like usual, she pushed them away. It was easier to believe she'd done the right thing if she didn't ponder if she'd done the wrong thing. Wynn was better off without her. That was just the truth.

"Noelle?"

She turned at the sound of Lucy's voice. "Yes, Lucy?"

"I, uh, found this in your notebook when I was going through and documenting the client notes you made from your time in Nebraska." Her assistant held up a piece of paper, then nudged her glasses up. "I figured you might want it."

Noelle took the paper, ignoring the lump in her throat. "Yes, thanks, Lucy."

The girl nodded, hesitated, then walked back out and across the hall to her own office surrounded by modern glass walls. Noelle crossed back to her desk—the very one she'd first opened Mayor Leo's letter at months ago—and sat, unfolding the paper.

To my Son's Special Someone,

First and foremost, thank you. In the event you're reading this note, you and my son are quite clearly in love. And maybe you've eased into it slowly, or maybe it was love quickly like my husband and I. I'm writing this note when Wynn is only thirteen, but he's old enough that I know what kind of man he will become. God-willing, anyway.

And even though I'm biased, I know he will be a lot like his father—respectful, handsome, kind, and hardworking. Which means that you, whoever it is that he's fallen for, must be worthy of his respect, beautiful, soft-hearted, and driven.

This note isn't to give you my advice, and it's certainly not to make you second-guess your relationship. But it is to tell you thank you. I know that love can be hard sometimes. That there are moments when the last thing you want to do is try and communicate. When everything the other person does—and this isn't solely in romantic love, but it does happen in a relationship between a man and a woman—just grates on your nerves, even if it's not intentional.

It's not always easy, I will agree with that. John and I have had our differences throughout the course of our relationship, but not a single one of them was worth throwing away the amazingness of our love story. Hard or easy, it is so worth it when you get to be in love with a person as wonderful as you could ever imagine.

But coming from someone who's been married to a man who is about as Godly and compassionate as they come, it is so worth it. On the days when it doesn't seem like it, IT IS. To watch such a man take care of your heart, slide a ring on your finger, and then with your babies is a life-changing experience. Then to grow and learn and age together—it's one of the very sweetest experiences this life has to offer.

I hope you remember that, even when the going gets tough, God is tougher. When you feel like the tide has come up and swallowed you whole, remember that you can't necessarily control everything, but God can. And when there's love in your heart and God in your soul, everything will work out exactly how it's supposed to.

Love, Jackie

Tears clung to her eyes as she closed them. She should mail it back to Jackie. It wasn't hers to keep.

And yet...

She read through the words one more time, even jotted down a couple notes like Jackie had mentioned to that one day.

Then she sat back, praying this would be the right step.

— ⌁ —

CHAPTER

Fifty One

While this little coffee joint couldn't compare to Cozy & Grounds—no cinnamon rolls from Jess, no familiar chatter between townspeople who knew each other or tourists who wanted to live up their time in an idyllic town like Balsam Falls—it was airy, fast-paced, and welcoming in its own way. All things Noelle was going to need for this meeting.

After she read Jackie Bryant's note last week, she'd taken off early from the office and searched for a coffee shop in the area. Then, toting the notebook Wynn had given her, her laptop, and a mind full of ideas, she came here. The place named Java had white washed brick walls, lots of windows, and wooden tables. Sort of reminded her of the flower shop in Balsam Falls.

Every day following, she sat at the same table by the window with earbuds in, music on, and pencil to paper. And the result was the neatly typed plan in front of her now at the very same table.

Only today she wasn't the only one who'd be at her table. When the idea had first come to her, the first thing she'd done was send an email to her mother. Maybe her choice in men wasn't stellar,

387

and Noelle wasn't sure what would come of this, but she needed to try. Mom had responded and they'd set up a time to meet. One that'd allowed Noelle to prepare both emotionally and physically for the meeting, unlike that night at Spring Fling. This time she was aware of the circumstances of her birth. Understood why her mother made the choices she had.

Hadn't fully come to terms with George Fleming being her father, but she was getting there.

Not that she'd be open to having a relationship with him at the moment like she was with her mother. Things would have to change for that to happen.

The sun bounced off the glass door as it opened several tables down, and Noelle waved to her mother. Mom looked slightly healthier than in May. Her skin was a little more tanned, her eyes not quite as sad.

"Hey," Noelle said, hesitating as she stood. Should she hug her? Shake her hand? *No. Definitely not the latter.* "Was your flight okay?"

Mom pulled her chair out and sat down, setting her pink leather purse on the table. "It was smooth. Good weather. This place is very cute."

Even though a part of Noelle was disappointed her mother hadn't reached out to hug her, she reminded herself that this would be only their second conversation in Noelle's twenty-seven years. To take it one step at a time and enjoy the journey. Because that's what life was—a journey. And who was Noelle to try and interrupt the flow of her journey? Recently, Noelle had started to journal every day. She'd note Bible verses or quotes or things she was grateful for in her journal, and it had shifted her perspective on many things. It'd changed how she viewed herself, even. Helped her become aware of her humanly flaws while also exposing her to the mightiness of God and His day-to-day, seemingly ordinary miracles.

"Yeah, I thought so," Noelle replied, setting her hands on the stack of papers she'd tied together with a string. Mostly because it made her feel accomplished. "So... I wanted to run an idea by you. I have most of the facts or numbers here, and I can't say that it would for sure work, but I tried to cover all my bases."

Mom's eyes lit up, and she clasped her hands on the pale wooden table. "I'm intrigued. I admit, it's been hard to concentrate on much else since I got your email the other day. I guess I should apolo—"

"No, Mom, it's okay."

"No, I need to say this." Mom held her hands out and Noelle tentatively slipped hers into them. "I am so sorry I didn't step up to the role of motherhood, and I wish I could go back and change it. I wish I could see you as a baby and toddler and little girl and all the way through your teens until now. I think I always will. But I also know that isn't possible. So whether or not you're able to forgive me, I am sorry about all the confusion. All the secrecy. But I'm most sorry about what my showing up, what your father's words, did to your relationship with Wynn."

"Mom, it's fine." She didn't really want to talk about Wynn. That was still a sore subject, and if she wasn't careful, she'd start crying.

"No, it's not." Her mother smiled sadly. "He's a good man, Noelle. I knew it from the moment I saw you together that night. Believe it or not, so was your father when I met him. He was raised in the foster system, your dad was. And it wasn't until he'd aged out that he came to Balsam Falls. When we met, he was working full time at the marina in town, trying to save up for the bank he wanted to build. And at heart—"

"Wait, the bank he wanted to build?" Noelle pulled her hands away to dig out the photo of Mom she'd carried with her since she and Ember had found it. "This picture, it was tucked between two pages about a groundbreaking for an undisclosed new building in the Balsam Falls history book. Was that the bank?"

Mom's expression softened as she took the photo, her fingertips brushing over it. "Oh, this picture. Yes. It was. Years ago, I went to Balsam Falls on my way to New York—I drove from LA; can't say I recommend it solo—and for some reason I left the picture there. Did you find it?"

"Kind of. It was actually Wynn's sister who found it, found it. I was just there with her."

"Ah." Mom set the picture down and nodded. "I was proud to see that Tommy had accomplished his dream. I was only there long enough to eat and stop at the library, though, so I doubt anybody recognized me."

Then it clicked. Her mother didn't know about John Bryant's accident or the fact that Noelle's father had caused it. She had no idea about the disrespect Noelle's dad treated the Bryants with.

"Mom, I need to tell you something..." Noelle swallowed, daring herself to meet her mother's gaze. "John Bryant, Wynn's dad, was the chief of police in Balsam Falls for years. And then he was hit by someone who ran a red light...George Fleming—my dad—is the one who ran the light."

"Oh, Noelle." Mom's eyes closed, and her jaw tightened. "I—I had no idea. That's why you were so upset. Why you left."

Noelle nodded. "Yes. He's already treated them poorly since then, even though he's the one who should apologize. I didn't want them to sacrifice their peace for me to be with Wynn. So yes, I left."

"Oh, my goodness, I can't—I'm sorry. There's nothing else I can say."

"But that's not why we're here." Noelle cleared her throat. "I need your help with something, Mom. Will you help me? Please?"

Her mother only nodded, a faint hope in the whispers of her smile.

Rain. They needed rain.

Wynn wiped his forehead with the hem of his T-shirt, the hot early July sun beating down on his back as he pulled the boat up to the dock behind the inn. The Fourth was only a couple days away, and the forecast looked promising, which meant the lake would be packed.

Normally on a Saturday afternoon like this he'd rather be *in* the lake, but Marshall had wrangled his way out of boat duty by saying he had to take Jess somewhere, and even though Dad offered, Wynn really didn't mind. It was sort of fun to see the lake through the tourists' eyes every now and again. And since Ember had volunteered to be the tour guide, all he had to do was drive the boat around to the different locations on the Luxury Homes tour list in his binder.

He'd donned swim shorts and a T-shirt, but if a breeze didn't pick up at all, he'd be getting rid of the shirt. For as cold as Nebraska winters could and did get, they made up for it with summer's heat and humidity.

"Welcome aboard *The Jacqueline*," Ember said in her best tour guide voice after their guests—a couple with two twenty-something kids—climbed aboard. His sister wore black athletic shorts with a pink tank top, her ponytail swishing back and forth as she gestured with her hands. "My dad named this boat after Mom, even though he took some heat from her mother for not naming it *The Margaret*. Oh, and I'm Ember. Our boat driver today is my older brother Wynn. Anyway, this beaut of a boat is only five years old, and she runs like a son of a gun, doesn't she, Wynn?"

Wynn could hardly suppress his smile, considering the parents nodded over-enthusiastically, but neither of the kids even glanced up from their phones. "That she does. We've got life jackets for safety purposes under your seats, and if you want to stop at any time, let me know. Otherwise, are we ready?"

The mom's bleach-blonde bob, well, bobbed as she nodded, her giant sunglasses hiding nearly her whole face. The girl of the kids glanced up, and Wynn didn't miss the way her attention was suddenly on him and not on her phone.

Okayyy. He glanced at his sister, silently pleading for her to talk, and pulled away from the dock. Ember only grinned—go figure—and Wynn revved it once they were out of the no wake zone.

Ah. Now this was how a day was supposed to be on the lake. Hair tousling in the wind as the boat underneath sailed across the churned up lake. His shirt clung to his skin in front and billowed in back, water spraying up as he navigated boat's waves. Anyone and everyone was out today, either tied to other boats for floating and swimming, or just flaunting their wealth by cruising around the lake with what they thought was the biggest and bestest boat.

Wynn's phone vibrated in his pocket, and for a second, he wished he could answer the call. Probably because he foolishly hoped it was Noelle, even though it'd been over a month since she left. But answering wasn't an option right now. The person could leave a voicemail if it was that important.

Besides, he was getting paid to drive a boat on a hot summer day. Even if the girl to his left appeared to be trying to take a photo of him—thank goodness he'd kept his shirt on—he loved being out here. Loved the bright, brilliant blue sky. Craved the hot air on his skin. This was how he'd been raised, and even all these years later, the love of the lake life hadn't dwindled. Actually, it'd probably just increased.

He took the boat to the multi-million dollar homes around the lake, and Ember described the square footage or special features or wow factors for each property. How some of these people only lived here part-time, Wynn didn't know. Sure, lake living was more fun in the summer, but Balsam Falls didn't exactly lack fall or winter activities. There was a pumpkin patch and Christmas tree farm and sledding and ice skating.

Right now, Wynn could admit that he didn't want to think about those things, though. Not on a day like today. One that was about as perfect as a person could ask for.

If only that was Noelle sitting there next to him. Her long blonde hair whipping around. Her laughter washing over him.

But it wasn't and even if he wished it was different, that wasn't up to him.

By the time he pulled back up to the dock where Dad was waiting for them, Wynn's mood was lifted. No longer was he irritably hot from mowing this morning and wiping down the boat before this tour, but he was content. The ride had reminded him of how good he had it.

While Dad talked to the family and Wynn waited for the next group to get there, he pulled his phone out. It'd vibrated no less than six times, and he'd blown off every one of them. There were a couple photos of Sadie from Sarah, two missed calls from Seth, and two texts from Seth. What did he—

We just caught Robert for drugs.

Call me when you can.

Wynn's heart hammered as he reread the texts. He glanced at his dad, thankful the family had already started back up towards the inn. "Can you cover the next ride for me? Seth texted me."

"Everything okay?" Dad glanced at Ember, then back to Wynn. "Marshall and Ember...?"

"What? No. It's Robert."

Understanding that could only be from his policing days sprawled on Dad's face. "Let me guess. Drugs?"

"Wait, really?" Ember asked, her brown eyes wide.

"Unfortunately, yes," Wynn said. "I should probably call him back."

Dad motioned to the boat. "Em and I can take care of this tour and the next one. Go do what you need to do."

"Mr. Wynn!"

Wynn opened his arms as Sophie raced across the industrial grade carpet of the police station, and he smiled as he picked her up. Seth hadn't even had to ask if Wynn was interested in taking the kids again. Wynn had said he would do it before Seth had gotten so much as a "hello" out.

"Did you miss me?" Sophie leaned back, her hands on his shoulders. "I missed you. Devin did too, but he probably won't say that. Did you know that school is out now? I kinda miss it though."

Yes, and Seth had been worried about where the kids would go during the day. Wynn had said he'd take them to the office, or his mother would watch Sophie if they were on a job site and Devin could help out.

"Of course I missed you, Soph." Wynn glanced up as Seth led Devin over. "Hey, Dev."

"Hey."

"You're sure about this?" What Seth really meant was that this time probably wouldn't be so short lived, but he wouldn't say as much in front of the kids. Especially not Sophie.

Wynn nodded. "Absolutely."

"Okay, then." Seth set his hand on Devin's shoulder. "I'll figure out how to go about things, but you can go with him for now. They've each got some stuff I can bring by in a couple hours, if you'll be around."

"Sounds good."

"Can we have pizza tonight, Mr. Wynn?" Sophie asked, her eyes hopeful.

Wynn couldn't help but laugh. "Yes, Sophie, we can absolutely have pizza. That okay with you, Devin?"

Devin nodded, and Wynn put his other arm around the teen as he led them out of the police station into the hot summer air.

"Nice swim trunks, by the way," Seth called after them.

Sophie giggled, Devin chuckled, and Wynn could only smile.

— ✑ —

CHAPTER

Fifty Two

D id he have everything?

Beach towels—check. Sunglasses—check. Toys, sunscreen, extra towels—check. He was less than twenty-four hours back into the "Dad" thing and already he felt like days had passed. Granted, the kids had never gone with his family for a Sunday afternoon on the lake, but he was probably a little too worried about the details.

Part of that was because he really didn't want to mess anything up.

Which probably wouldn't go perfectly well for his whole life—things were bound to happen—but what had Pastor Jay said this morning? Done was better than perfect?

Yes, that was it, and he probably needed to repeat it on a loop as he got the kids ready to go.

"Sophie, where are your shoes?" Wynn had looked under the sofa, in the kitchen, in her room. "The dock is going to be hot."

Sophie came from the bathroom wearing the pink swimsuit his mother had bought her, then pointed at her feet. "I'm wearing them, silly."

Sure enough, her flip-flops were right there on her feet. Even Nova tilted her head as if he should've known that. Wynn only shook his head and draped towels over his arm, the beach bag over his shoulder.

"Dev, are you ready?" he called as he ushered Sophie towards the back door. "The bus is leaving."

"Don't you mean the boat?" Sophie tried unsuccessfully to hide her giggles.

"Somebody's funny today." Wynn winked at her. "You ready to go swimming? Oh, shoot, I forgot about lifejackets."

"Nana Jackie said she has them for us," Sophie said. "She told me she even has a pink one for me."

His mother to the rescue. "Perfect. Devin, are you—"

"I'm ready." Devin walked out from the hallway, carrying a board in his hands. "Um, I know we gotta go, but I wanted to give you this. You kind of inspired me to do some woodworking stuff, and my dad brought home some wood for me a couple weeks ago from work before, well, you know... So anyway, here."

Despite the towels and bag he held, Wynn took the sign from the teen and swallowed as he took in the *BRYANT* that'd been burned onto the wood in all capital letters.

"I got a wood burner from the dollar store," Devin explained, his gaze on the floor. "It was a cheap one, but I hope—"

"I love it, Dev." Wynn set the sign on the shelf by the TV and gave Devin a side hug. "And cost has nothing to do with the obvious care you put into it. Thank you."

Devin looked up and offered a lopsided grin.

"We'll find a spot to hang it when we get back later, okay?" After the teen nodded, Wynn gestured to the door. "Out we go. Who's excited for an afternoon on the lake? I bet you'll be ready to be in the water pretty quickly."

"Me!" Sophie darted forward, Nova beside her. "Nana Jackie told me there's fishies in the lake, but if we splash lots, they'll get scared and leave us all alone."

"Oh, she did, did she?" Because Wynn vividly remembered his mother telling him and Marshall to *stop* splashing when they were kids.

Sophie's head bobbed. "Uh-huh. Has a fish ever bited you, Mr. Wynn?"

Beside him, Devin laughed. "There's no fish in here that bite, Sophie. Right?"

"Right," Wynn confirmed. He waved to his sister, who was carrying Will down from the inn to the boat. "Okay, guys. Remember, no running on the dock. But because I know you're excited, you can run down *to* the dock where Nana Jackie is waiting. Sound good?"

Sophie needed no further encouragement. She shot off like a cannon, Nova on her heels, and halted when Mom held out the lifejacket for her.

"Thanks for taking us again." Devin, who had stayed next to Wynn, glanced up at him. "I guess I never really told you that before. But I know you didn't have to do it. Especially 'cause we're out of school now."

"School or no school, I would do it in a heartbeat. Trust me, you'll probably be wishing you were in school after Mom has you for long enough. I speak from experience—she was my teacher."

Devin laughed. "Your mom is pretty cool, though. So is your whole family."

"Your dad... Was he doing drugs that whole time? Not just when you guys were with him this time, but before that."

"Honestly, I don't know. Probably not, because Seth probably ran drug tests when he booked him the first time—even though, yeah, sometimes Seth is slow, so maybe he didn't—but Dad was...different after his stint in jail. I know he messed up again, but I also think he needs help and he knows he can't get it on his own. Seth had told him he'd line up rehab. Maybe he'll do it this time. Anita wanted him to go, even."

Wynn believed him—the woman hadn't ended up causing any real problems, and Seth had been impressed that her motive for bailing him out was to help him. As it turned out, Robert had called her for help, which she'd given. Unfortunately, Robert had made more poor choices following that. Hopefully this would teach him a lesson, because he wouldn't be given another free chance.

"I think you're pretty smart for your age and what you've been through, Dev." Wynn bumped his shoulder against Devin's. "And as far as your dad, I'll be praying that he does go to rehab. Because he does love you and Sophie, even if he struggles to show it appropriately. And until then, I'll be here, okay?"

"Thanks, Wynn. And I know Seth tried to locate my brother but couldn't. Thanks for that too."

"Don't give up on finding him yet. God can do great things. Now, how about you lose the adult conversational skills and be a kid this afternoon, yeah?"

Devin grinned and nodded. They reached the dock, where Mom was waiting with a lifejacket for Devin. The DNR required anyone thirteen and under to wear one—the Bryant family had extended it to fourteen. The only time it had been waived was when Dad had allowed Wynn and his siblings to swim at the dock without life jackets prior to being older than thirteen, as long as Dad or Mom were around to supervise. Perks of having homeschool parents—they taught you how to swim young.

The boat was nearly loaded down—Sarah and Chris and their kids, Marshall and Jess, Ember, Dad, Sophie, and the grandparents—but Dad would squeeze as many as safely possible on, especially when it came to family.

"Oh, you know what, I forgot my phone in the kitchen." Mom smacked her hand to her forehead and glanced at Wynn, her smile hopeful. "Would you be a dear and get it for me? It should be charging in the kitchen. I'll bet Devin can take the load you've got."

Devin took the towels and beach bag. "Hook, line, and sinker, man."

What? Wynn looked at his mother, who was grinning. "Go on, dear," she said with a wave of her hand. "Your father might just leave without you if you don't hurry it up."

Probably not, but Wynn pivoted and jogged up the green backyard to the inn, the grass tickling his bare ankles. Why his mother needed her phone on a boat, he really had no idea. There was at least one other person who would have theirs if she really wanted to take pictures. And if she wanted music, the boat had a built-in radio, so they didn't need her phone for that either. On top of that, she was the one who encouraged everyone to leave their phone in a basket when it came to family suppers. This was a family boat ride, so how was this any different?

But Mom was Mom and—

And Wynn came to a stop only a few yards away from the inn's back doors so fast he was surprised his feet didn't *screeeechh* across the grass.

There, standing on the patio under the inn's back pergola was Noelle. Wearing a loose white sundress and sandals. Her skin was tanner than it had been before and she looked...different. In a good way. Almost healthier, and less timid. Wynn couldn't make himself move as his gaze took in her face. Those beautiful blue eyes of hers. The freckles scattered faintly across her nose and cheeks.

And then the next thing he knew, he was smiling and she was in his arms, her head burrowed against his chest.

Until she'd seen Wynn jogging across the inn's backyard—wearing *only* navy blue swim trunks—Noelle had wondered if this had been a bad idea. If showing up here unannounced to him—she'd called Jackie the other day, and it'd probably made its rounds to the other family members—wasn't a good plan.

But then his gaze collided with hers, those brilliant blue eyes brimming with questions, the most beautiful smile broadened his lips, and all doubt had fled. She'd closed the gap between them and thrown her arms around him.

Now, tucked against his sun-warmed chest with his steady, if not a little fast, heartbeat in her ear, she let out a sigh. Closed her eyes. Inhaled the sticky Nebraska air and exhaled all the fears she'd unnecessarily created. Right here, back in Wynn's strong embrace, all she could do was praise God for leading her back.

After several prolonged moments, she moved back, daring herself to meet his gaze. "Hey."

"Hey, yourself." His eyes held hers, his hands resting on her waist. Oh, how she had missed this man. "What are you... You're here."

She bit her lip. "Listen, Wynn, I'm sorry. I—I never should've left like I did. And I knew that. I knew I was hurt and that I was hurting *you* and that's not what I wanted, but I know I can't change it now. And I'll understand if you need time or you're not interested or I'm too late, but I'm not going anywhere. I'm going to move here, Wynn. And my mom and I, we're going to open an event planning business together here. I don't have all the details and I don't even know how it's gonna go for sure, but I do know we're going to do it. And we're going to name it Events by Elle—a name that ties in my grandma's and mom's names and mine, plus it includes the alliteration I know this town loves." She let out a breath. "And you haven't said a word, probably because I haven't let you and did I say I'm sorry? Because I am. I'm really sorry."

His gaze flicked to her lips, then back to her eyes. "You done?"

All she could manage was a weak nod. Never had his fondness of using very few words been more nerve-wracking.

"You can try apologizing again, but three times is more than enough for me, Noelle Carter." His lips curved into that ridiculously handsome smirk he'd mastered. "And are you sure you're done? Because I have my own things to say, but I've learned that a gentleman doesn't interrupt a lady."

Was he flirting with her? He was definitely flirting with her. And she couldn't blame the Nebraska sunshine filtering through the pergola overhead for the heat in her cheeks. Because maybe it was supposed to be that a gentleman didn't interrupt a lady, but she could recall several instances when he'd done so. Maybe not vocally, but that smirk of his implied he knew exactly what he was saying.

"A new business, huh? What about Carter, Inc.?"

"That's another thing. I forgot about—"

"Oh, so you're not done."

Her flush deepened. "I guess not. Um, so, Carter, Inc. is going to be sold. It was actually sold almost two weeks ago because there was someone interested back in November and they were still interested now and so it's sold now. And part of that money will go into Mom and I's new business. The other part was used to buy those lots from Jeff Stanhoue. The remainder after that was put into a checking account, and it will be used to pay you for when somebody who can't afford it, like you wanted, stays at the cottages."

Wynn's jaw went slack. "You what?"

"Wynn, I may not agree with some of my father's choices— especially how he and his buddies treat your family—but something even Jeff Stanhoue can't resist is money. Sad as that is, it's also true. Oh, and I put the lots in your name. Hope that's okay. I mean, if you're still interested in doing the—"

And, like he'd quite clearly been waiting to do when she first started rambling, he kissed her. His arms wrapped securely around her waist as she set her hands on his tanned, muscular shoulders, his lips caressing hers. So familiar, but so unfamiliar. She released a little sigh, that floating feeling coming back to her all over again. His kiss was soft and gentle, but filled with a new sense of exhilaration. As if all the other kisses they'd shared had been tentative, unsure of how things were going to work out.

"I love you," he mumbled, then pressed another kiss to her lips.

"I love you too." Noelle's heart pounded like that jackhammer they'd used to tear up some of the unsalvageable sidewalks at The Gardens. "Um, Wynn?"

"Hmm?"

"I have something else to tell you."

He kissed her nose. "Okay."

She laughed and nudged him back, more than a little breathless, no small thanks to the intensity burning in his eyes. "I wrote a letter to my dad and mailed it to him. I told him I understood that my mom could've told him about me, but that I hoped he could forgive her. That I don't hate him. That I hope he can find comfort in the God who still loves him. I don't know what he'll do or if he'll do anything at all, but I want you to know that I did extend a figurative olive branch. I won't let him walk all over me or your family, but he is my dad, and I guess I just needed him to know that I acknowledge him as that."

Wynn tucked a piece of hair behind her ear, his fingers brushing her skin. "I think that's wonderful. I think *you're* wonderful, Noelle Carter. And even though I'd love to stay right here more than anything, Sophie is anxiously—"

"Sophie?" *What* had he just said?

"Oh. Yes. That's what I was trying to tell you a couple minutes ago, but you just kept talking, and then I kissed you and... Anyway, the kids are back with me for the foreseeable future. We'll talk about it later, but as I was saying, Sophie is anxiously awaiting the afternoon on the lake I promised her. Would you like to come along?"

Noelle's lips twitched. "Your mom might've mentioned that I should just plan on wearing a swimsuit under my clothes all the time in the summer, so yeah, I would love to."

"You talked to my mother?"

"I did." She pressed up to kiss him again. "And by the way, she has her phone," she whispered in his ear before darting around him.

"Unbelievable, Noelle. Unbelievable." Wynn's eyes crinkled as he caught up to her and caught her hand in his, tugging her down to the dock.

Noelle opened her arms as Devin and Sophie came running towards her, her laughter bubbling over as Wynn rested that steady hand of his on the small of her back.

She was home. With the family she loved in the charming town she loved. With the kids who'd wormed their way into her heart. With the man she couldn't possibly love any more if she tried.

To her, this life was perfect. In its own beautiful way, even with the mistakes she'd made and the roundabout ways she'd taken, God had led her back here.

Maybe the Serendipity Inn really was just that—serendipitous.

Epilogue

Ten Months Later

Even though he'd dreamt of this day for more years than he could count, he was still nervous. What if people didn't like the cottages? What if all the time, money, and love they'd poured into them didn't turn a profit? Had they chosen the wrong paint or trim colors? The wrong light fixtures or furniture? Should they have put bigger front porches on them?

But then he caught Noelle's gaze from where she was talking to Robert Clark, Anita, and the kids, and all his fears went out the window. Funny how that worked. Ever since that July day when she'd shown up—his entire family had been in on it, as he'd later come to find out, so it hadn't exactly been as out of the blue as he thought—he hadn't ever felt as close to a person as he did Noelle. Every look, every kiss, every conversation—they all had meaning. Some conversations were more laughing than talking, and Wynn wasn't sure she'd ever fully be competent alone in the kitchen, but every single moment together meant something.

"I'm proud of you, son." Dad rested his hand on Wynn's shoulder as he stood next to him on Falls Drive, facing the newly constructed cottages. "For many reasons, not only these cottages, but I do think you knocked them out of the park."

Wynn hoped so. He really did. All three little houses had two bedrooms and two bathrooms, completely ADA compliant. Gray siding, sunny yellow front doors, and white trim made them attractive on the exterior while modern but familiar decorations and design elements welcomed a person inside. And the views—nothing could beat them.

Hence the name Viewpoint Cottages.

"Thanks, Dad," Wynn said, glancing at his father. "They wouldn't have been possible without you, and you can't even try to deny that."

Dad grinned. "Then I won't try to. I will say that they wouldn't have been possible without your determination either, though."

"Or that pretty little blonde over there." Though Wynn knew his brother missed Jess, Marshall still wore that signature smirk of his. "We all know that these probably wouldn't have happened if it wasn't for Noelle, bro. And *you* can't try to deny that."

Wynn held up his hands, aware the smile on his face was probably a goofy, lopsided one. "Didn't plan to. And if you guys will excuse me, I'm gonna go on over to that pretty little blonde right now."

Dad clapped him on the shoulder with a laugh, then started talking to Marshall about the curb appeal of the cottages as Wynn wove through people to get to Noelle. Apparently the town had found this Saturday morning reveal to be as interesting as a new business opening up, because the paper had even sent one of their reporters to take photos, and he was supposed to do an interview for a write-up. Mayor Leo was here, mingling among the crowd of what had to be at least fifty townspeople, and Seth had joked about needing to close off the street for this morning.

Wynn couldn't deny that Seth might've been onto something with the idea. When Ember had insisted on posting about the "big reveal" to the inn's social media or wherever, he hadn't exactly imagined *this*. There were plenty of familiar faces, all there to celebrate the figurative grand opening of the cottages, who would be seeing their first visitors for the official start of summer next weekend, also known as Memorial Day Weekend. The cottages were already booked throughout most of the summer, and then Marshall planned to live in one of them for the off-season until he figured out what exactly he wanted to do.

As far as life, it really couldn't be any better. Even though it'd
been a transition when Robert's sentencing was up and his rehab
was completed four months ago, Wynn was still a part of the kids'
lives, as was Seth. He and Noelle regularly took them for ice
cream—nearly every week—and Devin, now fourteen, still came to
help them out with projects. Sophie, now eight, loved to hang out
at the inn here and there, and Wynn had made it a point to have
Robert, his wife-to-be again Anita, and the kids over for supper at
least once a week. And even though he sometimes wished the kids
were still with him, he wouldn't change it. Not when he saw how
happy Robert Clark was, how much he appreciated the second
chance he'd been given with his kids. And his first wife, for that
matter.

"I think people love what you've built here, Wynn." This came
from Robert Clark—the clear-eyed and clear-headed one with his
daughter on his shoulders and Devin standing proudly beside him.
Anita was off talking to someone else. "I'm impressed. They look
great."

Wynn slipped his arm around Noelle and smiled. "Thank you.
Can't say I'd want them any different. Hopefully vacationers will
think the same."

"Can we stay in one, Daddy?" Sophie grinned as she used the
word *daddy*. "I like the pink flowers under the windows."

Robert squeezed his daughter's legs. "We'll have to see about
that, Soph. Well, we should let you guys—" He cut himself off as
a tall, presumably twenty-something guy approached. "Justin?"

Wait, what? Confusion zipped through Wynn as the man
caught Devin in his arms. Justin? As in Justin Clark, the one Seth
hadn't been able to locate? The one who'd run off to the Marines
without a backward glance after Robert's second wife died six years
ago? How in the world was he here, hugging his siblings and his
father? Had Wynn missed something, or...?

"Where have you been, Justin?" Robert's voice was rough as he
stepped back.

Justin's jaw clenched. "I did one tour, then got discharged because I was injured at the start of my second. And even though I wanted to come back, I couldn't. I was hurt, both physically and emotionally, both from the war and everything before that. Once I was back stateside, I found a job in South Carolina at a marina. It allowed me to pay for a small rental while giving me time to…process. And then Seth Johnson got ahold of me a couple weeks ago. Gave me some food for thought. Told me where to come if I wanted to, as he put it, 'man up.'"

Sounded about like Seth, even if Seth himself had yet to man up in most areas of his life outside of his job.

"I'm sorry," Justin said quietly. "I shouldn't have been so selfish, and Seth told me everything that's, uh, happened. I'm so sorry I haven't been here. I—I'm just sorry."

"You did come back." Devin barreled into his older brother's arms again. "Thank you."

Wynn gently and hopefully discreetly guided Noelle away from the reunited family. It was moments like this, with Noelle close to his side, that he loved the most. Her mother was around here somewhere, probably talking to his mother. For the landslide of events Annabelle's showing up last year had created, good things had come out of it. Noelle and her mom had become closer, built a relationship, and their business was going successfully. The building they'd bought for a storefront housed two apartments upstairs, and each of them lived in one. Though George Fleming hadn't changed much, there had been a subtle shift since Noelle sent that letter. Instead of snide remarks or what seemed like premeditated run-ins, though, George seemed to keep to himself more often than not.

Which was what made Wynn so surprised when the man walked up to them—when had he shown up?—and stopped. Instinctively, Wynn's arm tightened around Noelle, even though he knew she could hold her own.

"I, uh, wanted to tell you that the cottages look good," George said, his voice resigned. His expression without any of its usual hardness. "And I'm sorry I didn't sell the lots to you in the first place."

Wynn was wholly unprepared for the apology, and his delayed response probably made it quite clear. "I... Thank you. This land was the perfect spot for them."

"It is." George looked at Noelle then, and either Wynn was seeing things or the man actually looked remorseful. But hopeful, too, maybe. "I was wondering if you would be interested in meeting me for coffee Monday? I'd like to talk to you, maybe hear more about you. And I'll understand if you're not interested."

God, you might need to slow down on the surprises or my head might explode. But also...thank you.

"I would love that," Noelle said softly. "Does nine or so at Cozy & Grounds work for you?"

George nodded, something like relief in his expression. He hesitated as if he had something more to say, but he only offered a brief smile before turning and walking in the other direction. His gait had slowed some, and his posture was kind of hunched, but he actually looked better than Wynn had seen him for a long time.

"I think I'm in shock," Noelle said, her gaze on her father's back. "No, I'm *definitely* in shock."

Wynn turned to face her, his arms around her waist. "Make that two of us."

"Well, as much as I'd love to hang out right here with you, there's a crowd," she said with a smile. Man, she was cute. "And I'm pretty sure you have an interview to take care of. I know you're stalling."

He groaned. "Do I really have to? You're the one who really wanted these cottages to—"

"Nice try, handsome." She pressed up on tiptoe to kiss his stubbled cheek, then bounced back and nudged him away. "But it's not going to work. Come on, you're going to rock it."

"'The inspiration for the Viewpoint Cottages originally came to me many years ago, but it wasn't until last year that I started to get serious about them,'" Noelle read from the newspaper article a couple days later. Water lapped at the dock's edges underneath the rattan wooden chairs she and Wynn were sitting in, and a frothy pink sunset painted the cobalt sky before them. "'With the help of a special girl, I actually pursued the idea. The cottages here today were built with donations, volunteers, determined townspeople, and God. They wouldn't be here if not for Him. And while I don't know what will come about now for sure, I do know that I want Viewpoint Cottages to be a place for everyone. I want people to feel welcomed and appreciated when they step inside, or even just when they first pull up to the curb. That's what I hope these cottages will provide—an inspiring getaway on the shores of Falls Lake.'"

She rested the *Balsam Falls Gazette* on her lap and glanced at Wynn. "You did an awesome job with the interview. Why in the world did you think you wouldn't?"

"Um, because having a news reporter copy down every single word I say while someone else tries to take my picture isn't quite up my alley. Or maybe because there were tons of people milling around and it was a little nerve-wracking."

"Well, it's perfect to me." She held up the paper. "Do you realize how handsome you look in this picture? Like, I might need to cut it out and frame it. I mean, technically, you should do that anyway."

"I should, huh?" He leaned toward her, his blue eyes sparkling. "Isn't that kind of conceited?"

"What, to hang your awesome article on this huge accomplishment up? Um, no. It's not."

"Well, if you say so." His eyebrows rose. "Woah. Look behind you, Noelle. Is that an eagle?"

"What?" Noelle twisted around, brows scrunched as she tried to locate the eagle. Jackie had been telling her about the bald eagle pair that came every year, and she'd yet to see them. The winter had been surprisingly mild, apparently, and they hadn't come except for a couple times when Noelle hadn't been around to see them. "Where? I don't see an eagle."

"Huh, I must've been seeing things."

Was that laughter in his voice? With a comeback on her tongue, she turned back to him and froze.

Wynn had lowered to one knee in front of her on the sun-weathered wooden dock, and a diamond ring winked up at her from the open, pale pink ring box in his hand.

"Wynn…" Her voice wasn't properly functioning as she met his gaze, tears filling her eyes.

"Noelle Marie Carter, I still remember the day we met." His blue eyes twinkled as he smiled. "When you tried to close the door on me, when in reality, I had just given you a way to escape. How you threatened to use that cast iron skillet on me. And I thought you were the prettiest girl I'd ever seen, even if you needed more layers on for that snowstorm and you wanted to have nothing to do with me."

She bit her lip as he reached for her hand, his thumb gently caressing her skin.

"And ever since that day, I've only fallen deeper in love with you than I thought possible," he continued. "With you I am happy, I'm joyful, and most of all, I feel loved. There hasn't been a day that's gone by since I met you that I haven't wanted to be the man you deserve. A man worthy of your love. And even though sometimes I'm pretty sure I fall short, I love you more than I can say. I love your beautiful blue eyes and infectious smile. I love how willing you are to try something new. I love your drive and your determination. I love watching you with kids, and I hope we have our own babies to love on down the road. I want to grow old together, sitting side by side on a swing and looking at this lake. Will you marry me, Noelle?"

Tears constricted her ability to do anything more than squeeze out a squeaky *yes* and nod. She nodded like a crazy woman, but she *was* crazy—crazily in love with the man in front of her.

Wynn's smile broadened as he slid the ring—a stunning square solitaire with tiny diamonds on either side lining the white gold band—onto her trembling finger. Even though she wanted to stare at the ring—*her ring!*—Wynn stood and tugged her up with him, barely allowing a breath before his lips met hers. Noelle wrapped her arms around his neck, elation shooting through her as he lifted her off the ground.

She was engaged. *Engaged!* To Wynn Bryant, a man who sent her flowers and took her on dates and kissed her intentionally, yes, but he was also just…there. Steady and dependable. Not a day went by that Noelle second-guessed his love for her. He always made time for just them every day, even if that was merely sitting on this dock or his back deck later in the evening to talk.

Wynn returned her feet to the dock as he eased away, his uneven breath filling the space between them.

"I love you," he whispered.

His breath fanned over her eyelashes. "I love you too, Wynn Bryant. So very much."

Wynn moved back and lifted her hand to his lips, sending a shiver down her spine as he kissed the finger he'd just placed a ring on. A stunning, prettier-than-pretty ring she'd probably catch herself staring at more often than not.

"Are we going to tell your family?" she asked, hoping he said yes. Even though she loved being right here in his arms, she couldn't wait to hear Ember's enthusiasm, to hug Marshall, for Sarah to squeal over the ring, to see John's fatherly smile and feel Jackie's maternal embrace.

And, of course, hear the talk of babies from Grandma Margie like she had been for the past ten months. To receive a hug from Grandpa Henry.

"Nah." He grinned and tilted his head towards the back of the inn. "They already know."

Noelle glanced up, her cheeks flushing as the group of people she'd grown to love beamed and let out whistles and waved. Wynn's grandparents. John and Jackie. Sarah's family. Marshall, with Jess on video call on his phone. Ember, wearing perhaps the hugest smile of all. Even Devin, Sophie, Robert, Anita, and Justin. Noelle's mother. And there, a little to the side of them all, stood her father too.

Their conversation at the coffee house yesterday had been somewhat stinted, a little uncomfortable, but it was a start. George Fleming—Dad, actually, hadn't snipped. He'd been...nice. And he'd obviously been interested when she'd talked about her growing up with her grandparents, how much she loved what she did, and whatever else had come up. They were in a different place than a year ago, and that was enough for now.

"I asked him if it was okay to propose," Wynn murmured as he drew her to him for another hug. "And not only did he give me permission to marry his beautiful daughter, but he apologized to my father. He's changing, love, and I firmly believe you are a big part of how that's possible."

Heat flushed Noelle's cheeks. "Well, I'm not a miracle worker by any means. But God is, and we have so much to thank Him for."

"That we do, future Mrs. Bryant, that we do." He slid his arm around her waist and kissed her temple. "Are you ready to go get hugs and more hugs from those people watching our every move?"

Noelle laughed and leaned into his side as they started up the dock. "With you, Wynn Bryant, I most certainly am."

Dear Reader

I hope you enjoyed *With You I Am*. This was the first book in a brand new series, and I have to admit that it took a little time and patience to actually get to the point of what this book turned out to be. It was very different for me to craft a brand new family in a brand new town with brand new storylines/side characters.

That said, it was SO MUCH FUN. While the *Faith to Love* series and McKay family will always have a special place in my heart, I loved writing this first book, and I already have plans for the following two books, Marshall's and Ember's. I was able to create a town I would absolutely love to live in with characters I would love to call my friends/family. From the tiniest little detail of a one-scene dress shop to the family's inn to creating Wynn Bryant, I had a blast.

I'm so excited to bring you more stories set in the idyllic little lake town of Balsam Falls, Nebraska, and I hope you enjoyed the introductory book into the Bryant Family series.

Please don't hesitate to reach out to me! You can contact me at cleo@cleopatramargot.com or head over to my website www.CleopatraMargot.com to find my social media links and other information!

May God bless you!
Cleopatra

With You I Am

Questions for Discussion

1) When Noelle receives the letter from Mayor Leo Mason, she doesn't expect to be asked to plan an event in her late grandmother's hometown. Have you ever had something unexpected come across your figurative desk that ended up changing your life?

2) Wynn is the second oldest of four siblings. Do you have siblings? What is your favorite thing about having siblings? What do you find the most challenging about having siblings?

3) Were there any events in *With You I Am* that surprised you? If so, what surprised you (the most)?

4) Throughout the course of Wynn and Noelle's story, both Wynn and Noelle are forced to reexamine things they have either wanted to forget or have never confronted. Have you ever struggled to confront things you know you need to but don't have the desire to?

5) The overall theme of *With You I Am* is a blend of healing and forgiveness. Throughout the story, Wynn and Noelle walk through trials that may have been difficult, but they emerged on the other side better than before. Can you point out certain parts that portrayed that the most in this story?

6) Which characters or situations or scenes in this book made you laugh?

7) Which characters or situations or scenes in this book made you cry?

8) Was there any one certain healing, forgiveness, or truth-filled scene that stayed with you after you'd finished reading *With You I Am?*

9) *With You I Am* is set in a fictional lake town in Nebraska. What parts of the town were your favorite? Did you enjoy reading in this setting? Did it enhance the story?

10) George Fleming is a man who grew up roughly, then made poor choices after he was grown, which led to a snowball effect of bottled hatred and unnecessary anger. Did you find the ending of the story, his desire to talk to Noelle and his apology to John Bryant, realistic? What were your favorite parts of George Fleming's character arc?

11) Which character was your favorite, and why?

12) Did you find any particular parts of *With You I Am* to be extra romantic?

About the Author

Cleopatra Margot resides with her family and their golden retrievers in small town, rural Nebraska. Inspiration for her novels comes from both real life + fictional storylines she dreams up. She was homeschooled alongside her two younger siblings, and she enjoys traveling with her family. When she's not writing, Cleopatra enjoys reading, time with family and friends, dancing, playing cards, being outside, and enjoying life.

With You I Am

.

418

Connect with Cleopatra

Find Cleopatra Online at

www.CleopatraMargot.com

to explore characters, book trailers,

previous books, and more!

- @cleopatra.margot

Made in the USA
Monee, IL
14 April 2022

94093752R00246